GLOOMSPITE

Collections

The Realmgate Wars: Volume 1
Various authors
Contains the novels *The Gates of Azyr, War Storm, Ghal Maraz, Hammers of Sigmar, Wardens of the Everqueen* and *Black Rift*

The Realmgate Wars: Volume 2
Various authors
Contains the novels *Call of Archaon, Warbeast, Fury of Gork, Bladestorm, Mortarch of Night* and *Lord of Undeath*

Legends of the Age of Sigmar
Various authors
An anthology of short stories

Rulers of the Dead
David Annandale & Josh Reynolds
Contains the novels *Neferata: Mortarch of Blood* and *Nagash: The Undying King*

Warcry
Various authors
An anthology of short stories

Champions of the Mortal Realms
Various authors
Contains the novellas *Warqueen, The Red Hours, Heart of Winter* and *The Bone Desert*

Trials of the Mortal Realms
Various authors
Contains the novellas *Code of the Skies, The Measure of Iron* and *Thieves' Paradise*

Gods & Mortals
Various authors
An anthology of short stories

Myths & Revenants
Various authors
An anthology of short stories

Oaths & Conquests
Various authors
An anthology of short stories

Direchasm
Various authors
An anthology of short stories

Novels

• HALLOWED KNIGHTS •
Josh Reynolds

BOOK ONE: Plague Garden
BOOK TWO: Black Pyramid

Eight Lamentations: Spear of Shadows
Josh Reynolds

• KHARADRON OVERLORDS •
C L Werner

BOOK ONE: Overlords of the Iron Dragon
BOOK TWO: Profit's Ruin

Soul Wars
Josh Reynolds

Callis & Toll: The Silver Shard
Nick Horth

The Tainted Heart
C L Werner

Shadespire: The Mirrored City
Josh Reynolds

Blacktalon: First Mark
Andy Clark

Hamilcar: Champion of the Gods
David Guymer

Scourge of Fate
Robbie MacNiven

The Red Feast
Gav Thorpe

Gloomspite
Andy Clark

Ghoulslayer
Darius Hinks

Beastgrave
C L Werner

Neferata: The Dominion of Bones
David Annandale

The Court of the Blind King
David Guymer

Lady of Sorrows
C L Werner

Realm-Lords
Dale Lucas

Warcry Catacombs: Blood of the Everchosen
Richard Strachan

Covens of Blood
Anna Stephens, Liane Merciel and Jamie Crisalli

Novellas

City of Secrets
Nick Horth

Audio Dramas

• REALMSLAYER: A GOTREK GURNISSON SERIES •
David Guymer

BOXED SET ONE: Realmslayer
BOXED SET TWO: Blood of the Old World

The Beasts of Cartha
David Guymer

Fist of Mork, Fist of Gork
David Guymer

Great Red
David Guymer

Only the Faithful
David Guymer

The Prisoner of the Black Sun
Josh Reynolds

Sands of Blood
Josh Reynolds

The Lords of Helstone
Josh Reynolds

The Bridge of Seven Sorrows
Josh Reynolds

War-Claw
Josh Reynolds

Shadespire: The Darkness in the Glass
Various authors

The Imprecations of Daemons
Nick Kyme

The Palace of Memory and Other Stories
Various authors

Sons of Behemat
Graeme Lyon

Also available

Realmslayer: The Script Book
David Guymer

GLOOMSPITE

ANDY CLARK

BLACK LIBRARY

A BLACK LIBRARY PUBLICATION

First published in 2019.
This edition published in Great Britain in 2020 by
Black Library,
Games Workshop Ltd.,
Willow Road,
Nottingham,
NG7 2WS, UK.

10 9 8 7 6 5 4 3 2

Produced by Games Workshop in Nottingham.
Cover illustration by François Coutu.

See Black Library on the internet at

blacklibrary.com

Find out more about Games Workshop
and the worlds of Warhammer at

games-workshop.com

Printed and bound by CPI Group (UK) Ltd, Croydon, CR0 4YY.

For my friends and loved ones; sorry in advance that this came out of my brain. I even made myself feel a bit sick a few times. Oh, and mum, you absolutely are not reading this one…

From the maelstrom of a sundered world, the
Eight Realms were born. The formless and the divine
exploded into life.

Strange, new worlds appeared in the firmament, each one
gilded with spirits, gods and men. Noblest of the gods was
Sigmar. For years beyond reckoning he illuminated the realms,
wreathed in light and majesty as he carved out his reign. His
strength was the power of thunder. His wisdom was infinite.
Mortal and immortal alike kneeled before his lofty throne.
Great empires rose and, for a while, treachery was banished.
Sigmar claimed the land and sky as his own and ruled over a
glorious age of myth.

But cruelty is tenacious. As had been foreseen, the great
alliance of gods and men tore itself apart. Myth and legend
crumbled into Chaos. Darkness flooded the realms. Torture,
slavery and fear replaced the glory that came before. Sigmar
turned his back on the mortal kingdoms, disgusted by their
fate. He fixed his gaze instead on the remains of the world he
had lost long ago, brooding over its charred core, searching
endlessly for a sign of hope. And then, in the dark heat of
his rage, he caught a glimpse of something magnificent. He
pictured a weapon born of the heavens. A beacon powerful
enough to pierce the endless night. An army hewn from
everything he had lost.

Sigmar set his artisans to work and for long ages they toiled,
striving to harness the power of the stars. As Sigmar's great
work neared completion, he turned back to the realms and saw
that the dominion of Chaos was almost complete. The hour
for vengeance had come. Finally, with lightning blazing across
his brow, he stepped forth to unleash his creations.

The Age of Sigmar had begun.

PROLOGUE

ASHES

Hendrick Saul was surrounded by a whirling storm of faces, transformed from meek villagers to twisted gargoyles by their fear, their anger and their hate. They pressed around him on all sides beneath a dark and clouded sky, the cadaverous walls of Stonehallow looming at their backs.

'Varlen!' he heard Romilla Aiden shouting. 'Varlen, stop! Please, you have to stop this!'

She was answered by an inhuman scream, a sound that seemed ripped from several throats at once, not all of them human. It pierced the torch-lit darkness and rebounded from the towering walls of ancient ruins.

'*It brings death!*' screamed the awful tangle of voices, the words so mangled they were barely decipherable.

'Get out of my way!' roared Hendrick at the crowd around him, and for a moment he was tempted to swing his heavy war-hammer, Reckoner, into their midst. His fierce temper surged, its flames stoked by fear of his own.

Fear of what was happening to his brother.

Fear of what Varlen had become.

He controlled himself with supreme effort, reminding himself these were good people who had not asked for this horror to be thrust upon them. Holding his warhammer two-handed like a quarterstaff, he thrust at the townsfolk around him rather than swinging for them with its weighty head. Ignoring the farming implements and rusty daggers they held. Ignoring their outraged cries of pain and their furious demands that he stop fighting them.

'What did you people bring into our home?' the village headman cried. Hendrick had already forgotten his name. In the midst of this horror, he had forgotten everything but his brother.

'Varlen!' he yelled, shoving his way through the jostling mass of angry townsfolk. 'Varlen, you have to stop this! You have to fight it!'

Bedlam surrounded Hendrick. The dark of night was full of panicked bodies crashing and grinding together like the bone-jarring confusion of a battlefield rout. Blazing torches threw hard light that danced wildly. One moment, screaming faces were lit in hellish hues, the next they were but dark silhouettes, limned by fire.

'That *monster* was your brother,' screamed an old woman, her eyes bulging and her spittle spattering his face. 'For Sigmar's sake, kill it!'

'Enwin…' another babbled, tears streaming down her face. 'It tore… It tore his head off.'

Hendrick stumbled over sprawled bodies and crashed down onto the cobbles, where he slithered in blood.

Varlen had done this, he thought wildly. His brother, his garrulous, good-hearted, courageous brother, the leader of the

Swords of Sigmar. He had transformed into... *something*. Some monstrous abomination had burst from within Varlen Saul's flesh as the crown on his brow pulsed with eldritch power. It had ploughed through the mercenaries of Varlen's company, battering Bartiman Kotrin aside with the tumorous flesh-mass that had been its right arm, gouging the flesh of Romilla Aiden with the thicket of talons sprouting from its left hand.

It had rampaged through ruined corridors and echoing chambers, and as it had come across knots of shocked townsfolk it had torn into them like a bladed hurricane. All the time its flesh ran like wax. All the time, that awful cursed crown upon its brow had pulsated with unclean light.

Hendrick and the others had pursued Varlen, or rather the thing that Varlen had become. They had gaped, appalled, at what their leader had done to the folk who had offered them sanctuary. They had chased it out onto the wide, grassy gathering space before the ruins that housed Stonehallow – but so had the townsfolk.

Filled with religious terror at the horror stalking their halls, the mob had flowed down upon Varlen. Hendrick's group had tried to intervene, to slow their cursed leader's rampage and subdue him before the mob could do so. Bartiman had cast an entropic curse upon Varlen that had made the monster stumble but had not slowed it. Romilla had compelled its taint to be gone in Sigmar's name, but though white fire had leapt at the priest's words, whatever power she could bring to bear could not overmatch that pouring from the cursed crown.

In desperation, Eleanora VanGhest had shot Varlen through the leg, hoping perhaps to slow or stop him. For her troubles she had been smashed aside by Varlen's mutating nest of appendages and only just escaped a messy evisceration. Hendrick had even struck his brother, more than once, and that at last had slowed the monster, though it had felt to Hendrick as though he struck himself with every blow.

Though more than two dozen of them had died in the act, the Stonehallow mob had bludgeoned Varlen to his knees and collared him with the long catch-poles they used for wrangling their gheln-hounds.

The Swords of Sigmar had tried to intervene, to protest that it was not Varlen's fault and explain that it was the cursed crown he had placed, all unknowing, upon his brow.

The folk of Stonehallow did not care.

Now Hendrick squinted against a sudden flare of light from ahead. Heat beat against his skin and a great *whoomph* filled the air.

A pyre, he realised, and his lips skinned back from his teeth in a desperate snarl.

'*The Moonshadow brings death!*' screamed his brother in a cacophony of ever-more-monstrous voices. '*The Moonshadow brings death to Draconium.*'

'Don't you dare!' bellowed Hendrick as the crowd surged and he saw a mass of terrified-looking villagers forcing his mutant brother towards the flames. The sight of Varlen knocked the breath from Hendrick's lungs. His brother's fine clothes had been torn to shreds by the masses of chitin and writhing muscle and quivering fat that had sprouted from the warped trunk of his body. He staggered on an uneven thicket of foul limbs that seemed ripped from a dozen species Hendrick couldn't even have named. Yet it was Varlen's face that filled his mind with horror, that stole his wits and made him howl with anguish. It was monstrous, deformed, the dark metal of the crown seared irreparably into the molten flesh of its forehead. Yet they were still Varlen's eyes that stared back at Hendrick. He saw fear and frustration in his brother's gaze, his true self thrashing frantically to stay afloat amidst the tide of revolting madness in which he was drowning.

Varlen.

They were going to burn Varlen.

'No, *no*,' shouted Hendrick, and now he did heft Reckoner. He would pulverise these superstitious fools. He would batter a bloody path through them to reach his brother and somehow, somehow, he would tear that damned crown from his head and –

Then Romilla was next to him, appearing from amidst the crowd to place a hand upon his arm. She stared at him with furious intensity, her eyes boring into his.

'Hendrick, you cannot. These are Sigmar's people. They are terrified, and Varlen has… Varlen has killed so many of them. Look at him, Hendrick. Look at him and see that is no longer your brother.'

'It's Varlen, Romilla,' snarled Hendrick, throwing her hand off. He dwarfed the priest but still she stood in his path and placed her hand on his arm again.

'It is not. Varlen is gone, lost to damnation, and these people are burning that which destroyed him. I am sorry, Hendrick, but they do Sigmar's work, just as we do.'

He stared down at her, the blood hammering in his temples, the screams of the crowd beating against him like storm waves. He saw, at last, the anguish in Romilla's face, the tears threatening to well in the corners of her eyes, and the strength went out of him.

Hendrick fell to his knees amidst the surging crowd. Reckoner slipped from his hands and hit the blood-wet grass with a thump. Romilla stepped close and placed a hand on his shoulder.

'I am so sorry, Hendrick,' she said.

Other sounds came after: sounds of a crowd baying and a

monster burning; the inhuman howls of something that had once been human as it ranted and raved of a moon, and of danger, and of death.

Hendrick heard none of it, and yet he heard it all. When it was over, he knew for sure that, though he might still walk and breathe and see, he was every bit as dead as the brother he had lost.

Hendrick sat on the corner of his stone bed-pallet and watched dawn creep back into the world. Rosy fingers of light caressed the ancient stonework of the monastery, spilling through an ancient archway then diffusing across the silk hangings in Hendrick's chamber. It limned the screens with soft gold and seemed to halo the depictions of Sigmar, acting out his great deeds of myth across their swaying surfaces. It was a beautiful sight, especially when accompanied by the soft sigh of the breeze through old stonework and the faint scent of the incense that the villagers burned to ward off evil.

Hendrick knew that it should have stirred something inside him. All he felt was hollow.

No, he realised. Not just hollow, he felt resentful. How could the light of Hysh return after what had happened the night before? How could it show its face in the skies above after witnessing such horrors? How dare it? How could the realms continue with such a gentle and lovely dawn when his brother was dead?

The first dawn without Varlen.

It should have been grim and grey as a dead crone's hair. It should have been dark as damnation. But no, the light bled back into the skies just as it had for all thirty-seven years of Hendrick's life, and the absence of his older brother gave it no pause at all.

A shape moved beyond the screens. Hendrick's hand twitched towards Reckoner. He found himself hoping that the townsfolk had reneged upon their agreement, that they were coming to take him now. It was only because the Swords of Sigmar had seemed to renounce their leader in the end that the villagers had permitted them a night's refuge before casting the mercenaries out. That, and the fear in their eyes at what they thought the Swords might be capable of if pushed.

He relaxed as Aelyn slipped between the screens and stopped, staring down at him. The aelf stood silent and unnaturally still. She regarded him with black-and-amber eyes that most humans found disturbing, but to which Hendrick had long ago grown accustomed. The two stared at each other in silence, long enough for Hendrick to draw and release a heavy breath.

'Have you slept?' Aelyn asked.

'Have you?' he challenged. A muscle twitched in her right cheek, a minute tell that Hendrick knew indicated her displeasure.

'You sat there all night, hmm?'

'And if I did?' He could hear his own belligerence, knew it was ill directed at this, his oldest friend. He knew, too, that she wouldn't take it personally.

'You'll be stiff, tired, sluggish,' she replied in a matter-of-fact tone. 'If they turn on us, you'll be damn all use.'

'They're not going to turn on us,' he said, feeling the truth of her words as he rolled his neck and winced at the ache that had settled there. 'We're too many, and, Sigmar help me, they saw last night what we can do. Besides, we have Romilla.'

Aelyn inclined her head slightly, a gesture of tacit agreement.

'We ought not linger,' she said. 'If you're not sleeping then get up off that palette. We've choices to make.'

Hendrick ground his knuckles into his sore eyes, achieving little other than triggering a dull pain at the backs of their orbits. He blinked and took another breath against the tight weight he felt in his chest. He ran a hand over his bald scalp, felt a few days' stubble rasp at his callused palm.

'Aelyn–' he began, but she twitched her fingers to cut him off. For a moment he saw the ghost of something like sympathy cross her sharp features. The surprise of it came close to unmanning him.

'I know, Hendrick,' she said. 'It was horrible. We all lost him, but you lost the most. You will mourn. We all will. The fact remains, we have choices to make.'

'And with Varlen gone...' his words trailed off. It was the first time he had voiced it out loud, the first time he had made it real.

'You alone lead our mercenary band, now. You alone lead the Swords of Sigmar,' she finished for him. 'So. Lead.'

Hendrick closed his eyes and ordered his thoughts. He took a tight grip upon the leash of his temper, the same temper that had propelled him and Varlen into this life in the first place. He wouldn't let it flare now, not when it might endanger his friends.

He'd lost enough in this wretched settlement already.

'Are you centred?' asked Aelyn. Hendrick opened his eyes, looked at her, nodded. She returned the gesture then turned and slipped through the screens, the muted browns and greens of her waywatcher's garb vanishing through the gold and silver curtain.

Hendrick took a firm grip of Reckoner and rose.

'I am centred,' he muttered, hands tightening on his hammer's leather grip until it creaked. 'Just pray, Sigmar, don't let them give me cause.'

With that, he followed his second-in-command through the silk screens and out, into the settlement of Stonehallow.

* * *

Hendrick followed Aelyn down a corridor whose alcoves had been turned into small shanty-dwellings, all empty. She turned through a stone arch daubed in gaudy fire-hues, then into a high circular shaft that had once housed a corkscrew stair. The two mercenaries had to clamber up a haphazard arrangement of wood-and-metal scaffolds that had replaced its crumbled ruins, pushing up through draped curtains of red and orange silk.

They emerged through another arch and into a larger chamber that might once have been a chantry. Half its ceiling had collapsed, the rubble cleared away and silken awnings hung over the ragged hole. Wood and silk structures crowded the chamber's wings, a small village's worth of lightweight dwellings hidden away within the shadows of the ruined monastery. Hendrick noted that all of Stonehallow was hidden in this fashion. It was how the people had stayed safe during the Age of Chaos, concealed behind a façade of hollow ruin and the lingering holy energies that permeated the monastery's stones.

It was why they had responded with such terror to Varlen.

This wing of the vast monastery had been abandoned, its inhabitants scurrying away elsewhere while the outsiders remained. They had enough space to work with, thought Hendrick; the monastery was immense, an inexplicable ruin left over from the Age of Myth. How else could you hide an entire town in its depths?

Three figures waited for them here.

Eleanora VanGhest sat propped against the stub of an old stone pillar, beside the heap of backpacks and satchels that contained their gear. She was clad in her ever-present engineer's smock. Her hair was tousled and she had a lens-monocle pulled down over one eye. She was tinkering with an arrangement of gears and delicate metal arms, and barely glanced at Hendrick and Aelyn as they approached.

Borik Jorgensson and Romilla Aiden both rose at Hendrick's approach. The former was a stocky slab of a Kharadron duardin. He had his helm hooked to his belt, and in the wan dawn light every wrinkle on his weathered face created its own sharp shadow. He appraised Hendrick with his steely gaze but said nothing. After a moment, the duardin mercenary went back to cleaning the considerable mass of the six-barrelled rotary cannon he lugged about with him.

Romilla came to meet Hendrick half way. She wore white and blue robes still stained with soot from the night before, and her tattooed scalp was shaven like Hendrick's.

'Sigmar's blessings upon you,' she said firmly, reaching up to clap one scarred hand on Hendrick's shoulder. 'I have prayed all night for your brother's soul. If intercession were possible, I promise you it has been achieved.'

Hendrick gave Romilla a grateful nod then looked past her pointedly.

'Bartiman is still asleep,' said Aelyn.

'Sigmar only knows how the old sorcerer has rested at all, after what occurred,' added Romilla, her distaste clear.

'Olt slept beyond the walls,' continued Aelyn.

'Not his gods, not his problem?' asked Hendrick.

'Nothing so callous,' replied Romilla reproachfully. 'Varlen was a friend to all of us, Olt as much so as any.'

Hendrick winced. 'I'm sorry, you're right. I'm exhausted and… out of sorts.'

Romilla sighed. 'That's putting it mildly. You had to witness your brother teeter upon the brink of damnation, and then pass through the fires of cleansing. I cannot begin to imagine how you feel this day. I only wish to remind you that your friends and allies remain just that. After what happened, Olt chose to absent himself lest fearful locals turn their eyes upon him next.'

'So, not his gods, but very much his problem,' amended Hendrick grimly. 'If they have laid a finger on him– '

'They'd have suffered for it,' said Aelyn. 'He's safe. He'll find us when we depart. He always does.'

Hendrick felt Borik glance his way again at the word 'depart'. The duardin held his gaze a moment, then cleared his throat and went back to his gun.

'Come, break your fast,' said Romilla, tugging Hendrick over to where the others waited. She pushed him down onto a broken length of pillar, then produced dried meat, a canteen of water and a slightly withered jashbin fruit.

'My appetite died with my brother,' said Hendrick, immediately regretting how melodramatic the words sounded aloud. Romilla pressed the provisions upon him regardless.

'As did all of ours,' she said. 'But the Lord Sigmar has work for us yet, and we cannot do it exhausted and half-starved. Eat what you can, Hendrick.'

He took a bite of dried meat, chewed, tasted nothing but ash. Hendrick forced the mouthful down with a dry click and swilled his mouth with brackish water. He took another bite, and another, attacking the mean repast like a begrudged enemy until it was gone. Hendrick wondered, distantly, whether he would ever enjoy food or drink again.

Romilla joined him in his meal. Aelyn stood and stared off into the distance, head cocked as though listening to something. Aside from the sounds of stolid chewing and swallowing, there was only the click and tick of Eleanora's tinkering, and the slow scrape as Borik cleaned the bore of another gun barrel.

'El, my dear, will you not eat?' asked Romilla. She had to repeat the question before Eleanora glanced up at her.

'No,' replied the engineer. 'I've nearly got this. The third fly-wheel is still sticking, and the gears won't quite mesh right until

I've figured out why.' With that, she returned to her work with an intensity calculated to shut everything else out.

'She's nearly got this,' echoed Romilla in exasperation. Hendrick ignored her and forced down the last of the jashbin.

Hendrick gave a low grunt. His thoughts were far away, filled with the darkness of the night before. He heard again the screams of the townsfolk and the raving of his brother, the crack and crunch as Varlen unmade them with hands that had become talons. He felt the awful shock up his arms as Reckoner connected with his brother's chest, the sensation so real that Hendrick's knuckles twitched with it. He heard his companions' cries as they fought to subdue the monster that had once been their leader and friend, and he smelled the smoke as the villagers lit their great pyre. He jumped as he felt a hand-clap land on his shoulder, half fearing as he looked up that he would see his brother's twisted visage and melting pupils.

Instead, he saw Romilla crouched before him.

'It doesn't do to dwell, Hendrick,' she said, her tone stern but not unkind. 'What happened was too terrible to keep reliving.'

'What *did* happen?' asked Aelyn. 'Are we sure we know?'

'It was that damned crown,' replied Hendrick. 'I told him to leave it where it lay.'

'You know Varlen,' said Romilla, then winced at the faux pas. 'Knew. Sorry. We had fought our way through Sigmarknew-what to get to the heart of that Dreadhold. If there was a prize to be had for all that effort, he was going to claim it. And once it was on his brow–'

'It wouldn't come off,' growled Hendrick. 'We all saw him trying to pry the damned thing off his skull. We all saw what it did to him!' He took a breath, lowered his voice. 'There's no sense indulging in should-haves or would-haves. Varlen put the crown on, and saw visions, and they led him here to his death.'

'The Moonshadow brings death,' said Aelyn. 'That's what he was shouting, at the end, when he… burned. "The Moonshadow brings death to Draconium". What do you suppose it means?'

'Varlen was under the influence of a malefic artefact,' said Romilla. 'It didn't mean a thing.'

'Yes, it did,' said Hendrick, and even he was surprised at the iron he heard in his voice. They were all silent for a few moments, and he felt his companions glancing uncomfortably at one another. Eleanora's tools clicked relentlessly, dry and irritating jags of sound in the sepulchral quiet of the chamber.

He drew breath, wanting to shout at her to leave the damn mechanism alone. Before he could, Aelyn spoke.

'We need to decide what to do.'

'The townsfolk are undoubtedly winding themselves up to something even now,' said Romilla. 'They lost loved ones last night, in horrible ways, and it was us that brought that horror into their home. They won't care that it wasn't intentional, and they won't stay too frightened to act forever.'

Aelyn looked pointedly at Hendrick. He felt the weight of their stares turn upon him, felt his shoulders hunch defensively and his heavy brow settle into a frown. He'd just lost his brother, for Sigmar's sake, could they not give him the time to mourn?

But no, he thought; they were right, and hiding away from his responsibilities behind brooding silence was a luxury he could no longer allow himself. Varlen had always been the charismatic one, the people person, always ready with a quick quip and an easy smile to put folk at ease. Hendrick had been more of a silent partner, the menace that backed up his brother's charm and decisive sense of purpose.

Purpose. That was a word his mind could latch onto, a star

by which he could steer. Varlen's death had to have had a purpose, and Aelyn had shown him what that was.

'We make for Draconium,' he said. His comrades stirred awkwardly around him. Borik cleared his throat again.

'Hendrick, where even *is* Draconium?' asked Romilla. 'I've heard the name, but...'

'Draconium is a large fortified border city located two hundred and eighty-two miles to the north of Hammerhal Aqsha, and forty miles north of where we are now,' said Eleanora, still not looking up from her work. 'It dominates the pass known as the Drake's Jaws in the volcanic Redspine Range. Its thermal springs form the source of a canal that bears trade barges and troop barques through the reconsecrated lands north of Hammerhal.'

'Thank you, El,' said Romilla. 'But even if we do know where it is, what reason would we have for going there?'

Hendrick looked at the priest as though she were slow of thought.

'Varlen's words, at the end, when they were... when he... burned. We know that they were a prophetic warning, one that he died to deliver. We are going to see that it reaches the right ears.'

'Hendrick, we know no such thing!' exclaimed Romilla. 'Sigmar's hammer, he was *transforming* into something unclean, gibbering like a lunatic! For all we know, his words were some diabolical utterance designed to drag us into damnation along with him!'

'I don't believe that,' said Hendrick, feeling the familiar hot anger trying to well up and overwhelm his better judgement. 'He saw things, knew things, once he put that crown on. For months before... Things he couldn't have known. He predicted the Gor-kin ambush in the Ash Hills, didn't he? He saw that spine-trap and stopped you treading in it, didn't he, Romilla? Varlen was still Varlen. It didn't beat him, not even at the end, and he was still trying to aid us even in death.'

'We're meant to be bringing the rest of the treasure to the rendezvous at High Crag,' said Borik. He didn't look up as he spoke, carried on working an oilcloth over his weapon. 'We miss that meeting, we don't get paid, and maybe the Olmori tribe come looking for their ancestral treasures.'

'The Olmori tribe were cowards enough to send mercenaries to recover those treasures in the first place,' said Hendrick. 'They can wait a few more days while we deliver this message.'

Borik shot Hendrick a quick glance from beneath his heavy brows but made no other reply.

'Look, *if* Varlen was lucid, if he was still seeing visions... what if this is a warning from Sigmar? What if we ignore a warning from Sigmar and compound failure with faithlessness? All we have to do is to reach the city and make sure that someone in a position of authority hears our warning. Then that's it, job done. Who knows, if you're so concerned they may even provide some fiscal reward for our efforts.'

'We're mercenaries. Fiscal reward is our *only* concern,' the duardin said.

'We're a sight more than that,' said Hendrick hotly. 'Varlen always made sure we did Sigmar's work first and thought of profits second.'

'I'm sorry, I know you don't want to hear this, but as I said to you last night, Varlen may not have *been* Varlen anymore,' said Romilla, rising to her feet and looking around for support. 'Surely we're not going to break faith with our employers just because some unnatural being possessed our friend and used his face to tug upon our heartstrings?'

Hendrick felt the disapproval coming off Borik in waves.

Eleanora's tools clicked away with panicked intensity, and he felt frustrated fury build in his chest.

'Listen,' continued Romilla in more conciliatory tones. 'Perhaps we should–'

'No, we shouldn't,' Aelyn said. They all stared at the aelf, Hendrick included. Aelyn was so quiet, so still, that it was possible to forget she was even there until she spoke, but when she did her voice was sharp and clear as cut crystal.

Romilla drew breath to speak again but Aelyn talked over her.

'Before today, Varlen and Hendrick led the Swords of Sigmar. Now Varlen is gone, Hendrick is our only leader. We are mercenaries, not vagabonds. If our leader gives us an order, we obey it. The matter requires no further debate.'

Romilla blinked, scowled, but subsided. She looked at Hendrick.

'And do you so order, sergeant?' she asked.

Hendrick shot a grateful glance at Aelyn but she ignored him, and he felt the rebuke in her eyes. He had to do better, had to be firm not furious, a leader not a bully. He would try, he told himself, for Varlen's sake. This would all, ultimately, be for Varlen's sake. Nothing else would make his loss bearable.

'I do,' he said. 'We will deliver the message as quickly as we can and then return to the Olmori, and if they are angry then I will pay whatever reparations or face whatever judgement they deem right. You won't suffer for this, I'll make sure of it. But for Varlen's sake, we have to deliver his last warning. Maybe then something good can come out of this damned tragedy. Maybe it'll be enough to save lives.'

Borik grunted noncommittally. Romilla looked somewhat mollified.

'Very well then,' she said heavily. 'For Varlen.'

'Ah! Got it!' said Eleanora in sudden triumph, her tools giving a final flurry of clicks. She looked around at them and smiled. 'It'll work now,' she said, holding the inexplicable gadget up for their inspection. 'We can go.'

Hendrick sighed, shook his head, and stooped to gather his gear.

'For Varlen,' he echoed.

ACT 1
GLOAMING

'Listen child and heed me well,
A grave warning you must fear.
Get to bed and silent stay,
Lest the blackencap might hear.
Shuttered must the windows be,
Your eyes, quickly, close them fast!
Or the Bad Moon's light you'll see,
And the sight will be your last.'

– *Azyrheimer nursery rhyme*

CHAPTER ONE

SHADOWS

Tobias Kench stepped from the tavern door into the cobbled street beyond. He wiped the blood from his knuckles and took a deep breath of cool evening air.

'That's better,' he sighed, rolling his shoulders. The Wayward King rose at his back. The tavern was a slab-like architectural pile that looked as though it had been carelessly discarded rather than built. Its bottleglass windows were webbed with cracks, its heavy roof slates had begun to erode, and the rain-proofing was peeling down its frontage where the landlord had been remiss in his duties of care.

Tobias wouldn't have drunk in this dive if his life depended on it. He wouldn't have drunk anywhere in the Pipers' District, come to think of it. But the Wayward King was always good for working out the stresses of a bad day. It had got so that the regulars knew to get very quiet and attend their flagons of rotgut when Tobias walked in, but there was always some-one who didn't know better: docksnipes off the barges that came upriver from Hammerhal Aqsha, spending their ingots before they'd earned them; a local piper who'd scraped together enough dust to drink their resentment away in the cheapest dive in town while cursing their betters for their own misfortunes; ne'er-do-wells making sure to celebrate their latest score a safe distance from any who would place their faces. Some days it was just outsiders that he judged to be lacking in piety, or those Tobias suspected had turned from Sigmar's light.

Tobias would never take his fists to good, God-King-fearing folk. He would have been horrified at the thought. But the Wayward King never let him down.

'Such impious souls always stray when the daemon drink takes them,' he muttered to himself as he readjusted his watchman's cloak and took a moment to work the sparker of his lantern. It stubbornly failed to fire, reminding Tobias that he had meant to hand it in for repair and draw a replacement from stores. Evening was drawing in and the shadows of the volcanic mountains flowed along Draconium's streets like ink, pooling between the city's tall, slate-roofed buildings. 'I am merely preempting their transgressions, reminding them that Sigmar is always watching.'

Behind him, the tavern was quiet, as it always was after he left. It would become rowdy again soon enough. They'd light the lanterns, mop up the blood and carry on as though he'd never been there. Tobias, meanwhile, would continue his watch.

Ever was the pious man's burden thus.

Lightning blossomed high overhead, drawing Tobias' gaze to the sky. Up there, amidst the jagged peaks and rumbling calderas of the Redspine Range, storms brewed and broke with ferocious speed. The storm's wrath was a sign that Sigmar watched over them all, thought Tobias, as arcing bolts were drawn from the sky to strike the metal prayer rods of the shrines that dotted the mountainsides. He wondered if any pilgrims were up there now, knelt upon narrow ledges of stone, their rapturous expressions illuminated by the arc and flare of one lightning strike after another. If so, there'd be bodies to bring down by morning, those who had passed into the realm of the dead and whose charred mortal remains were no longer required.

'Not my task,' Tobias told himself. 'Not for many years now.' Pilgrim retrieval was a duty given to the watchmen fourth class, and these days Tobias was second class. He touched a fingertip to the silver clasp, inscribed with Sigmar's hammer, which held his cloak in place and denoted his rank. A habit, ever since Iyenna had left him to the affections of what she described as his twin mistresses – his job and his religion.

As it always did, the thought of Iyenna soured Tobias' mood. He squared his shoulders and set off down the street. His normal patrol route took him from here through the fringes of Docksflow before he doubled back west to reach the factories and workshops of Forges, before angling back uphill through the more affluent streets of High Drake and thence to the watch blockhouse atop Gallowhill. It would only be a short detour, however, to angle through the dive streets of the Slump. Tobias was sure he would find more impious souls to punish down there.

The watchman had taken only a few steps before a subtle movement caught his eye. Shadows shifted in the alleyway beside the Wayward King. Between a broken crate and a heap of burlap sacks, something moved. There was a scratching sound. Tobias frowned, shifting his grip on his halberd and pacing closer to the alley. Vagrants and fengh addicts were a constant problem in Draconium. Life was hard in the realms beyond the heavens, Tobias could attest to that, but he would never understand how desperate someone must have to be to lean on the rotted crutch of drugs.

His scowl became a smile as his eyes adjusted to the gloom and he made out glinting yellow eyes and a long, waving tail.

'Hah, Saint Klaus, you old rogue. Where have you been? It's been weeks, I thought the God-King might have taken you up for reforging!'

Tobias sank to his haunches and held out a hand. The cat padded from the alleyway, its gaze switching hopefully between his gloved hand and his smiling face. It shoved its head against his fingers, an insistent nudge that elicited a chuckle from Tobias. He scratched the cat's ears.

'Still no owner, lad?' asked Tobias. Klaus purred, danced back from his hand for a moment then wound under it again with his tail twitching. 'Oh, very well.' Tobias' smile broadened, and he reached into a pouch at his belt for a strip of dried saltfish. Klaus snatched the food from his hand, and Tobias watched with pleasure as the cat chewed and swallowed, then looked expectantly at him again.

'One of these days, I'm going to carry you back to the blockhouse and we'll take you on as a mascot.' Tobias reached for a second piece of fish but paused as a fresh volley of lightning broke high overhead. In its strobing glare, the alleyway behind Klaus was momentarily illuminated and Tobias saw something strange.

The watchman's frown returned, and he rose, trying again to light his lantern. It sparked and died, sparked and died, then at last sputtered fitfully into life. Klaus meowed a question, but Tobias ignored him, brow furrowed as he raised the lantern and played its beam along the alley. *There.* Halfway along, at the darkest point where buildings loomed high overhead, Tobias saw a deeper darkness surrounded by lumpy shapes.

'Klaus, old boy, I think you may make a watchman yet,' murmured Tobias. 'My cloak if that's not a tunnel of some sort, dug right in under the Wayward King.'

Thoughts full of smugglers and thieves, Tobias opened the clasps on the haft of his watchman's halberd and affixed his lantern beneath its blade. A twist of the mechanism and the clasps snapped shut, securing his lantern so that, when his halberd was lowered and pointed blade-first ahead of him, its light would shine out to light his way and blind potential miscreants. Tobias always thought of it as Sigmar's light, an inescapable glare that transfixed wrong-doers and aided the God-King's rightful servants.

Stepping carefully past Klaus, Tobias advanced into the alleyway. Lightning cracked on high, whitewashing the walls and floor then plunging them back into shadow. To Tobias' right rose the flank of the Wayward King, all crumbling stone and a couple of small, dirty windows high up. To his left hunched a tenement, one of many built to house dock workers, and Tobias noted that the only windows on this side of the building were long-ago broken and boarded. It was a good spot for secretive deeds; no eyes upon it at all.

None but his and Sigmar's.

In the beam of his lantern the dim suggestion of shapes resolved into something clear and, to Tobias' mind, incriminating. A hole had been dug here, right into the foundations of the Wayward King. It was surrounded by rough heaps of spoil, dirt and old broken cobbles piled a foot deep on the alley floor.

Sloppy work. Professionals would have removed the debris to avoid attention being drawn to their efforts. And surely pointless, he reflected with puzzlement. The hatch that led to the tavern's beer cellar was around the back of the building, in Drover's Lane; he knew from experience that its lock had been broken and repaired so many times that a good kick was all it took to snap it off and gain access below. So why go to the trouble of digging a hole?

He paced closer, lantern beam swaying with his footsteps. Tobias' body radiated tension. He was ready at any moment for some malcontent to spring from the pit, cudgel swinging.

Nothing moved but him.

Lightning flashed again as he reached the lip of the hole and saw that, sure enough, it led straight down into the tavern's cellar. Or rather, he realised as he stared at it, it had been dug up and *out* of the cellar. The way the soil had been pushed up and heaped around left him in no doubt of that fact. Tobias' frown deepened. He sank down on his haunches, playing the beam of his lantern around the edges of the pit.

'This was dug with... claws? Burrowed by something?' He glanced back and saw that Klaus had followed him a short way down the alley, but that the cat had now stopped, wide eyed and watchful, some way back. Klaus' tail twitched with agitation. His fur bristled.

Something was awry here, and Tobias aimed to find out what. If some vermin or beast had been allowed to make its lair in the cellar of the Wayward King then his next visit wouldn't be the usual social call, but an official inspection that would undoubtedly end in the negligent owner's business being shut down. Tobias felt a momentary pang of regret that his visits would have to end. It was eclipsed by the greater surge of pious satisfaction at the thought of doing his duty to Sigmar.

'Nothing for it, lad,' he said, setting off for Drover's Lane. 'That lock's getting broken again.'

A few moments and one swift kick later, and Tobias was treading carefully down into the darkened cellar of the Wayward King. He pointed his halberd ahead of him, its lantern light flickering as he played it across stacked kegs and boxes of foodstuffs.

'City watch,' he said in a loud, clear voice as he advanced. 'If anyone is here, step out into the light now or it will go worse for you.'

He paused at the bottom of the steps, waiting, but nothing moved. Tobias had been half-ready for some belligerent duardin smuggler or worshipper of the Dark Gods to burst out and assail him. If he was honest with himself, he had rather hoped for it.

It was cold here, the district being too poor to benefit from Draconium's thermal heating-pipe network. Ironic, he thought; they toiled to build and maintain the system that drew volcanic heat up through the pipehouse and funnelled it to the richer regions of the city, but they had not earned the right to benefit from it themselves.

From above, Tobias could hear a muffled din of rowdy conversation, singing and the clink of glass. Trickles of dust fell sporadically through the floorboards above his head, drifting in his lantern light.

'How in Sigmar's name can they have a hole in their cellar and not know about it?' he wondered aloud, but a moment later Tobias' question was answered as he realised that he couldn't see the hole at all from where he stood. Pacing across the cellar to where he knew the hole must be, Tobias instead found a wooden wall barring his path, empty ale tuns piled up against it in a heap.

The boards were rough-cut yarrenwood, festooned with splinters.

'Cheap,' muttered Tobias. 'And comparatively new.' It had clearly been put there to hide something.

Quick and quiet, Tobias set aside his halberd, propping it so its light was pointed at the false wall. He moved the empty tuns one by one, stacking them to his right until he had cleared a good space, and then slid his gloved fingers into the gap between two boards. A quick, sharp wrench and the board he had grasped came away with a splintering crack of wood and nails.

Tobias peered through the gap he had made. Sure enough, there was another few feet of space back here, and a ragged-edged tunnel connecting cellar and alleyway. He saw Klaus staring at him through the hole.

Repeating his wrenching procedure several more times, Tobias made a large enough gap to squeeze through. He thought about grabbing his halberd, but the weapon would be unwieldy in the confined space and besides, its light would serve him well enough from where it was.

Tobias pushed his way into the hidden chamber and immediately saw what it was for. Heaped at one end were several wood-and-iron strongboxes, hidden away behind the false wall.

'Ill-gotten gains, I'll wager,' he said with a satisfied smile. 'The watch coffers are about to receive a generous donation.'

Then he registered another hole, this one yawning in the dirt floor at one end of the hidden chamber. This pit was wider, around five feet across and vanishing back and downwards into darkness. Again, it looked to have been excavated with large, heavy claws. A damp reek wafted from it, causing Tobias to wrinkle his nose in disgust. Small, glistening fungi sprouted around its entrance, half-visible in the spill of his lantern's light.

'What in the realms did this?' Tobias wondered aloud. He edged tentatively closer to the hole, peering into its depths. Suddenly, he felt the lack of his halberd keenly. He was about to turn back for it when his lantern's light suddenly winked out.

Tobias cursed as he was plunged into inky darkness.

'That damned lantern,' he snarled, then stopped as he heard

a scuff of movement from the direction of the main cellar. The sound came again, something or someone trying to move stealthily across the dirt floor. Someone coming closer.

Tobias tensed, then jumped as Klaus gave a yowl from somewhere up above. Heart thumping, Tobias turned, trying to locate the gap in the boards that led back to the cellar. The hole up to the alleyway gave next to no light at all.

He fumbled at his belt for his coglock pistol.

'City watch,' he barked, hoping to banish his panic with the weight of his authority. 'Whoever is there, you are interfering with an official investigation. Spark that lantern at once and step back, or face Sigmar's justice.'

He heard a sound that might have been a mean chuckle or might simply have been an animal snarl. Tobias' heart beat faster. Nothing human had made that noise. He strained to see, the darkness seeming to smother him. He fumbled his pistol free just as another scuffing scrape came from the cellar, the sound close enough that it made him recoil involuntarily.

Tobias stepped smartly back and pointed his pistol blindly.

'I'm warning you–' he began, then something struck his legs from behind with tremendous force. Tobias felt hot agony sear its way up from his calves, felt himself flung forwards and a sudden crunching impact as the floor rushed up to meet his face. He tasted blood. His ears rang. His throat closed over the winded shriek of pain that tried to escape his lips.

Something was ripping at the flesh of his legs, like a dozen knives driven into his calves and thighs all at once. Tobias tried to cry out, to yell for aid, but shock seemed to have sealed his voice inside him as sure as a stopper rammed into a bottle. He heard grunting, felt a wash of stinking breath, felt warm wetness, the slither of something muscular and slick across his flesh and a crushing weight.

No.

Not knives.

Teeth.

'Oh, Sigmar,' croaked Tobias, swinging his pistol down to point at whatever had surged from the hole and sunk its fangs into him. There came a violent dragging motion, a wrench that hauled Tobias across the dirt floor and cracked his chin against the lip of the hole. His gun spilled from his nerveless fingers. Consciousness wavered.

Tobias felt another ferocious tugging sensation, a crushing pressure and an explosion of unbearable agony from his legs, then a deeper darkness swallowed him whole.

CHAPTER TWO

OMENS

'What in the realms am I to make of all this?' Captain Helena Morthan of the Draconium City Watch asked her lieutenant, Taverton Grange, gesturing at the three-dozen parchment missives glaring up from her ironoak desk.

'Captain?'

Outside the heavy leaded windows of Captain Morthan's office, the sounds of the city bustled by. Cart wheels creaked. Voices rose in song or shouts or as the cries of hawkers. Animals brayed and instruments played.

Inside her office, however, the air was stuffy and still, and resonated with the captain's frustration.

'There's thrice the normal number of fresh reports here, Grange. Sigmar knows Draconium is a border city, and it's always been a touch wild. Our city has spirit! But this?' She gestured disgustedly at the reports, picked one up at random. 'A break-in at the Alchemists' Guild,' she read aloud, eyes scanning quickly over the parchment to pick out the pertinent details. 'Entry forced from below, through the bottle cellars. Supposedly some kind of tunnel that has since collapsed. No money taken but they were cleared out of alembics, test tubes, glass beakers...'

'A peculiar theft, captain,' said Taverton, his expression neutral. Helena nodded, raised her eyebrows, snatched up another report.

'A wild animal attack *inside* the common grazing paddocks on Westslope,' she read. 'The herdguards swear nothing crossed their fences, yet three runtin were, and I quote here, Grange, "ripped to pieces and scattered about the place as though a gargant had got hold of them".'

'So... not rustlers then, captain,' said Grange. Helena snorted, but her expression soured as she continued to read aloud from the reports.

'Eighteen separate fights last night alone, four involving naked blades, two in the streets of High Drake no less. Six accounts of what has been euphemistically termed *family disturbances* and Sigmar knows how many more that went unreported. Old Posver has been spewing predictions of doom and damnation again in Fountains Square, so much so that the men have had to move him on three times in the past day alone. Krysthenna the bloody Lantern Bearer has been preaching her Shrine of the Last Days' Warning nonsense again. She claims that "the signs are all there", or some such nigh-heretical twaddle. Drunken and disorderly conduct, including from two of our own.'

'Surely not, captain,' said Grange, frowning.

'Oh, it gets substantially more unpalatable,' she said. 'An elderly grandfather, snatched, presumably dragged through an open window, down in Rookswatch. The man's daughter is understandably inconsolable and demanding something be done.'

'One can hardly blame her,' said Grange, his aristocratic features twisted into an expression of muted dismay.

'No indeed,' said Helena. 'But for now, our highest priority must be these three reports,' she brandished a fistful of parchment. 'Three of our own, Grange. Two found dead, one not found at all. Watchman Second Class Ulswell, or what was left of her, found in an alleyway in Forges in what's described as "a near skeletal state". Watchman Third Class Phenswick, face-down in a dung heap behind a row of homes in Docksflow. He was found with *eighteen* separate stab-wounds in his back, neck and limbs, one ear missing, and what are described as "growths of a fungal nature" splitting his skin.'

Grange gave a disgusted grunt. 'Clearly these are not normal attacks,' he said, folding his arms in a defensive gesture that Helena thought betrayed his age. 'Skeletal, fungal, these aren't words you'd expect to read in such reports. Is there some kind of dark magic at work here, captain?'

'No idea, Grange,' said Helena. Grange was young, and he had been foisted upon her as a political appointment in exchange for the favour of the Grange family, one of Draconium's largest self-made mercantile dynasties. It was a mercy, thought Helena, that he just happened to be an efficient and no-nonsense officer most of the time. Still, there were occasions when he looked at her as though expecting the answers to just fall out of her open mouth, and in those moments her lieutenant irritated Helena Morthan considerably.

'You mentioned a third watchman, a disappearance?' he asked.

'Watchman Second Class Kench, vanished shortly after resolving a violent altercation in the Wayward King on Catchman's Street,' Helena read. 'No one reports seeing Kench after he stepped out of the tavern's door. It's like he just,' she snapped her fingers, '*vanished*.'

She watched her lieutenant think hard before opening his mouth to speak. This, at least, was a trait Captain Morthan approved of.

'There's no common method here, and no apparent concentration of incidents,' he said.

'No,' allowed Helena.

'So, are we treating these issues as simply a particularly bad night of unrelated disturbances, or...?' he left the sentence hanging.

'If it were just this last night, I would be inclined to do so,' said Helena. 'It isn't, though, is it? Let's say aloud what we're both thinking. There's been a notable uptick in civil disturbance, inexplicable violence and... what else to call them, odd incidents for several weeks now, hasn't there?'

'You have to step back and look at it as a whole, captain, but yes, I would concur with that assessment. There were the Pole Hill killings a fortnight back, that even the threat of the Etched didn't prevent. Those rain-scalded Sigmarite priests put the fear of divine retribution into even the city's most hardened ne'er-do-wells, and yet... Then there was that business down at the docks, all that grain spoiled and workers choking on whatever it was that billowed out of the holds. And there's been more violence and disquiet in the last turning than I've seen in my entire service to date.'

Keeping to herself the thought that Taverton Grange's *entire service* had been just over ten months, Helena instead said, 'I'm glad you concur. But what in Sigmar's name does it mean? Dark magic and malfeasance? Some kind of criminal sect or cult? Azyr forbid – a curse, or even an upwelling of Aqshyan energies?'

The Realm of Fire was a place of elemental passions whose influence could make emotions run hot in sentient beings. They had all heard reports of border forts and villages consumed by sudden eruptions of inexplicable rage and violence. Helena hoped fervently that such a thing was not occurring here. But no, she thought, the pieces didn't fit. Those possessed of elemental fury didn't steal bottles. And then there were the dreams, which Helena was becoming convinced couldn't be entirely natural. For a moment she almost raised them, but then she thought better of it.

Helena had been jolted awake, night after night, by garish, half-remembered nightmares that left her in a cold sweat. The truth, had she voiced it aloud, was that she could still feel the feather-light brush of insect legs against her skin, and that she was exhausted from being chased out of sleep by sickly pale light and vast, staring eyes.

She liked Grange, trusted him in a professional capacity, but he was still the son of one of Draconium's most notorious social climbers. She wasn't about to admit to her nightmares in front of a Grange, even if the bags under his eyes, and the short tempers and sallow faces of the men and women who served her, suggested to Helena that she wasn't alone in her suffering. The Grange family hadn't got to where they had without an aptitude for exploiting weakness.

She had no desire to usher in the reign of Captain Grange just yet.

Instead, Helena rose from her desk and snatched a rolled parchment from a nearby shelf. Gathering up the reports and piling them in a loose stack, she unrolled the map of Draconium across the top of her desk and pinned its corners down with lead weights. Helena took a wooden pot of brass pins and jabbed them, one by one, into the map.

'Lieutenant, send a runner to the short archives and have them yield all the reports of major crimes please. I want to add them to this.'

'Should we ransack the long archives, also?' asked Grange.

Helena considered.

'No, I think we can both agree this a relatively recent phenomenon, yes? There's nothing in the long archives less than a year old. But you could do worse than to request some breakfast for us.'

Grange saluted and hastened to the door, opening it a crack and conversing with the runner that waited outside. Helena tuned them out, focusing her entire attention on the map as she drove pins in to mark each incident that had occurred the night before. Everything else faded around her as she frowned down at the map, tracing lines between the pins, totting up crimes-per-district, furiously seeking any kind of pattern to what seemed just an anarchic upswell of violence, theft and mutilation.

Helena jumped when Grange cleared his throat beside her. She realised that he held a silver tray on which sat spiced breakfast pastries, rashers of salted runti-flank, two crystal glasses of jashbin juice, two drake-glaze cups and a pot of steaming metha. There was a heavy satchel hanging from one of Grange's broad shoulders, scrolls protruding from its top in neat rows.

'That's a lot of reports,' she said.

'Captain,' agreed Grange, setting the tray down on a corner of the desk and pouring her a mug of metha. Helena gratefully took the hot herbal infusion and sipped at it, accepting slightly scalded lips in exchange for the invigorating tingle it sent through her body.

'Best get started then, hadn't we?' said Helena.

An hour later, Helena stepped back from the map. She frowned down at it, ignoring the drift of reports scattered on the floor and the crumb-strewn tray that had been shoved aside until it teetered on the desk's corner.

She tilted her head, drew a deep breath and blew it out. The map was festooned with pins, a frankly alarming number of them.

'Do you see any pattern here, Grange?' she asked.

'None whatsoever, captain. It's… anarchic,' he said heavily.

'I was afraid you'd say that,' she said, folding her arms and scowling at the map.

'Should we petition the regent militant for additional resources?' asked Grange. 'We could certainly cite a time of exceptional travails, based on the evidence we have here.'

Regent Militant Selvador Mathenio Aranesis. The man was a war hero, had been a young initiate amidst the ranks of the Sigmarite crusade that had claimed this region all those years ago. He'd slain a champion of the Dark Gods in single battle while standing protectively over the fallen form of the arch-priest he followed, and his rise thereafter had been meteoric. Helena had a healthy respect for the regent militant's drive, his faith and his belief in the ongoing war of reconquest. However, he was an old man now and Helena had long suspected that, unable to stride out and claim his own glories, Selvador sought to live vicariously through those he ruled. He raised ever larger and more magnificent shrines to Sigmar in the richest districts of the city and surrounded them with statuary that imitated the glory of Azyrheim itself. He pushed recruitment drives every turning, Sigmarite warbands training under the watchful eyes of the city's militia-militant and then setting out into the wilds to the north with hammers and flails in hand.

Helena could well imagine how the regent militant would respond, were she to request a diversion of funds away from his grand undertakings. Was the faith of her watchmen not sufficient, he would ask? Was she perhaps incapable of discharging the duties she had sworn to perform? Had she tried increasing the prayer rotas for the men and women under her command, or issued them with fresh Sigmarite charms, or perhaps enforced the application of new faith tattoos?

None of this she said to Grange, however. Instead, Helena walked over to her desk, recovering the coglock pistol from her drawer and the scabbarded blade that leant against the table's side. She buckled both onto her belt. Taking her captain's cloak off its hook and fastening it with the ruby brooch of her office, she smiled humourlessly at Grange.

'We don't ask for help with that we can do ourselves, lieutenant. Get a team of scribes in here, second class or above, and have them go over everything again. They're to look for patterns, links, common cause, anything we may have missed.'

'And what will we be doing in the meantime, captain?' asked Grange looking, she thought, a touch too eager.

'Our duty, Grange,' she replied.

Helena and Grange picked up an honour guard of two watchmen first class as they strode through the blockhouse and out into Hangman's Square. Gallowhill was the highest district in Draconium, spreading as it did across a hilltop of quite some size, and the City Watch blockhouse stood at its highest point. The cobbled expanse of Hangman's Square was featureless barring the stark row of gallows that lined its northern edge, and despite the slab-sided administration buildings that huddled around it, the square still afforded a magnificent view of Draconium.

Slate roofs marched away down the hill's slopes, and beyond them Helena could see the city she had dwelt in all her life – the city she loved, spread out in morning tableaux. To the north lay Hallowheart, the regent militant's palace, glittering amidst a collection of martial structures, Sigmarite shrines and the homes of the local nobility, all hemmed in behind a high wall of marble and iron. Beyond it, the homes and businesses of Rookswatch marched away to the northern wall, the old Rookswatch towers looming precariously over the surrounding structures. To the south she saw Pipers, Docksflow, High Drake, Forges and the Slump. Fountains Square sat amongst them all, a broad expanse near half a mile across dominated by the magnificent statue-fountain of Sigmar Triumphant. The south wall closed off the pass some miles from her, both road and canal gates heavily fortified and pugnacious. She caught the distant glint of daylight on metal where militiamen patrolled the ramparts, and felt her heart stir at the sight of the banners of Draconium flapping in the warm winds that rolled down off the volcanic slopes. East sprawled Pole Hill, with its shrines ruled over by the acid-burned priests known as the Etched. Westward from her lay the common grazing-land of Westslope, fenced off by tall wooden stockades, the impressive spectacle of the Statuegarden, and the sprawling mass of Marketsway district.

Dry lightning crackled through the pale sky above, reaching out to brush the mountainsides, and reminding Helena uncomfortably of the touch of insect legs in her nightmares. The recollection soured her moment of pleasure at the sight of her city. Squaring her shoulders, Helena set off down the hill, gaggles of administrators and scribes parting before her purposeful stride.

'Let's get to the bottom of some things, shall we?' she said, as much to herself as the two watchmen who marched in her wake.

Helena made first for Fountains Square. Since her earliest

days as a watchman fourth class, she had been dealing with Old Posver, and now she had a mind to do so again.

'Go on Grange, ask,' she said as they walked.

'Captain?'

'Ask your question, I can practically hear you wondering.'

'Very well, captain,' said Grange, clearly uncomfortable at questioning his senior officer in front of two watchmen. 'Why *are* we prioritising a doom-saying vagrant over taking a hand in the murder cases?'

'Posver happens to be a very useful source of information,' said Helena. 'I've known the poor man ever since I was a watchman fourth class. Most people think he finds his omens at the bottom of a bottle of cheap drakesbreath, and that certainly isn't untrue, but it's also not the whole story.'

'I suppose people are less guarded around a broken down old drunk,' said Grange. 'Ne'er-do-wells speak things they shouldn't in his earshot, no doubt.'

'They do, and actually that helped us crack that smuggling ring in Forges a few years ago, but there's more. Foolish as it may sound, Grange, Old Posver *knows things.*'

'Captain?'

'It's only been a handful of times, but when bad times have been on the way in the past, Posver has seen them coming. Oh, of course he rants about a new doom each turning and most of it is drunken nonsense. On the other hand, he saw the orruk invasion from the dust planes three weeks before the greenskins hit our walls. He was ranting about the Cult of the Twisted Hand before any official investigation discovered them, so loudly in fact that they gave themselves away in their attempt to silence him! Strangest of all, it was Posver that put me onto the trail of the Grey Ghoul. I'd never have tracked that child-snatching monster down without Posver's rambling insights.'

'The man hears things, sees things, is sharper than he looks,' allowed Grange. 'But to say he *sees* things?'

'An hour ago, you were willing to consider the possibility of dark magic or some form of curse afflicting Draconium, but you baulk at the notion of an old drunk also being a legitimate seer?' asked Helena. 'Careful, Grange, your prejudices are showing.'

Grange set his jaw at the sharp rebuke and followed her in silence, through a network of cobbled streets and down to Fountains Square.

The square was huge, a place for grand markets to bustle and armies to muster. Already it was lively, city folk patronising the businesses around its edge or drifting across it in small groups. Several raised flowerbeds broke up the cobbles, artful arrangements of sparkblooms and ashenpines rising from them. At the square's heart stood the huge marble-and-gold mass of Sigmar Triumphant, depicting the bearded God-King brandishing his hammer, Ghal Maraz, above the shattered carcass of a monstrous Chaos daemon. Water rushed from the horns of lightning-wreathed cherubs around the fountain's base, cascading down through three stepped pools before flowing away along a deep channel cut through the stones of the square. That was the source of the Hammerhal Canal.

Sat beside it, dangling his crooked old feet in the water, was Posver.

He was a small man, wrinkled, scarred and rendered quite bald by rain-scalding. His eyes were puffy and red as if he'd been punched in both, and his toothless mouth was puckered. Posver wore a mishmash of ragged garb and was possessively cradling a bottle despite the early hour. A wooden sign lay next to him, kept within easy reach as a warrior might keep their weapon close to hand.

Posver looked up and flinched as he saw watch uniforms moving towards him across the square. He clutched his bottle tight to his chest and squinted before recognising her and relaxing. She glanced pointedly at the watchman third class who had been lurking in a side street and keeping an eye on the old doomsayer. The woman saluted and left her post, released to recommence her slow patrol around the square.

'Enwin Posver, how are you, my old friend?' asked Helena as she crossed a narrow stone footbridge over the channel.

'I'm all right, captain, and I hope today finds you in good health,' said Posver, gumming at the words in an accent so thick it took Helena a moment to decipher them. Posver struggled to his feet and set his bottle down with exaggerated care. Expression solemn, he bowed deeply to her, and as he straightened painfully up again she saw his eyes dart to the other watchmen who accompanied her.

'Grange, would you all mind terribly giving Mister Posver and myself a few moments to converse?' asked Helena with a slight warding gesture. 'We're old friends, you see, and we've much to discuss.'

Grange nodded stiffly and backed off, herding the two watchmen with him. Helena turned back to the old vagrant, smiling at him with genuine warmth.

'How have you been?' she asked.

Posver worked his gums and rubbed his palms together, stepping from one bare and soggy foot to the other.

'All right this morning considering what's coming, captain,' he said, blinking furiously at her then glancing down at his bottle. She gestured consent and he snatched it up, taking a grateful swig.

'And what is coming, Mister Posver?' asked Helena.

Posver shook his head, blinked some more, shuffled his feet.

'Come now, Enwin, we've had reports that you've been

getting yourself a bit excitable the last day or so. Have you seen something?'

Posver's face crumpled, and Helena felt her disquiet deepen at the sight of the honest misery she saw there. The shadow was there and gone in a moment, the old man rubbing his hands over his scalp and blinking again. She decided to try a different approach.

'Enwin, what is on your sign? May I see?'

He looked at her, looked down at the sign, and one hand worked in a curious clawing motion as the other raised the bottle to his lips again. He seemed to come to a decision, setting the bottle down carefully and gripping the sign's handle with both hands. She wondered idly where he found the wood for the placards he'd been waving these past years.

'Watchmen didn't like it,' he said, not looking at her. 'Said they'd smash it if I waved it about again.'

Helena felt a flash of irritation and made a mental note to get the names of whoever had been so heavy handed with the old man. A turning's night-duties in the Slump would adjust their priorities as to what crimes required the threat of violence, and which should be handled with a little more finesse.

'I won't let anyone smash it, Enwin,' she said. 'But I would like to see. Please?'

Sucking in a short, sharp breath and blowing it wetly out through his gums, Posver rose and turned. Helena recoiled as she was confronted with a nightmare. The sign's flat wooden boards had been daubed with a crude greenish-white paint and marked with splatters that she realised queasily were crushed spiders and other bugs. Yet it was the eyes that held her – huge, cruel, weirdly amused, staring out to transfix her just as they had in her dreams.

'Oh,' she gasped, taking a step back. Posver cringed at her

reaction, dropping the sign with a clatter. Helena heard a scuffle of movement, turned to see Grange and the watchmen hastening her way, their expressions angry. She held up a hand to stop them, realising to her surprise that it had been curled around the hilt of her sword.

She turned back to see Old Posver cowering over his bottle, one hand rubbing at his scalp and tears leaking down the contoured map of his wrinkled face.

'M'sorry,' he said. 'M'sorry, it's coming, it's what I've seen.'

'It… it's all right, Enwin,' she said, recovering her composure. 'It's all right, you're in no trouble. But I wouldn't show anyone else that sign. It is rather alarming.'

'It's coming, it's what I've seen,' he repeated, though whether in agreement or rejection of her request she couldn't tell. Helena looked out afresh at the square, at the people milling across it or tramping along on errands or business. How many faces looked tired, she thought, how many pale and drawn? No wonder Posver had been causing a stir. Just what *was* this?

'Enwin,' she said gently, placing a hand on his shoulder and feeling sorrow at the thin, birdlike bone structure she felt there. 'What's coming? What did you see? If you tell me, maybe I can help.'

'Can't nobody help,' said Posver, shrugging off her hand. 'That's why I'm having my drink. Know it's early, but it's late too, captain. Terribly late. The Bad Moon's going to rise.'

'Bad Moon?' asked Helena, feeling an inexplicable chill run down her spine. Posver just stared at her, blinking his tired eyes, then sat back down without another word and raised his bottle to his lips.

Half an hour later, Helena, Grange and their escorts had joined a gaggle of watchmen, scribes and apothecaries stood in an alleyway in Forges. They were gathered in the shadows of a hunched factory on one side, its stacks belching black smoke into the lightning-hazed sky, and a row of communal houses on the other. A light drizzle had begun, and a couple of the watchmen fourth class held up a scaldshade, a heavy leather parasol, to shield everyone from the acidic precipitation.

They stood over the remains of Watchman Second Class Ulswell. Scraps of Watch uniform still clung to her ravaged form. White bone showed through a red and grey pulp of flesh and muscle. Half the watchman's face was still recognisable, one eye staring up in glassy horror.

'And she was found like this in the early hours, yes?' asked Helena. Watchman Third Class Ilvik, the first watchman on the scene, nodded and looked nauseated.

'A gang of urchins found her, captain. Came running straight to find a watchman. Eyes wide as saucers and half of 'em crying just with the sheer shock of it.'

'And you say that when you got here there were insects on the body?'

Ilvik shuddered and shook his head in horror at the recollection.

'Beg your pardon, captain, but that's like saying there's the odd skirmish on the Flamescar Peninsula. I get here and all I see is this sort of... *squirming*... in the dark, and I think well maybe she's not dead, can't be if she's still moving can she? But the urchins won't come any closer so I raise my lantern and take a proper look and I realise it's not *her* that's moving, its...' Ilvik raised a clenched fist to his mouth for a moment, coughed, took a breath and continued. 'It's insects, captain. Hundreds of insects, some black and shiny as onyx, some all pale and see-through, and all of 'em just a tangle o' too many legs and wavy...' he mimed antennae with his fingers and looked at her helplessly.

'And you believe that these insects, what, *ate* Watchman Second Class Ulswell?' asked Helena, fighting to keep the note of incredulity from her voice. 'I assume you mean that they were drawn to the body after it was dumped here, yes?'

Ilvik looked at her with frank dismay.

'Captain, I'll remember it until the day I pass on into Sigmar's light. They were still eating her when I got here, and they didn't scatter at my footsteps like they ought. No, they...' he swallowed with a click. 'Some of 'em broke off chewing on Ulswell and started scuttling *towards me.*'

Helena stood for a moment, watching Ilvik's face to make sure she was not somehow being mocked. There was nothing but horrified sincerity in his haunted expression.

'Well, they're gone now,' she said. 'But we need to know where they came from and what they were, in case there is some infestation we must be–'

Grange gave a sudden bark of revulsion, causing Helena to jump as he took an involuntary step back. She followed his gaze and her eyes widened as she saw something come squirming out of Ulswell's hollow rib cage. It was a millipede of some sort, but worm-white and bloated looking, its slimy hide slick with Ulswell's blood. The thing moved on legs that were splayed and spider-like and beat a busy tattoo against the watchman's ribs as it scuttled out into the light.

The insect kept coming, impossibly long and large, eliciting cries of horror and a frantic stir of movement from the watchmen. A scribe vomited noisily. Meanwhile, the insect slipped from inside Ulswell's carcass like some obscene, chitinous rope. Feathery antennae waved as it reared up and turned its thumb-sized head towards the gathered watchmen. For a moment, Helena felt again the revolting caress of insectile legs moving over her sweat-slick skin.

Then came a loud bang that made her jump. The top few inches of the monstrous creature vanished, splattering in a viscous spray across the factory wall, and its body fell back, thrashing and flailing atop the mangled corpse before laying still.

Helena looked down at the smoking pistol in her hand. She hadn't even been conscious of drawing it. Gulping a breath, she holstered the weapon.

'Nobody touches these remains,' she ordered. 'We won't be removing them for apothecary's augury. We will be burning them, right here, right now. You–' she began, pointing at Ilvik, but before she could continue she heard running footsteps pelting down the alley. Rainwater slapped under booted feet and echoed from the enclosing walls.

Helena and her companions turned to see a watchman running towards them. Helena frowned as she recognised the woman from Fountains Square. The watchman, in turn, pulled up short, no doubt startled by the array of horrified expressions in front of her. After a beat she collected herself and saluted.

'Captain, you'd better come back to the square quickly, there's been an incident.'

'What now?' barked Helena.

'The vagrant you were speaking to, captain, Posver...' the watchman trailed off, her eyes widening as she took in Ulswell's corpse and the revolting carcass atop it.

'Watchman,' snapped Helena. 'What about Posver? Why do you need *me*?' The watchman's eyes snapped back to her as though she had just remembered where she was.

'Captain, about ten minutes after your conversation with him, Enwin Posver purchased a second bottle of drakesbreath from his usual vendor on Wagon Lane. I followed him as per your instructions, and he returned to the square. I expected...

he… Captain, Posver began shouting about a moon, so loud and frantic that I moved to pacify him as he was alarming the city folk. Before I could reach him, Posver emptied the contents of the bottle over himself then lit it on fire. I rushed to him, pushed him into the fountain, but it was too late. He's dead, captain.'

Helena shook her head in mute horror. She'd known poor Old Posver a long while and, though he had come out with some impressive rants in his time, she'd never seen him so much as raise a hand in violence, to himself or any other.

What did you see? she heard herself asking him again. *Enwin, what's coming? What did you see…?*

CHAPTER THREE

CLOUDS

Olt Shev pushed past a screen of ashenpine boughs. He stared through the rain, across a stretch of fuming marshland, at the city they had come to save.

Or warn.

Or fleece?

He wasn't entirely clear on the details. Olt struggled with subtleties of the Azyrite languages, which shared only an ancient base root with his own Pyremouth Tribe dialect. Hendrick had definitely ordered the Swords of Sigmar to Draconium, though, Olt had made sure of that much when he rejoined the party south of Stonehallow.

Olt was tall and wiry, and if he was honest with himself only his scraggly brown beard stopped him looking about twelve kindlings of age. His spare frame was covered with tribal tattoos that depicted raging fire-deities and sigils of arcane warding, and all flowed into the screaming pyreskull design that covered most of his face beneath his short-hacked hair. He wore furs and leather armour scavenged from a dozen dead, wore a pair of curve-hafted axes at his belt that could be wielded or flung with equal ease, and bore a patchwork of scars and obsidian piercings across his flesh. In all, he was an alarming sight to the majority of civilised folk; there was a reason he had chosen to remain in his native wilds, rather than brave the small and fearful minds of Stonehallow.

'No avoiding this place, though,' he muttered to himself glumly. 'Chief isn't going to let me stay beyond the walls this time. Why these Heav'ners can't learn to read their own maps I don't know. They'd get lost in a sulphur swamp in a day without me, though.'

'You underestimate us,' came a voice from directly above, which made Olt jump and grab for his axes. He looked up, squinted, and relaxed as he made out the half-visible form of Aelyn crouched on a high bough. Her garb blended with the undergrowth to a degree that seemed almost supernatural. For all Olt knew, it was. He touched two fingers to the warding flame tattooed in the hollow of his throat, then to the heart-spark inscribed on his chest.

'Careful with gestures like that, in there,' said the aelf, pointing with her chin at the city ahead. Olt looked back at it, a long, curving wall forty feet high, made from iron and marble and painted with some oily treatment to ward off the acid rains spawned by the volcanoes that rumbled high above. Rooftops and spires and flags jutted above that wall. A hill rose towards the city's centre with more buildings crowding its slopes and clinging to its crest.

'Before the Heavensgates opened, I never seen more than a dozen or so buildings in one place,' he grumbled to Aelyn. 'Small tribes, high walls, sharp spears and everyone knew everyone else. What do you Heav'ners need so many buildings for anyway?'

'Olt...' said Aelyn.

'I'll wear my cloak, don't worry,' Olt replied. 'Go tell the chief we've found it. And stop sneakin' up on me!' he called after Aelyn as she melted back into the canopy.

'Stop making it so easy, then...' her voice floated back to him.

Olt settled into the underbrush with a scowl and watched Draconium with wary eyes.

Metal glinted, the helms and speartips of guards patrolling the walls.

Lots of guards, he thought.

A wide waterway emerged through a heavy metal portcullis in the city wall, a broad roadway running alongside it, both cutting through the marsh and punching into the forest a few miles to Olt's right. A few heavily laden barges sat on that waterway as though waiting to enter the city, but he noted that nothing was moving.

The brutish flanks of the volcanic Redspines marched away to the east and west, soon lost in a haze of sulphur-smoke and rain. Overhead, clouds were gathering thick and dark, thunderheads flowing down in waves from the north and piling up over the city. Lightning sparked in their depths. It reached crooked fingers down to jab at the mountainsides.

An uncomfortable tightness settled in Olt's gut as he stared at the city. He glanced at the twin calderas that overlooked Draconium and offered up a silent prayer to their guardian spirits.

'We get in there, we do what the chief wants, and we get out again,' he said to himself, touching his warding flame again. 'And we do it flickerswift.'

Hendrick stepped from the shadows of the forest eaves and scowled as the rain stung his bare scalp. The others emerged behind him: Romilla, their priest; Eleanora carrying her engineer's tools; Borik with his cannon and Aelyn pacing whisp-light with bow in hand. At the rear, leaning heavily on his gnarled staff and clad in the black robes of a death wizard, came the elderly figure of Bartiman Kotrin.

'Hood up, chief,' said Olt, lurking beneath his heavy hide cloak. 'Firemountains make the rain here bad. The imps in it'll burn you if you give them the chance.' Olt said something else in a dialect Hendrick didn't understand, but he caught the tone of a curse all the same. The tribesman was not happy.

Rightly so, Hendrick thought. None of them was happy. Not with his brother gone. Not with him in charge.

'Sigmar curse whatever deviltry was at work in those woods,' said Romilla from behind him. 'I can only assume the local priests failed to properly reconsecrate the ground, for surely the malice of the Dark Gods itself haunts the damned place.'

'No malice,' said Aelyn. 'Why should the realms be any more accepting of our yoke than they are of our enemies'?'

'Well, something in there hated us,' retorted Romilla. 'That was not an easy march.'

'The bite on my foot still hurts,' said Eleanora. 'It was a spider that bit me, I think. I saw it and I think it must have been at least the size of my fist. It was horrible, but at least it scuttled off when I swatted at it. I'm sure I could make something that would repel those sorts of nasty biting creatures, maybe a spray or something that makes a sound they don't like, but I'd need a proper workshop and some time. Hendrick, do you think there'll be time for me to access proper workshop facilities in Draconium?'

'Enough. All of you,' said Hendrick. He closed his eyes and took a deep breath, letting it out slowly. 'Hoods up and skin covered wherever possible. Stow your weapons, I don't want to march up to the gates looking like a gang of killers. No matter what we actually are,' he added to forestall any arch comments.

They did as he instructed.

'Hendrick, I'll only need a couple of days and–'

Romilla laid a hand on Eleanora's arm, shook her head at the engineer with a gentle smile. Eleanora frowned, made a quick counting motion on the fingers of each hand, right then left, then pulled up the hood of her cloak and hunched her shoulders miserably against the rain.

'Aelyn, what do you make of it?' asked Hendrick quietly as the waywatcher came to stand alongside him.

'Loaded barges idling outside a closed portcullis,' she replied. 'No foot traffic on the southward road. Lots of guards. Trouble.'

Hendrick gave a grunt of agreement. 'Could be our warning comes a little too late,' he said.

'No, the storm still gathers,' she replied. 'We should be swift. You don't need omens to feel there is something deeply wrong here.'

'Let's be about it then,' he said, and set off for the distant city walls.

The marshes were easier to cross than Hendrick expected. Packed-earth pathways extended through them, some wide enough for carts to pass two abreast and patched where necessary with wooden planks. Smaller paths wound away towards scattered peat-diggers' huts and shepherds' lean-tos.

'Looks like there are some folk unwilling to trade their independence for the protection of the city's walls,' commented Bartiman. His voice was deep and mellifluous for one who looked so wrinkled and old. It only matched his eyes, which sparkled impishly.

'Fools. The realms are dangerous enough without eschewing what Sigmar offers,' said Romilla.

'Where they are, though?' asked Olt. 'I see the homes, but not the people or their herds.' Hendrick saw their scout was right; no whisp of smoke rose from any sod hut, no herd-beasts chewed at the tough grass of the marshes.

'Maybe not such idiots after all,' he said, taking in the full scale of Draconium's southern wall. It ran from one craggy mountainside to the other, its end-towers carved right into the craggy rockfaces. The wall blocked off the pass entirely and loomed like a menacing shadow over the fringe of the marsh.

Mud squelched underfoot as Hendrick crossed into the long shadow of that wall, over which loomed the smouldering volcanoes and, above them, a slowly massing immensity of black storm clouds. For a moment he felt a claustrophobic sense of panic, as though the whole lot might come thundering down to bury him alive.

'This is for your brother, coward,' he muttered to himself. 'Just get the job done.'

Ignoring Aelyn's amber-eyed glance, Hendrick led his small mercenary band into the shadow of the wall, to where a wide and well-maintained roadway ran along its base. That road, he saw, ran off along the feet of the Redspines to the west, while to the east it passed before the wall's formidable gatehouse, then slid in alongside the Hammerhal Canal and sped away southwards.

'If we'd have come from the other direction, it would have been a much easier march,' said Eleanora, counting on the fingers of her right hand, then her left, oblivious to Olt's irritated glare. 'When we get into the city I'm going to find a map of this region and see about buying it, so that we don't make that sort of mistake again. And I'm going to get access to a workshop so that I can make my spider repeller.'

'*If* we get into the city,' said Borik. 'Gate's shut.'

Hendrick squared his shoulders and led the way along the base of the wall, ignoring the stares of curious guards who peered over the top. He stopped before the huge mass of the gatehouse and took a moment to study it. Two blocky towers of iron-banded marble flanked a deep-set archway with a drake's head crest worked in relief above its keystone. An imposing portcullis closed off this end of the tunnel leading into the city, while further back he could see slab-like inner doors doing the job from the city side. Hendrick could feel the stares of dozens of guards upon him, but he remained silent, as did his followers as they clustered around him.

'Good luck, friend,' came a distant shout, and Hendrick glanced over to see one of the bargemen leaning on the rail of his craft. 'We've been waiting out here in the rain for three cheffing days. City's shut, and they're more than happy to let my produce rot rather'n open the cheffing rivergate for five minutes.'

Hendrick turned back to the gate, made a show of considering the bargeman's words and the lack of address from the guards on the ramparts above. Then he cleared his throat and strode up to the portcullis.

'Hello, up there?' Hendrick cried. It had been years since his temper had seen him ejected from the ranks of the Freeguild, yet he could still drum up that sergeant's booming shout when he needed to. He saw shapes move behind the battlements, saw the tops of spears stir. No response. 'We've come with important information for the rulers of your city,' he tried. 'We've a warning they need to hear.'

Still nothing. Hendrick let out a grunt of annoyance.

'I'll try knocking,' he said.

Hendrick slid Reckoner from its back-scabbard, hefted the massive hammer and swung it at the portcullis. The weapon's head connected with the iron bars hard enough to send numbing shocks up Hendrick's arms. The clang of its impact rolled out like a flatly tolling bell. The bargeman's delighted laughter sounded in its wake.

Bow strings hissed somewhere above, and half a dozen arrows feathered the ground around Hendrick's feet.

'Those were a warning,' came a gruff voice from the battlements. 'Piss off, baldy. Take your bandit friends with you.' At his back, Hendrick heard the ratcheting clank of Borik engaging the mechanism of his rotary cannon. The duardin would now have it levelled at the battlements, Hendrick knew, and he was only too aware of how much damage it could do if Borik got the excuse to fire. Still, he waved a placating hand at his companion.

'Stow the gun, Jorgensson, there's a lot more of them than there are of us,' he said, eliciting an unintelligible mutter from Borik. 'I just wanted to get a conversation going. Now,' he barked, turning his attention back to the half-seen figures atop the battlements. 'I'm sure you've got your orders, but a good man lost his life getting this warning for you so why don't you be good lads and lasses, stop holding us up and let us in so we can talk to someone in charge? We just want to deliver this message then we'll be on our way and you can go back to hiding behind your walls.'

This time Hendrick definitely caught Borik's grumbling, something about getting paid for their troubles, not shot at.

'The city is closed by order of the captain of the Draconium City Watch and the arch-lector of the militia-militant,' came the reply from the walls. 'If you've got a message to deliver, feel free to shout it up and I'll be sure to see it goes as far as it needs.'

Hendrick was certain he knew how far that would be. He planted his feet, leant on the pommel of his hammer and squinted up through the rain at the battlements above.

'We're not bandits, we're mercenaries, and I'm willing to bet we've seen more blood and strife in the last turning than you've seen in your entire career,' he called. 'So, when I say this message is important, and we suffered to get it here, I'm not wasting air. Now go and get one of your superiors so I can talk to someone with some sense.'

'Step back from the gate and get gone, or the next shots won't miss,' came the reply, the voice from the wall clearly angry now.

'For Sigmar's sake, just listen, will you!' shouted Hendrick, his temper flaring in turn. 'We're trying to help!'

'Last warning,' came the voice. Hendrick was half tempted to take another swing at the gate, just out of frustration, but he knew that giving the soldiers on the wall an excuse to shoot him was stupid. Instead, he turned on his heel without another word and stalked back to his comrades.

'We'll move back out of bow range and wait,' he said.

'You can't be serious,' said Bartiman. 'We tried, Hendrick, but they don't want to listen. This was sunk the moment we walked up and found the city's gates shut and its guards ready to shoot anything that moves.'

'But what's got them so spooked in the first place?' asked Romilla. 'There must be a reason for the over-caution, the lockdown. I believe we're doing Sigmar's work here after all, Hendrick. I don't think we should give up so easily.'

'We've existing employers waiting for us to deliver their goods,' said Borik. 'That takes precedence. Shouldn't have diverted to begin with.'

'The Moonshadow brings death to Draconium,' shouted Eleanora, making them all jump. Her voice, normally quiet and hesitant, rang out clear as she recited Varlen's last ravings word for word. 'The Moonshadow brings death to Draconium. Beware the squirming beasts and the eyes that see into your soul, trust the omens, watch not out but down, for moonrise brings the lurking ones and their tainted curse.'

Hendrick felt a chill run down his spine. He hadn't remembered his brother's exact last words, had been too lost to the mayhem and the horror of the moment to take them in. Now Eleanora's recitation brought that awful night flooding back. It ripped away the comforting veil of a half-turning's slow forgetting and filled his mind's eye with the image of his brother, flesh twisted, body burning in the pyre's flames, eyes wild but horribly clear as he screamed out the words the crown had made him say.

'We have to give them the warning,' said Eleanora, shying from his sudden, fierce glare. 'If they won't let us in then we have to give it from here.'

Hendrick took a deep breath, glared up at the gatehouse and around at his companions, then stomped off into the fringe of the marsh.

'We wait,' he said in a tone that brooked no further argument. 'Olt, Romilla, get us a shelter up. Bartiman, hot food. The rest of us will stand guard in case they get any stupid ideas of running us off.'

'If they let us in then I can use their workshop,' he heard Eleanora explaining to Romilla as he stomped away. He scowled, feeling bad for upsetting the young engineer but too angry to trust himself to speak right now. They would wait in this biting rain, he could sit and hate himself for a while, and if nothing had changed by dawn tomorrow then Hendrick promised himself he'd think of something. But he wasn't going to just give up.

He owed Varlen that much.

An hour passed, then another. The rain drummed upon the thick canvas of the shelter that Olt and Romilla had raised. Water dripped from its edges and found its way in on gusts of wind to dampen their spirits and their cookfire both. Romilla prayed quietly for guidance. Aelyn faded into the marsh, saying she preferred to keep watch where she could commune with the land. Bartiman pored over an old tome, shielding it with the hem of his cloak and tutting occasionally at some gust of wind or rain. Eleanora had dug some new gadget from her pack to tinker with, breaking off every now and then to stare longingly towards the city gates, while Olt crouched near the fire and sharpened his axes over its flame with a whetstone.

Borik spent a while patrolling out in the rain, which pinged harmlessly from the shaped metal of his Kharadron armour. He looked like some golem or automaton, Hendrick thought, no hint of bare flesh showing, breath hissing through his armour's tubes.

Eventually, the duardin clomped over to where Hendrick stood just under shelter, staring balefully at the gatehouse from under his hood.

'Those fellas on the barge offered us shelter,' said Borik, halting beside Hendrick and fiddling with one of the gauges on his cannon. 'They've thirty sellswords between their three barges. Firearms. Food.'

'We're fine here,' said Hendrick.

Borik grunted, finished the adjustments on his weapon, stared at the city.

'Don't feel right here,' he said after a pause. 'Even I'll admit that. Surprised those bargemen are still here.'

'Aelyn said something the same,' replied Hendrick.

'Look at them,' said Borik, lowering his voice and gesturing to their companions. 'Read the mood, Hendrick. That's not right.'

'We lost Varlen a matter of days ago–' began Hendrick, but the duardin cut him off.

'You and your brother, Grungni rest his spirit, hired me to be your bodyguard did you not?'

'That we did,' replied Hendrick.

'So, if I tell you that I can feel something… *wrong*… here, and that it's obvious everyone feels it too, you should listen, because I'm doing my best to fulfil the contract I drew up with Varlen. There's a sense of menace hanging over this city. Those clouds are building up like the whole place is holding its breath. I've no desire to be sailing these aether-currents when that storm breaks,' said Borik.

Hendrick gave the duardin a level look. 'That was more words than I've heard you string together in turnings,' he said.

Borik didn't reply, just stared back through the hazy green eye-lenses of his helm.

Hendrick sighed and shook his head. 'If those idiots would just hear us out… Sigmar's hammer, if they'd just let us through the portcullis to speak with someone in the gatehouse that would be enough.'

'This isn't our city, it isn't our responsibility, and it isn't going to get us paid,' said Borik flatly. 'A captain's got to command, I understand that. But he's got to read the aether, Hendrick, and he's got to read his crew. I sailed the skies a long time, and I've seen even the finest bands of privateers become a mutinous mob when they were pushed far enough. I'm not saying that's us, not for a moment, but–'

Just then, a shout came from the battlements. A woman's voice, strong and clear, carrying through the rain.

'Hey, you out there. The mercenaries.'

Hendrick stepped out from cover. He stared up at the battlements. The daylight was beginning to fade as the hour grew late and the storm clouds massed, but he could make out a tall figure leaning over the battlements. Her shock of red hair was vivid in the twilight.

'Are you someone with the sense to listen to us?' he called

back. 'Or am I going to have to dance around a few more arrows first?'

'The former,' came the reply. 'You've got five minutes until I open this gate, then two more after that before it shuts again whether you're inside or not. And if you mean the city any harm, Sigmar help me I'll run you through myself. Clear?'

'Clear,' Hendrick shouted back, feeling something loosen a little in his chest. He ignored the indignant shouts of the bargemen as he and his comrades broke down their shelter and traipsed towards the gate. They were getting somewhere.

The gatehouse backed onto a broad courtyard, from which cobbled streets thrust away into the city like splayed fingers. Buildings rose on all sides, large and small, dilapidated and newly built, lantern-lights flickering in their windows and doorways as the evening drew in. Factory stacks rose from nearby streets, smoke rising from them to add to the malaise above the city. The sounds and smells of civilisation filled the air, though muffled by the curtain of steadily falling rain. Lamplight danced on slick cobbles in the twilight.

As they stepped through the second set of gates, Hendrick and his companions found themselves halted by a thicket of halberd blades. The men and women who confronted them wore black uniforms and cloaks clasped with sigils wrought from various precious metals. Cogwork lanterns and pistols hung from their belts.

At their head stood the woman who had addressed him from the walls. She was tall and powerfully built, and accompanied by a rangy and rather aristocratic young man that Hendrick took to be her second. Both wore more ornate versions of their followers' uniforms.

'Welcome to Draconium,' said the red-haired woman. 'Now,

who in the realms are you, and where did you come by your warning?'

'Hendrick Saul, sergeant of the Swords of Sigmar mercenary company. My companions and I...' his throat clicked, but he swallowed over it and pressed on. 'Our leader was recently slain by the curse of a malefic artefact, but before his death he garnered a mystical revelation that danger threatened your city.'

Hendrick saw the young officer's lip curl at his words, saw his distaste at the Swords' rag-tag appearance. He caught the boy's eye and favoured him with a dangerous smile. The officer paled slightly.

'If you're done intimidating my lieutenant, Hendrick Saul, then you'll follow me. All of you, we've carriages waiting.'

She had half turned away before Hendrick asked, 'Who are you, and carriages to where? We're not going anywhere until we know that much, at least.'

'I'm Watch Captain Morthan, and I'm taking you to the regent militant's palace,' she said over her shoulder.

Hendrick hastened after the captain, his companions following. The watchmen kept their halberds levelled menacingly as they herded the Swords of Sigmar across the square. Hendrick glanced up at the gatehouse as he went and saw figures in blue-and-white tabards clutching spears and staring down at him from the inner rampart with hostile eyes.

The coaches waited in a broad side-street, heavy constructions of dark wood and brass drawn by lithe beasts with scaly hides and no eyes that Hendrick could see. He recognised them as gnarlkyd, one of the more unsettling Aqshyan beasts – yet far more docile and benign than their monstrous appearance suggested. Spark-lanterns were flickering to life along the street, and in their wan glow the rain turned to silver streaks and the shadows between the buildings deepened.

'I take it that was the militia-militant on the walls,' said Romilla as they approached the coaches. 'They appeared less receptive to our message than you, captain. Why is that?'

'My watchmen will relieve you of your weapons,' said Morthan, ignoring the question. She held up a hand to forestall any protest. 'I am about to bring you straight into the presence of this city's divine ruler, so appointed by Sigmar himself and beloved of all. You can either go unarmed, and thus deliver your warning as you say you came to do, or you can enjoy a night manacled naked down in the scald-cells. They're called that because the rain gets in, really floods them on a night like this. The skin on your legs would be a dear and distant memory by morning, I assure you. Now, weapons, please. You'll get them back after we're done.'

Hendrick barked a laugh despite himself, then shot a warning glare at Borik. The duardin shrugged as though to say *'Why single me out?'*, but a pair of watchmen had almost to wrestle his cannon out of his hands. Hendrick handed over his hammer, the pair of daggers in his belt and the spare in his right boot, then climbed up into the waiting wagon. He locked eyes with Aelyn as he did so.

'I don't like it any more than you,' he muttered to her as she followed him into the coach. 'But we're getting what we came for, aren't we?'

Aelyn said nothing, only slid in on the bench opposite him. The interior of the coach was roomy and lantern-lit, its benches padded. Hendrick, Aelyn, Eleanora and Borik climbed into one coach, Romilla, Bartiman and Olt into a second. Hendrick found himself also sharing the space with a pair of watchmen, as well as the captain, who placed herself next to Aelyn and gave Hendrick an appraising stare. Thuds and creaks came from the outside of the coach and it settled more heavily;

additional watchmen clambering onto the running boards, Hendrick assumed.

He heard the whicker of a lash being plied, then they pulled away with a lurch.

Streets and buildings passed by in a rain-grimed blur as the carriages sped deeper into the city. Hendrick stared out into the gloom for a few moments, watched the spark-lamps drifting by like will-o'-the-wisps, then turned back to find Captain Morthan still watching him.

'Where did your comrade hear those words that she shouted at our walls?' asked Morthan.

'Why did you believe us when the men up there so clearly didn't?' he countered. Morthan turned her attention instead to Eleanora.

'Name?'

'Eleanora VanGhest.'

'Where did you hear those words, Miss VanGhest?' asked Morthan. 'And why are you dressed like an Ironweld engineer?' she added with a slight frown.

'I heard them from Varlen as he was dying,' replied Eleanora. 'They were his last words, so I remembered them because last words are important. And I'm dressed like an Ironweld engineer because I *am* an Ironweld engineer, second cog-circle and–' she halted mid-flow as Hendrick held up a hand to forestall her.

'Thank you, Eleanora, but Captain Morthan doesn't need to hear all of it.'

Eleanora nodded, counting rapidly off on her fingers, right then left.

Morthan blinked, then turned her attention back to Hendrick. The carriage lurched over an arching bridge, shaking them all in their seats.

'What am I to make of you all?' she asked Hendrick. 'Humans, a duardin, an aelf of the Wanderer tribe if I'm not mistaken, a lady engineer, supposedly… that was a wizard and a priest that got into the other carriage together, yes? And whoever you've got stashed away under that bloody great cloak. And you, ragged band that you are, turn up shouting about a warning, though what you're warning *of* seems a trifle vague. Then she,' the captain jabbed a finger at Eleanor, 'comes out with squirming beasts, and eyes looking into your soul, and dark omens…'

'You recognise some of this, don't you?' said Hendrick, realisation dawning. 'That's why you let us in instead of ignoring us out of hand.'

'Part of me fears you are complicit, the other part believes you may be the very thing I need to sway the regent militant,' she said. Hendrick could see fierce calculation going on behind her piercing green eyes.

'We just want to deliver our warning and then be on our way,' said Hendrick. 'I can see something's got your militia jumpy, but honestly, captain, I don't even know what you think we might be complicit *in*.'

'I hope that's true,' she said as the carriage began to slow. 'Because I'm about to put you in front of the ruler of the city, and if you harbour any hostile intent whatsoever you'll soon be found out and drowned in scaldwater for your troubles.'

Hendrick and his companions stepped down from the carriages to find themselves on the edge of a wide plaza, surrounded by magnificent buildings, patrolled by tabarded militiamen and lit by copious ornate lamps. Hendrick saw a column-fronted structure, huge and boxy with statues of Stormcast Eternals battling daemons running along its frontage. There was a great structure of glass and banded iron, lit from within and housing what looked like a captive jungle. Tall mansion houses jostled one another self-importantly along one edge of the plaza, and beyond them through the rain Hendrick could see another, lower wall with its own ramparts, towers and patrolling guards.

However, his attention skated from these lesser sites of magnificence to the awe-inspiring monolith that reared over all of it on the plaza's eastern edge.

'The Palace of the Regent Militant,' said Captain Morthan, sounding, Hendrick thought, somewhat sardonic.

The palace looked more like a castle or fortified cathedral, its buttressed walls and high towers wrought in black and white marble and gleaming gold. Beautifully worked frescoes decorated its walls. Braziers burned all over the structure, making it glow like a star brought to earth, and Hendrick could smell incense and hear plainsong floating from within.

He couldn't help but notice an especially prominent fresco of a heavily-thewed warrior in the robes of a Sigmarite novice, striking the head from a grotesque Chaos champion directly above the palace's main doors.

'The regent militant?' he guessed, gesturing. Captain Morthan snorted.

'In his younger days, he was quite the hero,' she said. 'Now, come on, I sent Lieutenant Grange ahead with word of your coming. We're expected.'

They might well have been expected, but that didn't mean they were considered important. After being marched through the piously opulent interior of the palace, Hendrick and his retinue wound up in a richly appointed ante-chamber to await their audience. Under the stares of the watchmen and the gold-robed palace guards, surrounded by beautiful crystal lanterns, ornate furnishings and religious statuary and artworks, Hendrick became more conscious than ever of his and his companions' appearance.

They dripped rainwater onto the thick crimson rugs and tracked marsh-mud across them. They looked ragged, patched and dirty. He was in little doubt from the expressions of their guards that the Swords of Sigmar could all have used a bath, not just Bartiman.

Captain Morthan had vanished a few minutes after their arrival, looking irritated and tired. She hadn't returned since.

'It's been, what, an hour? More?' asked Bartiman. 'They could at least have offered us some sort of refreshments, couldn't they? Its barbaric.'

'You think they seem barbaric?' muttered Olt. 'Better hope no one in this pretty place asks me to take my cloak off. Your God-King don't like those who worship the competition, does he?'

Romilla shot the tribesman an irritated look but kept her peace. Hendrick was relieved. Since Olt had joined their company a year before, he and Romilla had nearly come to blows over matters of faith several times. To Olt, Sigmar was not *the* god, just *another* god, whereas Romilla had almost died for her beliefs more than once. Here in the heart of the regent militant's palace was not a place for them to revisit that old dispute, however.

'We're for the cells after all,' said Borik, sounding morose.

A door swung open at his words, and Captain Morthan beckoned them from beyond it.

'Maybe not,' said Hendrick.

They followed the captain down a long corridor, then into a grand hallway crowded with columns, statues, icons of Sigmar and beautiful religious artworks. At its end, beyond a cluster of palace guards, arched stained glass doors led into a softly lit chamber from which choral singing echoed.

Morthan led the Swords of Sigmar past the glowering guards and on, through the glass doors.

The chamber beyond was roughly one hundred feet square. Its vaulted ceiling rose high above their heads and was illuminated with a beautiful bejewelled frieze of Sigmar sat upon his throne in High Sigmaron, surrounded by clouds, stars, cherubs and Stormcast Eternals.

The singing came from a choir of children arranged in a pulpit partway up one wall. Incense smoke drifted from censers that hung from the four fluted columns that held the ceiling aloft. Beyond them rose three marble steps, atop which the regent militant sat upon a metal throne.

'That's sigmarite!' blurted Eleanora. Hendrick couldn't imagine what strings the regent would have had to pull to have a throne of that most precious of metals crafted for him, or even who might have had the skill to do so.

The regent militant himself was a large man in every respect. Tall, broad of shoulder and wide of middle, he had a mane of white hair shaved in a line straight down its centre, a large nose and a wide, generous mouth that looked made for shouting or smiling. Hendrick could see he was old, old enough to have liver-spotted skin and more than his fair share of wrinkles, yet as he stood and opened his arms wide in greeting, the regent appeared to have the vitality of a much younger man.

A pair of ornately armoured warriors flanked the steps of his throne; Hendrick was surprised to realise they were aelves – lithe figures in crested helms, gold armour and flowing white cloaks who stood to attention as the regent descended from his throne, and who prowled at his side radiating elegant menace as he strode forwards.

'Welcome, my children, welcome to Draconium!' he said in

a booming voice. Hendrick wasn't sure what he had expected, but it was not this.

'My lord regent militant,' said Captain Morthan, dropping to one knee and motioning for the Swords to do the same. All of them but Borik complied, Romilla going so far as to prostrate herself with a heartfelt 'Your divine grace.'

The regent militant laughed, taking Romilla gently by the shoulders and raising her to her feet. He smiled broadly at her.

'Sister, there is no need for formality. You are all to call me Selvador, for we are all but humble equals beneath the gaze of the God-King, are we not? Come, all of you, stand, stand.'

Hendrick rose, feeling thoroughly wrong-footed. Romilla's expression was almost comical in its amazement, and Bartiman was smiling with relief. Surely, his expression said, here was a man who would listen to what they had to say.

'Helena, my dear, how fare my brave watchmen?' asked the regent militant.

'As well as we can, my lord,' she said, and Hendrick noted that the captain hadn't relaxed despite the regent militant's avuncular nature. 'The problems persist, and dark omens continue to manifest.'

'And I do not doubt for a second that, just like my dear Arch-Lector Hessam, you are more than equal to this trying time,' said Selvador, smiling indulgently. 'Sigmar tests us all, does he not, but we will not be found wanting! Now, I understand that these brave souls have fought their way to our gates to deliver a message, is that not true?'

'My lord, they come with a warning, bought at great price. I believe they may have been sent by Sigmar himself,' said Captain Morthan. Hendrick felt his heart beat faster, felt the predatory stares of the aelven guards and the sudden pressure as the moment they had worked for arrived all too suddenly.

Selvador turned to look at him, then at each of his companions in turn. His expression was grave.

'Well, by all means deliver your message, and I shall hear each and every word as though it came from the lips of the God-King to my unworthy ears.'

The next ten minutes felt like an eternity. Hendrick did his best to explain how they had come by their message, though he was acutely aware that his rough soldier's voice sounded jarring and out of place in this magnificent chamber with its soft choral song. Eleanora delivered the words again, exactly as she remembered them, and the regent militant frowned and nodded with solemn severity throughout the entire account.

'Your divine grace, we are aware that this is an unusual, perhaps even a bizarre message to bring to you out of the blue,' said Romilla after Eleanora had fallen silent. 'I myself questioned it at first, believed that it might be some machination of the Dark Gods sent to twist our purpose or trick us from our path. But now, seeing all this, feeling the pall of disquiet that hangs over this city, my conviction is absolute. The God-King sent us to deliver this warning to you, that you might act before it is too late.'

Hendrick felt a swell of gratitude towards Romilla, who had earnestly and clearly explained something he would never have been able to vocalise.

The regent militant took a deep breath and let it out slowly.

'Before it is too late for what, precisely, my dear?'

Romilla blinked, wrong-footed. 'Well, your divine grace, to prevent whatever dreadful danger approaches.'

Selvador nodded slowly to himself, as though at some confirmed suspicion. 'And what would you have me do, all of you? What is it you believe that I am not doing that I should?'

'My lord, the prophecy says to watch not outwards but

downwards,' said Captain Morthan. 'I have told you of the incidents that have been–'

Selvador cut her off with a raised hand, closing his eyes as though her words somehow pained him. 'Helena, my dear, we have spoken of this. You have sufficient watchmen for your duties, you have sewer patrolmen to watch over the pipes and waste tunnels, and we all have our faith. My child, you may doubt yourself, but I do not. You and yours will prevail whether a time of testing lies ahead or no. And when did this warning become a prophecy?'

Selvador's voice was so gentle, so reasonable, thought Hendrick, as though he were reassuring worried children. Before he could stop it, part of him felt foolish for even troubling the regent militant with such nebulous concerns. The rest of him felt a vertiginous sense of the conversation sliding away from his control, and in very much the wrong direction.

'My lord, my brother's words made the danger sound dire,' he said, trying to drag things back on course.

'I am sure that they did, and I am deeply sorrowful for your loss,' said Selvador, placing one large hand on Hendrick's shoulder. It wasn't often the sergeant found himself at eye height with someone, but the regent militant was tall enough to look at him square. He did so now, compassion and faith brimming in his gaze. 'You have lost much, I see it in you, and you desperately wish for your brother's death to have a deeper meaning. And perhaps it does. Perhaps it did. Rest assured I shall pray to Sigmar for guidance and contemplate the matter at length. But young man, the pain I see in you tells me that your brother meant enough without his needing to be the sainted saviour of this proud city.'

Hendrick felt a whirl of confused emotion at the old man's words, an intense rush of frustration and sorrow and gratitude and anger so intense that it tightened his jaw and clenched his fists. He saw the aelven guards tense as they watched him, and took slow, deep breaths to calm himself.

By the time the rushing sound had left Hendrick's ears and the band of iron had relaxed around his chest, the matter was as good as done.

'...but my lord, surely if Sigmar himself has sent us messengers–'

'Captain Morthan, that is enough.' The regent militant's voice held a note of steel that Hendrick hadn't heard before. 'It is not for us to presume the will of the God-King. Draconium has faced trial and tribulation many times and prevailed every time. We overcame the orruk invasions of the Bloody Season, did we not? We weathered the pyrothaumic storms and all they wrought. By Sigmar's grace we even overcame the summoning of daemons within the very walls of this city! I know what you want of me, but I will not send to Hammerhal for Stormcast aid. Sigmar's holy warriors have wars enough to fight, and we have weapons enough to look to our own defence. This warning,' he stressed the word 'is every bit as vague as everything else you have brought to me these last days. If there are a great many crimes just now, I suggest you stop allowing the distractions of doubt and fear to rule you, and instead strike out to solve them with faith in your heart. And if your faith is wavering then you might consider following our friend here's example, and swap your blade for a hammer.'

Captain Morthan looked like she wanted to say more, but instead she clenched her teeth and bowed.

'Yes, my lord,' she said.

'As for you all, you have my eternal gratitude,' said the regent militant, smiling beatifically at the Swords of Sigmar. 'I shall mention you in my prayers to the God-King for your efforts, thank you. Now, Captain Morthan will show you to the exit.

Go, enjoy the delights of this strong city and I am sure you will soon see that your concerns, while righteous, were ill-founded. And rest assured that I *have* heard you this night my friends. I shall pray upon the matter at length.'

With that, the regent militant turned and resumed his throne. Hendrick was still trying to work out what to say, some fresh argument to make the old man understand the horror he'd heard in Varlen's voice, when Morthan ushered him and his companions out of the palace and into the plaza beyond.

And then they were outside, and the rain was falling upon them once again.

The palace guards didn't even spare them a look.

They'd delivered their warning. Nothing had changed.

'What now?' asked Hendrick, feeling as lost as he ever had in his life.

CHAPTER FOUR

DOWNPOUR

Krysthenna the Lantern Bearer stood in the doorway of an old warehouse in Docksflow. Outside, rain fell through the night's darkness from the deeper black of the clouds. Krysthenna leaned from the doorway and tilted her head back to let the deluge batter her face. The rain was cool and refreshing, and its acidic sting made her skin tingle. She feared no scald-burns. Those were the mark of the impure, those without the moral fortitude to withstand Sigmar's infinite tests. She knew herself to be pure, shriven, strong.

Movement at the far end of the street caused Krysthenna to duck back into the shadows.

'Catching raindrops like a foolish child,' she chastised herself. 'A Lantern Bearer cannot afford distractions.' She peered into the dark, praying silently to Sigmar that she would not see the distinctive glare of watch lanterns suddenly sparked. The Shrine of the Last Days' Warning was not strictly illegal in Draconium, for settlers were free to worship the prescribed gods of Sigmar's pantheon in whatever way they saw fit. However, the truths that Krysthenna and her flock spoke were unpalatable, and so the city watch had taken every opportunity to shut them down. They had been repeatedly refused permits to preach openly on the streets, and of late the watch had taken to breaking up their prayer meetings wherever they found them.

Some sects might have railed against such actions, might have protested of ill treatment or prejudice. The Shrine just recognised it as another test. Krysthenna felt a moment's satisfaction that they had proven resourceful enough to overcome it.

Sister Bulpen had been the one to suggest they meet in secret, in one of the dilapidated Docksflow warehouses. There were several such hulks slumped shoulder-to-shoulder along the Highwharf Road, abandoned since the canal was redirected to better serve Pipers two decades ago and the business went with it. Krysthenna had been surprised that no one had ever torn the structures down or repurposed them, but the thought that Sigmar provided for his chosen soon dispelled such concerns. She had purposely chosen the dampest, most rat-infested of all the warehouses, reasoning that such surroundings would keep their faith keenest. They had re-established the Shrine there, had circulated word to all the chosen brothers and sisters, and for three full turnings they had been able to practise their faith in peace.

'Not for much longer though, praise Sigmar,' murmured Krysthenna, feeling her heart flutter at the thought. 'The Return is nigh.'

The movement at the end of the street came again, and she relaxed as she saw several furtive figures break away from the deeper shadows and hurry down the street. There were only a couple of functioning spark-lamps along Highwharf Road, and as the figures flittered through their light she caught glimpses of nervous, soot-smudged faces.

Krysthenna stepped back from the doorway and ushered them through, three big, rain-slicked figures breathing hard from their dash through the city's shadows. She closed the door and turned a gentle smile upon the new arrivals as they stopped in the entrance chamber to peel off sodden cloaks and shake away stinging rainwater.

'Welcome, Chosen,' she said, raising her hands to them with her fingers interlocked then untwining like an opening gate. It was the sign of their Shrine, the Opening Gates, and the three factory workers returned the gesture.

'Were you seen on your way here?' asked Krysthenna. They shook their heads.

'No, Lantern Bearer. We were careful like you said,' replied one of them.

'Well done, Chosen,' she said. 'Now, hasten within. You are the last, I think.'

The factory-men hurried through a set of rotting wooden double doors that led into what had once been the warehouse proper. The doors had been hung on their inner faces with heavy black velvet, and as they parted candlelight spilled out, bearing with it the scent of incense and the loud murmur of prayer. Krysthenna followed the Chosen into her shrine, ensuring that the doors were properly closed behind her, then turned to survey They Who Heard the Warnings. Dozens of Chosen thronged the centre of the empty warehouse, stood in a great huddle of praying, swaying figures clad in the garb of labourers, clerks, butchers, artisans, alchemists and countless other occupations. The Shrine made no distinction between rich or poor, erudite or ignorant; they cared only that their Chosen believed, and that they proselytised their belief to others.

Her order required few trappings for their faith, for all things not of the heavens were tainted. Still, various of their ancestors had preserved some meagre objects of Azyrite origin, and these holy relics had been arranged around the shrine and surrounded by candles set on rude earthenware saucers. There was little other light in the warehouse's interior, for more black velvet had been nailed up over windows and skylights; no sight or sound of their worship could be permitted to escape to alert the authorities of their presence.

The drapes did not stop the rainwater from finding its way in through the cracked ceiling or shattered windows. It sluiced down the walls and pattered steadily from on high to dampen the congregation gathered below and collect in rippling pools underfoot. Krysthenna frowned as she saw parents usher their children away from the acidic waters.

'Faith is protection enough,' she reminded her flock as she moved between them, heading for the low wooden platform to their fore. 'Recall, Chosen, that all here is tainted. All is impure, even our mortal forms. There is no safety but the illusion of safety or the reality of faith. To shy from Sigmar's challenge is to render yourself deaf to his warning. Only in Azyr will we find sanctuary, and only upon the appointed hour.'

Krysthenna stepped up onto her crude stage and turned to her Chosen. She was a small woman, slight and careworn with grey-brown hair scraped back in a severe bun and features that she would humbly describe as singularly unremarkable. Yet when she stood before her Chosen and the light of Sigmar flowed through her, Krysthenna felt like a giant. Her flock had told her that she underwent a visible change, seeming to become greater than her mortal self, a Lantern Bearer carrying the light of Sigmar, possessed of a saint's voice and a hero's piercing gaze.

She took a deep breath, smelling cloying incense mingled with rain-stink, mouldering damp and the collected body odour of more than three hundred Chosen. All tainted, she thought, and in that moment, she despised their surroundings and the corrupt flesh she and her followers were forced to wear. In the next heartbeat the light of Sigmar surged within her again, until she felt she must almost glow.

'Chosen, welcome once more to our shrine,' she said, spreading her arms wide, then bringing her hands together to form the sign of the Opening Gates. The Chosen repeated the gesture, young and old alike mimicking the prophesied opening of the Gates of Azyr.

'What is this life?' she asked, falling easily into the rote prayer of her order.

'Corruption,' they choroused back at her. 'Suffering. Pain.'

'What must we do?' she asked them.

'Wait,' they replied. 'Watch. Endure.'

'For what do we wait, and for what do we watch?' she asked, her voice as strident as any priestly rhetorician.

'We wait for Sigmar's Last Warning,' they answered in voices brimming with fervour. 'We watch for the signs.'

'And when the last warning comes, my Chosen, what then shall we do?' she cried.

'We shall return! We shall pass through the open gates of Azyr and be offered succour in his realm forevermore.'

'And what, my Chosen, what shall become of the unbelievers?' she demanded, voice hard as stone.

'Eternal suffering in the fires of the Dark Gods as they consume the Mortal Realms and transform them in their blighted image!' they answered, some descending into wails of religious horror, others tearing at their garb or their hair. There were some, newer converts or the less suggestible, who looked alarmed at these outpourings of religious fervour, yet not one of them took a step away. Krysthenna smiled a hard smile and produced a tattered chap-book from within her robes. Riffling its well-thumbed pages, she opened it to a passage she knew well and read aloud.

'And lo, though the tribes of Azyrheim did return to the Mortal Realms, their exodus was but a test from the God-King to ascertain their worthiness and their faith, for the heavens had no room for the unbeliever. And the Mortal Realms were beyond salvation and only the Realm of the Heavens had known not the touch of the daemon nor the daemon's deluded thrall. And in those places where Chaos had lain its taint, there the servants of Sigmar would know no true succour, but only suffering and pain and the slow erosion of the soul. For we are made of the stuff of the stars themselves, my Chosen, and unto them the truly faithful shall return when the clarion call doth sound. But to his truly faithful Sigmar did tell this secret, and he did instruct that they seek his signs, and answer his challenges of their worthiness, and listen always for his warning upon the last day. And on that day Sigmar did say that his Chosen should return unto him through the gates of High Azyr, abandoning all those too foolish or too lost so that the fires of Chaos might consume them and all of these tainted realms forevermore.'

She slammed the book shut, sweeping her gaze across the faces of the Chosen, reading the avid hunger, the self-righteous fear and single-minded faith that burned in their eyes. Prayers rose from the assembled mass, which heaved and stirred like a single beast. An electric charge of faith filled the warehouse, seeming to expand until the rafters must surely creak and the windows shatter with its pressure.

Krysthenna held up her hands and her followers stilled.

'You know, do you not, my Chosen?' she asked, knowing well the cause of their fervour.

'It comes, Lantern Bearer,' cried one old crone.

'The last day!' shouted a young nobleman near the front of the mob.

'The return is nigh,' enthused a grubby dockman, one of his arms wrapped around the waist of a stocky woman, the other cradling a little girl no more than two years of age. Excited happiness shone from that faithful family, thought Krysthenna, and yes, no little self-satisfaction. And who could blame them, when they had proven faithful where their perceived betters had not?

'*That* is what protecting your loved ones looks like, Chosen,' she shouted, pointing at the man and his family. His little daughter looked around in alarm at the sudden regard of the congregation and buried her face in her father's broad shoulder. He beamed, and he and his wife held each other a little tighter.

'You have all seen the signs, for your eyes are open and your minds alert,' continued Krysthenna. 'You know the corruption all around you, and you recognise that no physical labour nor worldly possession can amount to ought but tainted lies while we remain within this realm. You have heard of those who have gone missing in the streets at night, the lost and the luckless swallowed by the darkness. You have seen the omens as birds have flown backwards through the skies, and water has run uphill, and vegetables have yielded heart's blood when bitten into. You have felt the building malice all around us, the growing pressure as the madness of Chaos gathers like a tidal wave to sweep away all our foolish fellows have wrought! In their ignorance! In their arrogance!'

She saw her congregation stir at these words, felt their understanding and heard their prayers.

'You have all had the dreams, felt the terrible squirming tide wash across you, felt the ground groan and tear beneath your feet, seen the dread visage of the Dark Gods fill the skies above and try to drive your souls from your bodies with its malevolent gaze. *And you have endured! You have waited! You have watched!* And soon, my Chosen, you shall have your reward.'

A sigh of religious ecstasy passed through the throng, peppered here and there with pious exclamations and oaths of faith and preparedness.

'What must we do?' shouted one of the Chosen.

'How much longer should we wait?' asked another, and, 'Do we leave now, Lantern Bearer? The nearest Realmgate is many days to the south!'

Krysthenna clapped her hands briskly, the sound bringing instant silence.

'Still your questions, Chosen, for questions are the words of the Dark Gods forced through your minds and spat from unwilling lips. Know that I will tell you when the hour to depart is upon us, for am I not Sigmar's Lantern Bearer in this place? Go, prepare yourselves for a long journey through the gathering dark. Surely, we shall be tested one last time before our return, and those without sufficient faith will not endure the road. Gather food and water, for though all in this realm is tainted it is our duty to sustain this mortal flesh until we may shed it for the starlight of the God-King's realm. For is it not said that our mortal frailties are but another test that we cannot ignore? But leave all other possessions – they are but flotsam adrift upon a sea of poison, to which drowning fools cling and so are swept to their doom upon the currents of complacency.'

By the time she stopped speaking, Krysthenna was breathing hard, sweat trickling down her back, nostrils flaring and eyes wide. Her Chosen stared at her with fervid adoration and then, having made the sign of the Opening Gates again, they turned and began to file from the warehouse. They went in small groups, quick and quiet, furtive so as not to draw the notice of the watch.

And then Krysthenna was alone in her empty shrine. She moved slowly from one collection of candles to the next, extinguishing their light with sharp pinches of her fingers, unmindful of the building pain from one small scorch after another. Her thoughts were full of the warning, so close now, the last day approaching. She felt tears of gratitude threaten, forced them down along with the trepidation at what challenges Sigmar might set his faithful before the return. Would she be equal to them, she wondered?

'I must,' she whispered to herself as she slipped out of the warehouse's door and into the hammering downpour of the storm. Overhead, lightning crackled through the black clouds, illuminating the stark tangle of rooftops that reared above her.

'Thank you, Sigmar,' she said. 'I will stay strong.'

With that, Krysthenna set off down the street with a sense of purpose burning in her heart.

'We're stuck here, then,' said Hendrick, a sour look on his face. Aelyn could hear the bitterness in his voice, and the underlying tremor of self-doubt she'd detected these past few days. She could smell the old sweat on his skin, mingling with the acidic tang of rainwater and the hoppy scent of the ale in his tankard. Aelyn could filter such smells from amidst the fug that filled the inn's common room, just as she could tease out the specific sounds of her companions' voices, their breathing, even their heartbeats if she wished, all despite the tumult of conversation, scraping stools, clinking glass and the ferocious roar of the rain against windows and roof. Aelven senses were far sharper than those of humans or duardin. Aelyn had spent centuries honing her control over hers.

It didn't take such heightened senses to detect the mood of despondent anger that had gripped her comrades since their brusque dismissal from the regent militant's presence. Hendrick and Bartiman both looked sour and tired. Romilla had an air of betrayal. She kept shaking her head and touching her fingers to the hammer talisman she wore about her neck. Borik hadn't spoken a word, but when he removed his helm upon entering the common room his thunderous expression had spoken volumes. Eleanora simply seemed anxious; after her initial entreaties that she still be allowed access to a workshop had fallen on deaf ears, she had fished tools and a gadget from her bag the first chance she got and was now working at it with a frown of furious concentration on her face. Only Olt had seemed ambivalent, perhaps even relieved. Yet his mood, too, had soured the moment Captain Morthan revealed they couldn't leave the city. Olt now sat silently at the inn table with the rest of them, his hood still up and dripping rainwater into the ale clutched in his tattooed hands.

Captain Morthan sat opposite. She had shed her watch cloak and insignia, foisting them on one of her underlings in exchange for a heavy rain-cloak and one of the leather scaldshades covered with holy warding sigils that Aelyn had seen the city folk carrying. She had then led them to the nearest decent inn outside the Holyheart Wall, a place named the Drake's Crown, and bought them a round of drinks.

'You shouldn't be here at all, the city's entirely locked down,' she said before taking a long, angry pull from her flagon and thumping it back onto the table. 'I only let you through because I thought you might be able to convince Selvador to see sense.'

'You used us,' said Bartiman, jabbing a bony finger at her. 'That was not the first time you've tried to sway the regent militant to your point of view, was it?'

'Of course I used you, it's my duty,' Morthan retorted. 'What, you think I just make a personal exception for every band of vagrants that appears at the city gates with some fantastical excuse for why they should be allowed entry? You think those bargemen haven't assured the militia on the rivergate that their cargo is absolutely essential to the city's survival? It is my job–'

'Our warning *is* essential to–' Romilla interrupted.

Morthan raised her voice and spoke over her.

'It is my job to deal with threats to the security of this city, and to make use of whatever resources are at my disposal to neutralise any dangers within the walls. Arch-Lector Hessam Kayl and his militia watch for dangers from outside, my watchmen keep the inside safe. That's the deal. That's what Sigmar expects of me. It's not like we've got a Stormkeep sat in the heart of the city – a brotherhood or two of Stormcasts just ready to sweep out and save our arses every time something goes wrong, is it?'

'You don't feel that you're holding up your end,' said Bartiman, sipping at his tumbler of dark spirits.

'The regent militant simply will not see the danger,' said Morthan, the words escaping her like an exhaled breath too long held. 'I shouldn't say such a thing out loud, especially not to the likes of you, but there it is.'

'Precisely what danger do you think threatens?' asked Bartiman. Aelyn thought he sounded intrigued.

'I… a Chaos cult? Some hidden cabal? Sigmar's throne, a curse, maybe? You're the ones with the warning, I hoped you might know,' said Morthan in frustration, taking another swig.

'My brother died for that warning,' said Hendrick, and Aelyn tensed as she heard how dangerously low his voice had dropped. Ten years she had known Hendrick, a long time by human standards, and she had come to know his temper's tells very well. 'My brother died, and we brought his last words here to those who needed to hear them so that his death would mean something. Then you snatched us up and paraded us in front of that man as part of an ongoing feud. You must have known it would prejudice him against our words.'

Captain Morthan had become still and moved her hands away from her drink, down towards whatever weapons she wore at her belt. Good at reading people, Aelyn wondered, or just professionally paranoid? The waywatcher adjusted her own stance so that she could drive a knife through the captain's wrist if she went for her gun.

'Your warning had resonance with everything we've been going through here,' she said carefully. 'I genuinely believed that even Selvador would listen.'

'Well he didn't,' said Hendrick, his knuckles turning white where he gripped his tankard. The metal creaked slightly at the pressure. His eyes were locked on Captain Morthan. 'We had one chance to make Varlen's sacrifice mean something. You spat upon it.'

'The only reason that you delivered your warning at all was because I permitted it,' Morthan replied, and to Aelyn's surprise the captain didn't sound alarmed. She sounded every bit as angry as Hendrick. 'You'd be sat outside the gates getting rained on if it weren't for me. Do not hang the blame around my neck for your abject failure. Sigmar's throne, man, had you even thought about what you were going to say?' She made a sharp gesture to Eleanora. 'If she hadn't recalled the words of the bloody warning and managed to recite them to Selvador you would have landed in the cells! No wonder he dismissed it with the same old saw about Sigmar's will. Do not make the mistake of believing you were the only one in that room with a lot to lose, Sergeant Saul.'

'You didn't lose a brother,' he growled.

The captain's eyes hardened. 'I may yet lose a city,' she returned.

'A city that is *still* in danger because our warning was ignored!' Hendrick pounded his fists on the table hard enough to spill ale. Aelyn placed a hand on his shoulder and, when he glanced at her, she shook her head, once, sharply. She saw Hendrick become aware that the hubbub of conversation around them had died at his parade-ground shout. Alarmed glances were aimed their way.

He subsided, glowering. Hating himself again, no doubt, she thought.

'Carry on, good people, carry on,' said Bartiman, hands raised placatingly and voice as grandfatherly as he could make it. 'Our friend has had a dram too much, and he's had a very long day.'

There was some muttering from the folk around them, but the buzz of conversation returned over the next few moments. It did not touch their table, however. The Swords sat and glowered over their drinks. Aelyn listened to the relentless drum of the rain against the windows. The hiss of water hitting cobbles intensified for a moment as another drenched and cursing figure swung the inn's door open and lunged inside.

Captain Morthan took a deep breath, blew it out slowly. She looked directly at Hendrick.

'I'm sorry,' she said, and Aelyn heard her sincerity. 'It was not my intention to hijack your quest, and had I truly realised its significance to you...' she paused, shook her head. 'No. I would have done exactly the same thing. If there was even a chance that you could have woken the regent militant to whatever this threat is, I'd have paraded you all in front of him until Hysh's light dawned again.'

'Why is it you believe the warning we brought is prophetic?' asked Bartiman, leaning forwards on his elbows. 'We barely know its true meaning ourselves, and only came this far to deliver it because of the circumstances of its acquisition. But you overrode the authority of the militia-militant and rushed us straight to the heart of Draconium on the strength of a few cryptic lines.'

'I hoped you knew more than you had said, the actual nature of what Chaos-spawned horror approaches,' said Morthan.

'Be that as it may,' Bartiman continued, his airy gesture making the bangles on his thin wrist clank together, 'what little we do know clearly resonated with you. I think I speak for all my comrades when I say that we are intrigued to know why.' Borik snorted, but Bartiman pressed on. 'So, since we're stuck here anyway, and thus the consequences of any impending threat may well be ours to face as well as yours, indulge us. What has you so unsettled, Captain Morthan? I think you owe us that much after this evening's events.'

'Helena,' she said, raising her tankard then pulling a sour face as she realised it was empty. 'I'm Captain Morthan when I'm on duty, and this is definitely off the books.'

'Helena, then,' said Bartiman, looking expectantly at her.

'I'm not sure where to start,' said Helena. 'It's been weeks now. We've had fights, disappearances, civil disturbance, religious agitation.'

'Nothing unusual for a large city like this,' said Romilla.

'No, but the unrest has risen like a flood-tide,' said Helena. 'And there have been all manner of strange circumstances. Grown adults dragged down and eaten by swarms of insects, if you can believe that. Babes and pets snatched from homes, incidences of sudden and inexplicable insanity that have spread like plague. Why, two days ago there was a riot in Fountains Square when a homewife started screaming of great eyes in the sky, and then others near her took up the panicked cry, but then another faction attacked them. Shouted at them to stop "angering the face in the darkness". Six people died during that fracas and another thirteen were injured, but worst of all was that everyone touched by the violence was found afterwards to have pale purple fungi growing right out of their flesh.'

A couple of the Swords made disgusted noises. Bartiman leaned so far forwards that Aelyn thought he would crawl onto the table.

'Fascinating,' he exclaimed. 'Do you think that the fungus was the cause of the madness? There have been cases, so I have read, of fungal spores driving men mad with fear, anger, even cannibalistic hunger.'

'Perhaps, but it's far from an isolated incident,' said Helena. 'It's just... I don't know, everything, I suppose. There's been inexplicable subsidence, animal attacks, break-ins that I simply can't perceive motive or method for. Then there are the omens.'

'Omens?' asked Romilla.

'Runti born... wrong,' said Helena. 'Ashwings seen flying backwards across the sky, which I wouldn't have believed but for the fact that I saw it myself just this morning. The poor thing took to the wing, shot backwards on itself with a cry of alarm and struck the blockhouse window hard enough to leave a blood smear. It was most unsettling. The lightning shrines on the mountainsides have started to rust, so badly in some cases that they've collapsed. We've had actual lightning strikes on city buildings for the first time in years. Then there are the dreams.'

'The eyes that see into your soul,' said Eleanora without looking up from the bulky nest of gears and wiring she was working on.

Aelyn looked around at the engineer in surprise, as did all her comrades. Eleanora continued to tinker, oblivious to their stares.

'How did you know that?' asked Helena.

'I saw them too, last night,' said Eleanora, not looking up from her work.

'Why did you not tell us this?' Romilla asked in a concerned voice at the same time as Helena said, 'You've seen them too? Outside the city?'

Eleanora looked from Romilla to Helena and back.

'I didn't feel safe,' she said. 'I didn't want the eyes to come back while I was awake. And I thought if I mentioned it then you might decide not to come here, and then I might not get access to a workshop...' she trailed off miserably, clearly remembering that she was no closer to that goal.

'It's all a bit vague, isn't it?' mused Bartiman. 'Alarming, certainly! But how does it all tie together?'

'Not our problem,' said Borik. 'We have a job to finish and neither business nor pay here. The moment those gates open, we leave.'

'It may well be our problem, if whatever is coming happens before the gates open,' said Bartiman.

'And I can tell you now those gates will not open again until whatever threat we face has been dealt with,' said Helena. 'Though how precisely I'm meant to deal with a threat I can't place or understand, Sigmar only knows...'

'There are always routes in or out,' said Borik, glowering. 'Hendrick, this is hullrust, we should be about our business and you know it.'

'Try it, duardin,' said Helena. 'You'll be in the scald-cells before nightfall tomorrow.'

'Look. Perhaps we could be of aid?' asked Romilla. 'As Bartiman says, we're stuck here anyway, and we've skills that might be of use to you. If there really is a threat to Sigmar's subjects...'

'What skills, precisely?' asked Helena. 'You'll excuse me, but so far I've done most of the talking and frankly, you don't look like any mercenaries I've seen before. Normally they have numbers, swords a-plenty and faces like an Ogor's knucklebones. You're... unconventional.'

The Swords of Sigmar hesitated and looked to Hendrick, all except Borik who grunted in disgust and got up to elbow his way to the bar.

Hendrick stirred himself, and looked around at them all as though surfacing from a reverie. Aelyn virtually felt him crush down his emotions and come to a decision. Suddenly brisk, he pointed at each of his comrades in turn.

'Romilla Aiden, Sigmarite warrior priest and military veteran. Eleanora VanGhest, brilliant, outcast, and if there's anything she can't blow up it's not worth the black powder. Aelyn Melethryl, Wanderer, waywatcher, if you mean us any harm at any point she will know and you will die with an arrow in your skull. Bartiman Kotrin, death wizard, does very much what it says on the keg. Olt Shev, scout, another veteran from Azyrheim's glorious armies just like me, and the surly arse at the bar is Borik Jorgensson, who my brother Varlen hired as a bodyguard a couple of years back and who, I'm sure you will have noticed, carries a very large gun. There, you know us. Now, hire us and then we can get some damn sleep.'

Helena seemed taken aback, but Aelyn detected a hint of something else behind her apparent surprise, something like satisfaction.

'Hire you? Why should I hire you? You don't know anything more about this madness than me, perhaps less, and I've an army of watchmen at my disposal who I trust a damn sight more than any of you.'

'You need more resources, you said so yourself. We've got a varied skillset that your watchmen lack, and if we had their authority we could aid you without coming to blows with your people. We want to leave, and never see Draconium again, and whatever in Sigmar's name is coming we want to avoid being caught by it as much as you do. Sitting around ignoring the situation won't achieve any of those ends, but taking a hand in dealing with the impending threat? That might.'

Aelyn heard the words her sergeant didn't say, that this was still about Varlen, about Hendrick proving his brother hadn't died in vain, but she said nothing. Now was not the time to undermine him and besides, she agreed with him. They were better off taking action than sitting and drinking themselves into a stupor in this inn for however long it took for the nebulous danger to manifest. She just wished it didn't feel so much like Hendrick was inadvertently giving Captain Morthan precisely what she had wanted all along.

'Our fee is naught but bed and board in this inn, on the city's tab. And Eleanora wants access to an Ironweld workshop.'

Helena blanched slightly. Eleanora looked up with sudden delight.

'You wouldn't require payment?'

'We have cash to spare, captain,' said Hendrick matter-of-factly. 'We can hole up in this inn and start looking for a way to escape your city tomorrow if you've no use for us. We'll likely do some damage on our way out, hazard of the job. And I understand you're already short on watchmen.'

'You can spend the next few turnings in the scald-cells instead, if you like?' asked Helena, cocking an eyebrow.

'You can try to arrest us,' said Hendrick. 'It'll cost you. And besides, what use would we be to you in the cells?'

Aelyn felt her lips quirk slightly in amusement. Hendrick wasn't as good with people as Varlen had been, but she had always admired his blunt courage. Evidently, Helena felt something the same as, after a moment, she laughed.

'Very well, Sergeant Saul, consider yourselves hired. Find rooms here and I will send a scribe across first thing tomorrow to swear you all in and draw up a contract.'

'Send the details of whichever matters you want us to look into, also,' said Romilla.

'We're quite happy with the stranger cases,' added Bartiman with undisguised relish. Olt shrank lower in his chair but made no comment.

'Well–' began Helena as she stood from the table, but she was interrupted by a phenomenal crash of thunder so violent that it shook the window panes and killed conversation in the common room quicker than a headsman's axe. Outside, the ferocity of the rain redoubled. Then came a cry of alarm and disgust.

'Oh, Sigmar! Oh that's revolting!'

There came the sound of a tankard hitting the floor, then others. Cries of alarm and horror rose throughout the common room, shocked shouts of disgust and oaths to Sigmar filling the air. Aelyn looked down at the glass of spring water she had been nursing and slowly, carefully, took her hands away from it. The water had turned thick and clotted, and now gave off a rancid stink. Something moved in it, something black and squirming pinwheeling in circles as it drowned. She looked around the table; all of her comrades had recoiled from their own drinks while Borik, who had just thumped another three ale tankards down on the table, was cursing roundly in Kharadron.

'Whatever this is, Captain Morthan, we need to resolve it swiftly,' Aelyn said to the horrified captain. Helena could only nod in return, as outside the rain fell harder.

CHAPTER FIVE

CRACKS

Dawn brought no cessation to the rain, and for the next five days the downpour continued. Overflow drains gurgled and sloshed as they struggled to keep pace with the whitewater flows that filled the gutters to bursting. Building frontages peeled and began to erode, their owners unable to apply fresh coats of scald-proofing with no break in the torrential rains. Great covers had to be raised over the Statuegarden, over the runti paddocks of Westslope, and over the canal channels where they flowed out of Fountains Square.

The city folk hurried through the streets, swaddled against the rain and muttering darkly about the unending storm. Wagon and carriage traffic on the streets thinned to a trickle, most drovers being unwilling to risk their animal teams being scalded in their traces.

From atop Gallowhill, Captain Morthan watched it all through eyes of paper and ink, poring over the reports that flowed in from her watchmen and supposing that she should have been glad of the slight lessening in crime rates that the storm brought. Even ne'er-do-wells had more sense than to venture out for long amidst such an unheard-of deluge.

Still the strange reports came, however; earth tremors causing one of the Rookswatch towers to lean so perilously that the watch had to evacuate its inhabitants; a fungal blight spreading amongst the runti herds on Westslope, causing frightened whispers to spread that the Plaguefather must surely have turned his eyes upon Draconium; a street performer running mad, bludgeoning three onlookers to death with his lute, screaming about 'the eyes in his mind' and the 'pallid pale'.

No, mused Captain Morthan as she sipped metha at her desk and listened to the rain battering at her office window; storm or no storm, this was only getting worse. At least the Swords of Sigmar were making good on their end of the deal, she thought, shuffling through a few more reports and casting a critical eye over their efforts. They'd investigated several strange disappearances. Their priest had talked down an angry gathering of folk from Marketsway and Pipers that could easily have turned into a mob. They had even aided her watchmen in a raid on what they had initially hoped was the hideout of the cult responsible for the disturbances. It had turned out to be a ring of kidnappers and extortionists. Largely dead kidnappers and extortionists now, she noted; she was glad she hadn't pushed Hendrick too far that first night in the tavern.

'Damn it, Selvador, when will you open your eyes?' she muttered, fighting down the compulsion to go and speak to the regent militant again directly. He had been cloistered away for days now, allegedly deep in prayer, but he had issued no new edicts and offered no additional aid. Her entreaties to the arch-lector had produced nothing, either. The man was a climber, who was no doubt hoping she would appear the alarmist and allow him to expand his control to the watch as well when she was inevitably dismissed.

And still her dreams continued.

Hendrick, Bartiman and Olt stood outside the Alchemists' Guild beneath a pair of wide leather scald-shades. Hendrick was trying to avoid the worst of the downpour. Captain Morthan had sent the scald-shades along with their first assignments, seals of marque that would allow the Swords of Sigmar to operate under her authority, and enough heavy leather rain-capes for all of them. With the weather this dreadful, her note had explained, they would all be scalded by nightfall if they didn't wear them. The sergeant and his followers had made use of all the captain's gifts every day since.

The guildhouse loomed over him now, an impressive brick pile painted in thick layers of rain-proofing whitewash and adorned with dozens of weird gargoyles above its arched windows.

'Not many folk stupid enough to be out in this,' commented Olt, glowering up and down the empty street. They had seen precious few people on their way from the Drake's Crown, and those they passed hurried along under the lowering thunderheads, swaddled in rain-cloaks and not looking one another in the eye. This street boasted several well-to-do looking shop fronts, and lamps burned hopefully in a couple of windows, but most were dark and quiet.

'It's not just the rain, though, is it?' asked Bartiman. 'Whatever deviltry is at work here, why, you'd have to be a lump of rock not to feel it. Or Borik,' he added speculatively, and Olt snorted.

'Is there a difference?'

'Borik and the others have their own assignments,' said Hendrick, his tone communicating he was unamused. 'We're here for this place. The report said they've had two separate break-ins now, both times via tunnels penetrating the building's basement level.'

'And Captain Morthan thinks someone stealing bottles from alchemists is worth our attention, does she?' asked Bartiman. 'I mean, it's her time, her money, but after all that about deaths and disappearances... omens... what have you...' He trailed off with a wafting of hands, then leaned heavily on his staff and harrumphed to himself.

'Did she strike you as a time-waster?' asked Hendrick.

'Nope,' Olt replied without pause. 'Steel 'n' fire, that one.'

As though to underpin Olt's words, a rumble of thunder rolled through the still air. As it did so, Hendrick thought he felt the ground shift, almost imperceptibly, beneath his feet. There was a slight juddering, and as he watched he saw the surfaces of nearby puddles rippling. Just the rain, he wondered? Or something else?

'Then there's a reason we're here,' said Hendrick. 'Come on.' He led them towards the building's arched front door, striding up the rain-slick marble steps to pound a fist upon the treated ironoak.

'I'd have preferred to get a look at some of these insect attacks,' grumbled Bartiman as they waited for the doors to open. 'Fascinating necro-entomology there, I'll just bet. I've been asking about that for days now, you know, and I'm not getting any younger.'

'I don't care what we look at, so long as I can get away from the rain imps,' replied Olt, pulling his cloak tighter around himself. 'Let's just get off the street, and we can worry about the rest after.'

A few miles away from the Alchemists' Guild, Borik, Romilla and Aelyn stood on a metal gantry and looked down upon a sea of putrefaction. Rotting grain filled the warehouse floor where its swollen mass had split the storage sacks and spilled out in reeking drifts.

'That stench is truly unholy,' said Romilla, covering her nose and mouth with one hand and clutching her hammer talisman with the other.

'Wouldn't know,' said Borik, his voice rendered tinny by his helm.

Aelyn shook her head slowly. The grain hadn't just spoiled; it had turned black, puffing up until it looked more like mountains of black maggots. It was drenched in a mucal-looking slime, and busy with buzzing flies and slithering white worms. Their constant motion was dizzying. Shapes poked up from amidst the drifts of ruined grain, white and purple nubs that Aelyn realised were fungi. Romilla was correct, the stink rising from the ruined food stocks was beyond nauseating.

'You say it was found like this?' she asked the warehouse overseer, a man named Toftin, who had escorted them in. He had been so distracted that he had barely even glanced at their seal of marque, nor questioned their presence. Now Overseer Toftin looked at her with an expression of helpless horror over the cloth he had wrapped around his mouth and nose.

'This morning,' he said. 'Bastley and Jens ran the checks last night and reported nothing amiss. No rain getting in, no sign of vermin, nothing.'

'Does anyone guard the food stores overnight?' asked Romilla.

'Of course, the company employs a couple of night watchmen to keep an eye on things. Grain's hard to come by this far north of Hammerhal. We have to guard it against thieves…' Toftin trailed off, looked over the horror of spoiled food below and swallowed.

'Where are the watchmen?' asked Aelyn, thinking that if

anyone was likely to have seen what took place, surely it would be them. Her hopes were dashed as Toftin raised a shaking hand and pointed down at the mounds of oozing sludge. Aelyn followed his gesture and felt a twinge of horror as she realised that what she had first taken to be a clotted lump of spoiled food was in fact a pale hand rising from amidst the foulness. It was as bloated as the grain, thrice the size it should have been with taut skin purple and blue, slime and worms slicking it.

'Oh, Sigmar's throne...' gasped Romilla.

'No one has dared touch the stuff, in case...' Toftin shrugged helplessly again. 'But no one has seen either watchman since we left last night and, well, it seems a safe assumption.'

Romilla began to pray for the departed souls of the watchmen. Borik craned over the railing to peer at the befouled grain, then looked back at Toftin with his helm-lenses glinting.

'How much of the city's food reserve is this?' Borik asked.

'There are three warehouses, each a private concern endorsed by the regent militant's office,' said Toftin as though reciting from a script. 'You're stood in the main warehouse for Grange Grain. The Hazyrtein and O'Phennik families own the others.'

'About a third, then,' said Borik, turning back to the railing with a grunt. 'Anyone know if it's like this at the other warehouses?'

Aelyn hadn't thought Toftin could look any more alarmed, but the thought clearly hadn't occurred to him and now he turned white as a sheet.

'Do you think it could be?' he asked. Aelyn could see fear for the city warring with the selfish thought that, if all the warehouses had suffered a similar fate, he would not receive sole blame when fingers began to point. None of them answered, too busy staring down aghast at the slime-ridden crops.

Romilla concluded her prayers for the dead. 'What now?'

she asked. 'There's no way that this is natural. Is it the work of the Plaguefather, do you think?'

Aelyn heard the careful control in Romilla's voice. The priest had never fully recounted what happened to the army she accompanied out of Azyrheim all those years before, but Aelyn knew that it had been some curse of Nurgle that had spread through their ranks.

Romilla alone had survived.

The experience had plunged her into a crisis of faith, a spiralling descent into alcoholism and self-abuse in the slums of Hammerhal Aqsha that had almost been the death of her. Varlen, Hendrick and Aelyn had pulled her from her pit of self-recrimination and despair and helped her to find her faith and purpose again. Still, the priest's horror at disease and decay remained, a spiritual canker that she could only keep locked away behind ironclad gates of faith.

This spectacle of unbridled foulness could not be easy on her.

'It may be,' Aelyn allowed. 'A clue, perhaps. If so, we should not expose ourselves to this foulness any longer than we must.'

Toftin looked at her with fresh alarm. 'Do you think it's catching?' he asked. 'Bad air, curdled humours?'

Aelyn shrugged. A muscle twitched in her cheek. Her mind had already leapt ahead.

'Are there other routes in and out of here?' she asked.

'The... er... the big doors at the street end,' said Toftin, gesturing. 'There's another entrance like this at the back, another set of steps down for labourers. Oh! And there's the culvert, empties right into the sewers down there by the far corner.'

'Rain drainage?' asked Borik. Toftin shook his head.

'Smouldergrain,' he said, and when they offered him blank looks he elaborated. 'It sweats when you bag it up. The runoff sours the grain if you leave it to stand, and in extreme cases build-up can even be explosive. So, we let it drain into the sewers. That way it doesn't… um… spoil.'

'Didn't work,' said Borik, earning an angry glare from Toftin.

'There's food ruined, livelihoods lost. Sigmar's hammer, there's lives lost. Is this a joke to you?' asked the overseer.

'Hardly,' grunted Borik.

'Overseer Toftin, thank you for your aid,' said Aelyn, capturing his gaze with hers and holding it. Toftin seemed for the first time to become aware he was standing in the presence of an aelf, registered her alien features and the piercing amber eyes that shone beneath her cowl. Aelyn had found that many humans, especially the less-well-travelled, could be knocked off their stride by her 'otherness'. Toftin nodded absently, taking an involuntary step away from her.

'Of course, that is, er…'

'We will circle around to inspect the rear entrance in case anyone has used that to gain entry and commit malfeasance,' said Aelyn. 'I would ask on behalf of the city watch that you don't permit anyone in here in case there is a contaminant that may spread.'

'Of course,' said Toftin again. He looked relieved when they swept past him and out through the meagre office chambers of the warehouse into the rainy street beyond.

'That'll all need burning,' said Borik.

'The rear entrance, really?' asked Romilla as she swathed herself in her leather cloak and raised a scald-shade over her head. Next to them, Borik's armour emitted a constant chorus of metallic pings and plinks as the heavy rain rebounded from it.

'No,' said Aelyn. 'Captain Morthan spoke of tunnels, did she not? Things move beneath the surface here.'

'The sewer culvert, then,' said Romilla with a sigh. 'Sigmar's grace, won't that be pleasant.'

'You want pleasant, go back to the inn,' said Borik, stomping away past a gaggle of cloaked city folk who were hauling a cart down the cobbled street. Rainwater sluiced about its wheels, splashing up their legs, and Aelyn believed she could almost see the wood of the cart smouldering where the acidic rainwater worried at it.

'Why did Varlen hire him again?' asked Romilla as she and Aelyn set off after the duardin.

'The big gun,' replied Aelyn.

'Of course,' said Romilla, and Aelyn fancied she could hear the priest rolling her eyes.

Eleanora VanGhest sat at her workbench, enjoying peace, an absence of other people and the familiar comfort of a workshop. Hendrick had instructed her to go and take advantage of the facilities in the Ironweld Guildhouse to which Captain Morthan had granted her access. It had been all Eleanora could do not to run there flat out, and she had returned every day since. Hendrick would call on her if they needed her skills. It had been turnings since the Swords of Sigmar had last worked out of a civilised location, and while the presence of her friends and her bag of tools gave Eleanora familiar touchstones with which to reassure herself, the uncertainty and anarchic conditions had made her ever more unsettled.

Of course, there had been stares and mutters when she entered the guildhouse. There always were. Eleanora had endured the unfriendly scrutiny of artisans and engine-smiths ever since her father had first brought her in to test for the Ironweld Academy in Hammerhal Ghyra. She found their glares uncomfortable, and of course there had been more than one such supposed man of learning willing to impede her progress simply because of her gender.

That sort of thing had typically just been an inconvenience for her; Eleanora couldn't really connect with most people, couldn't empathise with the unfriendly engineers around her, and so their discomfort at her presence didn't increase or decrease her own in any meaningful way. And even the most obstreperous old-guard master couldn't deny her ability with mechanisms and machinery. It was as though the pieces already fitted together in her mind's eye.

She had never been able to articulate any of this to her proud but frustrated father, or to the jealous peers who had eventually torched her workshop and caused her expulsion from the Academy. Eleanora's father had died in that blaze, as had several other engineers, and after the entire thing had been pinned on her supposed carelessness, Eleanora had been exiled.

Bewildered, alone, and shocked mute by the sudden ripping away of all she had known, Eleanora had been sent through the city's great Realmgate and onto the streets of Hammerhal Aqsha. She supposed, in a detached fashion, that she would have died there, impoverished and starving, had not blind chance brought her and the Swords of Sigmar together. She had been with them ever since, she their ticket to all manner of ballistic and explosive devices, they her driftwood spar in the turbulent ocean of the realms. Romilla had nursed her back to health, had got her talking again, acting more like a mother than a virtual stranger.

Her presence made Eleanora feel stronger. Safe.

So yes, Eleanora endured the usual stares from the engineers around her when she entered the Draconium Ironweld Guild-house, but after all that she had faced in the last few years of her life, those stares had even less purchase upon her than before. And soon enough she had been led, albeit grudgingly, to a workshop where she could at last lock the doors, spread out her tools and components in the proper and orderly fashion, and get on with some work.

Eleanora's foot still hurt. She shifted and winced, but she paid it no real mind. The others hadn't seemed to be very interested when she tried to tell them about the spider, and it seemed to have been driven from Romilla's mind by other events, so Eleanora assumed it must not be all that important. If she concentrated on her work, she could ignore the dull throb and the heat radiating up her ankle. Hendrick had requested bombs, explosives large and small, anything clever she could come up with 'in case things got interesting'. Bombs, Eleanora could do. There was already a small stack of munitions by her workbench that attested to the fact.

Clever, she could do also. And then there was that spider repeller that she had been thinking about ever since she was bitten. She was sure she had some time to work on that too, in amongst everything else.

Distractedly she brushed her hair back from her eyes and tied it out of the way with the ribbon her father had given her on her tenth birthday, the one that had been on top of her largest gift. He had fashioned her a set of tools at his workbench. He had presented them with a proud gleam in his eye.

She still used the tools now.

Eleanora wiped away a couple of tears at the memory, not even truly conscious she had shed them, and set to work.

There was a lot to get done, after all.

'Strange enough for you, Bartiman?' asked Hendrick.

'Well. I mean. Yes!' The death wizard sounded oddly delighted, Hendrick thought, for a man staring at one of the most unpleasant and unnatural sights he'd ever seen.

Their brief had explained that the previous tunnel dug into

the Alchemists' Guild had collapsed by the time the watchmen arrived. This time, that was not the case.

Hendrick rather wished it had been.

He, Olt and Bartiman stood in one of the dusty sub-basements of the guild, in a section that the alchemists themselves referred to as the bottle-shop. The chambers down here were lined with shelf upon shelf of alembics, potion bottles, cut-crystal beakers, lead crucibles and other, stranger receptacles fashioned from substances of every colour. Some of the chambers appeared to be in regular use, but further back along the corridors, the bottle-shop took on a dusty air of disuse. Too many bottles, not enough alchemists creating potions to fill them, one of the old men had explained as they led the Swords of Sigmar down into the basement.

At least the disused chambers were tidy. Not so this one. Shelves had been torn bodily from the walls. Glassware and crystal had shattered, leaving sprays of glittering debris strewn across the floor. The jagged wreckage mingled with brick dust and rubble; much of the back wall of the chamber had collapsed inwards as though forced from without. Bare earth had been left exposed, and in this yawned a noisome hole a good five feet high and just as wide.

Olt touched his throat and muttered something in his tribe's dialect. It sounded superstitious and fearful.

'That is truly horrible, isn't it?' said Bartiman, still sounding too pleased by half.

A hole would have been alarming enough, but this gaping rent gave off a reek like wet mould, spoiled soil, faeces and what Hendrick could only think of as the feet of an entire regiment after a week's hard march. Thick tendrils of mycelium billowed from the hole's edges to dig eager roots into the surrounding brickwork. Pale fronds drifted in a cool and stinking breeze that blew from somewhere within the black pit, and fungal blooms of a dozen rotten hues jutted from the tunnel's walls, floor and ceiling. Several had fibrous spikes growing from them, while others resembled flyblown meat, chitinous carapace and in one case a screaming human skull. Thick-bodied white mites crawled all over the fungi and spilled out across the chamber floor.

'You believe that the thieves came through this tunnel?' Hendrick asked the gaggle of nervous looking alchemists packing the doorway behind them.

Several nodded in reply.

'And you believe that they used the same tunnel as their exit?'

More nodding.

'Has anyone explored the tunnel to see where it leads?' Hendrick asked, expecting the shaken heads and nervous muttering that he got in response. 'Right, then,' he said to himself.

'Chief, that's the home of the bad spirits down there,' said Olt. 'We're not going down there, are we?'

'We're no use just stood here,' replied Hendrick. 'The watch has spent plenty of time guarding holes from what Captain Morthan was saying, but they've not sent anyone down one.'

'I would imagine that is because it looked so very inadvisable to do so,' said Bartiman.

'We've braved worse,' said Hendrick.

'Not out of choice,' said Bartiman.

'Morthan hired us because we can do things, brave dangers her watchmen can't,' said Hendrick firmly. 'That begins with delving into evil-looking pits like this to find out who or what has made them. Find your courage, the pair of you, and let's go. Olt, you're the best at reading signs and spoor, you lead. Bartiman, give us some light. I'll take rearguard so that nothing unpleasant can sneak up on you from behind while you're concentrating on your cantrips.'

Muttering under his breath, Olt shed his cloak and dumped it in the far corner of the chamber, along with his scald-shade. The alchemists looked perturbed at his feral appearance, but Olt just favoured them with a wolfish grin. Hendrick and Bartiman followed suit, shedding anything that would act as an encumbrance in the tight confines of the tunnel. Hendrick's only concession was to leave Reckoner strapped to his back, reasoning that if they found a wider space further down he might have occasion to swing the hammer into the faces of whatever lived there.

'Are we sure that we don't want to gather the rest of the Swords first?' asked Bartiman.

'We're just doing a recce, they've got their own matters to attend to,' said Hendrick. 'If we meet anything we can't handle we back out fast. And keep your talismans close to hand, this has the reek of Chaos about it to me.'

Olt touched his fingers to his charm tattoos. He unslung his hand axes and picked his way over the spongy mycelium into the tunnel entrance, making little noises of disgust as he did so. Bartiman followed, cupping his hands and muttering an incantation that conjured a ghostly light between them. Hendrick drew a pair of daggers as he followed his comrades into the tunnel. He curled his lip in disgust as the stench intensified, and the crawling mites began to blunder over his feet and up his ankles. The tunnel closed in around him, forcing him to stoop. He found he desperately wanted to avoid the touch of the pallid mycelium against his head and neck.

The three of them shuffled along the tight confines of the passage, taking shallow, disgusted breaths. The light from the Alchemists' Guild rapidly faded until their only source of illumination was the pallid flickerlight conjured by Bartiman. Things scuttled through that light on swift little legs, their segmented bodies and feathery antennae brushing Hendrick's legs and arms.

'Remember what Captain Morthan said about insect attacks,' he said quietly. 'Keep an eye on these bugs.'

'An eye? Hendrick, I'm kicking myself for not bringing some specimen jars,' replied Bartiman.

'Quiet, both of you,' hissed Olt from up ahead, his voice sounding muffled. 'Tunnel starts heading down pretty steeply up ahead. Getting narrower too.'

Hendrick's face was a frown of concentration as he continued to press forwards. Sure enough the ground began to slope away, and the tunnel shrank in until his shoulders knocked loose soil from its walls. Claustrophobia threatened. The touch of the fungi that clung to the walls was foul, and worse, the walls themselves had begun to ooze a kind of thick, clear slime that was cold and tingling to the touch. The trail of glass fragments continued down the tunnel, and translucent insects crunched underfoot.

Hendrick kept his breathing steady and focused on the thought of finding a solution to the mystery of what threatened this city. Things had not progressed how he had hoped, thus far, and he desperately wanted a real enemy to fight. Racketeers didn't count.

If he was honest with himself, Hendrick had pictured their arriving in the nick of time to warn of some invading army. He had hoped to reap a tally of Chaos worshippers in return for his brother's death. Perhaps some part of Hendrick had hoped to follow Varlen into death's embrace, that he might be reunited with his sibling. Instead, they had mysteries and holes, ominous signs and a religious autocrat who believed Sigmar would save them from all of it.

Hendrick was keeping his temper reined in by the thinnest of margins, and the events of the night of their arrival kept playing out in his mind's eye. How he had stammered himself to a stop in front of the regent militant. How their warning had fallen on deaf ears. He felt as though he had let Varlen down, one last time, and the familiar sense of self-loathing had returned in force. That, in turn, frustrated Hendrick as he knew it was horribly counterproductive, but the anger he felt at his own weakness only made him loathe himself more.

Bartiman stopped so suddenly that Hendrick bumped into him, nearly knocking the old wizard from his feet.

'What is it?' he asked.

'Olt's stopped,' hissed Bartiman.

'Something doesn't feel right,' said the scout, placing a palm against the slimy soil of the wall. A moment later, in a voice of tightly controlled panic, he hissed 'No, no, go back, back, back now!'

Hendrick had fought alongside Olt for a year now. He knew well enough not to argue. However, as he tried to turn and retreat up the passageway the horrible realisation struck him that he couldn't.

'I can't turn around,' he hissed. 'There's not space.' Hendrick felt his body trying to freeze on him as intense claustrophobia clamped its hands around his throat. He sucked in a tight breath.

'Back, go, now!' shouted Olt, abandoning all pretence at stealth. Swearing, Hendrick forced his limbs to move. He began to scramble backwards along the tunnel as quickly as he could. His head banged the ceiling, dislodging clots of soil and fungus that showered down on him. Something wriggling dropped down the back of his neck, causing him to grunt with disgust. Bartiman, who had managed to turn around to face the right way, pressed close, his old features drawn with alarm in the wavering illumination of his light.

Hendrick could feel it now too, a shuddering in the earth

around them. He felt more than heard a subsonic rumble that shuddered through the bedrock and caused the tunnel to shake. Soil spilled down from above, finding its way into his eyes, his ears, his mouth.

'Move, Hendrick, I've no desire to be buried alive!' gasped Bartiman.

'What in the realms is going on?' he shouted, spitting mouthfuls of sour-tasting soil.

The only answer was an increase in the violent shuddering. Bartiman's concentration slipped and his light extinguished, plunging them into absolute darkness. Hendrick caught his heel on something that gave with a spongy crunch, and almost fell backwards. His heart hammered as he found his feet and kept going, praying to Sigmar almighty that the tunnel would soon widen enough for him to turn and run before it came down on top of them all.

Hendrick realised in that moment that he truly didn't want to die.

Not like this.

Not yet.

The sewer tunnel echoed with the furious roar of rushing water. The sound rebounded from the curving brickwork arch of the ceiling. It filled the air with a hammering tumult as thousands of gallons of acidic wastewater poured along the tunnel and away through other channels.

Aelyn kept one hand on the railing as she and her comrades picked their way along the gantry above the torrent. She had wondered if the stench down here would be unpleasant, but with so much water sluicing through the sewers the main concern wasn't the stink so much as it was getting snatched by the acidic waters and borne away to a horrible death.

The gantries down here didn't exactly fill Aelyn with confidence, either. Simple arrangements of wooden planking and ironwork bolted directly into the walls, they felt rickety and unstable. They creaked alarmingly under Borik's armoured weight, so much so that she had considered ordering him back to the surface. The spark-lamp on his armour's shoulder served as their main source of light, however, and besides, if they did run into anything dangerous down here then his cannon would prove very useful.

Of course, they had been down in the sewers for over an hour now and all they had run into was alarmed-looking rats attempting to stay above the rising floodwaters.

No, she thought, that wasn't quite true. They had found *something* else.

'The trail continues along the right-hand fork,' she said. They had been tracking a trail of slimy smears and purple fungi that began at the emptying-out point for the grain silo and led deeper into Draconium's tangled sewer network. Aelyn had a sense they were onto something concrete here, if they could just avoid getting swept away.

'How much further are we going to press this?' asked Romilla, rubbing at her arms. 'Should we not gather the others?'

'Probably,' replied Borik.

'Our trail is scuffs and smears, and a few small fungal blooms,' said Aelyn. 'How long before it is eradicated in these conditions? Even I cannot follow a trail that has been scoured away in a flood.'

'So, we press on until, what, we encounter the source of all this corruption?' asked Romilla. 'There are three of us, Aelyn. Sigmar helps those who help themselves, you know.'

'There are four of us,' said Borik, hefting his cannon meaningfully.

'I wish to find where our quarry entered the sewers,' said Aelyn, raising her voice to be heard over the rushing water. 'I don't believe anything could dwell in these tunnels. To whit, they must have entered them from somewhere else to make their way to the grain stores and do... whatever they did to them.'

'So, we find their entry point and that gives us something to work from,' said Romilla. 'But then we get out of here and find backup, agreed?'

'Agreed,' said Borik.

'There are a lot of pipes affixed to the walls of this next tunnel,' said Aelyn. 'Be careful not to scald yourselves.' The pipes that provided thermal heating to Draconium's more well-heeled properties ran through the sewers, threading in and out of the brickwork and sometimes vanishing off down their own, smaller side-tunnels. They gave off a constant wall of heat, and frequently belched clouds of steam that Aelyn and her comrades had so far been careful to avoid.

'I've served on Kharadron airships, crawling around tangles of endrinworks in spaces far narrower than this while two miles straight up in the sky,' muttered Borik. 'I think I can avoid–'

His sudden pause caused Aelyn to halt, holding onto the walkway railing with one hand.

'Avoid what?' asked Romilla. Borik held up a hand.

'Pressure differentials,' he muttered then, louder. 'Out. Now.'

Aelyn drew breath to speak, then felt it too. A rising wave of air pressure, a sudden oppressive sense of something stirring. She felt the vibration that ran through the railing, and her eyes locked with Borik's where they stared from behind his helm's eye lenses.

'What? *What?*' Romilla's voice sounded tight with alarm.

'There was an entrance back that way,' said Aelyn. 'Swiftly.'

She spun and, as she did so, a violent jolt ran along the tunnel.

Mortar dust puffed from fracturing brickwork. Water leapt and splashed high, causing Aelyn to hiss with pain where it hit her bare skin. The walkway groaned beneath them.

'Go!' urged Borik, and they broke into a run. Aelyn led the way, footfalls pounding the wooden boards as they creaked and shook. She heard her comrades behind her, Romilla's quick, light footfalls, Borik's slower, heavier gait.

Aelyn felt another surge of force, a sudden shift in air pressure violent enough to make her ears pop. The tunnel seemed to buckle around her, a jagged crack racing along its ceiling and vomiting mortar and dirt into the torrent below.

'What in Sigmar's name is happening?' yelled Romilla over the rumble of the earthquake and the roar of the water. Aelyn kept running, almost pitching from the walkway as a board broke loose and fell away with a chunk of railing attached to it. The water snatched the wreckage hungrily and swept it away, smashing it to flinders against the tunnel walls.

'Rust it all, just move!' yelled Borik, his voice amplified by some duardin artifice in his helm. The light from his shoulder lamp jolted madly as they ran, strobing the tunnel to illuminate frothing water, shuddering brickwork and cracking wood.

Aelyn rounded a corner and saw a metal ladder ahead, its rungs reaching down from a circular shaft to meet the wood of the walkway.

Another surge hit, and Aelyn watched with incomprehension as the raging waters flowed impossibly up the tunnel walls. Wobbling globules of sewer-water broke away and drifted up to splatter against the cracked ceiling. At the same time, Aelyn felt her feet leave the gantry. She snatched at the railing and managed to get a hand to it. Desperately, she tried to work out what was happening, attempting to reconcile the violent dizziness and the weightless feeling of her body as it drifted up from the walkway. Behind her Romilla yelled in alarm. Then came the thudding footfalls of Borik, moving fast like a drunk trying not to topple over his own feet as he runs.

Aelyn felt an impact as Borik slammed into her and bore her down the tunnel, Romilla colliding unceremoniously with her. Aelyn looked down to see that Borik was running as though on tip toe, his feet just making contact with the floor. He had them both, his gun locked to his back by lodestones, his arms wrapped around his comrades' waists as he made for the ladder.

His armour, she thought in bewilderment. His armour is heavy enough to weight him down, just.

Then came another pulse, a shockwave of pressure thundering up the tunnel behind them. Pipes buckled and burst from the wall. Brickwork exploded. The floodwaters fell with sudden fury and smashed down so hard that they sent hissing geysers spraying up towards the ceiling. Borik cursed as the gantry gave way with a crunch of buckling wood and a scream of twisted ironwork.

Aelyn twisted in the air. In a feat of agility, she kicked one foot against the buckling railing and, at full stretch, got a hand to the ladder. The aelf curled her long, strong fingers around an iron rung and grabbed hold. She snatched Borik's ammo harness with her other hand.

'Romilla!' she yelled.

The priest managed to snatch the ladder as the wood of the walkway plunged away into the raging waters below. She swung, banging hard against Aelyn and nearly dislodging her grip.

Aelyn screamed with the effort of hanging on to Borik. The duardin's armour-clad weight was enormous, and Aelyn felt tendon and muscle strain and begin to tear in her limbs as she clung on. Her shoulder was going to pop from its socket any moment. Her fingers were white hot agony. The ladder groaned ominously. Aelyn tasted blood in her mouth as she pushed her body past its limits.

'Drop me, or we'll all drown,' yelled the duardin.

Aelyn dimly heard Romilla speaking low and fast. A prayer, she thought incoherently. Then she felt something give in her wrist, felt something else blossom hot and awful somewhere in her chest, felt her fingers begin to slip.

White light filled the tunnel, the sudden flare of a lightning bolt unleashed from the heavens. Through a haze of pain, Aelyn felt Borik's weight taken off her as Romilla reached down, grasped the duardin by his other shoulder guard and hefted him upwards with no apparent effort.

Aelyn blinked as she saw the corona of holy light wreathing Romilla's head, the lightning crackling around her limbs.

'Climb,' spat Romilla, her voice underpinned with a rumble of thunder. 'Sigmar's miracles are brief.'

Limbs shaking, her left arm screaming with pain and virtually useless, Aelyn dragged herself up the ladder towards the metal cover above. Below her she heard Borik's gauntlets and boots clanging against the ladder's rungs. The holy light flickered out as suddenly as it had come, and the shuddering in the brickwork around them redoubled.

With a last surge of strength, Aelyn heaved the sewer cover aside and dragged herself out onto the rain-slick cobbles, uncaring of the downpour that engulfed her. She felt it scald her skin, but simply didn't have the energy to shield herself. Behind her, Aelyn heard her comrades pull themselves, coughing and gasping, into the light. The street convulsed beneath her, then someone was lifting her up, wrapping a rain-cloak about her. She saw Romilla's concerned face, skin pale, eyes red-ringed, then nothing.

* * *

Eleanora looked up from her work in surprise as a shudder ran through her workbench. Metal clattered as cogs toppled from their neat stack and spilled across the table. Her carefully arranged tools jumped and danced.

She sat back, frowning, swivelling the lens of her monocle away from her face.

'What is happening?' she asked the empty air.

As though in answer, the shaking increased. The tremors ran up through her chair, seeming to vibrate through her bones. From somewhere else in the guildhouse, Eleanora heard a muffled bang. Someone's volatile experiment going wrong, she thought. Distantly, she heard running feet, and a voice yelling about fire. Yet her attention was drawn back to her workbench, where the cogs and wires, and even her tools, were engaged in some sort of strange dance.

Eleanora watched in rapt fascination as small metal components drifted free of the desk and floated gracefully into the air. They wobbled on obscure trajectories, spiralling around one another as a constellation of wire and metal and glass rose in slow motion from her workbench to fill the air before her.

Another jolt shot through the chamber and Eleanora let out a shriek of surprise as the violent motion toppled her chair, and her with it. The next instant the air was full of hurtling metal shards, and she screamed again as hot pain blossomed across her back.

Panicked, uncomprehending, Eleanora scrambled on all fours beneath her workbench. Only then did she grope at her back and find small, cold objects embedded there. She hissed and whipped her hand away. Her fingers were red with blood.

The floating metal. It had, what, exploded? But no, she realised. It hadn't exploded. As she stared out from under her workbench with wide eyes, Eleanora realised that only her fall had saved her life. Across the chamber, cogs, wires, tools, bolts and glass had struck the far wall with enough force to embed themselves. Wrought in wreckage was a crude face ten feet wide, arcing outwards on one side, curving concave on the other so that it resembled some great leering moon. And its eyes… Eleanora stared fearfully across the chamber, into the same eyes that had cursed her dreams since the night before they came to Draconium.

'The eyes that see into your soul,' she whispered.

It was a good ten minutes before Eleanora gathered the nerve to emerge from under her workbench, and another twenty before she could finally bring herself to start prising shrapnel from her back, and then the wall.

CHAPTER SIX

BLAME

The common room of the Drake's Crown had become less crowded with each passing night. Where before folk had sought company and tried to reassure one another in bluff tones that all was well, the endless days of driving rain and ill omens had dampened all but the most ardent spirits. Hendrick suspected that most Draconium citizens who didn't have to be out of doors were huddled in their homes, doing their best to keep the rainwater out and a semblance of heat in. He felt a certain sympathy for the poorer folks down in Rookswatch and Docksflow, not to mention the Slump.

'The rain can't eat away the homes of the poor, nor the poor themselves, not all at once,' Captain Morthan had commented when she checked in with them two days earlier. 'But if this storm keeps up, it'll be their dwellings that start to come apart first, their cases of rain-scalding that will fill up the charitable apothecarions and the shrines on Pole Hill.'

Hendrick supposed that the tattooists would be doing a

roaring trade in faith-marks to cover scald-burns once the storm finally subsided. If it subsided.

He looked wearily around the table, noting with mild distaste that creeping mould had taken hold in the gaps between its wooden boards. The Swords of Sigmar were by far the largest single group seated in the common room and, as far as Hendrick could tell, the only out of town guests staying in the inn's rooms.

'Not been a good day, has it?' he asked.

Bartiman chuckled wearily. 'A fair assessment, sergeant,' he said. 'Frankly, I'm surprised we're all still here.'

Aelyn was withdrawn; salves streaked her skin over several livid scalds, one arm and the other shoulder were encased in bandages and poultices provided by Romilla. The priest looked scarcely better, pale and exhausted as she always was after calling upon the God-King's aid. Even Borik was quiet. He worked away with a scalthing-iron to smooth the dents out of his shoulder guard where Romilla had gripped it with her miraculously enhanced strength.

Eleanora sat as close to Romilla as she could get, her bandaged wounds hidden under a fresh tunic but clearly paining her. She seemed caught in a loop, going to pull her tools from her satchel then halting, staring at them uncertainly as though they might bite her, pulling a miserable face and counting off on her fingers, right then left, looking around to check Romilla was still there then absent-mindedly reaching for her tools again. She was favouring her left foot also, Hendrick noticed, and he had almost thought to ask her about it, but the moment had passed and now he didn't feel like distressing the young engineer further.

Hendrick was aware that he, Bartiman and Olt looked little better. They had barely made it out of the tunnel before it fell in. Hendrick had an assortment of contusions where rocks and roots had jabbed at him. Bartiman kept coughing into a black handkerchief, and his breathing had developed a distinct wet wheeze. Olt had fared worst, being forced to dive from the tunnel mouth as it caved in. He had badly twisted one knee, and his palms and forearms were cut to shreds where shards of glass and crystal had ground into them as he sprawled onto the chamber floor.

There were a fair few empty tankards collected on the table between the Swords of Sigmar. After the day they'd had, even Aelyn was drinking, though she had curled her lip at the human-brewed ale. The inn's barkeep, a stocky man named Gathe, slowly polished his glassware and watched them with an appraising eye. Hendrick supposed, glancing around at the near-empty common room with its guttering fire and smattering of lone drinkers huddled in dark corners, that their coin had been keeping the Drake's Crown going these last few days.

'We've had worse,' said Hendrick, trying to sound solid and reassuring. To his own ears his slightly slurred assurances just sounded foolish.

'When?' asked Olt, who had given up hiding under his cloak, having declared that the city folk had worse things to worry about than some tattooed heathen. 'Before I met you Heav'ners, yes? Because I don't remember a turning this cursed in the last year.'

'What is going on in this city?' asked Romilla, staring around at them.

'More's the point, what are we still doing in the middle of it?' asked Borik.

'We took a contract with Captain Morthan,' said Hendrick, frowning. 'And more to the point, we seek to honour Varlen's passing.'

'Aye, and we took another contract before that with the Olmori tribe. Last I checked, their loot is still sitting in our bags and we're overdue returning it, and meanwhile Varlen is just as dead as ever and far beyond caring what we do or don't do to honour him,' said Borik, setting his dented armour down with a thump. 'Now, I'll ask again, why aren't we getting out of here tonight, now?'

'Borik, the watch–' began Bartiman.

'Have their rust-taken hands full, and most of them are too busy hiding under the nearest roof to care anymore what's happening in the streets!' exclaimed Borik. 'With the skills we've got, *hrukni,* we could be out of here in half a night at most and long gone by dawn.'

'And when we hear that Draconium fell, and we weren't here to help prevent whatever horror transpired?' asked Romilla. 'Could you live with that on your conscience, Borik?'

'They've an entire city militia, the whole watch,' he said, exasperation causing him to raise his voice loud enough that Hendrick winced. 'What difference are a handful of injured, tired, *pissed off* mercenaries going to make, eh? This isn't our problem.'

'When Varlen died for this, it became our problem,' said Hendrick.

'I'm sorry for the loss of your brother,' said Borik. 'But he's dead. He's gone. In my fleet, we give our dead the burial of the winds, then we move on. A corpse is just ballast, Hendrick, and a memory doesn't care how it's kept.'

'Borik, enough,' said Aelyn quietly, her voice raw with pain. Borik glanced at her and Hendrick was surprised to see something like guilt flash across the duardin's craggy features. Borik subsided without another word, though he still glowered at Hendrick from under beetling brows.

The Swords were quiet for several minutes. They drank with the steady determination of those for whom reality has become something to be escaped. Hendrick finished his ale, the fifth or sixth he thought, and made his way to the bar for another round. If there was one thing he'd learned before being ejected from the Freeguild, it was that soldiers' troubles can often be salved with a generous application of alcohol. In the short term, at least, and after a day like this that was as far as Hendrick was willing to think. Any further, and he would feel the black pit of despair threaten to open beneath his feet again, feel the onset of doubt and self-recrimination at the thought he might have led his comrades into a death trap the moment his brother wasn't around to clean up his messes.

When Hendrick returned to the table, the conversation had turned to the city itself.

'From what the barkeep said earlier, that earthquake hit the whole city,' said Bartiman, gesticulating broadly. 'Knocked two Rookswatch towers over and killed a couple of hundred people. Brought down an alarming number of slum dwellings and poor-houses and what-have-you.'

'I heard that between the fungal pestilence and the fear-madness caused by that quake, they've lost most of the runti on Westslope now,' said Romilla. 'The grain, the beasts... even if the curse upon this city lifts, they'll need urgent aid from Hammerhal if they're to avoid starvation when the ashwinter hits.'

'That's if they've not all been swept away or drowned by then,' said Olt. 'Clouds so thick over the city today, you couldn't see the mountainsides no more. Just the calderas blazing away up there like a big old pair of burning eyes.'

Eleanora made a small moaning sound at this, and Romilla laid a hand on her arm. She shot a glare at Olt, who shrugged.

'It wasn't an earthquake,' said Eleanora in a small voice.

'Say again?' asked Hendrick, leaning forwards.

'People keep saying earthquake, but it wasn't an earthquake,' said Eleanora. 'It made everything float. It put the natural forces askew, like the engines of the heavens were turning wrong. It wasn't an earthquake.'

'Eleanora is correct,' said Aelyn. 'What we saw down in the sewers was no simple ground tremor.'

'It's all linked, it has to be,' said Bartiman. 'Listen, tomorrow I vote that I and whoever else wants to accompany me go up to the watch blockhouse and take a look at these reports of Captain Morthan's. Perhaps a set of fresh eyes, and a few fresh intellects would–'

Bartiman was interrupted by the door of the Drake's Crown banging open amidst a flurry of wind and rainwater. A watchman burst in and made straight for their table, throwing back her hood as she came closer.

'Oh, what now?' muttered Hendrick.

'You are the Swords of Sigmar, yes?' The watchman looked them over with a critical eye, dragging her fingers through her short dark hair to rid it of rainwater and then swiftly shaking the droplets from her hands.

'We have that dubious honour,' replied Bartiman.

'Captain Morthan requests your presence at the south gate at once. She said to come prepared,' said the watchman.

'Why, what's happened?' asked Hendrick. He set aside his ale and reached for Reckoner, ignoring the surge of weariness that made the hammer feel twice its normal weight.

'There's a disturbance – just hurry up,' said the watchman. Her message delivered, she raised her hood and vanished back into the rain-slick darkness.

'Is this… *it*… do you think?' asked Romilla, unhooking her hammer from her belt. Her comrades followed suit, gripping their weapons in ready hands.

'One way to find out,' said Hendrick, the alcohol fug clearing at the threat of danger. He found himself hoping that this was, indeed, 'it'. Anything was better than this awful waiting.

When they reached the south gate, bundled up in rain cloaks and huddled under scald-shades, the Swords of Sigmar found a strange situation developing. Beneath the lights of the spark-lanterns, hundreds of people had gathered in the square behind the gate. They wore all manner of garb, and carried backpacks, walking staffs, satchels, water bottles, all the paraphernalia of a group about to embark upon a long march. They looked odd, though Hendrick couldn't quite place why.

None were armed that he could see, yet they had been surrounded by a ring of angry looking watchmen with pistols and halberds levelled. The watchmen had their lanterns glaring into the faces of the corralled gathering, trapping them in a bright corona of light. Strangely, though, the trapped mob were doing little to shield their eyes, squinting into the light with a sort of grim determination. They made equally little show of concern about the bows pointed at them from the south gate ramparts, the militia-militant adding their own menace to proceedings.

'Young and old,' said Aelyn as the Swords approached the rear of the watch cordon. 'Rich and poor, all manner of folk. And they're not wearing anything to protect against the scald.'

Hendrick realised with a start that she was right. That was why they looked so strange; it was days since he had seen anyone outdoors not swathed in protection against the rain. Now he winced at the thought that these fools were standing out beneath the downpour utterly unprotected.

'Sigmar's hammer, they'll be lucky to have skin or hair by morning!' he exclaimed.

'That is the least of their worries,' said Captain Morthan,

turning from the muttered conversation she had been having with Lieutenant Grange and several watchmen first class. 'Thank you for coming so promptly.'

'Who are they?' asked Aelyn.

'They call themselves the Shrine of the Last Days' Warning,' said Helena, exasperation clear in her voice. 'A bunch of fanatical cretins who are convinced that Sigmar never meant for us to inhabit the Mortal Realms. They're demanding that we let them out of the gates right away. Supposedly they've heard the last warning and it's time for them to return to Azyr.'

'So, let them out, and us while you're at it,' muttered Borik. Captain Morthan made no sign she'd heard him.

'Why aren't they wearing scald-cloaks, are they a flagellant order?' asked Romilla, her eyes straying to the young, the elderly and the infirm amongst the flock. 'Is there nothing we can do to get them under shelter while this is resolved?'

'They won't have it, some nonsense about the rain only harming the impure,' said Captain Morthan. 'I'm this close to just having my watchmen rush them, but if we can avoid bloodshed it would be preferable. Besides, things are a little more complicated.'

From amongst the rain-soaked, praying mass of people a figure suddenly emerged, hoisted up onto the shoulders of those around her to stare imperiously at the watchmen.

'Captain Morthan, you have detained the Chosen long enough,' cried the woman, and Hendrick winced at the fanaticism he heard in her voice.

'Krysthenna, their Lantern Bearer,' said Helena. 'Not a woman to be negotiated with.'

'We do not wish to damage the defences of this city, but we will not hesitate to do so, for all of you impure souls face damnation whether you have walls to cower behind or not,' declared Krysthenna loudly. 'The bell chimes. The gates open. The warning has been heard.' This provoked wails and cries of rapturous fervour from many of her flock. 'Now allow us to pass or, like Sigmar opening the way for his Chosen, we shall thrust aside the gates of this city and leave them smouldering in our wake. Do not test me in this, Captain Morthan, for my faith is the greater and my determination to protect my flock is absolute.'

'By the gates, see them?' said Captain Morthan.

Hendrick stared past the mass of people in the square to where several figures loitered in the shadows by the inner gate. He hadn't noticed them until now.

'Those three claim to have home-made explosive devices and they've threatened to knock the inner gates down with them if I don't permit them egress. We've been unable to risk getting any closer to them in case they follow through with their threat.'

'Could they do that?' asked Bartiman. 'I mean, do they even have explosives? Have you seen them?'

'The arch-lector has made it clear that he would prefer I didn't take that chance,' said Captain Morthan sourly. 'If a threat to the city is impending, and note the *if* there, he doesn't want any risks taken with the integrity of the city's gates.'

'Where is the arch-lector?' asked Hendrick.

'Warm and dry in the shrine-militant, sending messages by runner,' said Captain Morthan. 'His holy and militant lordship takes a rather different approach to command than I.'

'Captain Morthan!' bellowed Krysthenna. 'This is the last time that I will beg your indulgence. I am the Lantern Bearer of Sigmar and you ignore my words at your peril!'

'All right, all right, you self-important little witch,' muttered Helena, pushing her way through the cordon of watchmen to stand on the edge of the ring of light. 'This ends now. You are endangering your flock with this foolish display. They will be scalded at the very least.'

'Heretic!' yelled the massed Chosen. 'Unbeliever! Damned!'

'I will not argue with one who stands already with one foot in the fires of the Dark Gods' realm,' cried Krysthenna, gesturing grandly down at Captain Morthan. 'It is not for the faithful to explain themselves to those who will not see the truth, whose ears are deaf to the warnings that Sigmar has given. If you wish to damn yourself in your ignorance, Morthan, then that is your mistake to make. But to impede They Who Have Heard the Warning? That is heresy of the worst sort, for you defy the will of the God-King himself! Let us through or I shall order holy fire unleashed upon these tainted and impermanent gates.'

'For Sigmar's sake, Krysthenna–' Captain Morthan began.

She didn't get any further. At that moment a mighty peal of thunder rolled through the clouds, and lightning exploded like a spider's web above the city. A ferocious gale swept across the rooftops and funnelled down the city streets, snatching up roof slates and hurling them through the air. A spark-lantern on the western edge of the square shattered, gas fire exploding from within. The Chosen wailed and prayed frantically. The watchmen looked askance at one another, shifting their grips on their cold and rainslick weapons.

'Sigmar has nought but fury for the words of heretics!' howled Krysthenna, turning, Hendrick assumed, to give the order for her followers to detonate their bombs. Yet she stopped as a new voice, a deep and booming baritone, answered her.

'That he does, Krysthenna, and this night his fury is reserved for you.'

Hendrick spun to see that while everyone had been staring fixedly at the exchange between the watch captain and the cult leader, a gilt-chased coach had rumbled down Herald's

Street and come to a stop on the edge of the square. His eyes widened as he realised that, alighting from the carriage beneath the cover of a metal scald-shade held up by a pair of liveried servants, was the regent militant of Draconium. It was Selvador who had spoken, and who now approached across the cobbles, flanked by his aelven guards.

'The arch pretender!' screeched Krysthenna, levelling a rain-dripping finger at Selvador as he came closer. 'The liesmith, the deceiver, the gilded tongue whose poisoned words have led this city's foolish faithful astray and would see them burn in the fires of damnation!'

'All of these are names that I could ascribe to you, Krysthenna,' replied Selvador in the commanding voice of a battlefield general. 'But that is not why I have come. I have prayed long and hard for guidance from Sigmar, for a sign as to why these terrible omens and dark days have plagued our city. Now I know. It was not our paucity of faith, not some failing of the good people of Draconium. No, it was the poison that drips from your lips, serpent temptress, that has brought the wrath of Sigmar down upon our proud city. I grant you this boon for which you so stridently pray. I grant it though surely it will be your damnation, for you lead your foolish flock unprepared out into the wastelands and you shall not be given succour here again. Take your false faith and get hence from my city, and in going take with you the curse that has benighted all of our days!'

At the regent militant's order, the south gates of Draconium rumbled open. Uttering strident prayers and rapturous exclamations, Krysthenna and her flock flowed through the arched tunnel, beneath the murder holes and the iron spikes of the raised portcullis, and out again into the rain-soaked night.

The regent militant took the steps up to the gatehouse ramparts, his retinue moving awkwardly with him up the cramped stair. Captain Morthan followed close on his heels and Hendrick, never one to wait for permission, led the Swords of Sigmar in her wake.

'My lord, is this wise?' asked Morthan as they reached the top of the wall. Iron braziers burned along its length, and in their flickering light Hendrick could see the Chosen spilling from the outer gate in a jubilant mob. There was still one barge left on the river, he saw, its captain particularly tenacious or desperate; the bewildered bargemen lined the rail of their craft and stared groggily at the jubilant flock whose cries had woken them.

'My dear Helena, it is the wisdom of Sigmar himself,' replied Selvador. 'We are a city of faith. We have no Stormcast Eternals to shepherd us, for the God-King trusts us to keep our own faith. That we have allowed a cult such as this to flourish within our walls... we believed that we were being magnanimous, but I see it now for the weakness that it was. They are practitioners of a false faith, deceived by the lies of Chaos and spreading their insidious mistruths through every strata of our society. Helena, they brought all of this upon us.'

'If that is so, my lord, should we not detain them?' asked Captain Morthan. 'Many of these people may simply have been duped.'

The regent militant shook his head sorrowfully and spread his gloved hands upon the stones of the battlements, watching intently as the Shrine of the Last Days' Warning flowed out into the night. 'No, my dear Helena, they are tainted one and all,' he said. 'Worse, their taint has brought a curse down upon Draconium. Why else would Sigmar have sent a raging storm to show his displeasure? These heretics must be expunged from our city in order that the God-King's wrath may be appeased. That they have chosen to depart of their own free will spares us the risk of a costly civil conflict, does it not?'

'My lord, this doesn't feel right,' said Morthan. Hendrick heard the frustration in her voice. 'They go unarmed into the wilderness. You know as well as I the dangers out there, even in these supposedly reconquered lands. These are folk of our city, we have a duty to them.'

'They are cursed, and they spread their curse to all they touch, and we shall harbour them no longer,' said Selvador in a voice that brooked no argument. Hendrick heard in that moment the uncompromising strength of faith that the regent militant possessed. He could well imagine that voice bellowing righteous imprecations across a blood-soaked battlefield. The man was every bit as fanatical as those he was exiling into the night. Hendrick just hoped that he was right.

Seeming to recognise that the regent militant was immovable, Captain Morthan took a place next to him behind the battlements, as did her lieutenants. The driving rain beat a tattoo upon the leather awnings that shielded the ramparts. The wind howled, and thunder boomed like a gargant's war drum. Militia-militant packed the firestep, staring down at the mass of people departing the city into the storm; it was easy enough for Hendrick and his comrades to squeeze in amongst them and watch for themselves.

'Should we try to stop this?' he asked Romilla.

She shook her head. 'Hendrick, the regent militant may be right. The Moonshadow brings death, remember? What if this storm that occludes the moon is that shadow, and the eyes haunting people's dreams belong to the God-King? What if our suspicions of Nurgle's taint were wrong, and it is their heresy that is the source of Sigmar's displeasure?'

'Do you really believe that?' he asked as he watched the last of the Chosen flow from the gate to join the massed gathering beyond. The ramparts trembled slightly as the portcullis lowered back into place, and the inner gates closed with a boom. Lightning split the sky, a vast web flashing there and gone. 'Do you really believe they brought the animal attacks, the insects, the omens and tremors, all this just for wrongly interpreting the will of Sigmar?'

'I do not know anymore,' said Romilla. The anguished doubt he saw in her eyes was enough to stay any further questions. Instead, Hendrick squinted against rain-mist and brazier smoke as he watched the faithful preparing to depart.

'Light the sacred torches, that they may show us the way back to the heavens,' commanded Krysthenna.

Her Chosen obeyed, pulling out the torches they had soaked in blessed unguent and igniting them. The rain made it difficult, but they persisted. Krysthenna felt pride as she watched, for what was this but a microcosm of all they had suffered and prevailed over? They were going home, at last. They had kept the faith that their parents hid in secret, and their parents before them, and in these last dark days they had spread their message far and wide through the doubtful populace of Draconium. Where her flock had numbered less than a hundred souls a turning earlier, it was more than five times that number now.

'We have saved so many,' she breathed, ignoring the fierce tingle of the rain saturating her skin, the burning in her scalp and eyes. This mortal frame might be as corrupt as everything else around her, but it needed to support her soul for only a few days more and then she, and all her followers, would be blessed by Sigmar. In passing through the Gates of Aqshy they would be cleansed of the sins of the tainted realms. They would be shriven, purged of sin and corruption and made fit to dwell once again in the Realm of Heavens beneath holy Sigendil's light. The thought sent rapturous joy surging through her.

'Praise be to Sigmar,' cried Krysthenna, unable to contain herself. 'Gather the procession, my Chosen, and let us take the road south to salvation.'

'Will you lead us, Lantern Bearer?' asked a red-faced old man in merchant's garb. His impure skin glistened red in the torchlight where the rain had scalded it, but the expression on his face was one of unalloyed joy.

'Of course, it has ever been my honour and my blessing, Pieter,' she replied. Taking a torch, Krysthenna led her faithful along the base of the wall and, as the road turned south alongside the canal, she followed it. The rain hissed from the surface of the waters. In the torchlight, thick mists rolled half-visible over the marshland to Krysthenna's right. Behind her, Draconium hunched massively in the dark, its lights defiant.

'Their defiance shall not long last,' said Krysthenna, and if she was more smug than sorrowful in that moment could she truly be blamed? How many times had she tried to warn them? How many times had she been ignored, spat upon, shunned? Let them face the coming horror, she thought, for there were naught but sinners now left in her wake.

With her flock praying and chanting at her back, Krysthenna led the march towards the distant line of the dark forest. To her right, the mist continued to thicken, and she smelled something sour on the air as its tendrils began to creep onto the road. Truly, the corruption of the Mortal Realms was becoming all too apparent, she thought with disgust.

'It is fortunate, is it not, that we are departing this ghastly place before damnation descends?' she said, and several of her followers agreed effusively. Yet a glance showed Krysthenna that many eyes had turned to the thick fog bank now rolling in from the marsh, and nervous expressions were creeping over rain-slick faces as the grey-white vapour rolled like a smothering wave over the road and engulfed the procession of Chosen.

'Steady your nerve, my Chosen,' called Krysthenna. 'We knew that this march would take us through lands overbrimming with damnation. Sigmar has tests for our courage and our fortitude yet, but keep your faith and you shall be saved.'

'Lantern Bearer, where are you?' came a muffled voice, floating from amidst the mists.

'I am ahead of you, and my light leads the way!' cried Krysthenna, shouting loud to ensure her flock could all hear. 'Your torches are holy stars amongst these tainted mists, just as your souls are celestial lights amongst the tainted darkness of the realms! Follow the lights, hold tight to the Chosen at your fore and let the Chosen at your back take a hold of your garments. Watch the Chosen to your sides that they might not stray, and those beside the marsh, those beside the canal, stay a solid course! Azyr lies ahead!'

Affirmations floated back to her. Dark shapes moved in the fire-lit fog. Krysthenna pressed on, her pace slow but determined, the hands of her nearest followers gripping her threadbare robes.

Then came the first scream.

It was sudden, shrill and so warped by the dense fog that it took Krysthenna a moment to understand what she had heard. Then came another, and a deeper yell of alarm, then a cry of pain from elsewhere. Krysthenna spun, staring hard into the fog to see what was happening to her Chosen. The faithful near her massed protectively, more of them piling up by the moment as they stumbled from the fog to join the frightened mass of steaming bodies.

'Lantern Bearer!' came a thin shriek.

'Oh, Sigmar. Get it off! *Get it off!*'

'Yannick? Yannick where are y–'

'Pray, my Chosen, pray with all your might and hold your lights aloft,' ordered Krysthenna, her heart thumping in her throat. 'This is a test. Only the truly faithful shall be permitted to walk the path of the heavens. Only they shall pass the cleansing gates and walk the road to beauteous Azyrheim. Think of that golden road. Picture those glimmering fields, the starlight that makes them glow. Believe it all shall soon be ours, our reward well earned and paid for in pain. Pray with me now.'

And, as cries echoed through the thickening mist, she led her flock in the prayers she knew would keep them safe.

'Oh Sigmar, God-King of the heavens and all the Mortal Realms...'

A flurry of screams and cries, growing closer.

'Shield us, your humble servants, in our hour of greatest want...'

A heavy splash from the direction of the canal, and a terrible wet gurgle.

'That we might continue on along the path of the faithful...'

An inarticulate shriek of pain, and a crunch that Krysthenna knew was bone.

'And return to you upon the day of the Last Warning...'

A flare of fire somewhere to the right as something was engulfed in the flames of a torch.

'With our hearts full of faith and our songs full of love...'

Doubt, creeping into Krysthenna's mind like poison as the awful sounds continued and something dark flitted overhead, there and gone. She fought it desperately, for if she, the Lantern Bearer, allowed the worm of doubt to creep into her soul then they would all be lost to the rot. Yet how did one *not* think a thought? The more she tried to focus upon something, anything else, the more the doubt forced its way in. Krysthenna took a step back and something crunched underfoot. She looked down and stiffened as she realised that fat black beetles carpeted the road in a squirming mass. She gave a small, involuntary moan of horror. A figure to her left shrieked as something snatched him away into the fog. Krysthenna's heart pounded as she strained to see through the mists, trying to work out what was taking her flock, trying to understand why their prayers were not working. Was it her doubt? Had she damned them at the last?

Something flitted behind her, and a terrible cry echoed over her diminished Chosen, something bestial and wholly inhuman.

'For we are your Chosen, and to us alone shall the bounty of the heavens be revealed,' Krysthenna finished, her voice wavering as she felt insectile legs scratch at her shins and smelled the dank reek of corruption. 'For we are your Chosen,' she repeated, as terror and pain wore away her shield of faith and the mists swallowed her flock whole. 'For we are your Chosen,' she said, as she clutched her torch close and spun in a crunching circle, all sense of direction gone. 'For we… are… your…'

Dark shapes closed in around her.

Red eyes gleamed in the torchlight.

On the ramparts, Hendrick heard a last, shrill scream rise from the dense fog bank. He saw one last torch wink out. His heart pounded, his knuckles hurt where he gripped the ramparts. There was a sour taste in his mouth.

'And so it is done, Sigmar's divine judgement delivered and the curse ended,' said the regent militant, and Hendrick felt anger at the satisfaction he heard in the man's voice. 'Captain Morthan, make preparations if you would. We shall open the city tomorrow at dawn. The danger is ended, the necessary sacrifices made. Praise Sigmar.'

With that, Selvador swept from the battlements leaving horrified silence in his wake.

ACT 2

NIGHTFALL

'It comes now rising high above,
It's heard your hue and cry,
The Bad Moon fills the velvet dark,
And beady is its eye.
Those naughty children that it sees,
No, Sigmar cannot save,
Grobi-the-Blackcap comes for all,
A-squirming from his cave.'

– Azyrheimer nursery rhyme

CHAPTER SEVEN

CALM

Hendrick opened his eyes to rosy dawn light. It spilled through the half-open curtains to limn the tired old furnishings with a reddish-gold glow.

It took the sergeant a moment to realise the significance. When it clicked, he untangled himself from his sweaty sheets and padded across to the window. He squinted blearily against the daylight, the after-effects of a late night and one too many ales causing his head to throb.

Hendrick pushed back the curtains and looked out through the dirty windows to see the light of Hysh beaming down upon Draconium.

Cobbles and slates gleamed like quicksilver, still slick with the last of the storm's rainwater. Rain-awnings, saturated by days' worth of downpour, steamed in the morning's heat. Despite the early hour, dozens of folk were out in the street; they talked excitedly and revelled in the simple act of venturing out without scald-shades and rain cloaks. Some were setting up produce stalls, eager to hawk wares that had spent days languishing in cellars and back rooms. He saw a man in gaudy leggings and little else dancing up the street, his fingers a blur as he hammered out a tune on a local instrument that Hendrick didn't recognise, a cheerfully-coloured arrangement of tuned strings and small finger-cymbals. A ragged group of children followed in the man's wake, and smiling city folk dropped coin into the wide-mouthed wicker basket strapped to his back.

'Can't be,' said Hendrick thickly. He stared blearily at the scattered scraps of cloud that were all that remained of the seemingly-endless storm. The volcanic mountainsides were easily visible all the way up to their smouldering calderas. The forge-red glow of the volcanoes' fires contrasted sharply with the cobalt blue of the sky.

'Barely a damned cloud,' he croaked, before shaking his head and turning away from the surreal cheer of the morning. He needed water, and something fried, and he needed to think about what this all meant.

Hendrick found several of his comrades at the inn's rear. Behind the Drake's Crown was a wide yard with a high, whitewashed wall around it, stables on one side and a half-hearted attempt at a rock-garden on the other. The carved stones had been artfully arranged, with various mossy plants and small, tough trees grown up around them by someone with a decent eye for landscape. Hendrick assumed that person wasn't the current landlord, as Gathe had clearly let the garden grow wild and hadn't repainted the flaking wooden benches that lined the garden's edge in a long while.

Still, with the morning light beaming down upon it and rain-steam rising from the tough mosses that clung to the weathered stones, the scene had its charms. Clearly Romilla, Eleanora and

Bartiman thought so as they were all tucking into breakfast and mugs of metha while enjoying the simple fact of sitting out-doors. Borik, meanwhile, could be seen over near the stables. He was examining a bulky old wagon that sat on resting blocks just inside the stable doors, a speculative expression on his face.

'Good morning, Hendrick,' said Bartiman. The old wizard favoured him with a crinkle-eyed smile. 'You look about how I feel. Come, sit here in the Hyshlight. It is *most* invigorating.'

Hendrick sat, closing his eyes and letting out a small sound of contentment as the warm light soaked into his skin. His head was still pounding, and his mouth had that 'ogor's latrine' flavour that too much drink brought on, but he couldn't deny the day-light felt good.

'So, no need to state the obvious,' he said, glancing mean-ingfully up at the sky.

'Aelyn felt the change in the early hours,' replied Bartiman. 'She'd been out into the streets and come back before I even rose. Apparently, people have been out from first light giving thanks to Sigmar for their salvation. The shrines on Pole Hill are thronging, from what she observed.'

'Where is she now?' asked Hendrick.

'Gone back out to do some more scouting,' said Bartiman. 'Our aelven friend doesn't trust this sudden meteorological miracle one bit, was the impression I got.'

Hendrick's next question was interrupted by the appear-ance of a serving girl, the first he had seen turn up to work at the Crown for two days. She quickly took his order of toasted oat-bread, fried runti haunch and metha, then bobbed a curt-sey and hurried back inside.

'Well the smile on her face suggests that *she* has no such reservations,' said Romilla. 'One would suspect that is true for most of Draconium's folk.'

'Just like that?' asked Hendrick, frowning. 'Days of dark omens and gruesome deaths, and suddenly the rain lets up and they're all celebrating their salvation?'

'The regent militant put out a decree at dawn's first light,' said Romilla. 'Cryers carried it through the streets. He's pinned everything on the Shrine of the Last Days' Warning, and made it known that he commanded them with Sigmar's own voice to martyr themselves, that the curse on our city might be lifted. He's opened the gates, he's stood down the militia... and, I mean...' Romilla gestured at the beautiful blue sky above.

'People whose houses were disintegrating around them will be out on their ladders with rain-wash, treating the walls and roofs, saving hearth and home,' said Bartiman. 'Folk who couldn't perform their trades will be out making coin again. People who thought they were going to starve, or scald to death, or die of disease crammed into overcrowded poor-shelters, have all just breathed one great big sigh of relief and stepped out into the light of a dawn I suspect many feared they wouldn't see.' He gave a sudden, surprised laugh. 'That tenacious bloody bargeman probably got let in this morning, eh?'

'For the first time in days, I didn't have the dream last night either,' said Eleanora.

Hendrick blinked as he realised that his sleep, too, had been untroubled.

'But still,' he said, frowning. 'They cannot believe that it is over simply because one little band of fanatics strayed into the marshes.' He heard again the shrill screams in his mind. Goosebumps rose on his skin and suddenly the morning light didn't feel so warm. 'What *happened* out there last night?'

'Perhaps it was divine vengeance,' said Romilla, avoiding his eye and sipping her metha.

'Really?' asked Hendrick. 'Is Sigmar so jealous in his worship?

Does he truly have time to inflict a curse of displeasure upon an entire city because a deluded cult worshipped him the wrong way?'

'Hendrick, the regent militant was a mighty servant of Sigmar back in his youth,' said Romilla. 'He founded an entire city upon faith alone, defeated a mighty champion of Chaos and all his armies, defended this place without any aid from the Stormcast Eternals. His deeds are little short of miraculous. Doesn't it seem plausible that the God-King might take a personal interest in this place? And can you not at least entertain the notion that perhaps the regent militant's prayers were answered with clarity, and a terrible blight was expunged?'

'Didn't get plucked up in lightning though, did he?' asked Bartiman. 'Surely someone that marvellous should have been reforged, no?'

'From what I saw, Romilla, those fanatics were dead-set on leaving anyway,' said Hendrick, giving the serving girl a brief smile as she placed his breakfast before him. 'What did the regent militant really do?'

The girl's return smile faltered at his words, but she kept its remnants plastered on her face as she hurried back into the inn.

'For all we know, it was the strength of his faith that repelled the heathens and drove them to go marching out into the storm as they did,' replied Romilla. 'I do not disagree that last night was unpleasant, cruel even. But this is a cruel time, Hendrick, and deviance swiftly brings the curse of Chaos down upon us all.'

'Doesn't matter why it happened,' said Borik as he joined them, and his manner was brisk. 'Fact is, the city's open, we've done what we were hired to do, and we've an overdue contract to complete. I'll talk to the barkeep about hiring that wagon and a beast to pull it. We can be gone by noon.'

'You want to leave?' asked Hendrick, finding himself unsurprised.

'Why would we stay?' asked Borik, sounding genuinely surprised. 'Whatever this was, it's done. We've a job to finish.'

'I'm not convinced we've finished *this* job,' said Hendrick.

Borik's expression darkened. 'We're done with Draconium, Hendrick,' he said, his words hammered out like flint. 'We warned them. We helped. We're done.'

'It doesn't tie up,' said Hendrick stubbornly. 'Varlen's warning wasn't about some band of deluded cultists. And just because the storm's stopped–'

'Enough,' Borik growled. 'Varlen was possessed, or gibbering nonsense! For all we know, we were never here anyway by anything other than ill chance! We've a fair wind and a clear heading, Hendrick. Now, are you captain enough to lead us, or are you going to stay here chasing a deeper meaning that doesn't exist until the Olmori tribe send another mercenary band to take their treasures back by force?'

'People were eaten by insects!' exploded Hendrick, thumping the table. 'The food rotted! The livestock were taken by beasts and plagues! Does any of this sound like Sigmar's work to you? Does it?'

He glared angrily around at his comrades. Romilla was drawing breath to answer when a new voice replied instead.

'No, Sergeant Saul, it does not.'

'Oh, rust take me,' spat Borik as Captain Morthan emerged from the Drake's Crown with a pair of watchmen in tow.

'Captain, you don't agree with the regent militant?' asked Romilla.

'I don't wish to sound unconvinced of the regent militant's divine wisdom, but no, in this instance I do not,' replied Morthan, sitting. She waved her two watchmen back. They took up positions either side of the inn's rear door, and to their credit Hendrick saw that they remained every bit as vigilant as if the rain had still been hammering down and the dark signs abounding.

'The storm has gone, the dreams have stopped–' began Romilla.

'And yet three more of my watchmen vanished overnight,' interrupted Helena. 'And something, Sigmar only knows what, rampaged through an overcrowded poor-shelter in the early hours and left the place looking like an abattoir. *And* two separate drinking wells were found congealed into green slime this morning. This isn't over just because the rain has dried up.'

Hendrick looked closer and realised that, behind her mask of professionalism, Morthan looked tired and close to panic.

'What do you need from us?' he asked.

'The militia have stepped down their presence in line with Selvador's decree, but I think I can get away with keeping the watch fully mobilised for another day, perhaps two under the justification that public order needs to be restored and the celebrations are likely to be rowdy. What I can't do anything about is the feast of thanks that the regent militant is throwing at the palace tonight. He's already ordered a minimal presence of both my watchmen and Kayl's militia in case we "send the wrong message". He's forbidden either myself or the arch-lector from attending, if you can believe it. *But* I've managed to wrangle an invitation for all of you on the basis that you came to us with a warning that may well, in some way, have pertained to what's transpired. At least in Selvador's eyes, at any rate.'

'You would have us attend the feast as, what, security?' asked Romilla.

'Just go along and watch for anything *untoward*,' said Captain Morthan. 'I don't know what – Sigmar knows, I wish I did – but I can't shake this dreadful feeling that today is merely the calm before the *real* storm.'

'A disturbing notion, and not one without merit if what you say is true,' said Bartiman. 'But our duardin friend is not wrong. We do have another contract that is now quite pressing. We should really be away.'

'I'll find you extra coin for tonight, if payment is your concern,' said Morthan, and Hendrick heard the deep worry that underlaid her voice. 'Selvador may be a deeply infuriating man, but he is a good one. He is the beating heart of this city. If anything should happen to him, I fear Draconium might not recover.'

'We'll be there,' said Hendrick, staring at Borik and daring the duardin to gainsay him. Borik just set his jaw and looked away angrily. 'At best, we get paid to attend a feast. At worst...'

'Just keep your eyes open and your wits about you, and keep the regent militant safe,' said Morthan. 'Please.'

The rest of the day was spent in preparation. Olt was no happier than Borik to be staying, and Hendrick half-expected both to be gone by the evening. Romilla seemed angry with him, but he left her alone; whatever conflict of faith she was undergoing, Hendrick trusted the priest to speak to him about it if it became a real issue. Aelyn, by comparison, confided quietly that she agreed with Captain Morthan. Something felt off, but even her keen aelven senses couldn't place precisely what.

They were no closer to a solution by the time the Swords of Sigmar assembled before the Drake's Crown, clad in what passed for their smartest attire. They were all there, Hendrick saw with relief. Everyone – except Olt, who lurked under his cloak with a sour expression – had made some effort to look presentable. Borik had buffed his armour. Bartiman appeared both splendid and ominous in his full wizardly regalia. Romilla looked the part of the noble priest, Eleanora the astute, if somewhat awkward-looking artisan, Aelyn the regal aelven Wanderer with her hooded cloak set aside and a thin circlet of bloodwood and silver on her brow. Hendrick wore his own approximation of an officer's dress uniform, richly coloured and well starched garb he had put together with great care the year after he had been thrown from the Freeguild. It paid to be able to impress rich clients, after all, and showing up looking like the archetypal grubby sellsword rarely had the desired effect.

Their only concession to their true natures was that everyone went armed, with additional munitions, blades and other tools of the trade concealed about their persons.

'After all,' Hendrick had said earlier, 'we'll be damn all use if anything *does* occur, if we're stood there empty-handed.'

'Speak for yourself,' Bartiman had replied with a sniff, while Olt had just smiled a wolf's humourless smile.

The streets were thronging as their carriage pulled up and the Swords clambered on board. City folk drank and cheered, offering raucous praise to the skies above. The crowds had thickened throughout the day, at least in the more affluent parts of the city, and from what Hendrick had seen most of the population of High Drake, Gallowhill and Docksflow had taken to the streets.

'I wonder what the poorer folk are doing?' said Romilla as their carriage-driver shouted imprecations and herded jubilant drunkards from his path. 'I doubt they have the means for such celebration.'

'They remain in their homes, watchful and cautious,' said Aelyn. 'At least, those with homes left to hide in.'

'It's like prey beasts in the wild,' said Olt darkly. 'The rich, they can afford to take risks, and believe it when they're told everything is okay. Pampered cattle. But the poor, they've got to watch for danger all the time. If the poor are still hiding, I'm inclined to believe Hendrick and Aelyn that something isn't right.'

'I moved all of the explosives and the firearms and the other inventions that I've been working on back to the inn earlier,' said Eleanora. 'If anything happens, we'll be able to go and get them and use them to protect ourselves.'

'Sigmar's hammer, I hope you didn't tell the innkeeper,' said Hendrick.

'They're all perfectly safe unless they're activated,' said Eleanora, looking suddenly alarmed. 'Do you think he would be angry if he knew they were in my room?'

'I can't imagine why anyone would be unhappy to find an arsenal of bespoke ordnance tucked under a bed in their establishment,' said Bartiman with a chuckle.

'Oh, all right,' said Eleanora, looking uncertain. She counted quickly off on her fingers, then went back to looking out the window.

No one else spoke as their carriage ploughed through the crowds around the Holyheart Wall like a floe-breaker traversing icy waters. The claws of the team-beasts, the gnarlkyds, rang on the cobbles as they passed through the inner wall and into Draconium's ruling district.

Beyond the gate, the crowds thinned. Those folk who promenaded the streets between the private manses, the temples and the buildings of office were well-to-do merchants, minor nobles and prominent holymen. They travelled with their own retinues and celebrated in an altogether more refined fashion than the raucous mobs who could still be heard beyond the walls.

'He's spared no expense here, has he?' commented Bartiman as their carriage rumbled to a halt on the edge of the statue-lined square. As he alighted from the carriage into the warm evening air, Hendrick saw what Bartiman meant. The front of the palace had been illuminated with ornate crystal lanterns that lent it an artfully magical air. As the rich and powerful of Draconium approached the palace entrance they passed between a twin row of gold-robed palace guards, who held crackling spark-lanterns in their left hands and heavy ceremonial hammers in their right.

Off to one side of the palace entrance, Hendrick saw to his amazement that a troupe of entertainers was putting on an elaborate performance. A bulky iron fuel-wagon sat just out of the lantern-lights, hoses snaking out to power a huge mechanical pipe-organ and a number of burning braziers by whose firelight grease-painted figures capered and danced.

'Is it a play of some sort?' he asked as the Swords approached the palace.

'I could be mistaken, but that looks like a mummers' tale recounting the very events that have just transpired,' said Bartiman.

'That is in very poor taste,' commented Romilla archly.

Hendrick couldn't help but agree with her. Faces painted into grotesque masks or twisted by the addition of prosthetics into monstrous aspects, the players capered about in time to the music and imitated insect attacks, terrible nightmares, abductions and the eventual departure of Krysthenna's cult. The Swords stood and watched for a few minutes, Hendrick feeling increasingly dismayed at the gruesome parody being played out before him. How would he feel, he wondered, if he saw Varlen's end reduced so?

'Can't have been without cost, either,' commented Borik.

'In Hammerhal Aqsha, their fuel wagon would cost in the region of five hundred flaregilt,' said Eleanora. 'The organ is a *Hegson's Triumphal*, which are only made to order and cost eight hundred flaregilt.'

'No, not without cost,' said Hendrick, shaking his head. 'But cheapening, all the same.'

'When desperate and fearful folk find sudden relief, they sometimes wish to lampoon that which terrified them,' said Bartiman.

'Doesn't make it right,' said Hendrick. 'Come on, we're wasting time here.'

The Swords moved on, striding between the palace guards and their shimmering lanterns. They were stopped at the foot of the steps by several more guards, who looked at them haughtily.

'Weapons,' said one, who wore a richly decorated tabard that Hendrick assumed denoted a rank of some sort.

'I don't think so,' said Borik.

'Weapons,' repeated the officer, beckoning impatiently. Behind the Swords, a richly garbed couple waited with thinly veiled impatience. Hendrick thought quickly and decided to gamble on a slight stretching of the truth. There didn't seem many other options. He motioned to the palace guardsman to lean closer, which the man did with a grimace.

'Watch Captain Morthan has ordered us to attend this gathering in an official capacity, if you follow my meaning,' he murmured. 'She has some lingering concerns about certain elements within the local nobility and perceived sympathies with the heretics. We're to apprehend them if anything untoward occurs, while your men protect the regent militant.' Hendrick took in the man's aquiline nose, his high cheekbones and sneering expression, and decided to push his gamble a little further. He'd learned enough about Draconium this past turning to make an educated guess at the officer's prejudices. 'There's evidence to suggest that some of those who achieved their station through commerce rather than breeding may have patronised the cult.'

Hendrick shot a quick glance back at the gaudily bedecked

man and woman behind them, and the equally haughty and irritated looking nobles now queuing up behind the pair.

He watched the calculation going on behind the guard's eyes, saw him weighing his dislike of obvious mercenaries and his love of his own unquestioned authority against the possibility that he might be to blame if one of the mercantile class turned out to be a threat to the regent militant.

'Very well, you hand over anything you can't conceal, and you don't go brandishing your blades without good cause,' said the officer. 'If I find out one of your ruffians got inebriated and menaced anyone with a weapon, it'll be the scald-cells for the lot of you. Understood?'

Hendrick drew himself up to his full and considerable height and glared down at the officer.

'Perfectly,' he said.

It still took a good few minutes to part certain of the Swords from certain of their weapons, but eventually they were permitted entry to the palace still carrying an assortment of daggers, pistols and various other lethal accoutrements concealed about their persons.

Inside the building, spark-lanterns and smiling servants indicated the route feastgoers were expected to take. Hendrick led his comrades along a richly carpeted stone hallway, beneath the sombre gaze of gilded statues of Sigmarite saints, and into a vast hall lit from above by crystal chandeliers.

'It's beautiful,' breathed Eleanora, and Hendrick had to agree. The floor was black and white marble, threaded through with whirling designs of rich gold. The walls were hung with rich tapestries depicting victories over the forces of Chaos, while fluted columns held up a vaulted ceiling that bore incredible frescoes. Through some visual illusion, the painted images seemed to recede up and up into the heavens themselves, depicting majestic storm clouds, wheeling stars, mighty Storm-cast Eternals in their sigmarite armour and the gilded spires of high Sigmaron towering over all.

'Quadratura,' commented Bartiman, pointing upwards. 'Style of painting that conjures a receding illusion. Clever stuff.'

'You do know some rubbish, don't you?' said Romilla, shaking her head.

The hall was lined with rows of ironoak feasting tables, spread with rich red and blue tablecloths and piled high with cooked meats, cheeses, steaming vegetables, huge loafs of oat-bread, tureens of richly scented sauces and carafes of blood-red wine. The great and the good of Draconium lined the benches that ran along either side of each table and had clearly not thought to stand on ceremony. A number of platters were already piled high, and a number of faces were already flushed with an excess of alcohol.

'They all look so damned happy,' muttered Hendrick as they searched for a large enough gap to seat all the Swords together. 'So why do I feel like there's a knot the size of an ogor's fist in my stomach?'

'Their cheer feels forced, manic,' said Aelyn quietly. 'I am not sure that many of those here do not harbour misgivings of their own.'

'Whistling past the boneyard, and dancing a merry jig in Nagash's shadow,' commented Bartiman with unseemly cheer.

'There's some protection, at least,' said Hendrick, motioning to the palace guards who stood quietly back in shadowed alcoves along the walls.

'Doing their best to look unobtrusive in case they panic all the delicate little nobles,' muttered Borik.

'I just don't know,' said Romilla, shaking her head. 'It has been a long and trying turning, my friends. I fear you are all jumping at shadows. I agree that the excess displayed here is unseemly, and unwise considering the damage done in the past days to the city's food stocks. What they have here must represent most of the city's remaining reserve, even assuming private citizens held their own stores back and contributed them to this merriment. But if the regent militant received divine guidance from the God-King himself then who are we to second-guess? Perhaps we should simply sit, and enjoy this repast, and pray to Sigmar that what Captain Morthan saw last night were the final aftershocks of disquiet, and that whatever malign influence beset this city, it has been driven out.'

Hendrick smiled at Romilla, he couldn't help himself.

'It must be good to have such strength of faith,' he said.

'It is hard-won, as well you know,' she said with a tired smile, reaching up to place one hand on his shoulder.

'Let's try it your way, then,' said Hendrick. 'But I'd ask you all to keep your wits about you. No alcohol for the time being, understood? And for Sigmar's sake try not to offend the locals.'

Finally finding a suitable space near the front of the hall, Hendrick ushered his comrades to sit either side of a feasting table and fill their platters. He nodded to the small group of Sigmarite priests who sat just down from them, and the holy-men and holywomen nodded back with reserved smiles that didn't reach their eyes.

Hendrick applied himself to a haunch of runti, piling up roasted tubers, some kind of tough brown stalks with a spicy aroma, and a generous helping of khenouine gravy on his plate, then digging in. He attempted to look the part of the simple mercenary, eating better people's food with great gusto. In truth, he was watching the hall, observing the feastgoers, cataloguing exits and escape routes, possible hazards and potential blind spots.

Yet the feast progressed and nothing untoward happened, beyond a relatively poor turn from a group of local musicians who looked frankly terrified to be playing to such a grand assemblage. Servants moved amongst the tables, replacing the empty carafes with small gold and black serving tuns fitted with gilded spigots. The meat course was replaced by a fresh selection of fish, fowl and dairy. People chattered animatedly, got steadily more inebriated, loudly thanked Sigmar for their city's deliverance – as though daring any to challenge the assertion.

The best part of an hour had passed when at last Selvador Mathenio Aranesis himself graced the hall with his bombastic presence. He strode in amongst much fanfare, clad in his full sigmarite finery and flanked as ever by his aelven bodyguards. Priests followed him, bearing lit censers that gave off sweet-smelling lilac fumes. Selvador climbed a short flight of steps to a pulpit that overlooked the feasting hall and absorbed his guests' applause and cries of thanks with a warm and humble smile.

After the tumult had gone on long enough for Hendrick to find it uncomfortable, the regent militant raised his hands for quiet. It fell slowly, the more drunk and raucous having to be quieted by their fellow guests. Hendrick's heart thudded, and his eyes roamed the crowd, the shadows, the exits for any sign of a threat. He saw again his brother's firelit features, twisted and tormented, and felt a dreadful foreboding settle upon him. A glance at Aelyn showed she felt it too. He longed for the comforting weight of Reckoner strapped to his back.

'My friends, my friends, we are here this night to give thanks, but not to me,' said Selvador, his smile widening until his wrinkles almost hid his eyes. His baritone voice rolled through the hall with the consummate skill of a born rhetorician. 'We are here to give thanks to Sigmar, who in his wisdom and his mercy saw fit to test our faith and to reward our wisdom! Praise Sigmar, God-King of all the Mortal Realms!'

'Praise Sigmar!' cried the assembled masses, and it was several moments before the beaming regent militant could once again restore quiet. He laughed with what sounded to be genuine delight.

'Your fervour does you credit, my friends, just as your faith and prayers bolstered my own and gave this city the strength it needed, when it needed it most. A toast, then, to all of you, and to Sigmar almighty, for without your strength and his guidance this humble old priest could never have sent the heretics out into the night to perish!'

Selvador motioned for one of his priests to bring forth another tun, and swiftly decant a measure of wine into a simple silver cup. This, the regent militant raised. The great and the good of Draconium echoed his gesture and, as he drank, so did they. To his irritation, Hendrick noticed Borik did too, in defiance of his orders.

Selvador set down his cup upon the edge of his pulpit and smiled around the room.

'And now, my friends, to make...'

He stopped with a slight frown, and Hendrick found himself tensing.

'And now...' the regent militant tried again, stopping and swallowing hard. His mouth turned down in consternation. A murmur rippled around the hall. Hendrick felt the dread that had been gnawing at his guts surge up like bile into his throat as Selvador leaned heavily on the edge of his pulpit and thumped himself in the chest.

Poison? thought Hendrick. Or was it something in the food, or in the wine? He was half way to his feet, ready to rush to the regent militant's aid when the old man gave a convulsive cough, and his eyes widened as a great cloud of glowing purple motes billowed from his mouth and drifted down upon the feasters below.

Then, bedlam.

CHAPTER EIGHT

MOONRISE

Hendrick felt a surreal sense of horrified fascination as the glimmering purple cloud hung in the air. It coiled languidly, then began to drift downwards. By the time those feastgoers nearest the pulpit broke their paralysis, the motes were settling on them like snow.

Selvador shuddered and gave another convulsive cough. Another cloud billowed from his lips, and this time Hendrick saw the glisten of blood mixed in with what he realised with a lurch must be spores.

'Someone fetch a healer! Attend the regent militant, damn it!' shouted Hendrick, his sergeant's bark shattering the silence like a hammer-blow. Selvador Mathenio Aranesis clutched his throat, staggered forwards and pitched over the low railing of his pulpit. His body fell with a crash onto a banqueting table ten feet below, splattering feastgoers with mashed vegetable and splatters of cooling sauce. Madness erupted as guests across the hall pushed themselves to their feet, some trying to make for the regent militant to offer aid, others turning for the exits, many of them drunk and all of them quickly entangling one another in a heaving mass of panicked bodies, toppled chairs and spilled wine.

Hendrick's eyes widened as those who had had the spores fall upon them pushed themselves to their feet and began to convulse. Bloody foam squeezed between their teeth and trailed down their chins, and their veins stood out dark and purple against their skin. A man who had not been touched rose to help the woman next to him, who had. Confusion and concern were plastered across his features, but they gave way to shock as she spun with a feral snarl and lashed out. Her nails dragged red lines across the man's cheek and he reeled back.

The woman wasn't done. She pounced on her would-be helper, her furs and finery whipping incongruously about her. Her face was contorted in a look of absolute fury and her eyeballs had turned a reddish-purple, as though the blood inside them had burst its channels. The table was only a dozen or so feet from where the Swords had sat themselves, and so Hendrick had a perfect view as the woman pinned the man to the table by his shoulder. Her chest hitched, her jaws yawned wide, and Hendrick's gorge rose as she vomited a torrent of purple, porridgey slime across her victim's face. Frantic with disgust, the pinned man managed to get an arm free and land a punch on his assailant's jaw, knocking her back.

Even as he staggered, dripping, to his feet, the male feast-goer started to shudder and whine, spitting up clots of bruised foam. Unperturbed by a blow that should have stunned her at the very least, his attacker darted past him with a shriek and launched herself at a merchant's wife who was trying to extricate herself from her bench-seat. The two went over in a mass of flailing limbs, screaming and vomit-spatters.

'What in the Eight Realms is going on?' exclaimed Bartiman, hauling himself to his feet and leaning on his staff.

'It's begun!' said Hendrick, before adding, 'Whatever in Sigmar's name *it* is.'

'Where are the guards?' asked Romilla.

'Trapped back in the shadows in those stupid alcoves,' answered Olt. 'They'll be lucky if they don't get crushed in the panic.'

'*Hrukni*, up to us then,' said Borik.

'That's if you've not been poisoned like the regent,' snapped Hendrick. 'I damned well told you not to drink.'

Borik tossed his goblet aside and spat. 'Duardin constitution lad,' he growled, but Hendrick thought he detected a note of concern there all the same.

'Hendrick, orders?' asked Aelyn. For an instant, he froze as the realisation struck him that it was he, not his brother, who would have to set their course. He, not Varlen, whose job it was to keep them alive and get the job done. Whatever the job even was, now, with the regent militant possibly dead and some form of spore-madness sweeping through the hall.

He saw Varlen again, as he had been at the end, with his flesh running like tallow and one eye bulging forth on a distended stalk, with his tongue split in two and a nest of three-foot, lashing worms where one arm should have been. Varlen, covered in the blood of the villagers, with that damned crown still embedded in the flesh of his forehead, the stone in its centre still blazing blue. Varlen, who he'd failed.

'Hendrick!' snapped Romilla.

'The regent militant,' barked Hendrick in reply. 'Captain Morthan ordered us to keep him safe, and if there's a chance we can still save him then we've got to take it. We can't let her down.'

Bestial howls rose from the feastgoers who had already contracted the spore sickness. The crowd surged and heaved around the Swords of Sigmar, threatening to sweep them away from one another. Glass shattered, metal rang against marble as plates scattered to the floor, people wailed and shrieked and sobbed. Some, who had made the theoretical connection between the regent militant's last drink and his horrible fate, rammed fingers down their throats to make themselves vomit. By the stench, others had soiled themselves in terror amidst the crowd. For an instant, Hendrick was struck by how swiftly the veneer of genteel civilisation was stripped away to reveal little more than frightened animals fighting for their lives.

'We need our real weapons!' said Borik. 'I don't fancy our chances fighting those things off with shivs and side-blades. I want my damned cannon.'

'They put them in the guard-post just inside the main entrance on the left as you come in,' Eleanora said rapidly, a look of barely contained fear on her features. She was sweating, Hendrick saw, and looked almost feverish.

'All right, whatever this is we can't fight it here, like this. Not with side-blades. Aelyn, take Eleanora and secure the rest of our weapons. Don't try to get them all back to us, you'll never fight your way back here against the human tide carrying all that. Get them ready and we'll come to you.'

Aelyn shrugged off her sling bandage and winced as the crowd surged against her. She grabbed hold of Eleanora's arm and set off, all but towing the young engineer behind her.

'Borik, Bartiman, Olt, get as many people out of here as you can,' Hendrick continued.

'Why waste time on these fops?' snarled Olt, shoving a portly, panicked man in a skewed hat away from himself.

'Whatever this thing is, it's spreading from one person to the next,' said Bartiman, nodding understanding as he clung on to Hendrick's arm to steady himself against the crowd. 'They might deserve saving, they might not, but it's a question of limiting the exponential explosion of enemy numbers.'

'What he said,' said Hendrick. 'Just do it!'

'And what are we doing, Hendrick?' asked Romilla as the others began to shove their way towards the exits, bellowing at those around them to do the same.

'You know,' he said, reaching down and wrapping both hands around the leg of a fallen bench. Hendrick's muscles bulged like rocks under his dress shirt as he heaved at the leg, snapping it off with a loud crack of splintering wood. Hendrick hefted the three-foot club, testing its weight. It was no hammer, but it would do.

'The regent militant,' said Romilla, hoisting herself up onto the table and sliding off again to land next to Hendrick. The guards had let her keep the smaller warhammer she carried at her belt, on the understanding that it was purely ceremonial.

It was not.

Romilla unhooked the weapon now and brandished it, her other hand going to her hammer pendant.

'Sigmar, lend us your strength and your protection,' she intoned, glancing at Hendrick with serious eyes. 'Realms know, we're going to need it.'

The two of them made for the banqueting table beneath the pulpit where Selvador had fallen. The human herd had thinned slightly, allowing them easier passage, but that only meant that the spore-sickened could come at them all the quicker.

Hendrick saw the first one coming, scrambling along a table-top on all fours and scattering food and cutlery in all directions as he came. The man wore a priest's robes, but nothing holy remained in him, nor anything remotely human. His face was contorted in a rictus of hate and Hendrick realised with revulsion that the man's flesh was covered in bulging white lumps.

His teeth seemed to have elongated, also, until they resembled yellowed tusks, and his nails had twisted into jagged talons.

'What *is* this?' shouted Hendrick as the spore-sickened priest sprang at him. Hendrick swung his improvised club double-handed, throwing all his strength behind the blow. It caught the leaping man in the face with an appalling crunch of bone and a spray of blood. His momentum through the air violently arrested, the priest crashed to the floor and thrashed like a dying insect before lying still.

'Something dreadful,' replied Romilla, swinging her hammer in time to catch a charging nobleman in the face. Yellow teeth sprayed through the air and the nobleman crashed backwards onto a table with a tinkle of shattering glass. 'Something unclean and corrupt. Surely something sent by the Plaguefather.'

'Are you all right?' Hendrick asked, sidestepping the next shrieking attacker and ramming the splintered end of his club into her gut to double her over. A brutal upward swing caught her under the jaw and flipped her onto her back, heels drumming the marble.

'You mean can I remain stalwart in the face of Nurgle's foul works?' asked Romilla. She spared him a momentary glance, a pallid smile. 'I must, for that is the task Sigmar sets before me.'

'Oh, Sigmar save us,' exclaimed Hendrick as they rounded the end of a table and came into sight of the regent militant through the scattered crowd. Here, those first infected seemed to have completed whatever horrifying transformation was overtaking them. Their jaws had stretched and cracked, yellow tusks forcing their mouths open and allowing froth to pour constantly over their blackened gums. Purple veins stood out all over skin gone waxy pale and somehow spongy, like the flesh of a mushroom. A pack of five were hunched over several more feastgoers and one of the regent militant's aelven guards; by the busy way their jaws were working and the wet crunching sounds they were making, they were enjoying an entirely different feast of their own.

Beyond them, Hendrick got a fleeting glimpse of Selvador lying spreadeagled on his back, chest bulging as though he had breathed in as far as he could, eyes rolling and more glowing motes billowing up from his mouth.

Then the spore-sickened realised that he and Romilla were there, and spun with vicious howls. They charged as one, scrambling and leaping like simian monsters. The first fell to a thunderous blow from Hendrick's club, the second to a meteoric impact from Romilla's hammer. The priest reversed her momentum and brought the weapon back down to crack the skull of another luckless feastgoer, while Hendrick grabbed the fourth by the throat before it could leap and stove the side of its head in with his club.

He hurled the body aside and looked for the last one. He got a fleeting impression of a crouching figure atop the table to his left and spun in that direction, raising his guard. It was pure instinct, and Hendrick's eyes widened as he realised his mistake a moment too late. Warm, putrid slime hit him in a gushing torrent. It spewed into his eyes. It squirted up his nostrils. It spattered into his mouth as he cried out in horror.

Instantly, Hendrick's body prickled with fever-sweat. He felt something wrench inside him, something bilious and squirming that began in his guts and spread through every fibre of his body like poison. Hendrick spat a lukewarm mouthful of someone else's vomit, feeling his own gorge rise at the sensation.

'Hendrick!' he heard Romilla's yell of shocked horror, but it was as though it echoed to him from the other end of a tunnel that was growing longer and darker by the second.

'Romilla… get… away from…'

His mind wasn't with her anymore, wasn't in the receding chamber with its echoing screams and dim shadows of pandemonium. Hendrick was in the darkness, searching, staring, feeling something rushing up towards him along the tunnel like a warm wind or a tide rising. He thought he could see something down there, something that glowed with pallid light, something with staring eyes of jaundiced yellow and a leering maw full of fangs.

'Varlen... I... sorry...' he heard himself gasp wetly, then rational thought fled.

Olt had shed his cloak the moment the panic started. These city-cattle had worse things to fear than a barbarian in their midst, he reasoned, and if the sight of him scared them, then good – maybe they'd stay out of his way.

Now he pushed his way through the shoving, yelling masses brandishing a dagger in each hand. Olt preferred to fight with paired weapons. With the unintentional arrogance of the naturally talented, he had never understood why many fighters restricted themselves to a single blade when they had two perfectly good hands to fight with.

'Get out of here!' he bellowed, doing his best to herd the terrified feastgoers towards an arch on the western edge of the hall. 'Move your pampered arses!' A bespectacled man jostled past him, his arm thrown protectively around a woman in a fine gown, who had blood pouring from a wound to her scalp. Ahead, a gaggle of merchants fought tooth and nail to push their way through the crowded archway. Olt almost stumbled over the prone body of a trampled guard, the man's face a bloody mess and his fine attire soiled and torn.

'Stop fighting each other and get moving!' Olt roared, and as he did so he felt the wyrd come upon him, as it always did when the gods lent him their power. Olt's skin tingled, and a crimson glow filled the air around him as his tattoos lit with inner fire. The merchants looked back, reacting with precisely the alarm he'd expected and squirming through the doorway in a sweating, finely garbed mass.

A palace guard came at him, hammer in hand. Olt caught the man's frantic swing upon his crossed blades, and his tattoos glowed brighter as he drew on their strength to push the guard stumbling backwards.

'I'm on your side, you fool,' yelled Olt. 'Stop fighting me and get these people outside!' The guard blinked, then seemed to grasp who Olt was, what he was saying. Still the man hesitated, and it was that indecision that saved Olt's life. The guard's eyes widened in sudden panic at something over Olt's shoulder, and the tribesman reacted. Instincts enhanced by the gods' blessings, he spun and ducked, thrusting out with both blades. He caught the charging spore-sickened in the chest and the gut and rolled, hurling the snarling monster clean over himself to crunch headfirst into the wall by the archway. There was a dry snap as his attacker's neck broke, and they lay still in a spreading pool of blood and purple foam.

Olt turned to find the guard still staring at him.

'MOVE!' Olt roared, the crackle of fire playing behind his voice, and at last the guard woke up, turned and fled. Olt shook his head in amazement and pressed on, herding the panicked city folk before him. He hoped the others were having an easier time.

'This is simply unacceptable!' snapped Bartiman as another fleeing noble barrelled into him, almost spilling him from his feet. The old wizard clung to Borik's armoured form, the stolid duardin like a boulder amid rough seas.

'I could just shoot us a way out,' came Borik's baritone voice from within his helm. He brandished a short cutlass in one hand, and what he had proudly announced to be a Grundstock Aethermatic Repeating Handgun in the other.

'No, let me deal with it,' shouted Bartiman over the cacophony of screams and cries. 'One should always practise one's art lest one becomes–'

'If you have to do something unnatural, just get on with it,' interrupted Borik. He levelled his pistol and fired it with a loud bang, the shot snatching a charging spore-victim off their feet. Gears clicked and spun as the gun reloaded itself.

'Very well, very well, bones of Shyish, rushing an old man,' grumbled Bartiman. He cleared his throat and raised his arms, allowing his capacious sleeves and jangling bangles to slide down and leave his forearms bare. He reached out with his senses and found the magics he had spent his long life learning to channel. By now, they were old friends.

'Ek'suneteh, melloch mel anar!' Bartiman intoned, his voice growing deep and echoing as he chanted the incantation. 'Asmosai, asmosai, ghastirith morbidaris Shyishia!'

Black energies leapt along his bone staff and coiled into the air. A howling gale blew up from nowhere and swept into the panicked crowd. It was an icy blast, carrying the howls and cackles of malevolent things as it battered the feastgoers and drove them bodily towards the nearest exits. Bartiman felt the exhilaration of unleashing his powers, caring not one jot that many of those closest to him stumbled away with their hair prematurely greying, or their skin beginning to wrinkle with sudden age. If it got them clear of the hall and away from those monstrous things then he didn't care what effect it had on them in the long run.

'There, we–'

He was interrupted as a heavy figure sailed through the air

and slammed into him. Bartiman felt something snap in his chest as a great weight landed atop him, then cold fire blazed in his collar bone as fangs dug deep.

Panicking, wheezing, Bartiman struggled against the great weight pinning him. His vision greyed at the edges with shock and pain, and his old fingers fumbled hopelessly for the dagger at his belt. There came another deafening bang, a hot wet spray, and then the twitching corpse rolled off him as Borik shoved one booted foot into its ribs.

'Up you come, you filthy old conjurer,' said Borik, grabbing Bartiman by his uninjured shoulder and hauling him unceremoniously to his feet. 'Let's hope they don't spread this thing with their bite, eh?'

Bartiman's mind had been swimming with pain, but that thought sent icewater down his back and brought everything back into sharp focus.

'Horrible... thought...' he grunted, fumbling with his good hand for a leather pouch at his belt. Managing to open the drawstring as Borik shielded him from the crowd with his body, Bartiman extracted a generous pinch of black salts and, after a deep breath, ground them into his wound. He swore effusively as the grave-salts went to work, black ash puffing from his wound as it dried out and sealed shut. He would need proper healing, Romilla's healing – and soon, if he wanted to keep using that arm properly – but at least he wouldn't bleed to death.

Bartiman had lived a long time, far longer than any of his comrades, except perhaps Aelyn, he suspected, and he had learned an interesting thing over that great span of time.

The longer one lived, the more concerned with going on living one became, and Bartiman Kotrin was keen to avoid the underworlds of Shyish for a long while yet.

* * *

Romilla backed away until she hit the feasting table behind her. She shook her head in mute denial as Hendrick doubled over and retched violently. The club dropped from his twitching fingers and a wordless snarl bubbled between his foam-flecked lips.

'Hendrick. No, please. This can't be happening. Sigmar, please preserve us, this can't be happening.'

Hendrick's head snapped round at her words, and she felt a lead weight settle in her chest at the sight of the redblooms clouding his eyes, the purple veins worming their way through his flesh. Hendrick retched ropey strings of slime and let out a low growl.

He took a step towards her, another, his fingers flexing into claws, his limbs shaking.

'Hendrick,' she tried one last time, knowing it was hopeless but praying for a miracle. Romilla grasped her talisman and prayed with all her might for Sigmar to intercede, to save her friend, her comrade of many years. To lose Varlen then Hendrick like this in so short a time, it was just too cruel.

'Sigmar, preserve your servant, I beg of you!' she cried, but no golden light flared, no warm rush of divinity spread through her like the rays of dawn. There was only her friend, his face twisted into a monstrous mask, frothing poison spilling from his gaping jaws, his heavy muscles flexing as he lurched towards her.

She had seen what they became, the infected. She knew deep in her soul that, just like before, once the corruption took hold there was no saving them. It *was* just like before, and she thought her mind might snap, her heart might shatter right there and then at the thought of it.

'God-King, why do you test me so?' she whispered, then hefted her hammer and said, in a clear, unwavering voice,

'Hendrick Saul, I offer you the mercy of Sigmar. I am so, so sorry old friend. Be with your brother now.'

Hendrick lunged with a howl. He was a huge man, heavily built, but Romilla had been fighting the spawn of Chaos in the Mortal Realms for nigh on twenty years. She had been through tests, endured horrors that would have seen most warriors curled foetal and ruined on the floor. This was no different. She told herself that as she stepped fluidly aside from his wrecking-ball punch, as she sprang back and swung her hammer down on the back of his skull. Bone cracked and Hendrick's face slammed into the tabletop in a spray of blood.

Romilla cursed bitterly as he stumbled to his feet again, blood-fouled eyes rolling, and heaved a great stream of glowing purple vomit at her. She sprang back, frantic to avoid the fluid's touch, and tripped over the half-eaten corpses behind her. Romilla hit the ground hard, managing to keep hold of her hammer, but he was on her in an instant. Bigger by far, heavier, stronger even with his skull broken and tongue lolling, Hendrick tried to pin Romilla down and vomit on her as she had seen so many other infected souls do already.

Squeezing her eyes shut and holding her breath, she did the only thing left to her, head-butting Hendrick in the face with all her might. Her forehead slammed into his already broken nose and drove shards of bone deep into his skull. Hendrick flailed backwards, blood squirting from his ruined face, and Romilla swung her hammer up from the floor and straight into the side of his head.

Hendrick was thrown sideways by the force of the swing, crashing against a fallen bench. He slumped over it, fingers twitching, and was still.

Romilla levered herself painfully to her feet, ignoring the tears threatening to squeeze themselves from the corners of her eyes. There would be time for grief later, she thought. For now, she would try to save the man that Hendrick had given his life for.

Yet the moment she turned to look at the regent militant, she knew it was far too late. In fact, she thought bitterly, they could never have saved him at all.

Selvador's chest was a distended dome, his throat a quivering sac within which things squirmed. Spore-thick froth drizzled down his cheeks and Romilla saw to her revulsion that questing tendrils of mycelium crawled out of his ears, his nostrils, even the corners of his eyes. The man's gaze rolled madly towards her and she recoiled as she realised that somehow, he was still alive.

There came a grotesque ripping sound and a series of awful cracks as something forced the regent militant's ribcage open. Blood fountained, mixed with glowing spores, and Romilla found herself backpedalling again to get clear of the lethal contagion. Unfolding itself from Selvador's burst torso came a great mass of rubbery purple fungus, which grew and spread by the second. Thick tendrils thumped down and quested across the tabletop, pulsing and growing even as she watched. Blunt and bulbous growths swelled from within Selvador's carcass like impossibly bloated organs that grew and grew, shedding more glowing spores as they went. In seconds, the fungal mass had obscured the regent militant's body entirely and was spilling off the sides of the table, which groaned and then cracked under the ever-increasing weight.

Romilla looked longingly at Hendrick's fallen form, already crawling with mycelium where the vile fungal mass was spreading over him. He was dead, she knew, and there was nothing of him left in that mortal flesh now. Nothing left to save.

With that knowledge came the thought that she must warn the others, that they must do something to stop the spread of this revolting daemonic growth. Who was to say when, or indeed if, it would stop growing?

Romilla spun on her heel and ran for the exits as behind her the pulsating fungal mass grew.

And grew.

And grew.

Aelyn cursed in frustration as she stumbled down the palace steps. Only her inhuman grace and poise prevented her from tripping and falling as panicked feastgoers barrelled into her. She had lost Eleanora when the press of the crowd drove her clean past the guard post and out of the arched main door.

People wailed in fear as they staggered out into the open space of the square before the palace. The mummers had long ended their performance, but now they sprang up from where they had been chatting and smoking jacu root, staring in frank shock at the panicked tide of people surging down the palace steps.

'The regent's dead!' screamed a disconsolate voice. 'Sigmar almighty, the regent's dead!'

'Plague!' cried another.

'Chaos, the taint of Chaos is upon us, the unbelievers defiled our city!' came another shout. Palace guards were trying to force their way back up the steps, but against the fleeing masses it was a hopeless effort.

Aelyn caught sight of Eleanora, staggering from the leading edge of the crowd, hobbling badly. Aelyn slipped through the milling crowd, wondering if those who had just kept running had the right idea.

'Eleanora, are you all right?' she asked as she reached the engineer.

'I couldn't get to the weapons,' said Eleanora, looking dazed. 'There was a big woman and she–'

'It will be well, it will all be well,' said Aelyn. 'Hendrick will get them out of there and then we can *all* go in and get our weapons back.'

'My foot really hurts.'

'I promise that Romilla will look at it as soon as we get everyone back together,' said Aelyn, attempting to sound soothing. She had never been especially adept at the finer points of humans and their limited emotional expressions. It was part of why she watched a lot and said only a little.

People were still spilling from the palace in their dozens, and as they came, several battered guards emerged with Olt close on their heels. 'The infected are coming!' shouted a guard, clearly retaining a bit more presence of mind than her comrades. 'Weapons ready, for Sigmar's sake! Civilians get out the damned way! Run, you idiots!'

That started a fresh stampede, and the guards from the square were forced to stand braced as exhausted, frantic people surged around them in a tide. More than one brave soul was knocked from their feet and vanished under the trampling of the herd.

Behind Olt came Borik, supporting Bartiman's sagging form. Aelyn had barely taken three steps in their direction when the first infected ran shrieking out of the palace doors. Bows hissed and Borik and Bartiman threw themselves flat as arrows whipped over their heads to thud into the wave of spore-sickened bearing down on them. Olt was there in an instant, grabbing his comrades and hauling them roughly down the steps with his tattoos smouldering.

'Where are Romilla and Hendrick?' Eleanora asked.

And then Romilla was there, bursting from the palace doors at a flat run, her chest heaving and eyes wild.

'The regent is dead,' she bellowed. Aelyn saw her skid to a stop at the top of the steps by the panicked-looking guards and begin an animated conversation. Where was Hendrick? Aelyn thought with growing alarm. Was he still trapped inside? Why had Romilla gone to the guards rather than coming to join her comrades?

With Eleanora limping at her side, Aelyn hastened through the last fleeing dregs of the crowd and met the Swords at the foot of the steps. Even as she got there, a wave of familiar pressure rolled across the square. Yet this time, it was far more ferocious. Aelyn found herself lifted bodily from her feet then thrown hard against the ground. She hissed in pain as her injured arm was hammered into the cobbles. Eleanora cried out in pain beside her, and as Aelyn staggered to her feet she saw that everyone in the square had been toppled.

Some did not rise again.

'Where's Hendrick?' she asked.

Olt shook his head, Bartiman and Borik stared blankly at her.

'Isn't he here already?' croaked Bartiman. Then Aelyn saw Romilla walking leadenly down the steps, and in that instant, she knew. She felt a bleak sorrow well up inside her, threatening to overwhelm her composure, her sense, everything.

'He's gone, isn't he?' asked Aelyn.

'I'm sorry,' said Romilla.

Perhaps they would have said more. Perhaps there would have been tears, denial, even recrimination. But at that moment another shockwave struck, and with it came a terrible groaning sound that seemed to radiate from the very air itself. Aelyn staggered, feeling pressure crushing her down to her knees then vanishing as suddenly as it had come. Her ears popped, and a sharp headache blossomed behind one eye. She raised a finger to her nostrils and was unsurprised when it came away wet with blood.

'What is happening?' she asked.

'Damnation,' replied Romilla.

Then came the leprous light, spilling across the square like a false dawn as something emerged slowly from behind the flanks of the volcanoes that loomed over Draconium. Aelyn's instincts screamed out a warning, and she felt suddenly as though she had woken from a deep sleep to find something monstrous standing over her bed, staring into her eyes. She felt an awful foetid touch spread over her skin as the pallid light found her, and as she turned slowly to stare skywards she already knew what she would see.

Vast, horrible eyes staring down, seeming to see straight into her soul. Tattered clouds scattering as though fleeing in horror from the lunar abomination that settled low and gibbous in the skies above. The jagged suggestion of fangs the size of mountains, set in a leering, pockmarked face whose sanity-blasting immensity dwarfed the city as an armoured warrior dwarfs an insect.

Aelyn beheld the monstrous celestial body as it rose. As its crushing malevolence bore down upon her she tried to scream, but her chest could not force the sound out.

CHAPTER NINE

EMERGENCE

Aelyn was driven to her knees by the monstrous spectacle above her. The lambent immensity dominated half the sky. It filled the gap between the two volcanic peaks, blotting out the stars of the heavens with its sickly light. Its glow glinted from cobbles and walls suddenly slick with cloying moisture. With a desperate effort, Aelyn dragged her eyes away from the grotesque spectacle to look at her comrades.

'What in Sigmar's name…' Romilla managed to gasp. The priest's eyes bulged with horror as she stared skywards, both hands wrapped around her hammer talisman so tightly that her knuckles were white.

'The Moonshadow brings death,' whispered Eleanora.

Screams rose from across the square as city folk and palace guards alike cowered. The vast celestial horror leered down at Draconium, and as its pallid light bathed her Aelyn felt her head spin and her gorge rise. She could not tear her gaze from the moon's pockmarked surface, the great craters that looked so much like shadowy eyes. She felt the malevolence and cruelty that radiated from those immense black pits, and knew as surely as she had ever known anything that these were the eyes she had seen in her dreams, only writ impossibly vast.

Aelyn could not have said how long she knelt, staring upwards, her mind and body both paralysed by unthinking horror. It was a sharp stab of pain in the back of her right hand that shook her from her stupor. She looked down and made a sound of disgust as she saw a white-tipped lump pushing up through the skin on the back of her hand. Even as she watched, revulsion tingling through her, the skin split and a white and purple mushroom the size of her fingernail pushed up from her flesh.

She snatched at the horrible growth, grabbing its rubbery flesh between the finger and thumb of her left hand and plucking it out of her skin. It came away with a slight tug, as though she had plucked out a hair, and a thin trickle of blood welled after it. Aelyn flung the mushroom away with a cry of disgust.

'Rust and iron!' cursed Borik, and as she glanced his way Aelyn saw that two small fungi had burst from the metal of his armour just as easily as one had poked through her skin. The others were exclaiming in horror now, too, and Aelyn suppressed a surge of panic as she realised that all of them had small, pallid mushrooms forcing their way out through flesh, metal and cloth.

The palace guards were similarly afflicted – as, it seemed, were the remaining feastgoers and mummers still scattered across the square. In fact, Aelyn realised as her aelven senses relentlessly drank in detail, there were patches of fungi bursting from every surface, forcing their way up between the cobbles, sprouting from the stained glass of the palace's windows and popping up across people's bodies like obscene pustules.

'Is it the spore sickness?' asked Romilla, aghast.

'No, look, its everywhere. It's in everything,' said Aelyn, her voice a weak croak.

A palace guard staggered past her, clawing at his face and wailing. She gasped as she saw purple-capped mushrooms forcing their way out of both of his eyes, thrusting through his tear ducts in dribbles of blood.

Then came a terrible scream from the palace. Aelyn spun, the painful prickling on her skin driven from her mind by fresh horror. Three of the infected charged down the carpeted hallway and burst from the arched door. Two hurled themselves onto palace guards, smashing the soldiers down the steps in clattering tangles of armour and hammers and flailing limbs. The third launched itself in a high arc and sailed towards the Swords. Instinct took over and Aelyn plucked a curved Wanderer's dagger from her belt, flinging it to thump into the creature's eye. She stepped aside, and the spore-stricken nobleman hit the cobbles with a wet crunch. Aelyn noted with distaste that pale fronds of mycelium had pushed through his skin like hairs. As his corpse lay twitching on the ground, the fronds sought purchase in the cobbles and began to dig in and spread.

'We need to move,' said Aelyn, shocked at how shaken she sounded. The attack of the infected had woken her companions, their mercenaries' instincts taking over. They looked to her with fear and disgust in their eyes.

'Where to?' asked Romilla, then cursed as another mushroom split the web of skin between finger and thumb. 'Where in the realms can we flee from such a malefic manifestation of the Plaguefather?'

'Not Nurgle. Not Chaos at all,' said Borik, sounding like he had been kicked in the chest. 'We had it wrong.'

Aelyn heard more screams from within the palace, accompanied by the groan of buckling wood and metal, the crack of splintering stone. Something huge was stirring inside. To her left, the palace guards bludgeoned their infected into bloody pulp, before staggering away from the bodies looking aghast.

Everything was happening with nightmarish speed. Aelyn felt overwhelmed, her mind close to shutting down in self-defence. She couldn't let that happen or they would all be lost. She wished for Hendrick. He would know what to do. She thrust the thought of him aside.

She could mourn later, but for now it was up to her to lead.

'We need to get back inside,' she began, forcing the words out, forcing herself not to stare up at the malevolent moon looming inescapably above her.

'There's something in there,' replied Romilla, and Aelyn could see the priest was struggling too. 'Some fungal obscenity. It grew out of the regent militant's body and just kept growing. It filled half the feasting hall by the time I got out of there.'

'Then we must be quick, before–'

Aelyn's words died in her throat as there came a splintering of glass and a groan of metal from part way up the palace's frontage. She looked up in time to see the epic stained glass representation of Selvador's youthful triumph split down the middle. The glass heaved outwards, then shattered and fell in a razored rain. Aelyn spun and shielded her eyes, feeling jagged shards nick her skin as they fell around her. When she looked back, a pulsating mass of purple and grey fungus was pushing out through the window, crumbling the stonework around it as it went. She dropped her gaze to the main entrance in time to see that same grotesque mass of rubbery mushroom-flesh pushing its way up the entrance hall. It packed the entire space, crushing statues, furniture, paintings and anything else in its path. Whipping coils of mycelium burst from its surface every few seconds, slapping wetly against walls, floor and ceiling and digging in before pulsating, growing rapidly thicker until they became fresh fungal tendrils to drag the mass forwards.

'What *is* it?' she asked, then cursed as another fungal growth split the skin of her neck. She plucked it away quickly.

'I know only that it burst from Selvador's body and it hasn't stopped growing since,' said Romilla.

'If it doesn't stop soon, I imagine the entire city may be in trouble,' gasped Bartiman. 'And this light doesn't exactly seem deleterious to fungal growth.'

'The light,' exclaimed Borik suddenly. 'We've got to get out of its light. It'll send us mad.'

'What in the names of the realms are you talking about?' asked Bartiman.

'You just have to trust me,' said Borik urgently. 'I know I'm right.'

Aelyn turned to ask him if he knew what this was, but a splintering crash from the palace dragged her attention back.

'Aelyn, we can't go in there now, it's too late,' urged Romilla as the fungal wall ploughed up the hallway fast as a man could walk. It was almost at the entrance. Aelyn cursed in frustration. Romilla was right. Her bow, Borik's cannon, Hendrick's hammer – all gone, vanished under that mindless mass of revolting flesh.

Still the moon leered above them, still its foul light bathed the square. The infected burst from other palace exits and sprinted off across the square. A few dutiful guards ran to intercept. Others simply ran. Fungi sprouted in thick outcroppings all around them. Screams rose from across the city and alarm bells tolled, sounding to Aelyn as though they floated from every district in Draconium.

'Borik, you say we need to get out of this light? We fall back to the inner gate, take shelter in its shadow and take stock.'

ANDY CLARK

Aelyn turned, hoping they would follow her, and set off with her remaining knife clutched tight. Crossing the square seemed to take a nightmarishly long time, exposed to the unblinking stare of the celestial monster above, her gaze darting back and forth trying to track the spore-sickened where they dashed to and fro, attacking everything they saw. Fresh cries rose, as the horrors smashed through the windows of mansions near the square and plunged into Sigmarite shrines to where terrified feastgoers and other Holyheart residents had fled.

Aelyn plunged into the shadowed tunnel that led through the city's inner wall, almost slipping on slime-slick cobbles. Above, on the wall's ramparts, militia-militant were milling and crying out, plucking fungi from their flesh and yelling in panic for orders. She knew the Swords couldn't remain in this tunnel for long in case they were trapped when the militia inevitably took it upon themselves to close the gates. However, it was shelter from the putrid moonlight at least, and she felt a blessed relief the moment she was away from those awful eyes.

Her companions joined her, breathing hard. They stared at her with wild eyes.

'Is Hendrick dead?' she asked Romilla at once.

'Yes, I told you that,' she replied.

'No. I mean is he *dead*?' repeated Aelyn. Romilla sighed and nodded, her shoulders slumping as she understood.

'I gave him Sigmar's mercy.'

'Then you did the best you could for our friend,' said Aelyn. 'Thank you.'

'Your best would've been not letting him get killed, uh?' spat Olt. Romilla turned with a face like thunder, but Aelyn raised a hand.

'Not now.' Her voice was hard as tempered iron. 'Borik, you said this wasn't Chaos. What is it, then? What do you know?'

188

'Sky-sailor's tales, is all I thought they were,' he said, shaking his head.

'Evidently, they're rather more,' grizzled Bartiman, who was pale and sweating from the pain of his wound.

'They call it the Bad Moon,' said Borik slowly. 'It's a dark omen, the very worst. They say its light brings madness and death, that it smothers the heavens and brings night everlasting, and that it calls the blackcaps up from the bowels of the earth upon a tide of squirming terrors.'

'The Moonshadow brings death,' repeated Eleanora again, counting rapidly on her fingers. 'I need to get my tools. And my bombs. From the inn.'

'The Bad Moon? The tales of Grobi-the-blackcap? Borik, these are children's rhymes, folklore,' exclaimed Bartiman. '"Get ye to sleep little one, and close your eyes up tight, lest blackcap comes a-calling and you see the Bad Moon's light." It's an Azyrite nursery rhyme!'

'My people aren't given to the flights of fancy yours indulge in,' growled Borik, looking for a moment as though he might shrug the injured wizard off to stand or fall on his own. 'I heard tell of the light that draws fungus from flesh and iron, like dawn rains in the forest. Does that sound familiar?'

'Blessedly, that at least seems to have ceased,' said Romilla with a shudder of revulsion.

'Only what it touches,' said Eleanora, fumbling a half-built gadget out of one of her many pockets and rotating it in her hands.

'What's that, my dear?' asked Romilla.

Eleanora shook her head, frowning, but Aelyn felt a surge of realisation at her words.

'She's right. It has stopped since we ducked into this tunnel. No more... fungi...' she grimaced in distaste.

'And none sprouting within the tunnel's shadow,' said Romilla.

'Plenty outside though, eh?' said Olt, gesturing to the cobbles directly outside the tunnel entrance. Wherever the pale light reached, the cobbles were slick with mucal moisture, and outcroppings of purple-capped mushrooms were pushing up between them. Nearby lay the body of a fallen feastgoer, fungi swelling up from his fine garb, sprouting out of the walking cane that had spilled from his nerveless fingers – even growing in profusion across his face and the palms of both hands.

'So, we stay out of that light as much as we can,' said Bartiman. 'Fine. I'll accept that much. Even the most far-fetched tales have a grain of truth to them. But what *is* this? What does it mean? And what in the name of the Land of Endings are we meant to do about it?'

Before Aelyn could answer, there came a cry from the battlements above. For a moment she feared the inner gates were about to shut. Instead, she heard the percussion of talons and wheels upon the cobbles. An instant later, a carriage was careering down the tunnel towards them from the city end, the gnarlkyd that pulled it hissing frantically. The coachman saw the Swords of Sigmar standing in his path and shouted a frantic command, drawing his team to a halt just a few feet from where Aelyn stood.

The aelf had a moment to take in the fungi sprouting from the carriage's chassis, the scrapes and cracks on its bodywork and the look of barely-controlled terror in the coachman's eyes. Then one of the doors opened. Two watchmen hopped down, pistols drawn and immediately levelled at the Swords. After them came Captain Morthan, who had a bloody cut down one cheek and the beginnings of a black eye.

'Coachman, what–' she stopped when she saw them, and her expression became stony. 'You,' she said. 'Why is it that wherever I turn to find trouble in this city, there you are? What in the name of Sigmar's hammer happened? Are the rumours true, is Selvador dead?'

'He is,' said Aelyn.

'How?' demanded Morthan, marching up to them. 'You were tasked with protecting him.' More watchmen climbed from the coach behind her and formed up in a menacing group at her back. Aelyn sensed her comrades subtly shifting postures, tightening their grip on what meagre weapons they held.

'Poison, we think,' she replied. 'He gave a toast, then immediately afterwards began coughing up spores that in turn have begun the spread of some terrible plague.'

'There's madness and panic in the streets,' said Morthan. 'Mindless, insane rioting in Docksflow and Marketsway and Sigmar knows where else. And damn me for a fool if I don't see your bloody Moonshadow now, eh? *What in the hells is that thing in the sky?* Tell me now, truthfully – did you have something to do with all this? Have I allowed the architects of this doom into my city? Because if it is so, I will execute you all where you stand.'

'You can't seriously think this has anything to do with us?' exclaimed Romilla, her tone incredulous.

'Where is Sergeant Saul?' asked Morthan, ignoring her. 'I'd have the truth of this from him.'

'He's dead,' said Aelyn, and felt something splinter inside her as the words made it real.

Morthan stopped and stared harder at them, seeming for the first time to see their wounds and their dismayed expressions. She paused, took a breath, then continued in a slightly calmer tone.

'How did he die?'

'The same spore sickness that claimed so many others at the feast,' said Romilla. 'I gave him Sigmar's grace.'

'I am truly sorry to hear that, he seemed a good man,' said Morthan.

'He was better than he knew,' replied Aelyn. There followed a moment's uncomfortable silence, in which screaming voices and tolling bells could be heard echoing over the city. Aelyn felt the tunnel shudder as another pressure wave rolled across Draconium. Mortar dust drizzled down from above, the tunnel creaked and her head spun.

'Do you know what this is? Is this what Hendrick's brother warned of?' asked Morthan.

Swiftly, they told her what little they knew.

'The Bad Moon?' asked Morthan incredulously. 'Grobi-the-blackcap and squiggling-squirms and all that?'

'There are monsters all over the realms, why not these?' asked Aelyn. 'And can you deny the evidence of your own eyes filling the sky?' She was surprised to find she believed Borik's tale without a great deal of effort. In her experience, most myths and fairy tales bore a seed of truth in the Mortal Realms; more often than not the reality of that seed was ghastlier than any tale could be.

She could see Helena Morthan struggling with the idea, but as she'd said, it was hard to deny your own eyes.

'*Whatever* we're dealing with, we need to control the situation and restore order swiftly,' said the captain, falling back on what she knew best. 'I've got the watch spreading out across the city to maintain order, but I've no idea where half of my men and women even are right now. It's anarchy. There are rioters in the streets, we've had reports of insects spilling up from the sewers and attacking people, and now you tell me there's a sickness spreading and something growing in the palace.'

'Public unrest can wait,' said Romilla. 'You haven't seen what the infected can do, how quickly their sickness spreads. And whatever that *thing* in the palace is, last we saw it was outgrowing the damned walls! Those have to be our priorities.'

Her words were punctuated by the groan and crash of masonry falling.

'That came from the palace,' said Olt, sounding rattled.

'Sigmar, how do you stop something like that?' said Romilla.

'What about the militia?' asked Borik.

'Arch-Lector Hessam Kayl should be massing their strength in Fountains Square,' replied Morthan. 'That's standard procedure in the event of a threat to the city itself. He'll march them out from there to restore order, using whatever force is necessary.'

'They'd be no use to us anyway – an army could assail that growth all day and it would simply roll over them,' said Romilla.

'Fire,' said Olt. 'The gods of plants and nature, they fear the deities of the volcano and the inferno.' He touched fingers to his heart then his throat reverently.

'The notion has merit, but where would we get a fierce enough blaze to kill something that vast and fecund?' asked Bartiman. 'No, the city is going to be overrun by spore-sickened and fungus, you mark my words. We need to get out of here now.'

'The Kazlag and Gephryn third type brimspark fuel bowser has a contained volume of over three thousand measures of liquid fuel held at a pressure of one point two parts to the unit,' said Eleanora as though reciting from an engineer's manual. 'The fuel itself is refined from crushed bellicosite and magma-oil, and must be fed through a triple-filtration control nozzle before it reaches the brazier in order to prevent compound flaring and uncontrolled detonation. Were the Kazlag and Gephryn third type brimspark fuel bowser to be pierced by an incendiary projectile or secondary explosive component, even assuming a two-thirds load due to persistent use over a period of no less than six hours at this point, the detonation would be the equivalent of in the region of ten thousand aqshels of force and heat.'

Eleanora subsided, becoming aware that everyone was staring at her in silence.

'What?' asked Morthan.

'Oh, you damned genius, El!' exclaimed Romilla. 'The mummers, their...' she flapped a hand. 'Their braziers and the fuel wagon thing powering them. She means that, don't you Eleanora?'

'Would that be sufficient, if we blew it up?' asked Bartiman.

Eleanora nodded, counting hurriedly on her fingers.

'All well and good, but we've only got pistols, and I couldn't guarantee even my piece would pierce through the hull of that tank,' growled Borik.

Eleanora rummaged in a pocket and produced a pair of compact devices that looked to Aelyn like banded metal eggs, each flat on one side and with several cogs and wires visible through gaps in its surface.

'One of these would affix to the Kazlag and Gephryn third type brimspark fuel bowser and detonate with sufficient force to rupture the tank,' she said. 'They have lodestone clamp mechanisms here, look. That will attach it. And each has a timer for remote operation.'

'You took bombs to the feast with you?' exclaimed Captain Morthan, aghast.

'They're the best ones I've made,' said Eleanora, as though explaining something simple to a child.

'That's hardly a comfort!' said Morthan.

'Not the time,' said Bartiman as they heard another groan and a crash. Screams echoed from the direction of the palace. Footsteps slapped on cobbles, and from above them they heard bowstrings hiss.

'Eleanora, show Borik how those bombs work, then you, Romilla and Bartiman go back to the Drake's Crown and get the rest of our gear,' said Aelyn. 'We can't keep fighting the infected with daggers. Borik, Olt – we're going to affix one of the bombs to the fuel tank and get it into the path of that fungal… thing.'

'Why not both?' asked Borik.

'Save one just in case the first doesn't work,' said Aelyn.

'I've got to run around with a pair of bombs in my arse pocket?' asked Borik dubiously. 'Are you mad? No!'

'It's that or let this whole city get buried by that… thing,' said Romilla. 'Even you're not that heartless, Borik.'

The duardin muttered something about her being surprised but he slipped the device into a pocket on his leather under-suit all the same.

'We'll help you,' said Captain Morthan, shooting Eleanora one last hard look. 'Then you and your people are to rally on Fountains Square and join the muster. They'll have use for warriors of your unusual talents.'

'We're charging you extra for this,' said Borik.

'Considering the situation, escaping with your lives should be payment enough, don't you think?' replied Captain Morthan, scowling.

Eleanora went over the workings of the bomb with Borik. As she did so, and while Captain Morthan issued quick orders to her watchmen, Aelyn slid up to the end of the tunnel and peered back into the square. What she saw made her heart lurch in her chest.

The palace was a crumbling ruin, walls and windows bulging outwards grotesquely. In places, sections of masonry had already collapsed or windows shattered, and from within spilled pulsating fungal growths so purple they were almost black. They were digging into the mushroom-festooned cobbles of the square, squirming blindly over the fallen bodies of feastgoers, palace guards and infected alike. Aelyn found her gaze drawn skywards, towards the ghastly spectre that hung above the city, and she flinched as she realised that its expression had changed subtly. Surely features wrought from mountainous stone couldn't change – and yet she was sure they had. The Bad Moon grinned ghoulishly, and she almost felt it was waiting for something.

As though the thought had brought it, the ground shuddered beneath her feet.

'Another shockwave,' gasped Bartiman, teeth gritted as Romilla did what she could to patch up his wounded shoulder.

'No, that was something else,' said Aelyn. 'Something from below. We need to move quickly, now!'

The ground shuddered again, and across the square she saw a drain cover fly into the air like a cork from a bottle of spice-wine. Aelyn grimaced as something black and undulating flowed up out of the ragged hole it left. Insects, she realised: thousands of squirming, scuttling beetles and millipedes and realms knew what else.

'Really, we need to move *right now*,' she urged. Borik and Olt appeared at her side, accompanied by Morthan and all nine of the watchmen who had crammed into the carriage with her. The captain's followers gaped in open horror at the state of the palace, recoiling as another wing burst asunder and collapsed to reveal more bulging, swelling fungus.

'We'll meet you in Fountains Square,' called Romilla as she, Bartiman and a limping Eleanora hurried away towards the city end of the tunnel.

'Cover your skin as best you can,' replied Aelyn, wishing she had not left her hooded cloak behind at the inn. 'Only what it touches, remember?'

Romilla waved understanding, and the three of them pulled sleeves down, dragged hoods forwards, and did whatever else they could do to keep the moon's light from their flesh.

'And stay alive,' muttered Aelyn as her comrades departed.

'Let's concentrate on doing that ourselves, shall we?' asked Helena Morthan, looking grim.

'Now or never,' said Borik, eyeing the spreading tide of darkness that was the insect swarm. It looked like oil, spilling over the moon-slick cobbles. 'I've no desire to get in the way of that lot.'

'On my word, then,' said Aelyn. Fear tried to clamp itself around her heart at the thought of stepping out into the open beneath that daemon moon once more, but she knew it had to be done. It was that or flee the city they had sworn to save, and for her, that had now become a quest that both the Saul brothers had died for. She would be damned to Shyish before she abandoned their memories.

'Move,' she hissed, and the small group burst from the mouth of the tunnel at a run. Morthan and her watchmen had thrown up their hoods and pulled cloth masks up over the lower portions of their faces, so they had precious little skin on show. Aelyn was not so fortunate, still clad in her blood-stained feast garb, and she felt the immediate crawling prickle upon her skin again as fungus began to push through her pores.

She tried not to think about it, nor about the onrushing tide of insects now only a hundred or so yards distant, nor about the fungal abomination overrunning the palace and the spore-sickened now vanished into the streets and causing Sigmar alone knew what carnage. Most of all, she tried not to think about the vast presence that loomed above her and radiated such a crushing weight of malice and hate.

They made straight for the fuel wagon. So vast had the fungus grown that it had wholly buried the palace steps, and was now only a few dozen yards from the bowser and its braziers. Aelyn hurdled the fallen body of a mummer with half his grease-painted face missing and skidded to a halt beside the bowser. Olt reached her a moment later, followed by a puffing and blowing Borik. Morthan and her watchmen formed a loose cordon around the three Swords, pistols out and eyes alert for danger.

'The insects are getting closer,' one of the watchmen sang out.

'Borik, get that bomb onto—'

Aelyn was interrupted by another tectonic lurch, this one so ferocious that it almost knocked her from her feet. Cracks erupted across the square and loose cobbles flew a dozen feet into the air before clattering back down.

'What was that?' gasped Morthan.

Her answer came in the form of an explosion of cobbles and mortar, which blew skywards like a geyser directly in the path of the insects. Something huge moved amidst the drifting dust, and Aelyn made out an arm as thick as a tree trunk pushing up from the hole. Huge, blunt talons sank into the ground, and a lumpen figure hauled itself into the moonlight. She saw rubbery flesh thick with fungal growths, grotesquely large ears, nose and jutting tusks, small eyes that glittered with idiot malevolence, and a gigantic body corded with ropey muscle.

'Troggoth!' yelled a watchman. 'That's some kind of troggoth!'

'Biggest damned trog I've ever seen,' breathed Borik.

The troggoth threw back its boulder-like head, opened its jaws and gave vent to a deafening roar. As it did so, smaller figures squirmed out of the hole around it. There were dozens, Aelyn saw, perhaps the size of a human adolescent, clad in mouldering black robes with pointed hoods, their green skin pale in the moonlight and their red eyes gleaming.

'Borik, the bomb, now!' she urged. The duardin hurriedly twisted the clamp on Eleanora's device and slapped it into place.

'How long?' he asked.

Aelyn looked up to see a wall of pulsating fungus rolling towards them, dripping tendrils spewing from its surface to grope for the fuel bowser and the bodies around it.

'Ten seconds, that's all we'll need,' she said. Borik twisted the mechanism again, and as he did so there was a ripple of pistol fire from Morthan and her watchmen. The troggoth, which was stomping towards them clutching a stalactite club taller than Aelyn, staggered as the volley of shots struck home. It gave a subsonic growl of annoyance and kept going. Behind it slunk dozens of hooded greenskins, fangs bared in cruel grins, hands clutching crude shivs and spears. Around their feet flowed the insect tide, rushing like a river towards the Swords and the watchmen.

'The bomb is set! Run!' shouted Aelyn.

'This way,' replied Morthan, discharging her pistol into the troggoth's face before turning and dashing away with her cloak flowing behind her. Aelyn felt the ground shake again as she pelted after the captain. The moonlight made her feel nauseous and light headed, and she almost missed her footing. She counted in her head.

'Four.'

'Five.'

'Six.'

One of the watchmen screamed as he stumbled, and insects flowed over him in a tide. For an instant there came an awful sound of massed chewing, and Aelyn glanced back helplessly before the troggoth's club whistled down and smashed the fallen man into bloody paste. Insects fountained into the air at the blow.

'Seven.'

'Eight.'

There came an awful creak of stressed metal, and another stolen look showed the fungal abomination rolling over the fuel bowser, spreading its tendrils into the corpses around it, polyps rising on its surface and bursting wetly to spew clouds of glowing spores.

This had to work, she thought, or they were all going to die.

'Nine.'

'Ten.'

'Eleven.'

She felt her heart sink and an awful tingle of dread at the lack of a detonation. Spears clattered from the cobbles around her, and she heard the clang as one rang from Borik's armour. Cloaked figures sprinted out to either side of her, fungi sprouting from their weapons and cloaks, the lambent moonlight lending the scene a nightmarish quality.

'Twelve.'

'Thirteen.'

The troggoth roared, the sound frighteningly close. Insects chittered and skittered.

Then came the blast. Aelyn felt it like a kick in the back from an enraged horse. Her feet left the ground and she was thrown through the air, her back hot with pain. She felt her skin sting in a dozen places at once, though whether from fungi or stone shrapnel she didn't know. The world spun, and instinct took over. Aelyn hit the ground on her uninjured shoulder and rolled, coming back to her feet with the sort of grace that only aelves could achieve. Still, bolts of pain shot through her and she stumbled, looking back. Her ears rang as she took in the devastation Eleanora's bomb had wrought.

The explosion had been ferocious; for an instant, Aelyn feared *too* ferocious. Lumps of blackened and burning fungus were strewn across the square, some still raining down hundreds of yards distant. The growth itself had been annihilated all the way back to the palace steps, simply blown to bits by the force of the blast. As the black smoke billowed, Aelyn realised with a surge of triumph that the fungal mass was burning fiercely. The flames crackled, spreading further into its enormity with every passing second. The fungus writhed, as though trying to squirm away from the inferno that was eating it alive, and Aelyn felt a sting of bitter satisfaction at the thought that this awful thing might feel pain.

The explosion had scattered the insect tide, burning many to windblown ash, and Aelyn spat a mouthful of charred bug-dust onto the slick cobbles. The blackened bodies of greenskins were strewn about, still burning. The troggoth was lying on its face, the flesh of its back aflame.

Three watchmen had also been consumed by the blast, Aelyn saw with a stab of regret, but the rest were staggering groggily to their feet. Captain Morthan stood, the cut on her forehead reopened and spilling blood down over one eye. Borik and Olt rose, the latter shaking his head as though to clear the ringing in his ears.

The ground shook again beneath Aelyn's feet, another savage tremor, and a fresh geyser of sundered rock spat skywards on the other side of the square. Diminutive black-clad figures spilled up from below. As her hearing returned, she became aware of fresh screams ringing from within buildings all around her, and crash after crash as more tunnel entrances burst open from below.

Captain Morthan spat a tooth, blinked twice, then turned and hauled one of her watchmen to her feet. 'Fountains Square,' she barked, and to Aelyn her voice still sounded muffled by the blast. 'We've done all we can here. Fountains Square!'

Morthan set off, weaving slightly as she ran. Aelyn and her companions shared a look, then followed the captain and her surviving men. Morthan led them along the square's western edge, as far away from the emerging greenskins as was possible, and hurriedly unlocked a postern door in the inner wall.

'We'll cut along Makeweave Street, down the back of the Red Firkin and across Tinker's Square to the Fieldway,' she said to her watchmen. 'That should bring us to the square from the west.'

Aelyn took one last glance behind her before she ducked through the postern gate after the watchmen. The fungal abomination burned, and the palace with it, a vast pyre for all those who had died at the victory feast.

'Goodbye, old friend,' she whispered, then ducked into the tunnel and was gone.

CHAPTER TEN

FALL

The dash through the city streets was chaotic and horrible. From the moment Aelyn emerged from the outer face of the Holyheart Wall, she found herself immersed in panicking, pushing crowds. Faces reared up, eyes wild, mouths yawning in cries of terror. Townsfolk shoved past, clutching children close or dragging maddened animals in their wake. Some fought, crazed with terror or moon-madness Aelyn could not tell. She saw a man in blacksmith's garb swinging his hammer indiscriminately at everyone who came close, screaming over and over that he felt the Bad Moon's gaze as he broke bones and skulls. White whiskers of mycelium had pushed out from his scalp and face and waved around him like a silvery halo. Three watchmen bore him to the ground, and his cries were silenced by a pistol shot. Only two cloaked figures rose again from the brawl.

Aelyn was almost run down as a carriage thundered down the street, scattering panicked city dwellers before it and crushing those too slow to clear its path. Olt grabbed her by her collar and wrenched her back before she could vanish under the vehicle's wheels.

'Thank you,' she said.

'You saved me enough times,' he said, and his awkward half-smile reminded Aelyn how young he was.

Captain Morthan bulled through the press, shouldering people aside and menacing them with her pistol where she had to. Her watchmen had raised their halberds and activated their blinding lanterns, and folk instinctively scrambled aside from the piercing beams that signified authority in Draconium.

Aelyn kept her eyes on the captain, trying to ignore the bloodshed and bedlam, her pain and nausea, and the building sense of horror as more fungal blooms pushed through her skin. As they passed an overturned stall, she gratefully snatched up a hooded cloak that had spilled onto the cobbles, grabbing one for Olt as well. The garments were trampled and torn, cheaply made, but as she pulled the hood up to shield her face Aelyn felt blessed relief. It warded away the moon's clammy touch and hid her from its leering gaze.

That was enough.

Morthan led them into a back alley beside a pub. Its frontage was sprouting vile green fungal fronds that spat streams of spores into the night air. Aelyn heard screams coming from within the building, saw that its windows were broken from the inside and that blood drizzled from several of them.

As she entered the alley, black-clad figures swarmed out of the pub's doorway and set upon the panicked crowd. They cackled and shrieked in a crude tongue she couldn't understand.

'What are those things?' she asked.

'Moonclan grots,' replied Borik. 'Or Grobi-the-blackcap, whatever you prefer. Folklore.'

They made swift progress along the alleyway, until another vicious earth tremor threw them against the wall of the pub. A scullery door smashed open in the building's flank, and three of the Moonclan burst into the alley. One raised a flintwood bow and loosed a black-fletched arrow from point blank range. The shaft struck a watchman in the face, snapping her head back and throwing her to the ground. Captain Morthan yelled and shot the archer, blasting away half of its face. Borik shot another grot in the chest, and the third was quickly spitted on a pair of watch halberds.

The group stepped over the corpses and pressed on, leaving the fallen watchman where she lay.

'They're grots all right,' said Olt. 'But they don't act like them. Big greenies, orruks and the like, sure they get a sniff of battle and they're brave as heroes. But I've never seen grots attack like this. Usually cowards, you know?'

'Only know what I heard,' said Borik tinnily, reloading his pistol as they approached the end of the alley. 'Something about the Bad Moon filling them with a sort of madness. Draws them up from their caves and tunnels like the ocean tides. They call it the Gloomspite.'

'Oh, damnation,' said Captain Morthan quietly as they halted at the mouth of the alleyway. She brushed a stray strand of red hair out of her eyes, rubbing away the crusted blood on her face with her knuckles. Aelyn caught up to the captain and saw what had caused her to halt.

Beyond the alley, lit a sickly green in the moon's poison light, was a scene from some gruesome underhell. A wide square sat at a confluence of smaller streets, flanked on two sides by townhouses and on its other two by some kind of eatery and what looked like a public library. The centre of the square had collapsed into a wide pit from which spore-laden fumes rose. A wagon lay half-in and half-out of the hole, its dray beast lying dead in its traces with great chunks missing from its flesh and mycelium crawling into its wounds.

A handful of palace guards and militia-militant were fighting against a swarm of bizarre beasts. The monsters were bulbous, each one easily three feet across and roughly spherical in shape, its flesh spongy and burnt orange in colouration. The creatures had stubby, muscular legs ending in vicious talons, short, jutting tails and the entire front of each one's body was taken up by a pair of piggy eyes set above a massive lantern jaw stuffed full of crooked fangs.

Squigs, Aelyn thought. These horrors she had seen before, after she and some companions disturbed a nest of the things amidst an ancient ruin south of Taelfen many years ago. Those creatures had scuttled through the undergrowth and gnashed ferociously at her and her comrades. By comparison, these squigs were bounding along in great arcing leaps, ricocheting from the walls and bulling headlong into screaming humans like huge rubbery cannonballs. Sat atop the back of each squig, clinging on for dear life and cackling with deranged glee, was a Moonclan grot.

Even as they watched, another wave of squig riders bounded up from the pit. Jaws gaping, the beasts ploughed into luckless militiamen, their fangs snapping shut in sprays of blood to sever limbs, crush skulls and eviscerate torsos. The grot riders flailed madly, clubbing and stabbing at anything in reach before their steeds bounded off in all directions like misfiring volley-gun rounds.

'We can't leave these men and women to die,' said Captain Morthan, drawing her blade.

'There are a lot of those beasts,' said Aelyn.

'Then we'll have to fight hard and kill them quickly, won't we?' said Morthan.

'And pay well,' muttered Borik, but Aelyn could hear the duardin's heart wasn't in it. His people had many reasons to hate greenskins. He would fight willingly enough, she knew.

The decision was made for them as one of the squigs caromed back across the square and shot straight towards the alley. The grot sat atop it spotted them and shrieked something at its comrades. The next instant, its steed slammed into the levelled blades of several watch halberds, the impact sending their wielders staggering back and the grot rider catapulting forwards amidst a shower of his steed's blood. Aelyn wove aside from the greenskin's awkward trajectory and heard its bones crack as it hit the cobbles. Borik's ironclad boot came down on its head before it had even finished rolling, splattering blood and brains across the alley floor.

'Charge,' barked Captain Morthan, and surged from the alley with her blade levelled. The watchmen and the Swords of Sigmar followed her. The beleaguered soldiers raised a ragged cheer and redoubled their efforts.

Aelyn swept a needle-like dagger from her belt and threw it in one smooth motion. The blade sang through the air and struck a squig in the eye just as it landed. The beast convulsed, throwing its rider and toppling onto its side with a weak kick of its legs. Another blade in hand, Aelyn slid in beside the fallen grot and slit its throat before it could rise. She plucked the first dagger from the dead squig, then dropped forwards onto all fours as she sensed a rush of air. Another squig hurtled over her, close enough for her to smell the rancid stink of its breath. She sprang to her feet and threw her blade again, sinking it into the back of the grot rider's neck and spilling him from his saddle. Riderless, the squig bounded high into the air, landed on a nearby rooftop in a shower of slates, then leapt away into the night.

Aelyn heard a cry, and spun in time to see Olt surge across the square with flames licking around him. His tattoos glowed furiously as he slammed bodily into a squig and smashed it from the air. The creature landed on its side, rider squealing with fury, the squig's legs kicking and clawing for purchase. Swift as thought, Olt drove his forehead into the grot's nose and slammed its skull against the cobbles hard enough to break it. He bellowed in his tribal tongue and conjured a swimming heat haze around his fist before driving it savagely into the squig's flank. Fungal flesh gave way, hissing and sizzling as it literally cooked. The monster's eyes bulged, and it bicycled its stubby legs in panic, but Olt wasn't letting his quarry get away. Ignoring the gouge it cut across his chest with its talons, he reached deep into the monster and, with a feral cry, tore out a smouldering fistful of its guts. Sparks belched from the squig's maw. It convulsed once more before lying still.

Pistol shots rang out across the square. Blades clashed, and voices rose in cries of hate or screams of pain. Captain Morthan hacked her sword through a grot's neck as its steed landed nearby, and the squig bounded on again with the headless corpse still clinging to its stubby horns. A squig landed on Borik from behind and Aelyn felt a surge of alarm, but the thing's fangs struck sparks from the Kharadron armour before Borik managed to squirm around, ram his pistol into the monster's mouth and fire. The back of its spheroid body erupted in a flash of fire and gore, and its rider was blown through the air to land twitching on the cobbles.

Suddenly, there were no more squig riders, just a smouldering pit surrounded by bleeding, dying bodies. Aelyn dragged her blades from the body of a fallen squig and took stock. Thirteen left standing, she saw: Captain Morthan and five of her watchmen, the three Swords, three militiamen and a single, bloodied palace guard. Most of them were wounded in some way or other, and all were breathing hard. Aelyn realised with alarm that they were all sucking down the spore-thick fumes with every breath, heard suddenly the wet congestion in her lungs.

'Let us get away from this pit,' she said, feeling nausea stirring in her gut.

Morthan coughed wetly, took her meaning and nodded. 'You soldiers, you're with us,' she said. 'We push along the Fieldway and join the muster at Fountains Square. No damned greenskin invasion is going to take Draconium from us, you hear me? This is Sigmar's own city, and we–'

She broke off, her inspiring words interrupted by a bout of phlegmy coughing. Morthan spat and scowled angrily.

'Just follow me,' she snarled, and was off again, leaving the square by its eastern edge. Aelyn and her companions followed.

The Fieldway turned out to be a wide arterial street that connected Marketsway to High Drake near the city's centre, and to Pole Hill in the east. Aelyn saw it had been built broad enough for ranked formations of soldiery to move along as easily as foot-and-trade traffic, and understood why Morthan had chosen this route to reach Fountains Square quickly. Yet it was clear that many others had had the same idea, friend and foe alike.

Grots roved in packs between panicked masses of city folk, who fought back against their leering attackers with whatever implements came to hand. Many fled screaming, only to be dragged down and knifed cruelly. Aelyn saw greenskins maliciously hacking off fingers and toes and stuffing them into dirty cloth bags tied to their belts.

She saw a spider-legged grot picking his way through the carnage, a gnarled staff in one hand with what looked like a beast's stinger jutting from its end. The awful creature had a cluster of red eyes scattered across its face, and a bulging wicker basket lashed to its back that clinked with bottles and vials. A militiaman charged the arachnid greenskin with a yell, spear levelled. The grot hissed and spun its staff, weaving aside from the man's blow and driving the stinger into his throat. The soldier staggered back, clawing at his neck as his flesh swelled and turned black around the wound. The corruption ran through his flesh like wildfire, bloating and distending his skin even as it turned it bruise-black and splitting it in splatters of fluids. He crashed to the floor, choking on his own swollen flesh, then lay still, a blackened and bloated ruin.

The grot peered at its handiwork with amused fascination, before fishing a vial from its basket and emptying the contents over its stinger-staff. Aelyn itched to slay the monstrous poisoner, but Morthan wasn't stopping for anything and the crowd swept the grot away.

Aelyn's shoulder hurt, her injured arm ached, and her mind churned with the constant terror of the Bad Moon leering down. She felt as though, if she could not escape its monstrous gaze soon, she might go mad. Instead, she kept moving. She wove around the fiercest knots of fighting and drove her knives into anything greenskinned that came too close. An arrow whipped over her shoulder – friend's or foe's, she didn't see – and Aelyn felt keenly the lack of her longbow. Her comrades were retrieving her backup weapon, she reminded herself. She would have a bow in hand soon.

'Providing any of us survives this long enough,' she muttered, grimacing as a troggoth smashed out through a shopfront in a shower of stone and broken glass to swing its club through a knot of watchmen. Broken bodies flew through the air, the one survivor screaming in terror as a spore-sickened nobleman pounced on him and vomited across his face.

'The sickness is still spreading!' shouted Aelyn, spotting several more gibbering infected tearing their way through the crowd.

'I know,' replied Morthan. 'We'll regroup with the muster then put them all down.'

Another earth tremor rocked the ground. Something huge and shadowy ploughed along a neighbouring street amidst a chorus of screams. Aelyn privately wondered whether matters were already too far gone, but she kept moving. At this point, a determined fight back from a secure position seemed the city's best bet. She tried not to wonder how they might even begin to banish the lunar monstrosity that filled the skies above them.

One problem at a time, she thought.

'Where the hells are the Heav'ner Stormcasts I heard so much about?' shouted Olt as they pushed through a mass of panicking city folk. 'Seems like the sort of thing they might take an interest in?'

'All off fighting their damned wars of conquest, just like most of our city militia!' replied Morthan angrily. 'I *told* Selvador he'd left us too weak. I damned well *warned* that old fool.'

They reached the end of the street, and at last Fountains Square opened out before them. Aelyn felt a sudden surge of hope. Around the square's edge, greenskins and soldiery were locked in violent conflict. Further back, arranging themselves with swift and professional determination around the fountain itself, she saw hundreds of militia. Watchmen were gathering there too, and mobs of what looked like citizens clutching makeshift weapons, old blades, broken bottles; anything they could find. Aelyn saw priests, too, clad in similar garb to that worn by Romilla, their flesh scarified and tattooed, their expressions fierce. The Etched, she assumed. Cannons were wheeled into place by sweating crewmen. The banners of Draconium hung lank and fungus-spotted beneath the Bad Moon's light, but they were raised nonetheless, and a substantial army was gathering beneath them.

Aelyn saw a figure she assumed must be Arch-Lector Kayl, astride a snorting demi-drake that wore hammer-inscribed barding of rich gold. The man was straight-backed and imposing. His beard was neatly forked and a halo of saintly power played about his head. A cloak of spun gold flowed behind him as he stood in his stirrups and bellowed commands at his swiftly mustering soldiers.

'Quickly now, we must join them,' said Morthan, and set off across the square at a run. The ragtag group followed, weaving around a mob of greenskins and discharging pistols into them, dodging their return spear-thrusts. Aelyn spun around an assailant and rammed a blade into the grot's eye, ripping it away bloody before running on. The ranks of soldiery were less than a hundred yards away now, closer by the footfall. Here was a chance to fight back. Here was a chance to survive, to take revenge for Hendrick's death.

The pressure wave hit like an avalanche.

Aelyn felt herself leave the ground, felt everything tumble madly around her. The floor hit her cheek like a punch. She blinked stars from her eyes, tasted blood and felt the tug of a loose tooth. Aelyn scrambled to her feet and saw the proud muster in disarray. Men and women were picking themselves up, dazed and bleeding. Cannons had been hurled onto their sides and one crewman was screaming shrilly where his legs had been pinned beneath a fallen field-gun. Around the square, several buildings had collapsed in avalanches of rubble, burying city folk and greenskins alike, and the square's ornamental trees now leaned at crazed angles, their roots jutting up from the ruptured soil of their beds.

'Are those stars?' asked a watchman as she staggered upright beside Aelyn.

'Stormcasts! It's the Stormcasts!' cried another, pointing up at the glowing points of light that stood out stark against the Bad Moon's visage. They were bright, glimmering sparks that grew larger by the second. Drawing closer, Aelyn thought. Could they be Stormcasts, riding the God-King's lightning down into Draconium to deliver vengeance and retribution?

Then she took in the subtle shift in the Bad Moon's ghastly visage and her blood froze in her veins. Its crater-eyes had constricted impossibly into narrow chasms. Its mountainous maw was twisted as though coughing, or retching.

'Sigmar, no...' she breathed, as the glittering lights swelled into roiling fireballs plummeting closer and closer. Her sharp aelven eyes picked out the shapes of jagged meteorites, mercilessly showing her the vast weight of loonstone hurtling down upon Draconium.

'Fangs of the Bad Moon,' croaked Borik. Across the square, fresh screams rose as soldiers pointed skywards and fleeting hopes of deliverance turned to panic.

The first rock struck far away across the city, ploughing through the distant towers of Rookswatch amidst eruptions of fire and shattered mortar. The structures had no time to topple, as the meteorite hammered into the ground and raised a roaring blast wave that snatched the towertops and blew them apart. Blazing lumps of stone and blackened bodies rained down for miles around.

Another rock struck closer, slamming into the slopes of Gallowhill and flattening a quarter-mile zone of buildings, streets and people in a heartbeat. Captain Morthan cried out as the proud silhouette of the distant watch blockhouse came apart amidst the devastation.

Another burning light consumed Aelyn's focus, a blazing projectile that grew and grew above the square until the entire area was lit by an apocalyptic false dawn.

'Get to cover!' she yelled. She turned, grabbing Olt and Borik by their shoulders and urging them towards the sagging shop-front of a milliner's on the edge of the square.

Fire blazed above them.

Their footsteps pounded the cobbles.

The cries of terrified city folk were drowned by the roar of the falling rock.

Then the impact. A blinding flash. A furious convulsion of air and ground, and Aelyn knew no more.

Across the city, near the southern edge of Docksflow, desperate eyes watched fires consume the skyline. Orlen Drell had scrambled from his barge before it was dragged below the waters and somehow, by the grace of Sigmar, he had made it through the bars of the river gate. He hadn't wanted to attract the attention of the city watch, and so he had slunk from one shadowed doorway and draughty corner to the next, a half-drowned shadow indistinguishable from the other homeless vagrants who haunted the city's poorest districts. His mind broken by the sights he had seen, Drell's only thought had been to hide amidst his fellow humans, to seek what comfort he could beneath the city's flickering lights. He had scavenged and stolen to survive, and for a few precious days he had believed he might be safe.

Now he crouched in a broken crate beside the Wayward King and knew he had been a fool. The ground shook. Orlen cried out weakly, a pitiful sound that might have brought folk searching for the source of the sound. They were all gone, though – fled to Orlen knew not where, or lying butchered and strewn across the street.

Another shudder ran through the cobbles, and the centre-most point of the alleyway rose briefly, before falling away into a deep pit. Cracks shot up the wall of the inn with a sound like cannonfire. The structure sagged alarmingly.

Orlen sunk lower in his packing crate, heart hammering. He would have fled, but the terrible face that hung above the city left him too frightened to move. Instead, he watched as black-clad figures with green skin and gleaming red eyes scrambled up from the pit. A sharp stink reached Orlen's nostrils. The creatures advanced down the alley and Orlen cringed into the deepest, darkest corner of the crate. He was desperate to escape their notice. These things stank of cruelty and malice. The black-robes scurried past Orlen's hiding place, oblivious to the rag-clad wretch praying silently to Sigmar. They spilled out into the street, some of them clanging away at crude copper gongs, others brandishing ragged black banners with stylised leering moon devices emblazoned upon them.

A third shudder ran through the alleyway, so violent as to shake Orlen to his bones. The man dug his nails into the splintered wood and stayed low, breathing in short, shallow pants. A moan of alarm escaped him as stone splintered and beams groaned, and the alleyway floor heaved. The edge of the pit widened rapidly, falling away in great chunks, and the Wayward King reeled like the drunks who had so often frequented it. Something massive moved in the pit and a huge hand emerged, a gnarled mass of flesh nearly as large as a wagon. Fungi and weird mineral deposits clung to the leathery flesh of that hand, and its talons sank into the stonework of the sagging pub with ease. A mighty heave, and something terrifying dragged itself out of the pit, even as it pulled a great chunk of the Wayward King down into it. Orlen Drell had an impression of a massive humanoid shape, hunching shoulders thick with stony growths, and beady eyes glinting from within the eyepieces of a crude helm. The thing stomped its way down the alley, smashing chunks from the stonework on either side and barely avoiding treading on Orlen where he hid, paralysed by terror.

Another of the massive things clambered up from the darkness, then yet another, each clad in segments of lumpen metal, each gripping massive clubs in their boulder-like fists. Their heads swung ponderously back and forth as though searching for threats, or perhaps for victims.

For all that the monsters were terrifying, it was only when the last figure emerged from the pit that Orlen's fractured mind finally snapped with terror. It wasn't large, this last being, barely bigger than the black-robes that had preceded it, but a bow wave of malice swelled before it and filled the alley until it felt as though the crumbling buildings to either side must surely collapse. The creature rose regally from the pit, its green-skinned scalp topped with a pale crown of glowing fungal growths whose mycelium dug deep into the creature's skull. Its red eyes crackled with power, lurid green sparks that danced in the air one moment and dripped like slime the next. One taloned hand clutched a short rod topped with a human skull, whose jaw-bone twitched and whose worn teeth chattered together. In the other, the creature gripped a long staff of gnarled wood from the top of which grew a pallid fungal moon as large as his head.

It was from this awful fetish that the wave of oppressive menace spilled, and as the figure raised its face and arms towards the leering moon in the skies above and screamed out in triumph, Orlen's basest instincts drove him from his hiding place in a scuffle of rags and splintered wood.

He ran as fast as he could along the alley, weaving frantically through the mass of surprised creatures, darting madly past the few jagged blades that flashed out to slice his skin and tear his ragged clothing. A stomping foot almost mashed Orlen into paste and then he was free, pelting down the street to he knew not where, eyes bulging out of his skull and heart hammering madly. Gales of malicious merriment and jeering shouts followed him into the night.

He knew only one thing. He had to get away from the creature with the moon-topped staff, the being that almost seemed the embodiment of the evil moon above, crammed into a living form and walking the city streets. He had to get away from its malevolent gaze, and its chilling peals of insane laughter.

CHAPTER ELEVEN

SHOCKWAVES

Romilla straightened up, Aelyn's quiver of arrows, third knife-belt, backup aelven longbow and a satchel of wickedly crafted snares clutched in her arms.

'Do you have everything yet?' she asked Eleanora, who had hurriedly but precisely laid out her stash of munitions on top of her bed and had been counting them methodically into a large backpack. As the engineer turned to reply, she let out a hiss of pain and stumbled against the bed. She took a limping step and sat down hard amidst the last few scattered devices, her face drawn.

'Sigmar's grace, what *is* the matter?' asked Romilla. 'Eleanora, is it your foot again? Will you let me look at it, please?'

'It's just a bite, it just hurts sometimes,' said Eleanora, looking uncomfortable. Romilla had tried to get a proper look at her friend's bitten foot for the best part of a week, but Eleanora had been remarkably cagey about it. She did this, sometimes, if something she mentioned was not immediately paid attention to; Eleanora had an odd habit of assuming if something wasn't addressed instantly then it must be unimportant and should be stringently ignored. If Romilla was honest, Eleanora had many strange habits that they had all simply adjusted to. They were just part of her genius, a side effect of the gifts that Sigmar had given her. But this one had caused her to hide injury and illness before, and if Romilla hadn't been so distracted by darker matters, she would have insisted she be allowed to treat Eleanora's foot before now.

As she knelt and stripped off the engineer's footwear, she cursed herself for not checking sooner. Eleanora's foot and ankle were both badly swollen, the flesh mottled red and blue and warm to the touch. Gently holding the foot still despite Eleanora's uncomfortable squirming, she found a green-black lump near the arch of the foot, presumably the original bite. Tendrils of the same unclean hue had spread out from the bite mark and begun to make inroads on Eleanora's calf.

'Damnation, Eleanora, this looks awful!' she exclaimed.

'It's just a spider bite,' repeated the engineer, brushing her hair out of her eyes and sounding less certain.

'Does it hurt?' asked Romilla.

'More since the moon rose.'

Her blood ran chill at Eleanora's quiet reply.

An image flashed unbidden into Romilla's mind, of Hendrick staggering to his feet, the spore sickness already ravaging his features. Behind it lay another memory, deeper buried, hidden behind a wall raised in self-flagellation and shored up with alcohol and self-hatred. It was one she hadn't seen in a long time, a glimpse of Freeguild soldiery sprawled about her feet, flesh thick with stinking pustules, bodies slowly mutating, mewling groans filling the air. Her friends, dying around her; she herself untouched yet utterly powerless to stop their demise.

Guilt nearly choked Romilla for an instant, but she forced it back, remembered all the tests of her faith she had passed to reach this point. She looked up at Eleanora, who was staring uncertainly down at her with the beginnings of real alarm in her eyes. Romilla forced her expression into something reassuring. She quietly promised herself that she would not let some horrible infection take Eleanora too. Sigmar's blood, she thought, I will fail no more of my friends.

'I have tinctures in my bag, and anti-inflammation unguents,' said Romilla, patting Eleanora on the knee. 'We'll apply those now, and then–'

The blast wave hit with catastrophic force. The window detonated, filling the room with a hail of razor-sharp glass that tore the curtains to tatters. The floor bucked as though a gargant had kicked it. Eleanora, who had her back to the window, was thrown from the bed to slam into Romilla with a scream. They both hit the back wall hard enough that Romilla had the breath driven from her body and felt a burst of agony as something cracked.

Dust billowed.

The air filled with a muffled whine.

Woozy and half-stunned, Romilla stirred and tried to stand. She gritted her teeth as bone ground together, somewhere inside her chest. Pain was an old acquaintance, however, and the priest ignored the feeling as she disentangled herself from Eleanora. For an instant she feared the worst as she saw blood pouring down the engineer's face, but a swift check revealed a scalp wound and some bruising, and nothing worse. Eleanora's eyes were open and wild with panic, but they focused on Romilla well enough.

'You've hit your head, but you're going to be all right,' Romilla said. All she heard was a distant suggestion of words, like someone speaking softly through a plaster wall. She realised Eleanora was trying to reply, but that her voice, too, was muffled and unintelligible. Falling back on the practical, Romilla quickly checked them both over for injuries. Aside from the internal break, which she could do nothing about, and a few stinging wounds where flying glass had cut her, she found herself to be more or less in one piece.

Eleanora, too, could have been hurt far worse. Her scalp wound looked nasty, but it was superficial and quickly staunched. The engineer had other small wounds where broken glass had peppered her back and nicked a sliver from one of her ears as it whipped past. Yet her insistence on always wearing the heavy, tanned leather garb of the Ironweld had been her salvation, as the thick material had stopped the majority of the vicious glass projectiles that could otherwise have cut her to ribbons.

Romilla surveyed the ruin of their room, working her jaw to try to encourage sound back into her ears as she did so. The window was a gaping hole, fringed with tatters of curtain. Their bags, the remaining equipment, and most of the chamber's furniture had been picked up and hurled against the back wall, and now lay in dust-plastered heaps. Romilla's eyes widened as she took in the heavy cross-beams that had fallen through the half-collapsed ceiling. They had crushed Eleanora's bed entirely.

'That could have been you,' she mouthed, pointing, and Eleanora nodded back in shock. They had been phenomenally lucky, Romilla realised, that none of Eleanora's bombs had been triggered by the blast. She offered up a prayer of thanks to Sigmar and dug through the rubble and dust for her bag of medical supplies. She didn't know what had caused that blast and right now, she didn't care. Romilla would attend to her duties first, and then face whatever trials Sigmar had in store for her next.

She was still seeing to Eleanora's cuts and doing what she could for the engineer's foot when Bartiman pushed his way in through the buckled door.

'We need to move,' he barked. 'Those things came down all over the city. I think one of them hit the square.'

'What things?' asked Romilla, her words marginally clearer to her own ears, now, as the whine there receded.

'Projectiles, meteorites – great lumps of rock from that accursed moon!' exclaimed Bartiman. 'Have you not looked out the… what's left of the window?'

'I was busy,' said Romilla shortly, but now she hastened to stare out of the ragged hole in the side of the chamber, being careful to avoid the sickly moonlight that spilled through.

Her heart almost stopped as she beheld the ominous clouds of smoke, dust and dimly-glowing green spores that rose over the city. They were billowing upwards from multiple impact sites, she saw, swelling and spreading even as they slowly tattered apart. The clouds looked for all the realms like vast and horrible mushrooms fashioned from the stuff of ruin and nightmares, and where their pall drifted over the shattered cityscape the spores they carried fell like sickly embers. Romilla felt dread at the thought of what might happen, were they to settle upon human flesh.

'Our friends were somewhere in all of that,' she breathed.

'Precisely,' replied Bartiman as he came to stand next to her. Romilla turned to see Eleanora dragging her boot back on with a wince of pain and shouldering her sack full of explosives and weapons.

'We have to go and help them,' said the engineer, looking scared but determined. Romilla nodded and, pausing to scoop up what she had managed to salvage of Aelyn's wargear, she made for the stairs.

In the glass-scattered shadows of the inn's common room, Romilla made for the front door but Bartiman grabbed her arm and pointed out the back. They passed Gathe and several of his serving staff, huddled behind the bar in terror. The man gestured at them, his intent clear. *Go away. Leave us alone.*

She shook her head and hastened through the back door, throwing up the hood of her cloak and pulling her sleeves down as far as they would go before stepping back into the curdled light of the Bad Moon. She stopped in surprise as she saw the wagon that Borik had been eyeing a few days earlier, parked up under cover with a gnarlkyd in its traces.

'That's us,' said Bartiman.

Romilla raised an eyebrow at him.

'Borik wasn't wrong, it's a solid wagon,' said Bartiman. 'We needed it more than Gathe, so I conducted a swift negotiation and paid the man a fair price. He seemed keen to be rid of us, did he not?'

'I won't ask how much,' she said, her ears still ringing. 'A fine idea, Bartiman. Let's move.'

They hurriedly loaded everything they had salvaged into the back of the wagon, tucking it under a heavy tarpaulin that had already sprouted several pale mushrooms. Then, bundled as thickly in cloaks and garments as possible to ward off the moonlight, they scrambled aboard the driver's bench and Bartiman took the reins.

As Romilla's hearing returned fully, she took in the rising cacophony that floated from across the city. Screams of pain and terror mingled with the howls of the hopelessly insane. Creaks, groans and crashes told a tale of structural devastation. Yet the worst sounds were those of the invaders. Gibbering shrieks and malicious cackles, great booming roars, terrible hissing sounds and the constant clangour of crude gongs and bells echoed from every direction. Romilla felt fear for the friends they had left out amidst this madness before the moon rocks fell. She prayed hard that they remained alive and unharmed, but she feared that amidst the fervent tide of prayers surely rising from Draconium in that moment, hers would be lost long before they reached the God-King's ear.

The moment Bartiman drove their draybeast out into the moonlight, the creature lowed in panic and discomfort. A row of blood-red mushrooms popped out of its spine as though emerging from the forest floor after a gentle shower, and Romilla squashed her revulsion at the little spurts of blood and pus that squirted out as each broke the surface of the creature's flesh. The gnarlkyd tried to buck and fight, but Bartiman plied the reins with skill. He muttered words in a strange tongue that Romilla couldn't place, causing the beast to stiffen as though with fear and then surge out through the inn's back gates and into the benighted streets beyond.

The journey that followed was a surreal and nightmarish experience. The Bad Moon leered down at them, its malice a palpable force beating upon their brows. Heaps of wreckage and the collapsed ruin of buildings forced them to detour, and then detour again, every delay driving them further away from Fountains Square and increasing Romilla's fear and frustration.

At times, they rattled along empty cobbled stretches where the only signs of life were the detritus dropped by fleeing crowds, and the occasional suggestions of pale and fearful faces peering through blinds and curtains.

Yet for every abandoned space, there was a square, or street, or alley or bridge drenched in gore and thick with heaving bodies. Romilla saw black-clad greenskins pouring along the streets in such numbers that they looked more like swarming insects, overrunning those who fled them and burying them in heaving, stabbing bodies. She saw an obese grot riding atop a many-legged toadstool as large as a man, pointing his glowing staff at people and transforming them into fungal statues with cackles of glee. Beyond them, lunatic greenskins with froth spilling from their jaws whirled through militiamen wielding massive iron balls at the ends of long chains. These fanatics clearly had no control over their direction of travel, for she saw more than one smash into a wall or spark-lantern and meet a bloody end. Yet where they ploughed through human bodies the results were sickening.

They crossed an arched bridge that spanned a dirty offshoot of the canal between looming houses, and as Romilla looked up she saw flesh-crawling shapes silhouetted against the skyline. Arachnid things the size of ponies picked their way across the rooftops, the exaggerated care of their many-legged gait belying the speed with which they moved. Sat astride each huge spider she saw the hunched silhouette of a grot, and as their wagon thumped down on the far side of the bridge a hissing hail of barbed arrows struck the cobbles behind its wheels.

They sped across an intersection, scattering snarling green-skins as they went, and Romilla felt the cart lurch as bones broke and bodies split beneath its wheels. She heard shrieks and saw several of the spore-sickened dashing madly after the wagon, gaining by the second, their yellow eyes locked on her.

'Behind us,' she cried over the whipping wind. Romilla hefted her hammer and tried to turn in her seat as the first of the crea-tures leapt high with gangling agility and thumped down on their fungus-thick tarpaulin. There was a loud crack, and the spore-sick wretch's face dissolved in a red blizzard. Its body was flung back from the wagon to thump bonelessly to the street in their wake.

Romilla glanced sideways and saw that Eleanora had pulled

a heavy firearm from her back, some fusion of coglock pistol and ferocious-looking blunderbuss that was churning with mechanical motion as it reloaded itself.

'Hendrick told me to make plenty of guns and bombs,' said Eleanora, as though apologising for something.

Romilla managed a faint smile at her. 'I'm glad that he did,' she said, then snapped her head back around as thumping sounds heralded more of the spore-sickened landing on the tarp. The first, a mutated woman still clad in the ragged ruin of her former finery, reared up with a shriek, and her throat bulged with infected bile. Before she could spit it, Romilla lunged upwards and smashed the head of her hammer into the woman's jaw. Tusks splintered, bone broke and Romilla's victim was thrown backwards with frothing vomit geysering from her ruined face.

The other, a grotesque that had once been a noble palace guard, crawled hand over hand towards them only for Eleanora's gun to roar again and fling him backwards in a tangle of limbs.

'Shadows of Shyish!' exclaimed Bartiman in alarm, and Romilla spun back around in time to see something bewildering hurtling towards them with the speed of a runaway avalanche. She had an impression of huge fungal forms, two spheroid monsters each a good twenty feet across that were all fang-filled jaws, madly-staring eyes and lashing talons. Her mind struggled to process the scene as she realised the two abominations had been chained crudely together, and that cackling grots had lashed themselves to the creatures as though attempting to ride upon them.

The monsters whirled around one another, pushing off with their stub-clawed legs, snapping their enormous fangs together with maddened fury, leaving cracked craters in building facades and street cobbles as they ricocheted closer.

'They're going to hit us!' cried Eleanora.

Romilla cringed as the shrieking grots rushed closer upon their enormous wrecking-ball steeds. With a sudden furious spasm, one of the chained monsters launched itself skywards, dragging its bellowing twin with it and eliciting a chorus of furious cries from the greenskins. Chains snapped tight and the entire deranged mass shot over Romilla's head, low enough that tusks as long as her torso snapped together a hair's breadth from her shaved scalp.

Then the creatures were gone, past them and careening away down the street to smash through an alchemists' tower at the far end.

'What in the name of the Mortal Realms...?' asked Bartiman, gripping the reins with one hand and plucking a toadstool from his robes with the other.

'Don't know, don't want to know,' said Romilla. 'Just get us to the square.'

'Almost there,' replied Bartiman. 'If I'm not mistaken, it's just up this rise.'

As they climbed a steep street thick with a miasma of dust and spores, Romilla pulled cloth over her nose and mouth and tried to take shallow breaths, motioning for Eleanora and Bartiman to do the same. The cart's wheels hissed through a shallow flood of groundwater that was spilling from the lip of the square above them. Romilla feared the worst as she saw red streaks polluting it.

Then their wagon was up over the rise with a lurch, and ploughing into thicker black clouds of smoke and dust.

'Stop, stop,' urged Romilla as their wheels hammered over rubble and bodies. Bartiman hauled on the reins, but their gnarlkyd was mad with fear and tried to keep going. Something burst wetly beneath their wheels, then there came a tremendous crunch and a violent sideways lurch. The wagon swayed madly, threatening to overturn and hurl them into the ground with violent force. Romilla cried out as another deafening crack sounded right beside her ear. The gnarlkyd convulsed and fell forwards, ploughing into the cobbles face first. Their wagon thumped into it from behind and they skidded to a bloody halt.

Romilla stared at Eleanora, whose gun was still smoking as it reloaded.

'We had to stop,' said the engineer. 'What if we ran over our friends?'

They disembarked from the wagon, which Romilla doubted was ever travelling anywhere again. Its panels were thick with fungus that was prying the boards apart, wet rot was spreading through one axle and the front right wheel was a shredded mess where they had struck some lump of rubble or wreckage.

'Quickly, gather the equipment and let us search,' she said. Yet Romilla felt far less hope than she did dread. Amidst the swirling smoke, the ashes and dust and glimmering spores, visibility was a matter of yards. The ground was split and crumpled as though someone had grasped one end of the square like a huge tablecloth and given it a violent tug, and dirty water swilled across it. Chunks of glowing moon rock and smashed fragments of statuary lay everywhere, and between them were heaped corpses. Grots and humans sprawled, their limbs snapped like twigs where the blast wave had flung them, their skulls crushed, or their bodies burst like gourds by the force of the meteor's fall. Some seethed busily with insects, which worried at flesh and scuttled in and out of nostrils and eye sockets. Others were thick with fungal growth, entire heaps of corpses disappearing rapidly under multicoloured groves of swaying spore-blooms.

'This is a nightmare,' intoned Bartiman. 'I can see scant chance that they are still alive amidst all this.'

'They're alive,' replied Romilla with a conviction she didn't feel. 'Until we see them laid out dead on the ground, Bartiman, they're alive.'

'The longer we spend here looking for them, the greater the chance we'll join them in the underworlds,' said Bartiman. Still, he hefted the satchel that he had recovered from his room and stalked into the gloom with his staff pointed out before him.

Romilla followed the death wizard, motioning for Eleanora to stay close. The engineer nodded, handing her a leather bandolier into which were tucked several metal orbs with cogwork innards. Romilla quickly buckled it around her waist.

'If the greenskins come for us, press down the brass stud on the top of the orb and throw it at them,' said Eleanora. 'It should take three seconds for the mechanism to fire.'

They picked their way through the roiling fumes. Romilla knew from prior experience that Bartiman's powers afforded him sensory perception that went beyond the canny, especially when it came to seeking out souls either alive or dead. She didn't waste breath asking him where they were going, she simply trusted him to lead the search.

Romilla felt nausea sweep through her at the touch of the airborne spores. She could only imagine what horrible effects they might have, and wherever she saw one settle on her skin she brushed it away before its tingling touch grew too intense. The fumes hid the face of the Bad Moon, yet she felt no relief from its malevolent regard. Her head swam, and ghoulish shapes reared up through the smoke, the screaming faces of diseased friends long dead that broke apart like phantasms whenever she looked their way.

Groans and the scuff of movement reached her ears, seeming

to come from all around. Metal clinked and clanged. Something heavy dragged against stone. Something else splashed noisily then stopped. She couldn't tell whether they were real or some awful auditory hallucination; couldn't trust her senses beneath the Bad Moon's gaze.

Romilla held her amulet with one hand and her hammer with the other, praying under her breath and concentrating on scouring the ground for signs of a familiar face. She both longed for and dreaded the sight of Aelyn, Olt or Borik amidst the sprawled bodies, for she desperately wished to find them but feared that, as Bartiman had said, they must surely be slain.

'What was that?' said Eleanora suddenly, spinning and pointing her gun at the swirling fumes.

'You're seeing things. We're all seeing things,' said Romilla.

'No, there, again!' said Eleanora, whirling and aiming wide-eyed. Her hand strayed towards the sack of explosives she carried.

'Eleanora–' began Romilla, but Bartiman raised a beringed hand.

'No, she's right, there's something moving,' he said. 'Stay close and keep a weather eye. We're not alone.'

Romilla's heart thudded as they paced slowly through the murk, shuffling along nearly back to back with their weapons raised. Something stirred amidst the fumes and she snatched one of the bombs from her bandolier, almost pressing the stud before she realised that it was a city watchman staggering towards them with a hand raised in supplication. The man's other arm was missing, and fronded fungi clung to his cloak and flesh.

'Please,' he croaked, then he arched his back and gave a gurgling cry as a metal point burst through his chest. The man toppled, revealing a snarling grot behind him with its spear buried in his spine. Eleanora fired, the crack of her gun loud amidst the unnatural quiet of the square, and the grot was flung back into the shadows.

Fresh movement sounded around them, the splash of footfalls, the whisper of cloth. Something laughed, shrill and deranged.

'Eyes peeled,' hissed Bartiman, fishing in a pouch at his belt and sprinkling what looked like glittering ashes over the tip of his staff. 'They're surrounding us.'

Dark figures surged forward amidst the murk. Bartiman spat a string of syllables and black energy leapt from his staff to reduce half a dozen charging greenskins to withered corpses. More movement, and Eleanora lobbed a brass sphere into the smoke. There was a fierce flash and a deafening bang. A green-fleshed arm slapped into the water at Romilla's feet, still trailing blood and smoke. She heard a wailing coming closer, a rapid slap of footfalls, and one of the infected burst from the swirling smog to her right. Romilla reacted with practised skill, side-stepping a swipe of clawed fingers and swinging her hammer into the thing's face. Blood and teeth rained down, and the infected hit the ground. She smashed the back of its skull in to be sure.

'No use for quiet any more,' she said, and raised her voice to a booming shout. 'Aelyn! Borik! Olt! Are you there?'

Groundwater rippled and leapt as something huge lumbered their way. The troggoth emerged from the smog-clouds with a roar, and Romilla realised with a lurch that it was wielding a buckled cannon barrel in both fists like a tribesman swinging a double-handed axe. The troggoth took three long strides and swung its weapon up with a growl. It jerked and staggered as Bartiman's staff spat darkness again and blasted a blackened crater in the beast's chest. Yet even as Romilla watched, the wound began to suck closed, the troggoth's unnatural flesh sealing as quick as it could be harmed. It bellowed and swung, and Romilla leapt aside just in time. The cannon barrel hammered into the cobbles, raising a spray of dirty water that drenched her.

Ponderous, the troggoth raised its dripping weapon and turned, its piggy eyes squinting as its slow intellect processed the fact that she had evaded its blow. It searched the ground and found her again, raising its weapon for another swipe and roaring.

Romilla realised she still had an orb in her hand. She pushed the stud down and flung the weapon at the troggoth's face. It flew straight into the beast's open mouth. The troggoth gagged, its roar choked off. It raised a huge hand to its throat, blinked in surprise, then the bomb detonated. Trogflesh sprayed in all directions. Chunks of bone shrapnel whistled through the air and skipped across the soaked cobbles. Mucal slime and gore sprayed Romilla, drenching her afresh. The troggoth, now lacking its head, one arm and most of its upper torso, took a staggering step and pitched over sideways into a pile of corpses. Within seconds, insects were swarming hungrily across it.

Romilla stood, spitting foul-tasting slime. She was angry now, revolted and furious at these vile monsters that had burst up from below to befoul a city of the God-King.

'Come on, you disgusting wretches!' she bellowed, and as she raised her hammer it flared with the divine energies of Azyr. 'Come and meet your righteous annihilation!'

Romilla spun as she heard footsteps splashing closer, yet this time it was several human figures that emerged from the fumes.

'Borik!' she gasped, feeling her heart leap at the sight of the duardin. He hastened towards her, his armour battered and scorched, a pair of bloodied watchmen flanking him.

'Thanks be to Grungni the maker, you made it!' he said, and Romilla saw none of the gruff cynicism Borik usually affected. He was exhausted, she could see despite his mask, dispirited and hurt.

'Borik, where are the others?' she asked.

'Not here, not now,' he hissed, beckoning them. 'The rust-damned Moonclan are everywhere. Come on.'

Romilla followed, unanswered questions burning in her chest. Eleanora limped along behind her, with Bartiman bringing up the rear, staff in hand, scanning around him in search of threats. Water sloshed deeper underfoot as they pressed on across the square, and Romilla almost slipped as the ground sloped away.

'Edge of the crater, watch your footing,' said Borik over his shoulder. Romilla felt heat rolling in waves from somewhere deeper into that crater, heard the tick and crack of cooling rock.

'The meteor?' she asked. Borik replied with a tinny grunt.

They pressed on, scrambling over scattered wreckage and picking their way between heaps of corpses. Romilla thought that perhaps the fumes were beginning to thin a little, that visibility was improving slowly. The thought didn't cheer her, but instead left her feeling more exposed. Any moment a horde of greenskins could pour into the square, if they weren't already, and it could only be a matter of time before the light of the Bad Moon punched its leprous shafts through the thinning haze to twist and taint all it touched. No, she thought, they needed to be well gone and somewhere safe before that happened. If anywhere was safe in Draconium anymore.

At last they reached the far edge of the square, and there Borik led them up a heap of rubble, through a narrow gap and into the unwavering muzzles of half a dozen pistols.

'Don't shoot, it's us,' growled the duardin as he clambered down the far side of the rubble heap into the remains of the building beyond. Romilla took in the ruin of what must have been a milliner's shop, its frontage now blocked off by the toppled remains of its upper storey. Hidden in the half-dark was a small group of city watchmen, every last one battered and bloodied. They visibly relaxed as the Swords of Sigmar skidded down the rubble heap, but not that much. Romilla had seen that expression on a lot of faces in her time. It spoke of the horrors its wearer had seen and prophesied a life never again wholly untouched by fear and sorrow. She felt for them, but her first thought was for her friends.

'Borik, what about the others?' she asked urgently, hurrying to catch up to the duardin as he passed through a hollow doorway.

Borik's expression was hidden behind the face-plate of his helm, but the slump of his shoulders spoke volumes.

'Through there,' he said, gesturing.

Romilla hastened through the door, Eleanora and Bartiman on her heels, trepidation filling her. It was an old stock room, she supposed, a gloomy space with wooden shelves packed with dusty hats clinging to the walls and blood staining its threadbare rug.

She saw Aelyn first. The aelf was crouched beside the bloodied figure of Captain Morthan, who lay propped against the back wall with her pistol still clutched in one hand. The captain's skin was alabaster-pale and streaked with sweat. Her legs were hidden beneath a dirty blanket, which was stained a dreadful dark crimson.

Then Romilla saw the shapes lying along the opposite wall. Forlorn mounds laid out with as much dignity as could be mustered, each hidden beneath their torn cloaks. She saw several blue militia garments, several other black watchmen's cloaks. For a moment she didn't recognise the cheap and tattered covering at the end of the row, and wondered if they had dragged the body of an unfortunate civilian with them. Then she saw the tattooed arm protruding slightly from beneath the meagre shroud and felt her throat tighten as she understood.

'I heard your shouts,' said Aelyn simply. 'It is good to see you alive, my friends.'

'How?' asked Romilla thickly, gesturing at the hidden shape of her slain comrade.

'It was the meteor, when it hit,' said Borik. 'A shard of flying stone... I don't think he felt a thing. Hope he didn't. We'd have prayed for him but none of us ever really learned much about his gods, did we?'

'I will offer my own prayers,' Romilla said stiffly, and knelt beside Olt's body.

'There isn't... time,' said Helena Morthan, her voice little more than a strained croak. Romilla gave a start; in her sorrow, she had forgotten the captain's presence.

'I will make time,' she replied angrily. 'He died trying to protect *your* damned city.'

'Draconium will die, too, if you people don't act quickly!' snarled Morthan, her fire flaring through the pain of her wounds. She broke off, coughing wetly into her fist, then stared straight at Romilla. 'Please,' she said. 'A lot of people are going to die.'

'A lot of people already have,' replied Romilla, but she rose and crossed to the captain's side, promising herself that she would attend to Olt's rites before they left. Never mind that he had been a heathen – he had served the God-King all the same, and his soul deserved what protection she could offer.

'Let me see what I can do for your wounds,' she said, taking hold of a corner of the blanket that covered Morthan's legs. The captain placed a blood-stained hand over hers and shook her head. A look of revulsion crossed her features.

'Don't. Please,' she said. 'I can't look upon that again.'

'The city is already lost,' said Borik. 'If it wasn't before, it absolutely is now. Have you seen it out there? The greenskin filth have won this fight.'

'Defeatist, for a duardin,' said Captain Morthan bitterly.

'Realistic,' replied Borik. Morthan seemed to dismiss him, looking around as though in a daze until her pupils focused shakily on Aelyn. Romilla realised that the captain wasn't just wounded; she was dying. Should probably already be dead, if the quantity of blood drenching her blanket was anything to go by.

Morthan grabbed Aelyn's arm, and the aelf bore her touch without pulling away.

'Take my seal. My brooch,' coughed Morthan, pointing weakly to the ruby clasp that held her cloak in place. 'The watch will obey whoever has that. Get it to Lieutenant Grange, if he lives. If not…' she coughed again, this time blood spraying from her mouth. She winced, before waving a hand in a gesture that eloquently said 'you figure it out'.

Aelyn took the proffered brooch and pocketed it.

'You wish us to aid Grange in the evacuation?' asked Romilla. Captain Morthan fixed her with a surprisingly fierce glare, for one so close to death's door.

'No!' she hissed, her words becoming more and more laboured. 'There are secondary armouries. Hidden safehouses. Stockpiles.' She paused, drawing in a wrecked, rattling breath. 'Grange *has* to lead the fight back.'

'For what?' asked Romilla, aghast. 'Even if the city does have hidden reserves, even if by some miracle they've not been found and looted, what would be the point? Borik is right, the greenskins and their awful moon have killed this city in a night. All we can do now is to save as many folk as we can.'

Morthan shook her head, urgent and pained. 'Please, there's more to this,' she said. 'Must be. Your warning. The omens. Why attack here? Why not...' she shook her head and her hand dropped from Aelyn's arm.

Romilla leaned close, one hand wrapped around her hammer amulet as she placed a hand to Morthan's neck and felt a fluttering pulse. Her ear was right beside Morthan's lips as the captain whispered a last few words.

'Been in the watch... all my life... trust my instinct... more to this than just... mindless death...'

Romilla sat back on her haunches and muttered a prayer to Sigmar for the captain's soul, before sliding her eyes shut and brushing her sweat-plastered red hair back from her forehead.

'What now?' she asked, as a pair of watchmen moved to their captain's side and laid her down beneath her cloak. Romilla felt exhausted, hollow from so much loss and terror, the fire of her earlier anger doused by the cold reality of fallen friends and failure.

'If I might?' said one of the watchmen. 'We can't stay here, it's too close to the square. But there's a safehouse nearby, where Gallowhill meets Marketsway. We could regroup there? Then you can decide whether you want to help us fight for this city or... not.' Romilla heard the effort the man made to control his voice, the anger and loss lurking just beneath the surface. She knew how he felt. Still, Aelyn was their leader with Hendrick gone. Romilla looked to the aelf, who gave a fluid shrug and plucked her longbow from the pack that Romilla had shucked off on the stock room floor.

'Lead us to this safehouse,' she said, nodding to the watchman. 'We will make our decisions there.'

ACT 3
WITCHING HOUR

'A crown upon the Loonking's head,
A staff clutched in his hand
Both twisted by the fungus moon,
Both blackened like his heart.
Don't let him see you little one,
Don't let him hear you cry,
Or down into the darksome depths
He'll bear you off to die.'

– Azyrheimer nursery rhyme

CHAPTER TWELVE

AFTER

Aelyn peered through the small gap between the wooden slats that covered the window. It should have been dawn by now. Instead, the moonlit twilight persisted. The feeling was surreal and surprisingly unpleasant. The natural order of things had been wholly upended, and any sureties she still clung to she could no longer trust.

Despite a journey of less than a mile through the city streets, it had taken them several hours to reach this safehouse. It was, at least, secure when they arrived; a solidly built townhouse that hid behind a facade of boarded-up abandonment. They had got through the door thanks to the presence of the watchmen they had rescued, coupled with the authority of the late captain's brooch of office, and had found a dozen watchmen and perhaps three times as many rescued city folk cowering in the rooms within, doing their best to stay silent as the grave.

Most of Aelyn's companions were now snatching what sleep they could. She did not feel the need, though her wounds ached and her mind churned with nightmare images she would rather forget. She wasn't sure she could have slept, even had she wanted to; the hours since the Bad Moon's rise had been too profoundly disturbing.

Instead she had offered to stand guard, along with a couple of watchmen. She could protect her comrades while they rested, and at the same time get a little peace and time to herself in which to think, and to try to come to terms with all that had happened. Both things felt very important to her, after what had transpired.

The view through the dirty window was less restricted than she had expected. The boards had been artfully affixed to give the look of long-term abandonment while actually affording good sight-lines in the event that the building required defending. Aelyn could look up and down the street quite a way. She could see the slime-slick cobbles that were slowly disappearing beneath a swelling field of fungal blooms. She could take in the wrecked carriage that had ploughed into a shop front across the way, a half-eaten corpse still dangling from one shattered window. She could look upon the other bodies of dock workers and militiamen and traders that were scattered amidst the debris, their poses unnatural, their bodies thick with squirming insects and swaying toadstools. Blessedly, what she could *not* see from this angle was the monstrous moon that leered down upon the city.

She could feel it up there, though.

Still watching.

Still leering.

Still hungry.

Aelyn tensed as she heard footfalls slapping the cobbles, approaching fast from the north end of the street. A man burst into her field of view, running hard, slipping and skidding on

the treacherous footing. He was dressed in colourful pantaloons that had been torn and stained, and the remains of a large
wicker basket dangled from his back. Aelyn tensed as she saw
him shoot a panicked look over his shoulder, then cry out as
his foot struck something buried in the fungi. The man pitched
forwards, landing amidst the foulness in a spray of slime. He
scrabbled frantically as he tried to rise. The aelf began to reach
for her bow, then stopped herself. The safety of her friends
came first. She couldn't endanger them by drawing attention.

More figures dashed into view, sprinting things with
deformed faces and revolting froth spilling from their jaws. A
mob of spore-sickened sprung onto the man before he could
rise, and his screams echoed along the street. Aelyn made herself watch until it was over, until the infected had risen and
stalked away, twitching and gibbering, a new figure in torn
pantaloons lurching along in their midst.

She heard movement behind her, turned to see Romilla
standing in the doorway.

'They're gone,' she said quietly in answer to the priest's unasked
question.

'So many we can't save,' said Romilla, shaking her head in
sorrow.

'There are those we can,' said Aelyn. 'But we need to decide
how, and whom, and we need to do it now. I don't believe that
this building will remain inviolate for long.'

'That's true enough,' said Romilla. 'There are patches of
fungi beginning to sprout from the walls on the ground floor,
and watchman Shen found insects spilling into the basement
armoury through a drain cover. He's blocked it, but…' Romilla's shrug was eloquence enough.

This was a temporary sanctuary at best. At any moment, the
horrors that prowled beyond its walls could come spilling in.

The two of them made their way along the house's landing and down its ironoak stairs to the ground floor. Despite its dilapidated outward appearance, the interior of the building was smartly appointed in the colours of the Draconium Watch. It had the feel of a fortress, its fixtures and fittings austere and functional but for a few portraits of previous watch captains that hung on the walls. Aelyn wondered if such a portrait would be commissioned of Helena Morthan. It was the least she deserved, but it seemed tragically unlikely. Barring a miracle, Aelyn wasn't sure there would be a city left for that portrait to be painted in soon.

They picked their way over the sleeping forms of exhausted city folk and nodded reassuringly to others who huddled watchfully in corners, their clothes stained with dirt and blood, their possessions or loved ones clutched close.

The largest of the ground floor rooms was what Aelyn took to be the office of whichever watch officer had run this place. It boasted a solidly-built desk and chair, a half-stocked weapons rack and scroll shelving along one wall that overflowed with rolled parchments. A large street map of the Docksflow and Marketsway districts dominated another wall, festooned with brass pins and faded notes; Aelyn assumed each pin related to a recent incident. She noted uncomfortably that, if she tilted her head slightly, they described the rough shape of a crescent moon.

Borik, Bartiman and Eleanora were all sleeping in this room, their bedrolls pushed up against the wall nearest the weapons. A couple of the watchmen had chosen to bed down here too. Watchman First Class Shen stood guard by the window. A pale sliver of moonlight made a sickly stripe across the man's face. It made him look pale and drawn.

As Aelyn and Romilla entered, he looked around.

'Who's in the upper lookout?' he asked softly.

'Currently, no one,' replied Aelyn. 'We've rested long enough. We need to make plans.'

'Not alone, you won't,' said Shen, and Aelyn couldn't tell whether his firm tone was meant to sound comradely or threatening. 'I'll wake a couple of the third class and set them on guard. If you mercenaries are planning your next move, myself, First Class Marika and First Class Thackeray should join you.'

'As you wish,' said Aelyn. The watchmen knew that she had been entrusted with Captain Morthan's brooch of office. No one knew what had become of Lieutenant Grange, and in his absence the watchmen seemed to have assumed that meant Morthan had also entrusted Aelyn with the fight for Draconium. When talking their way into the sanctuary of the safe house, it had seemed prudent not to disabuse them of the notion. She wondered, though, how they would feel by the end of the conversation she knew must be had. Were the Swords of Sigmar Draconium's saviours, or mercenaries who would cut and run now that the money had dried up?

Honestly, at that moment, even Aelyn herself didn't know the answer to that question.

While Romilla went in search of breakfast, Aelyn woke each of her comrades in turn. Borik, whose only concession to comfort had been removing his helm before he fell asleep, was surly and quiet. Bartiman was pale and drawn; the deaths of his companions seemed to have aged him, and he required some effort to wake. Eleanora smiled wanly at Aelyn when she woke, but her skin was clammy and warm to the touch.

Romilla returned with a few scant provisions and a warm jug of metha, then proceeded to move Aelyn aside and see to Eleanora's bitten foot. Aelyn winced at the sight of puffy flesh and blackened veins creeping up to Eleanora's knee. What could they do, though, except rely upon Romilla's knowledge as a healer and what meagre supplies she still possessed?

Watchmen First Class Marika and Thackeray arrived just as Eleanora was pulling her boots on, struggling with her swollen ankle. Marika was a short woman with an intense cast to her features and a long scar running down one cheek, while Thackeray looked far too boyish to be a watchman first class. Aelyn could read his calm composure, however; no matter that the world had gone to the hells around him, she sensed that Watchman Thackeray intended to do his duty to the last.

The Swords and the watchmen gathered around the desk. Everyone stared at each other. No one quite seemed to know where to start.

'We're leaving,' said Borik after the pause had become uncomfortable. Aelyn looked sharply around at him, but the duardin's expression was stubbornly unrepentant.

'We haven't decided anything of the sort!' exclaimed Romilla.

'Captain Morthan trusted you with a duty!' said Watchman Shen at the same time.

'Captain Morthan still owes us a substantial sum of money,' replied Borik. 'As it doesn't look likely that's going to be paid, our services are no longer available. Are they, Aelyn?'

'Typical cheffing mercenaries,' muttered Watchman Marika. 'No faith, no loyalty, no care for Sigmar's realm, just in it for yourselves.'

'We've lost three of our own to this nightmare,' Romilla retorted hotly, turning a furious glare upon Marika. 'One before we even got here! We didn't need to come to your damned city, didn't need to bring you our warning.'

'Oh, and what good did that warning do anyway?' asked Marika. 'The way I heard it, you fools turned up with a few scraps of prophecy and nary a clue how they related to anything. I heard the regent militant threw you out of his palace.'

'That much is true, and look at how matters have turned out,' said Bartiman sourly. 'Perhaps if your precious regent militant had listened to us when we arrived he'd be alive now and so would a lot of other folk.'

'Listened to what?' snapped Watchman Shen. 'A bundle of half-formed guesswork? The words of a tainted freak? Lieutenant Grange told us all about you lot, don't worry about that. He had no idea why the captain put any faith in you at all.'

'Maybe the captain recognised a company of proper warriors when she saw one, realised we'd be more help than you glorified night watchmen,' growled Borik. 'Doesn't matter anyway, she's dead and she's not paying us any more, so whatever task the captain had for us here, it's done.'

'She trusted you with her brooch of office!' cried Marika. 'You claim to be good servants of Sigmar! How can you possibly spit upon all of that and turn away when an entire city is at risk?'

'What damned city?' Borik shot back. 'Half of it's in ruins already, and how long before the rest follows? Open your eyes, human. You lost this fight before it even started. The best thing you can do now is evacuate as many folk as you can and leave the place to the grobs.'

'You'd like us to run away, wouldn't you?' asked Marika, her tone venomous. 'Make you feel better about your own cowardice, wouldn't it? I thought duardin were supposed have backbones.'

'It's not a lack of courage I suffer from, just a lack of stupidity!' yelled Borik furiously. 'There's neither profit nor sense in fighting an enemy that's already beaten you!'

'No one is running anywhere!' said Romilla. 'We haven't decided anything, Borik. You don't speak for us, Aelyn does.'

'Grungni's divine arse!' shouted Borik. 'Am I the only one who remembers who we are? We are *mercenaries*, Romilla. *Mercenaries*. We fight for *money*. Hendrick was the bleeding heart who decided we had to come here and get mixed up in all this madness. Gods give us Varlen back, he'd never have brought us within a hundred miles of such a profitless mess.'

'Varlen would have wanted to aid these people, just as Hendrick did, and you know it,' shouted Romilla. 'Varlen, Hendrick, Olt – the Bad Moon claimed all their lives and yet you just want to turn tail and run? What of vengeance, Borik? Do not our friends deserve to be avenged?'

'Against all of that out there? Amidst this madness?' asked Borik. 'Who's going to avenge us when we're all dead, Romilla? Because that's all anyone who stays here is going to be.'

'You see, they're just a bunch of damned cowards!' exclaimed Watchman Marika to her comrades. 'I *told* you we couldn't rely on them!'

'All of you, shut up.' Aelyn didn't raise her voice, but her words cut through the angry tumult all the same. Everyone turned to stare angrily at her. 'Keep your voices down, or do you want to bring a horde of greenskins down upon us?' she asked. There were a few uncomfortable glances towards the boarded window. People strained for any telltale sounds of scrabbling claws or animal snarls.

'Captain Morthan tasked us with the defence of this city,' said Watchman Thackeray into the restored quiet. 'It's a simple enough question. Do you plan to help us, or don't you?'

'It is not so simple as you imagine,' said Aelyn. 'I ask you, what do we face here? Why has this curse descended upon Draconium?'

'The Moonclan grots, we know that much,' said Bartiman, who was clutching his hot mug of metha to his breast like a talisman.

'What, Grobi-the-blackcap? The lurkers below?' asked Shen incredulously.

'Is anyone even still asking that question?' replied Romilla. 'You've all seen them out there. You've seen the Bad Moon in the skies above. Fairy tales are only fairy tales until they're sinking their fangs into your neck. They don't care whether you believe in them or not, they'll kill you either way.'

Shen looked ready to argue further, but Marika put a hand on his arm and shook her head.

'You haven't been out there, Shen,' she said, her former anger replaced by a haunted tone. 'Just believe us, it's all true and much more besides. There's things from nightmares roaming the streets. I saw a spider big as three coaches weaving its web right around a townhouse, for Sigmar's sake. The people inside were still screaming…'

'Strip away the fae-tales and underneath you find greenskins, albeit monstrous ones,' said Thackeray. 'They wreak destruction for its own sake, do they not? Surely the answer to your question is that Draconium is beset simply because we were unfortunate enough to stand in their path.'

'I don't believe so, and neither does Eleanora,' said Aelyn. 'Is that not right?'

The engineer looked stricken as all eyes turned to her. She counted quickly on her fingers then brushed her sweat-lank hair back from her forehead.

'Too much planning, too many omens,' she said. 'Unrest, unnatural phenomena, all chipped away at the city's capacity to fight back. Draconium was under siege but we didn't recognise it, because the methods were too strange. Food, morale, defences all eroded over a turning or so, then when the attack came it was coordinated all across the city. Who poisoned the regent militant? That wasn't random elemental violence, it was part of a deliberate strategy of terror and organisational destabilisation that suggests prodigious forethought.'

'Are we *sure* it's greenskins at all?' asked Shen. 'That sounds more like the machinations of some cult to the Dark Gods.'

'It's greenskins all right, but they don't fight like any I've ever faced before,' said Aelyn. 'Orruks come at you from the front, an avalanche that sweeps away all before it. This is insidious, cunning, a poisoned blade sunk into your back before you even know you are at war. But I ask again, in aid of what?'

'Conquest, ruin, pure and simple,' said Borik, in a tone intended to brook no argument. 'Greenskins can be wily but they don't plan ahead. It's as the watchman said, Draconium was just in their way.'

'I don't think that we can choose our path until we know for sure whether that is true,' said Aelyn. 'Perhaps you are right, Borik. Perhaps this is simply ill fortune, and the best course of action is to clear the path of the avalanche. We could make for the towns and cities to the south, warn them of Draconium's fate and call down the wrath of the Stormcasts to retake whatever remained of the city.' She held up a hand to forestall Marika's angry protests. 'But what if that is not the right move? What if that ghastly moon hanging above us... what if the greenskins have conjured it somehow? What if they have a wider-reaching plan, and its light ends up spreading to all the corners of this realm?'

'How do we know that isn't already the case?' asked Romilla darkly.

'You said it yourself, Sigmar made the Stormcast Eternals to deal with matters of such vast import,' said Borik, taking an angry swig of his metha. 'If there is truly some dreadful plan afoot here, let them be the ones to deal with it. But I don't believe it. I'll butcher greenskins as gladly as the next duardin, but I follow the Kharadron code, and its statutes leave no room for doubt – there's no profit in a losing battle, and the honourable dead are still dead all the same.'

'Krysthenna's cult tried to leave,' said Eleanora quietly.

'Rust it all, Krysthenna's cult were a gang of moon-eyed fools who marched out into the wilds without a blade between them,' snapped Borik.

'And how much better do you believe the people of this city would fare, if they tried to flee?' asked Marika.

'If they have any sense, they already *have* fled,' Borik replied. 'As we should. As we're going to.'

'We are called the Swords of Sigmar, not simply the Swords,' said Romilla. 'There's a reason Varlen and Hendrick chose that name, Borik. No matter how much you try to argue otherwise, you know that they cared more about their duty to the God-King than they did about the money they earned performing it. They became mercenaries because it suited their methods, not because they cared more about coin than they did about the war for the Mortal Realms.'

'And now they're dead,' said Borik. 'I don't intend to make the same mistake. You can all do what you like. Varlen hired me and my contract ended with his death. I've come this far on faith, but no further. This isn't our fight, it isn't worth our deaths, and if I can't make anyone else see that then I'll light a mourner's beacon for you all when I'm next aboard an airship.'

'The Swords of Sigmar will stay and aid you in your fight,' said Aelyn, addressing the watchmen as though Borik hadn't spoken. 'But we will not fight blindly. I propose a scouting mission to discover our foes' intentions.'

'We should also try to link up with other defenders,' said Thackeray, nodding. 'We can't fight back just the few of us, but I don't believe that we're the only ones left. There are other safe-houses, other arms caches. Perhaps we may still find Lieutenant Grange as the captain asked.'

'I don't believe I'm hearing this foolishness!' exclaimed Borik. 'If you–'

Aelyn spun, interrupting Borik with a raised finger. She marched past him to where the Swords' remaining bags had been piled in a heap. A moment's rummaging and she returned with a felt pouch, which she thumped down on the table before him with a heavy clink of coin.

'You are leaving. You have made that sufficiently clear. Does anyone else consider their business in Draconium concluded?'

Romilla stared back at Aelyn fiercely, her answer clear. Eleanora looked to Romilla, then looked back and shook her head. Aelyn felt her determination waver as she saw a complex mix of emotions pass across Bartiman's features. The wizard made her wait long enough that she thought perhaps they had lost him too, but then he sighed.

'Hendrick… Olt… no, this has gone far enough. It's personal, and I'll not leave their shades to roam unavenged.' He coughed wetly into his handkerchief, which by now was stained a ruddy brown. He huffed ruefully. 'Besides, I've breathed in too much of this city's muck, I suspect. My soul is long overdue in the Land of Endings. Perhaps it's time to come to terms with that at last. I'd rather die doing something meaningful than waste away knowing my last true choice was to abandon the few friends I have. Borik, for the gods' sakes stay, will you?'

The duardin's face had set into an impassive mask when Aelyn thumped the coins down in front of him. She knew that he was the most truly mercenary amongst their number, that his code compelled him to act in that fashion and that to a duardin such matters were of gravest import. Still, she dared to hope for a moment that Bartiman's words might have swayed him.

Moving stiffly, Borik took the coin purse and tucked it into a pouch on his belt. He looked around at them, his expression unreadable, then turned without a word and marched over to collect his equipment. No one spoke as the duardin donned his helm, hefted pack and gun, and strode from the room. Borik paused in the doorway for a heartbeat, and then he left. The door swung shut with a click behind him. Aelyn sighed deeply into the deafening quiet that followed.

Another comrade gone. Silently, she wished Borik luck in escaping the city alive. Then she turned back to those who remained.

'So, a scouting mission,' she said.

CHAPTER THIRTEEN

CURSED

Romilla felt the comforting weight of her hammer in her hand, and of the amulet that hung about her neck. She concentrated on those sensations as she picked her way along in Aelyn's wake. So much around her was nightmarish and gruesome, it helped to have something familiar upon which to centre herself.

The aelf slipped through the shadows, clad in a heavy watchman's cloak that she had strapped, slit and swiftly re-stitched to better integrate with her waywatcher's garb. Thanks to her deep hood, the bandana she had pulled up over much of her face and the lightweight gloves she had donned, not a scrap of Aelyn's skin was exposed to the foul moonlight that spilled down upon Draconium. Romilla had taken similar precautions; she had no desire to feel the awful sting of fungi pushing through her pores again and besides, they had no idea what further corruption the moonlight might bring.

Eleanora and Bartiman had been left behind at the safehouse, helping to shore up the defences and provide what aid they could to the watchmen and city folk hidden there. Instead, three watchmen accompanied Aelyn and Romilla on their intelligence gathering mission. Watchman Thackeray had insisted that he join them and had brought two watchmen second class with him. Romilla had been told their names but had forgotten them straight away. She had simply been overloaded these last few days, she supposed. Besides, she was fighting a constant battle with the feeling that all those around her had become transitory, fleeting presences who would soon enough leave her side again. The sensation frightened her, for it echoed the dislocation and isolation she had felt before her plunge into depression. Before Varlen and his comrades had found her, and helped to restore her faith in herself, in her deity.

She wouldn't lose herself again, she thought fiercely. Never mind that the brothers Saul were gone, that Olt had been slain and Borik had deserted them. She still had Aelyn, and Bartiman, and of course there was Eleanora. Romilla wouldn't let her down by breaking now. The thought of Eleanora's injured foot, of the corruption that was clearly spreading up her leg by the hour, preyed upon her mind. Romilla cursed herself for not insisting she check on the wound sooner. Perhaps they could have treated it, stopped the spread of whatever poison was working its way through Eleanora's body. She glanced up for an instant at the Bad Moon leering high above. Then again, she thought, perhaps not – not with that foul orb blighting the skies. If they passed any kind of an apothecarion, Romilla intended to ransack it for additional herbs and unguents that might help. Still, she couldn't help fearing that at best Eleanora was going to lose that leg. She had put the decision off thus far, but if the poison spread much further she would have to–

Romilla's attention snapped back to the present as they neared the end of the alleyway they were creeping along. On the advice of Watchman Shen, they had headed north from their safehouse, up the Threadway Road and thence into a warren of backstreets and workers' housing that bordered Docksflow. Aelyn had expressed a desire to find a vantage point from which to fully appreciate the condition of the city and the disposition of their foe. According to Shen, an unofficial rooftop highway began amidst the houses of the Docksflow fringe and led uphill to the Mercantile Guild building in High Drake. Providing the plummeting moon rocks had not annihilated it, that building's rooftops would provide the best view for miles around, or so said Watchman Shen. Besides, there was another objective to be reached in High Drake, one that Watchman Thackeray was intent upon.

The dash along the Threadway had been nerve-wracking, but though they had been forced to navigate thick fungal outcroppings and a minefield of half-buried corpses, they had seen no enemies. Once into the tangle of back streets, things had become less terrifying; the tight confines and high buildings conspired to hide much of the Bad Moon from sight most of the time.

Still, there was fungus growing from every surface, and Romilla had repeatedly had to stamp on hungry swarms of insects that had attempted to clamber up her legs to sink mandibles and proboscises into her flesh. A fat black-and-red spider had fallen onto her shoulder, and she had squashed it before it could bite her. Her skin tingled uncomfortably where its juices had soaked through her cloak.

They had heard movement several times, slapping footfalls and harsh, inhuman voices snarling and jabbering in a tongue she didn't recognise. Until now, though, they had been lucky. As Romilla came up behind the crouched form of Aelyn, she saw that their Sigmar-sent luck had run out.

Beyond the alleyway, several streets met around a stone well with a rain-etched slate roof over it. Something slimy and pulsating had sprouted from the well, its rubbery black flesh and thick tendrils bursting the stonework and sinking into the cobbled ground. The black tendrils were festooned with small red and green toadstools, and these were being busily harvested by a gaggle of Moonclan grots. The hunched creatures shoved and pinched, jostling to reach the best fungi. Their pointy black hoods bobbed, and sharp little daggers glinted in the sickly moonlight as they were brandished threateningly. She saw to her revulsion that most of the greenskins were grabbing fistfuls of the slimy fungi and stuffing them into their fanged mouths. They chewed greedily and, as they did, frothy black foam spilled from their jaws and dribbled down their chins. As Romilla watched, several of the grots began to shudder and gibber. They capered about the small courtyard, flailing their limbs and shrieking a single word over and over. To Romilla's ears it sounded like 'Gloomspite! Gloomspite!'

'Do we fight, or do we try to avoid them?' asked one of the watchmen softly.

Aelyn motioned upwards, and as Romilla followed the aelf's gesture her blood froze in her veins. Spiders moved up near the rooftops, horrible bloated things as big as she was, with crude saddles lashed to them. Grots sat in those saddles, primitive-looking creatures clad in loincloths, their pale green flesh pierced with stolen feathers and daubed with war-paint. They leered as their steeds spewed silk from their abdomens and worked it with their long forelimbs. Some of them looked to be weaving a sort of roof between the buildings, Romilla saw. Others were cocooning bulky shapes in layer after layer of slimy silks and hanging them from the gutters. It was a larder, Romilla thought, trying to ignore the way some of the bundles twitched and gave muffled moans of fear.

'Too many,' whispered Aelyn. 'We need to get above them. Thackeray, how do we reach the rooftop road?'

The watchman frowned as he thought, drumming the fingers of one hand against his chin.

'We double back down this alley, take the left-hand fork at the bottom. If we can get into the fishmonger's there, then there's a way up through the building's attic. There was a gang operating out of the fishmonger's at one point, until we shut them down.'

Aelyn nodded and gestured for Thackeray to lead. He set off, back along the alley and away from the gaggle of Moonclan grots. Romilla kept checking their rear as they retreated, alive for any sign that the greenskins might have seen them. There was no sign of pursuit.

They took the left fork and worked their way through several quick switchbacks that ran along the rear of a string of buildings. They passed beneath shattered windows like dark caves, and Romilla watched them intently for any sign of movement. Beneath one lay the corpse of a large man with a wicked grot shiv buried between his shoulder blades. A colony of mushrooms had grown from the wet gap in his cracked skull, and beetles were scurrying busily across his corpse. The sight caused Romilla barely a moment's revulsion, and she wondered dully whether she was becoming so saturated by horror that she could no longer feel its touch. If so, she doubted it was a good thing.

Stopping again at the last bend in the back alley, they peered out into the narrow street beyond. Shattered spark-lanterns lay scattered around where they had been torn out of the ground and flung. Broken glass twinkled in the moonlight. Some distance away at the street's far end, several stone-skinned troggoths were hunched over a butcher's wagon, stuffing fistfuls of spoiled meat into their mouths with noisy relish. Closer, Romilla spotted small bands of grots prowling through the ruins. One group picked through the smashed glass, pocketing the shiniest shards with glee. Another group was ransacking a blacksmith's partway down the street, while the last band were doing the same to the shop opposite. Romilla's heart sank as she saw it was the fishmonger's.

'We could creep up on them, then rush the ones in the fishmonger's?' suggested one of the watchmen, though she sounded singularly unconvinced of the proposition.

'Not without bringing the rest of them down upon us,' said Romilla. 'Those troggoths aren't as large as the one we saw outside the palace, but still, between them and the greenskins we'd be overrun.'

'Wait here,' said Aelyn. 'When I give the signal, stay low and fast and make for the fishmonger's. I'll meet you on the first floor.'

The aelf slipped from the alleyway, her bow slung easily on her back next to a quiver full of arrows. Romilla held her breath as Aelyn loped swiftly across the street, fully exposed to the grots' view, then leapt high and caught hold of a gutter outside a first floor window. As she moved, her outline seemed to blur. Aelyn became difficult to watch or to follow. Romilla had seen the waywatcher employ her strange talents before, but it never became any less unsettling. Aelyn swung her legs forward to gain momentum then swung back and out, twisting her body in a way no human could have emulated. She executed a neat flip and landed catlike upon the windowsill.

She sprang from one windowsill to the next, and then to the next, before bounding diagonally upwards in order to catch hold of a windowbasket outside the second floor of some merchant's house. Romilla tensed as the basket gave under Aelyn's weight and broke away from its moorings. Moving faster than even Romilla would have believed possible, Aelyn caught hold of the windowsill with one hand and hung onto the basket with the other, preventing it from falling and smashing in the street below. For a few heartbeats she dangled, and Romilla prayed fervently to Sigmar that none of the greenskins would think to look up.

Aelyn swung herself first one way then the other, back and forth several times before managing to hook one foot over the sill. Sinuous as a snake, she hauled herself up and placed the broken basket gently upon the sill. Then she vanished into the dark interior of the building.

'What is she doing?' whispered Thackeray as they waited. 'There are other routes we might have tried.'

'Any of them as direct as this, or any less likely to be infested?' asked Romilla. The watchman sheepishly shook his head. 'Trust Aelyn, she will handle this,' said Romilla. 'Just be ready to move when she signals.'

Romilla counted her heartbeats and tried to ignore the half-visible face of the Bad Moon staring down at them with hollow eyes. Its gaze made her want to take her hammer and smash it into her own skull as hard as she could. It made her want to swing the weapon into Thackeray's jaw, and then to scream out praise to the Bad Moon as the grots descended upon them all. It made her want to–

Romilla shuddered and shook off the vile waking night-mare, which left her with a sense of disoriented nausea. She leaned against the wall, then snatched her hand back as some-thing with a pale, segmented body and too many legs scurried across it.

'There,' said one of the watchmen, pointing. A thin silver line descended from the shadowed eaves below a jutting roof.

It slid down through the air, directly above the grots looting the blacksmith's. As Romilla watched, the line dangled down behind one of the greenskins and settled with a glint upon the hilt of a dagger thrust into his waistband. The next moment the dagger was rising skywards, caught neatly in a silken noose and reeled in like a crab on a line. The grot, who was hunched over a barrel and rooting about inside, didn't notice a thing.

The dagger vanished into the shadows, and again there was a pause. A second floor window creaked part way open above the blacksmith's, and the dagger flew out of it in a low, tight arc. The blade thumped neatly between the shoulder blades of one of the grots who was ransacking the fishmonger's, causing him to arch and shriek in pain.

Immediately, the grot's fellow looters spun and began to scream and jabber at the mob in the blacksmith's. Those grots turned in confusion, which rapidly became outraged anger. The group in the fishmonger's grabbed their weapons and stormed across the street, pointing menacingly at the other mob and spitting threats.

Seeing the developing fun, the smaller bunch of grots picking over the smashed glass forgot their glinting prizes and hurried over to watch. Inevitably, one of them was struck by a flying brick lobbed by one of the blacksmith mob, and with a chorus of angry screeches the third mob of grots piled into the developing brawl in the blacksmith's. Blood sprayed as daggers were drawn and used. One greenskin snatched up a heavy iron mace from a weapon rack and laid into his fellows with it. Meanwhile, at the other end of the street, the troggoths continued their meal, wholly oblivious to the developing carnage.

From the second floor window, Romilla saw a brief flash, moonlight reflecting on glass.

'The signal,' she said. 'Move, now, before they settle their fight.'

They ran quickly, doubled over in the hopes of avoiding notice. Romilla's heart pounded in her chest at the thought that any second one of the brawling grots might look round and see them. She tried to ignore the awful sense of the Bad Moon peering down at them, and did her best to avoid treading in puddles of congealed slime or on especially slippery-looking fungi.

She offered silent thanks to Aelyn and Sigmar both as she ducked through the smashed-in door of the fishmonger's. The place was a ruin, mangled produce smearing floor and walls, bugs crawling over everything. Romilla ignored it all and made for the shadowy doorway behind the counter.

She stepped through and came face to face with a grot. Romilla swung her hammer more by instinct than conscious thought, and it connected with the greenskin's skull. At the same instant she felt an icy pain in her side. The grot crumpled, leaving its six-inch shiv embedded in Romilla's ribs.

'Damn,' she gasped, pressing a hand to the wound and feeling blood well through her fingers. The others were right behind her, and she felt their confusion and panic at finding her stood frozen over a fallen grot in the shop's back hallway.

Move, Romilla told herself. *Hurt later*.

She mounted the stairs to the first floor, keeping one hand pressed hard to her wound as she went. She could feel blood dribbling down her side, and a cold, tugging pain shot through her with every step. Still, Romilla kept moving until they stood below the hatchway that led up into the attic. Only then did she lean against the wall and rummage in her bag for a healing compress.

'Who's bleeding?' asked Aelyn as she joined them. 'There's a trail up the stairs that they won't struggle to follow.'

'That would be me,' said Romilla through gritted teeth.

Aelyn moved wordlessly to her side and, while Romilla held the poultice in place, the aelf swiftly wound bandages around her midriff until the wound was properly bound. The watchmen guarded the stairs nervously, halberds at the ready.

'This will have to do,' said Romilla, checking that the bandages were tied off to her satisfaction. 'Idiot.'

'Just unlucky,' said Aelyn. 'Thackeray, how do we get up?'

'There used to be a ladder,' said the watchman, casting about with obvious agitation. Below, they heard the scuff of movement. Something broke with a smash. A cruel voice cackled. Then came a cry from the hallway. Someone had found the body.

'No time,' said Romilla. 'Boost me up.'

Aelyn knelt, making a stirrup of her hands. Romilla ignored the pain in her side as the aelf pushed up with inhuman strength and propelled her into the open hatchway. Romilla grabbed hold of the dusty boards and hauled, biting down on a scream as her wounded side ground against the lip of the hatch. She dragged herself onto the attic's part-boarded floor. Aelyn followed, springing straight up through the hole with remarkable grace and agility. The two of them lay on their stomachs by the hatch and lowered their arms through.

'Come on,' Romilla hissed. 'We'll pull you up!'

Thackeray came first, gripping their wrists as they gripped his and dragged him up to safety. Romilla reached down again, stifling a groan of pain. She could hear angry shrieks and jabbering cries from the shop's ground floor, then the thump of footfalls on the stairs.

'Sigmar, hurry!' Romilla hissed as the female watchman grabbed their arms and was hauled up.

Romilla groaned with agony at the effort and felt fresh blood spill down her side. Then Thackeray was there, ushering her gently but firmly aside as he and Aelyn reached down for the last watchman. Romilla rolled aside, sprawling on the dusty boards and staring up at the arched ceiling, half visible in the gloom. Her vision swam, but her hearing was still keen. There was no escaping the screams of the last watchman as the green-skins reached him. Romilla felt all the worse that she didn't even know his name.

'Damn it!' cursed Thackeray as he and Aelyn ducked back from the hatch. Several crude arrows and a flung blade whipped up to embed themselves in the joists overhead. The lost watchman's screams turned swiftly to bubbling gurgles, which were drowned out by cruel grot laughter.

'We can't stay here, they'll figure a route up,' said Aelyn. When Thackeray didn't show any immediate sign of movement, the aelf shoved him none-too-gently towards the back end of the attic. 'Watchman, where is the route up?' she asked.

Thackeray took a last angry look at the open hatch, then turned wordlessly and led them to the far end of the attic where a section of boarding had been levered aside. Romilla hobbled after him, praying to Sigmar that her bandages would hold long enough for her to get somewhere safer. She had no desire to bleed to death out here.

They crawled one by one through the hole, then up a tight crawlspace that emerged through a gap in the brickwork of a large chimney stack. Everything was badly eroded by exposure to the city's acid rains, and Romilla was glad of her gloves as she crawled through damp patches. She was doubly glad of them as she emerged onto a rooftop thick with worm-like fungal fronds. Those, she would not want to touch, she thought.

'The rooftop road,' said Thackeray, gesturing to an arrangement of badly rain-eaten boards that ran along the downslope of the roof and bridged the gap to the next rooftop along.

'How delightfully perilous,' gasped Romilla, wishing that blood loss had not left her feeling so woozy and light headed.

'Come on, that must be the guild hall,' said Aelyn, pointing to an imposing fortress of a building some way upslope across the rooftops. It was slab-sided, built from rain-treated granite and boasting what looked like a battlement's crenulations at its peak.

'We'll get our view from there,' said Thackeray. 'But we'll need to enter two floors down. That's where, Sigmar willing, they'll be dug in.'

'Very well, let's move,' said Aelyn and set off along the boards at an alarming pace. Romilla followed, her heart lurching at every creak, groan and sudden lurch of the boardwalk.

'Sigmar, if you can hear me, guide my steps,' she prayed as she ran, and tried to ignore the sickening drop to either side of her into the fungus-thick streets below.

They were halfway across the rooftops when Aelyn heard the cries of greenskins behind them. She glanced back, still running surefooted across the roofboards. Thackeray and his remaining watchman were close on her heels, Romilla lagging slightly further back, looking pale but determined.

A hundred yards or so further behind them, Moonclan grots were spilling up like insects from a collapsed attic space, swarming up the fungus-dotted roof tiles and onto the boards of the roadway.

'Romilla, faster!' shouted Aelyn, and saw the wounded priest dutifully redouble her efforts. Aelyn swung herself up onto a chimney stack and crouched there like a gargoyle. She swept her bow off her back and swiftly strung it. Thackeray and his watchman passed her at as close to a run as they dared, their cloaks flapping behind them.

'Get to the guild hall and secure our entry,' she ordered as they dashed past. Then she drew an arrow from her quiver, drew back her bowstring and, ignoring the foul Bad Moon hanging fat and low overhead, she loosed. The shaft whipped through the air, passing over Romilla's head and dropping neatly into the eye socket of a Moonclan grot. The creature shrieked as it was spun from its feet to topple bonelessly down the roof and into the void beyond. Its body hit the cobbles far below with a distant splat. By that time, Aelyn had loosed three more arrows that sped through the air and plucked three more greenskins from their feet.

As she had hoped, the rest lost their nerve and scattered to cower behind buttresses, chimney-pots and the like. Romilla kept running, reaching then passing Aelyn's position with a grim nod of thanks.

'It won't keep them back for long,' said the aelf, dropping from her vantage point and following her comrade.

She ran, and as she did black-fletched arrows the length of her forearm started to fall around her. One skipped off the roof tiles just feet to her left. Another thrummed over her shoulder and thumped, quivering, into the roofboards in front of her. Aelyn kept running, turning her innate talents to blurring her outline and blending with the shadows. Yet there was so little cover, exposed as they were, silhouetted against the skyline with the bloated Bad Moon shining its light down upon her like a beacon. At any second Aelyn expected to feel an arrow thump into her back and pitch her from the roof.

The tingle of her instincts warned her of something worse, however. Crying out a warning, Aelyn threw herself flat. Romilla heard her and half-ducked, half-fell onto her face. There came a crackling roar and a foul fungal stench, and a roiling orb of green energy flashed over their heads to hit a chimney stack two roofs ahead. The stonework detonated in a greasy green fireball, and Thackeray and his companion shielded their heads as blazing lumps of rock rained about them.

Aelyn spun, and saw a greenskin with a gnarled staff clutched in one hand and half a cat's worth of animal bones piercing his nose and ears. The creature was festooned with amulets and gewgaws, and pale green energy crackled around his head as he capered and shrieked. As Aelyn sprang back to her feet, the sickly moonlight condensed around the greenskin's staff then leapt out as another coruscating blast of energy. Aelyn flipped backwards, cartwheeling through the air and landing in a crouch on the roofboards a dozen yards closer to the guild hall. The roof where she had been standing erupted in a blast of green energy that left a twisted, glowing crater that belched spore-thick smoke.

'Shaman,' shouted Aelyn as she turned and pelted along the shuddering roofboards. She heard the cries of emboldened grots rise behind her as they gave chase again.

Ahead, Romilla turned and raised her amulet in her fist. All the pain and exhaustion left her for an instant as she raised her voice in a booming prayer, and blue light haloed her head.

'Sigmar almighty, God-King of the heavens, hear my prayers! Abjure the foul sorcery of thy base foes, that we might prevail in thy name!'

There came a crackling boom from behind Aelyn, and a flare of green light. She glanced back to see that the shaman's staff had shattered in his hand with such force that the grot's broken body was bounding away down the rooftops trailing smoke. The damage was done, however; dozens of grots poured from top-floor windows and shattered rooftops to join the chase. They swarmed after her, sure-footed and maniacally courageous beneath the gaze of the monstrous moon.

Aelyn reached Romilla, who was staggering with the effort of calling upon the God-King's aid. She looped the priest's arm around her shoulders, took some of Romilla's weight and urged her onwards.

The two of them kept going, limping as fast as they could across the rooftops. Fungi splattered and broke underfoot, more than once giving Aelyn a nasty shock as they threatened to pitch her and Romilla from the boardwalk. Arrows fell around them, several coming close enough to nick her flesh through her cloak. Aelyn hoped none of the heads were poisoned.

Ahead, she saw that Thackeray had reached the roof below the guild hall and was yelling up at an arched window full of dark, leaded glass a dozen feet above him. She was alarmed to see that the watchman looked angry and frantic as he shouted.

'I might be able to make that leap,' said Aelyn. 'But there's no way any of you can, and I won't leave you.'

'Much… appreciated,' grunted Romilla, who was leaning ever more heavily on Aelyn and who had gone alarmingly pale. Her side was blood-slick, and her hammer hung from her hand ready to drop.

'Looks like Borik might have had the right of it after all,' said Aelyn as they came up on Thackeray's position. His surviving watchman had already dropped to one knee on the wooden platform he stood on and was sighting along her pistol at the tide of greenskins flowing closer with every heartbeat.

'Piss on Borik,' spat Romilla.

'You don't mean that,' said Aelyn.

'I don't, but his guns would be useful right now, wouldn't they?' replied the priest with a wan smile.

Aelyn could hear Thackeray now, even over the demented chorus of the pursuing grots.

'Damnation, I know you're in there! We have Captain Morthan's seal! I order you in her name to open that window and lower the bridge!'

Aelyn skidded to a halt and lowered Romilla down next to the crouching watchman. She turned, reaching for an arrow to nock to her bowstring.

'What's your name?' she asked as she did so.

'Polenna,' replied the watchman, whose hand and pistol were shaking slightly.

'If we die here, know it was an honour to fight for your city,' said Aelyn. Polenna nodded to her but didn't take her eyes from the approaching greenskins. The creatures poured along the roofboards and made them shudder, their red eyes and bared fangs glinting in the moonlight.

'In the name of Captain Helena Morthan and the regent militant of Draconium, *I order you to open the window and lower the damned bridge!*' roared Thackeray, and at last the leaded glass window cracked open.

'Show us the seal,' came a querulous voice from within. Aelyn drew back her bowstring and loosed an arrow, slaying a grot who was about to take a shot of his own. The greenskin tumbled and put his half-drawn arrow straight through the cheek of the grot next to him, who howled and fell in a spray of blood. More grotesque figures trampled both corpses as they flowed closer.

'Just lower the cheffing bridge!' cried Thackeray, almost shrieking with frustration.

'The seal,' came the obstinate reply. 'You could be anyone. You could be bandits trying to gain entry.'

Thackeray's response was so littered with profanity that Romilla actually raised an eyebrow. Polenna took her shot and blew another grot sideways off the rooftops. Dozens remained, though, and they were bare yards away now. Dropping her bow,

Aelyn reached into a pouch and raised the captain's brooch high. It glinted in the moonlight.

For a moment she thought nothing would happen, that they would be left to their fates and overrun by stabbing grots. Then came a clatter as the windows along the guild house's second-from-top floor slammed open in unison.

'Fire!' came the bellowed command, and a hail of pistol shot and hissing arrows filled the air. The grots were decimated. Stunted green bodies bounced and rolled down steep slate slopes, their black robes flapping around them as they fell. Some screamed in terror as they plunged to their deaths.

'Again!' came the commanding voice, and another withering volley hit the remaining grots. The few who survived turned tail and fled, their black hoods streaming behind them.

Aelyn turned to see a long wooden bridge, rather like a gangplank, swing down out of the tallest window and thump into place. It spanned the gap between the platform they stood on and the guild house.

'Romilla, one last effort,' she said, helping her comrade to her feet. 'Beware the drop, have a care not to fall.'

'Oh, I won't,' Romilla replied with a scowl. 'I'm staying conscious until I've given the officious arse in that window a black eye.'

In the event, they all made it across the plank-bridge safely and into the guild house beyond. Aelyn clambered through the window, the last one across, to find herself in a large gallery that she assumed must take up most of the entire floor. Wood and brass candelabras hung from the vaulted ceiling. A well-built firestep ran beneath the leaded windows all around the chamber, and Aelyn saw that a mixture of militia-militant and watchmen stood upon it. They had spyglasses with which to keep watch on the streets and rooftops all around, and copious stocks of ammunition close to hand. Much of the space was given over to solid workbenches and copious weapons racks, while through a nearby arched door she saw barrels marked with the Ironweld sigil for black powder marching away into shadow.

Aelyn took in a fair number of men and women in the gallery – easily more than a hundred at arms, she thought. From the faint sounds and smells of numerous unwashed and uneasy folk that came from elsewhere nearby, Aelyn assumed there must be refugees hiding here too. What was this place, she wondered. The watchmen had been cagey, when they were planning. They had only spoken of another safehouse, but this was clearly something more.

Two militiamen were reeling the gang-plank back in, while a group of ten watchmen kept the new arrivals at halberd-point. Nearby, a man clad in what Aelyn took to be clerk's garb looked on with a face like thunder. She saw Romilla would not have to waste her energies; the man was already clutching a hand to what looked like a magnificently swelling bruise under his right eye.

'What in Sigmar's name was that?' demanded Thackeray of the watchmen who guarded them. 'We were almost killed!'

Another watchman first class, a tall woman with short-cut blonde hair, saluted and lowered her halberd.

'Precautions, Thackeray. I had to remove a bit of red tape before you could be given admittance,' she shook one fist ruefully and winced.

The clerk made a sound of disgust in the back of his throat. 'Let us see the brooch again, then – properly, now that we can,' he demanded, mopping sweat from his narrow brow with his free hand. 'I might be the only one here still following proper protocol, but I'd like to make sure we've not admitted agents of the enemy into our midst. If you wouldn't *mind*, Watchman First Class Kole?'

The blonde watchman sighed in exasperation. 'We've seen the damned brooch, Stephan, we don't–'

'My friend is wounded and bleeding,' said Aelyn, producing the brooch again from her pocket. 'Have your proof then aid her, please.'

Shooting a pointed look at Stephan the clerk, Watchman First Class Kole gave the brooch a long look then gestured for her comrades to lower their weapons.

'Get this one aid,' she said, pointing to Romilla, who was pale and swaying. Polenna and another watchman hastened to the priest's side and led her away to a row of nearby pallets where they laid her down and set to cleaning and sealing her wound.

'Since when did guild clerks give orders to the city watch?' asked Thackeray.

'Since you chose to site your reserve armoury in the upper floors of our guild house,' answered Stephan, stalking over to join them. 'The mercantile guild must be protected in these terrible times. We've got dozens of merchants, traders and their families ensconced one floor down from this… fortress… and I'll not allow the militia to draw hostile attention to them. I don't care how many palms your captain greased in order to hide this facility up here.'

'Families?' asked Thackeray, somewhat mollified.

'This is not a safehouse, that much is obvious,' Aelyn observed. She looked questioningly around.

'You are not a watchman,' replied Kole. 'How do you come to carry the captain's seal? What is this, Thackeray? And what's happening out there?'

'Aelyn, I couldn't tell you precisely where we were going in case anything happened to us on the way. The fewer people who know about it the better, you see? This is the city's reserve armoury. A shared facility between the militia and the watch, stocked in case of a disaster like the one that has occurred. You learn about it when you progress from third class to second. Kole, this is Aelyn and the injured priest is Romilla. They're… crusaders, in the captain's employ. She charged them to aid us with the city's defence before she passed.'

'The captain is dead? How?' exclaimed Kole, and a ripple of dismay radiated outwards through her fellow watchmen. While Thackeray explained as best he could, Aelyn had time to feel silently grateful to him for avoiding the term mercenaries. She supposed that crusader was closer to the truth, now, than mercenary. Certainly, vengeance for her friends had become a crusade to her, and Aelyn highly doubted she would be getting paid for her work here. If she even survived it.

The watchmen were interrogating Thackeray for more information on Captain Morthan's death, but Aelyn interrupted.

'Her loss is tragic. I have not long been in this city, and of all those I have met within its walls she was without doubt the most courageous and determined soul. But if I'm right, there is no time to discuss it now. I am sorry.'

The watchmen all turned to look at her, and Aelyn felt hostility radiating from many of them.

'Why do you say this?' asked Stephan sharply.

'The omens. The Bad Moon's rise. The level of planning the greenskins' attack must have taken. We believe this to be more than just a chance invasion,' said Aelyn, looking to Thackeray for support.

'We came here for the view, Kole,' he said. 'What have your people seen from on high?'

'Bloodshed, carnage and horror,' she answered, and for a

moment Aelyn saw just how tired and drawn the watchman was. 'The enemy have looted and rampaged, and we've been forced to sit up here out of sight and watch it all occur. No orders, no communication, nothing. And when the rocks fell from the skies...' she tailed off and exchanged looks with several of her comrades.

'There's the rock in the square,' said one of them. 'Whatever they're doing there.'

'The meteor that hit Fountains Square?' asked Aelyn. 'What of it?'

'When the fumes cleared, we saw that a few of the meteors had survived the impacts. Bits of them, anyway,' said Kole. 'That one's the largest by far, and the greens have been swarming round it like skitterlings. Last word from the rooftop came down an hour ago, said they were carving a face on it, but how that could put the city in any more danger than it's already in, Sigmar only knows.'

'Show us,' said Aelyn.

Kole looked to Thackeray, who nodded.

Aelyn stepped through an ironoak door and out onto the flat rooftop of the mercantile guild house. The view took her breath away, even dominated as it was by the bloated Bad Moon. The city spread out below, stretching away for miles around. Over there, Gallowhill loomed, smoke still drifting from the blasted crater on its peak. In every other direction she saw district upon district, street upon street, turning the foul colours of rot and ruin as fungi and squirming things overtook them. Up here, in the shadows of the looming volcanoes, one could truly appreciate the corruption that had taken root throughout Draconium. This was not a city they could save, she thought despairingly. It was already dead.

Still, Aelyn and Thackeray followed watchman Kole across

the rooftop to where a pair of lookouts stood next to a bulky brass telescope. Others were dotted around the roof's edge, she saw, concealed behind its bulky crenulations and watching silently as their city perished around them.

Kole issued brisk orders, and the two men at the telescope retrained it then stepped smartly aside. The watchman gestured, and Aelyn stepped forwards to stare through the telescope. Initially everything was blurred, until she realised that the watchmen had adjusted the device for human eyes. With their guidance, she gently turned the sighting wheels until the ruins of Fountains Square leapt suddenly into focus.

Aelyn almost recoiled from the telescope.

The square itself was still littered with heaps of corpses and piles of rubble, and the gnawed and blackened ruins of tree trunks lay strewn like discarded sticks. Fungi and insects were everywhere, and dirty water washed across the square in waves. She noted that it was still flowing in the direction it always had, and she winced at the thought of the poison and filth it must surely be emptying into the canal, thence to be borne south towards the settled lands and Hammerhal Aqsha.

The waters now bubbled up not from an ornate fountain, but from beneath the twisted remains of the Bad Moon meteor that still jutted thirty feet into the air at the square's heart. Grots were indeed swarming across it, chiselling and working frenziedly. Figures in shamanic robes capered and shrieked as they directed the work, brandishing their staffs or riding about on huge, lumbering mushrooms.

The grots had graven a leering visage into the meteor, whittling it into a moon-like shape. It was this monstrous grotesque that had caused Aelyn to recoil; its eyes were alive with deranged madness, and as she stared down upon the square she had felt those eyes stare back.

Taking a breath, she forced herself to look through the telescope again. Perhaps they were just carving idols? Greenskins did that, she knew, and if they worshipped the Bad Moon in whatever crude fashion then it made sense they would etch its likeness into things. Yet something made her stare harder, some instinct or inspiration that she could not quite place.

And then she saw it.

Aelyn straightened up from the telescope, her heart thumping sickeningly in her throat. She swallowed, turned to Thackeray and Kole who were watching her with alarm.

'What in the realms did you see?' asked Thackeray.

'There is a tunnel beneath the idol,' she said, forcing her voice to stay level. 'They are bringing them up from below. Dozens and dozens of them, and stacking them beside the waterway.'

'What? What are they bringing up?' demanded Kole.

'Barrels,' said Aelyn. 'Black and gold barrels. Barrels like the one your regent militant drank from before his horrific demise.'

'They'll empty them into the waters,' breathed Thackeray, growing visibly pale as the implications sank in. 'The villages to the south. Sigmar's blood, Hammerhal...'

'We have to stop this,' said Aelyn. 'We have to stop this right now.'

CHAPTER FOURTEEN

ESCAPE

Darkness.

A foul stench.

Throbbing pain that pulsed behind his eyes and ran in electric jolts down his neck.

Borik opened his eyes and quickly blinked them shut again. He had had a brief and bleary glimpse of something pressed close against his face, something fibrous and foul-smelling that he realised encased his entire head. He dragged in a breath, nostrils flaring as he fought back panic. He felt as though he was suffocating. There was something cold and wet jammed in his mouth that he couldn't spit out. It tasted utterly foul, and he gagged deep in his throat as he fought not to vomit.

He wasn't thinking straight, couldn't orient himself. He thought perhaps his aching body was in a sitting position, but when he tried to move he found that his wrists and ankles were locked tightly in place. Borik's breath came in short, fast gasps as he fought against the pain and the urge to frantically thrash his way to freedom.

Remember the code, he told himself. Remember the code. A Kharadron doesn't shame himself with humanish displays of fear. A Kharadron stays firm and true as the winds that bear him to his aethergold prize. Amidst the storm, a Kharadron is the riveted iron, unbending and impervious.

Still, though he repeated the tenets of the code to himself again and again, Borik couldn't entirely stop himself straining against his bonds. He was used to a mask upon his face, but this was different. Whatever it was felt awful, scratching and tickling his skin, bound close against his flesh as though whoever had captured him had given only the vaguest thought to whether he could breathe. That thought tightened his chest all the more, and Borik let out an involuntary groan around his disgusting gag.

He heard movement, and suddenly felt the need to stay very still. He couldn't feel the weight of his armour, he realised, just his leather undersuit. Borik felt suddenly exposed.

How had he got here?

Where even *was* here?

Hazily, he remembered leaving the safe house with his equipment and a small band of survivors in tow. He hadn't tried to talk them into it, hadn't cared whether they followed him or not. He had assumed that they must have heard the raised voices through the office door. A watchman – Kasmir? Kasyr? Something like that – had stopped Borik right before he left and said that he and a few others thought the duardin was right. They wanted to join him in his escape. Borik had shrugged and set off with the watchman in tow, a small band of nervous city folk following close behind.

Borik's plan had been to make for the rivergate. He had thought to steal a boat of some description and then lay low under a tarp, a cloak – whatever he could find – until the craft had drifted through the city wall and away.

He couldn't remember exactly how that had worked out, but some sardonic nugget of icy calm deep in his mind suggested that it couldn't have gone especially well. He had a vague memory of something huge and hulking, of a retched stink of rotting fish and the awful sound of spewing bile that hissed and bubbled as it ate away at screaming city folk. Borik remembered nothing else, but from the pain in his skull and his current predicament, he assumed that whatever had come for them had knocked him out and dragged him... where?

He didn't know.

He wasn't sure he wanted to know.

Harsh voices now, jabbering in grot tongue and sniggering evilly. Something poked him hard in the side of the head and made him groan in pain. More sniggering, then a harsh shout and the sound of scampering feet receding.

Through a haze of pain, Borik heard footsteps move closer. He smelt weird, acrid smells and heard low, muttering voices all around him. Suddenly a part of him wanted his hood to stay in place. It was irrational, it wouldn't help anything, but he just wanted to be left alone. Part of him was working furiously on anything that would offer him even the remotest chance of escape. But the first part just moaned over and over again that he be left alone. That whatever was coming next would be even worse than this.

He thought for a moment of his comrades and wished that he could have made them see sense. If they'd been together, perhaps they could all have escaped. But he had left them behind, and now he was here. Borik felt anger at being abandoned, and shame at his own act of abandonment, and then suddenly sharp talons were raking the flesh of his face.

He tried to recoil, and his head banged against something cold and hard. He tried to cry out, and instead gave a spit-wet gurgle. The clawing fingers closed in a fist, ripping at the material that covered his face and clawing it away in a thick fistful. They left stinging lines of pain across his cheeks and forehead.

Borik forced his eyes open, cringing back in his seat for fear of what he would see. He took in a shadowy room, a cellar maybe? Or a cave? He was strapped into a metal seat and in the half-light he could see a group of grotesque figures leaning over him. Grots, certainly, but freakish and distorted creatures. One wore a huge fleshy toadstool on his head like a hat, whose roots, Borik saw, had squirmed through the grot's scalp to emerge like wiggling worms from around his eyes. Another was scrawny and hunched, his pale red eyes saucer-huge in his wizened face. Borik saw his own bloodied visage reflected in those foul orbs, and his head began to spin. He looked away hurriedly and the creature chuckled to itself. Another of the grots was bloated and leathery, its skin covered in scar tissue from what looked like burns. It wore a bizarre arrangement of bottles, alembics and pipes on its back that jutted well up over its shoulders. Fluids gurgled through them, heated by glowing coals in a metal dish that the grot wore strapped to its head. The sight would have struck Borik as humorous, were it not for the faint stink of burning flesh and the cruel delight in the greenskin's piggy eyes. It was this one who had clawed the covering from Borik's face, and the duardin felt ill as he realised the grot was holding a fistful of thick grey spider's web.

'Oozit?' snarled the boggle-eyed grot in a shrill voice, poking at Borik's chest with a long talon. 'Wassit doon skarprin? Zoggin sneak, grokkit dunno. Kummon, zogger. Krakya jawz open.'

Borik shook his head, struggling to understand the mangled words. His eyes darted around the room and he struggled to make them focus in the hope of spotting some means to escape his tormentors. He saw his armour, his bag and his guns strewn in an untidy heap a few yards away. They looked to have been thoroughly rifled, but still, if he could just reach them. In his addled state, Borik actually strained against his restraints before reality asserted itself.

Somewhere behind him he heard a door creak, then the thud of heavy footfalls getting closer. The grots backed away, their expressions filling with fearful caution. Borik's eyes rolled as he tried to look around, tried to see what was coming.

A shadow fell over him. The metal chair groaned as something huge and heavy settled upon its headrest. Borik felt hot breath upon his scalp and smelled a rank stench of sweat and fungi and something deeper, colder and immeasurably older. He craned his head back and found himself staring up at a truly enormous troggoth. The brute was wearing a crude helm, its yellowed eyes peering at him from the shadows of its eye-pieces with dull hunger.

Borik grunted, and tried again to tug against his restraints. Again, he could barely move at all. He stared upwards, breathing fast and waiting for the thing to rip him from the metal seat and bite his head off in a single mouthful. Instead, the troggoth stepped ponderously aside to make way for a smaller figure who circled around to stand before Borik.

Only now did he realise that the grots hadn't been backing away from the troggoth. They had been retreating in fear of this ghastly figure instead. It was grot, but like none Borik had ever seen. Tall and rangy, the greenskin stood wrapped in ragged black robes with crude Bad Moon glyphs worked into their material. It wore a crown of pale fungi that burrowed their roots into its skull, and held a staff atop which a huge moon-fungus glowed with nauseating light. In its other talon the grot held a shorter staff topped by a human skull, while the train of its robes was borne aloft by a pair of weird moon-faced squigs, who clutched the cloth in their fanged mouths.

Borik could stare only at the greenskin's eyes, though. He saw cunning there – fierce, cruel intellect that studied him like a spiteful child studies a helpless insect. There was madness there too, Borik thought, sharp as a razor and every bit as deadly. This was surely the greenskins' leader, nightmare royalty stepped from the pages of a children's fae-tale to torment him.

The grot rapped its moon-staff against the ground, and its followers dropped to their knees. They bowed to their king and jabbered 'Gloomspite! Da Gloomspite!' over and over.

'Enough, shut yer mouths,' spat the grot king, its words thick and snarling but comprehensible. Borik felt sweat trickle down the back of his neck as the figure stalked closer and peered regally down at him. A cruel smile played at the corners of the grot's wide mouth.

'Oo are you then?' asked the grot. 'Talk, stunty, wot's yer name?'

Borik tried to speak around whatever was gagging him. He could produce only a groan. The grot king scowled, pantomiming noticing Borik's gag for the first time.

'Oh speak up, zog's sakes! And don't talk wiv yer mouth full! Don't yooz know yer addressin' Skragrott da Loonking? You ain't worthy, ya little scrutter. Someone get dis leg bone out of his gob, it's makin' me hungry!'

The grots cackled at their master's jest, and the one with the alembics on his back hastened forwards. Borik heard more spider silk tear, and then blessedly the awful tasting object was ripped from his mouth. He spat bile as he saw the rotting bone now clutched in the grot's hand.

'Come on then, oo are ya?' asked Skragrott, leaning closer. 'And why woz you trying to sneak out of my city?'

'Borik… Borik Jorgensson,' he croaked. 'I was leaving because… the place has… gone downhill of late.'

Skragrott blinked, then his face split in a broad leer.

'Oh, Bad Moon's blessings ladz, we've got one wot finks he's *funny*.' The grin turned hard and mean, and Skragrott brandished his skull-topped staff under Borik's nose. The duardin stiffened as the skull's jaw twitched, and a murmur of jumbled voices spilled from it.

'Listen to me, stunty. You don't want to be funny. You don't want to be clever. All yooz want to be is helpful, and maybe you get out of this alive. Now you don't look like dem uvver gits that fink they can stop us from taking wot's rightfully ours. You ain't a black-robe or a spear-boy. I should know the difference, we've snatched enough of 'em these last days. Nah, you're something else and I want to know what. And I'm Skragrott da Loonking, so I always get what I want.'

'I don't care… if you're the king of that rust-taken moon up there…' panted Borik, his mouth bone dry and still full of that foul taste. 'You're a filthy grot and I'll not tell you anything. Not that I've got anything to tell.'

Skragrott's smile widened, showing an alarming array of fangs.

'You best hope dat's not true, stunty,' he said. 'I can drive ya mad. I can turn you into whatever 'orrible thing I please. Know why? Coz I ain't da *king* of da Bad Moon. No, I'm its emissary!' He shouted the last word, brandishing his staffs and eliciting a worshipful cry from the assembled grots.

'You're… a *hrukni*-faced little monster in a crown made of mushrooms,' snarled Borik. 'I spit on you and your ugly damned moon.'

The crack of his cheekbone breaking echoed through the chamber. Borik's head jolted sideways with the blow, the ringing in his head redoubling. Skragrott hefted his skull staff, now spattered with Borik's blood. He looked as though he were contemplating another blow. Instead, he allowed his leer to resurface.

'I got business here, stunty,' he said. 'I'm doin' the Bad Moon's bidding, and I can't be leavin' nuffin' to chance. You might just be some nobody, but you got a lot of guns and gear if dat's true. Me, I reckon yooz a messenger or something, tryin' to run off and get help. Tryin' to spoil fings before the real fun begins. Well, lucky you, I got some time to spare. Da Loon-shrine ain't proper carved yet, and 'til it is we can't do our ritual. So dat means my ladz get to run rampant for a while and 'ave some fun. And meanwhile, I get to 'ave some fun of my own, wiv you.'

'Keen on the sound of your own voice, aren't you?' said Borik with a grimace. He tongued a loose tooth and winced. Blood trickled down his chin. 'Why are you doing all this anyway?'

The grot king threw back his head and shrieked with laughter. The lunatic mirth cut off as suddenly as it began, and Borik noted with alarm that the other grots had backed away further. Clearly, this was a recognised sign of Skragrott's patience wearing thin.

'You think I'm some stupid little grot chief, gonna try to impress you by gabbin' all my plans out just so yooz can run off wiv wot's in my brainbox and tell your mates?' asked Skragrott. He leaned in again, and this time Borik felt the crackle of barely suppressed power. The Loonking locked eyes with him, and it felt to Borik as though he teetered on the brink of some terrible precipice, powerless to pull himself back from the edge.

'I'm the Bad Moon's will made manifest,' hissed Skragrott, his eyes glowing fiercely. 'I'm malice, and I'm spite, and I'm cruelty and cunnin'. I'm da one that's worthy, and soon enough I'm going to be the one everyone calls Master. But not before I find out what's… in… your… skull…' He punctuated each word with a smart rap of the bloodied skull between Borik's eyes. The blows were sharp and painful, sending sharp jolts through Borik's brain.

'Not yet though,' said Skragrott, straightening up. 'For now, let's see how you enjoy a bit of the Bad Moon's generosity.' So saying, the grot swung his other staff around so the glowing fungus at its tip was pointed straight at Borik. The duardin squirmed, unable to stop himself, desperate for that horrible object not to touch him. He was powerless to stop it, though. Skragrott tapped it once against Borik's chest: just a gentle nudge, accompanied by a string of glottal sounds deep in the grot's throat.

Then he stepped away with a wicked grin and swept from the chamber. The other grots hurried after their king, while the troggoth stomped across the chamber and settled heavily in one corner. It locked its dull gaze on Borik and then became still as stone.

Borik barely gave the monster a thought. His heart was racing painfully and there was a tight pain in his chest that he knew was nothing to do with panic. He felt awful pinching sensations deep inside his torso, and groaned at the sensation of something squirming deep inside him.

What in Grungni's name should he do? Borik tried to restrain his panic. Was he about to burst open from within like the regent militant? He prayed to all the gods of Order that it wasn't so. He might not always have been his best self, but he didn't deserve so horrible a fate as that. The minutes dragged out, Borik waiting with horrified fear as the pinching, twitching feelings inside his chest continued. He felt his breathing getting ragged, and coughed hard, his chest convulsing as though something inside was tearing. His eyes widened as he saw glowing motes dancing on the air in front of his face. Had he coughed those up? What was going on inside his body? Borik's skin crawled and his thoughts spun. Revulsion made his skin tingle. The grot had put something inside him. He couldn't flee, couldn't try to tear it out, couldn't even move. He could only feel that awful squirming going on and on, only endure the tightness and convulsions of his chest, only give occasional wet coughs when he couldn't control his hitching chest any longer, then moan in horror at the sight of the glowing spores that drifted lazily from his mouth to settle upon his body.

They tingled where they landed, and his flesh crawled anew at the thought of whatever horrors their touch might bring. At last his shortness of breath and the awful dizziness of Borik's concussion conspired to plunge him back into a black well of unconsciousness. The duardin welcomed the feeling.

But oblivion didn't last nearly long enough. He was dragged back to wakefulness by a drenching splash of cold water that made him gasp and choke. His eyes opened to a chamber now lit by glowing braziers full of coals. Borik took in the gaggle of grots, now joined by several more freakish creatures. Spider-like clusters of eyes stared at him pitilessly. Weird fungal bat-things fluttered back and forth over pointed black hoods. Something in a huge, grotesque mask cocked its head as it stared at him.

Borik's peripheral vision was tinged with shimmering colours, warped shades of burned crimson and lurid green and sour blue that flickered in and out every time he moved his head. He coughed again, then froze in horror as he looked down at himself. Borik couldn't see his chest, only his arms and legs strapped into the chair's restraints. They were dotted with dozens of bulbous, flesh-coloured toadstools that glowed from within with a mottled light. He felt sick to his stomach as he realised some of the growths had sprouted tufts of body hair the same colour as his. They were fungi, but they were formed from his flesh. He could feel them now as part of him, pulsating, quivering. Borik couldn't help himself, his gorge rose and he retched dryly. All it achieved was to spill another cloud of glowing spores across his body, and he felt misery and madness threaten. What grotesque thing was he becoming?

'Don't have to stay that way,' said a familiar voice, full of mock pity. Borik turned his head to see Skragrott stalk around the chair. The grot reached out a claw and flicked one of the toadstools, which wobbled flabbily. Borik felt it as though Skragrott had poked him in the arm, and just managed to keep down another retching heave.

'I don't think he's so funny now, is he?' sneered Skragrott.

His grot attendants probably couldn't understand his words, Borik thought, but they surely caught his meaning as they all sniggered and hissed.

'I can stop it, and I can turn yooz back,' said Skragrott, who had halted next to one of the burning braziers. 'I got power over da 'shrooms, see? But first you got to tell me what I want to know. Who you workin' for? Why woz you running off, and where to? What d'you know about my plan?'

Borik shook his head and groaned. 'I don't know anything. I came here...' he stopped to spit out a mouthful of spores, trying desperately to avoid his flesh as he did so. 'I came here alone and I'm leaving the same way.'

Skragrott shook his head and pinched the bridge of his long, hooked nose.

'Dat's not what Nukkit here says, though, is it?' he asked, gesturing to the bloated grot with the alchemist's set on his back. 'Nukkit here is my number one Brewgit, and *he* says he seen you at dat big glitzy feast-thing wot the city's boss-king threw. Da one where we 'shroomed him good!' Skragrott cackled nastily. 'Nukkit likes to watch his best work, see. Spent years perfectin' that brew, had to delve into some dark 'n 'orrible places and make sum terrible dealz wiv terrible fings, so after him and his ladz switched dat barrel over in da kitchens, he snuck onto a balcony right up 'igh and watched da fun. And zog me, but what does Nukkit see? He sees yooz and your mates runnin' about tryin' to save everyone and *spoil everyfing!*' Skragrott's screech of rage was so sudden that it made Borik jump. The grot smashed his staff into the brazier with a resounding clang, and hot coals showered across the chamber's floor. Sparks danced in the air, and Borik felt Skragrott's red eyes boring into him through the rising heat haze.

''Urt him,' snarled the Loonking, and his grot underlings closed in around Borik. Daggers flashed in the gloom. Talons dripped poison, and flasks dripped acids. A green-skinned fist brandished a jar full of scrabbling beetles with vicious mandibles and spiky limbs.

The minutes that followed were the longest and amongst the most miserable of Borik's life, a cavalcade of horrors and agony that his mind fled from as best it could. When at last Skragrott recalled his underlings with a rap of his staff against the floor, Borik's vision was swimming and every part of him screamed with raw agony.

'That's it fer now,' said Skragrott. 'Not fun, lyin' to the Loonking, is it? I could stop the transformation, ungrow them flesh-shrooms, but you fibbed to me, stunty, and I don't like them wot fib to me. Makes me think they're up to sumfink sneaky wot I won't like. So, have fun sproutin' and we'll talk again later.'

Borik managed to grunt weakly, the best show of defiance he had in him, and Skragrott stalked from the chamber. As his consciousness wavered, Borik's eyes again settled on his gear.

There was no way he could reach it; that option was closed to him. But as he shifted uncomfortably in his seat, he felt a slight pressure against the base of his back. There was a cold lump there, and as he felt it, Borik realised that he had an escape plan after all.

He just had to work out how to enact it.

A workable scheme still hadn't come to him by the time Skragrott and his retinue returned. This time, as well as his gaggle of hangers-on, the Loonking had something in tow, a wagon of some sort heaved along on rusty wheels by another massive troggoth. Skragrott stopped and looked over Borik with a critical eye before shaking his head ruefully.

'Well you're a zoggin' state and no mistake,' he said.

Borik knew it was true. The fungal curse was consuming his flesh, he could feel it spreading and pinching with every passing minute. The fleshy toadstools had doubled in size since Skragrott's last visit, and to his revulsion a few of them were beginning to show signs of rudimentary features. A shallow pit here that flared like a snuffling nostril. A translucent blister there that could conceivably be an eye. One of the damned things was growing teeth, which jutted obscenely out of pink flesh that looked for all the realms like a gum. Borik could feel that his sanity was fraying along with his anatomy. He could feel skin and muscle softening and becoming rubbery and pliant, his physical form slouching and slowly breaking down. His body was one thirsty, hungry howl of agony, and each time he glanced at himself his revulsion at his own mutating flesh built. He wanted to claw at himself and scream. Instead, he could only sit and suffer as he felt himself teetering upon the brink of madness. He felt sick. He wanted to sob and giggle all at once. But he was Kharadron, and so he did neither.

'Let's try again, before you're too far gone to speak proper,' suggested Skragrott.

Borik grunted at him. Skragrott produced an amulet from within his stinking robes and brandished it in Borik's face. It was crudely carved, as though it had fought against chisel and awl. It looked like an idiot's approximation of a staring eye.

'Who are yer mates?' asked Skragrott. 'Where are yer mates? And what are they up to? Tell me all dat, and I'll fix ya. I swear it on the Bad Moon itself. But you lie to me, and dis here loonstone trinket is gonna light up like da Bad Moon isself.'

Insane as it seemed, Borik believed Skragrott truly would fix him. Even with his vision pulsating between psychedelia and the colours of putrefaction, even with his hearing echoing weirdly and vile itching sensations shuddering through his tortured body, Borik was sure he heard sincerity in the grot's tone. Skragrott could fix this curse, and if he was willing to swear on his deity, he must genuinely be prepared to do so.

The temptation was immense. Borik could save himself from this ghastly torment. He could stop the revolting transformation that was wracking his body, maybe even be set free at last from this damned city he had never wished to come to in the first place. What loyalty did he owe his former comrades anyway? They had cut him loose! They had let him walk away! The code was clear, you stuck your neck out for your shipmates but everyone else was just a mark to be profited from. What profit was there in continuing to undergo torture for those who were no longer a part of his crew?

A single thought cut through his exhausted delirium, a clear memory from maybe a thrice-turning before Varlen donned that damned crown. It hadn't been a special evening, hadn't mattered at all in the grand scheme of things, but it had mattered to Borik. They'd finished a job watching over some ore caravans travelling between Char-Vale and Hammerhal, and he remembered it now because he had almost been dragged into a Lashrat nest. He certainly would have been if his comrades hadn't risked their own lives to come back for him. After making it to their destination in one piece, they had taken their pay to their favourite ale house, the Vandus' Revenge. They had been well into their cups, just laughing about some stupid jest of Varlen's. Hendrick, quietly amused, happy in his garrulous brother's shadow. Romilla sat close to him as she always tried to be, and Eleanora close to her in turn, utterly absorbed in whatever gadget she was tinkering with. Bartiman had been holding court and Olt had laughed so hard he spilled his ale. Even Aelyn had raised a smile. Borik remembered that night – how he had felt, for just a moment, that if he never took to the skies again he might feel contentment with that, providing he had these good souls to guide his course.

They might not have understood the artycles of the code, might not have seen the sense of what Borik had been trying to tell them, but they had been good and true comrades. He wouldn't betray them now.

'I have nothing… to say to you… grot…' spat Borik. His voice sounded thick and weird in his ears, as though he might be melting from the inside out.

The crude stone pendant in Skragrott's hand glimmered with a sickly light that hurt to look upon. It turned one side of the Loonking's grotesque face corpse-pale, and reflected in his maddened eyes.

'I was very much hoping that'd be your attitude,' said Skragrott with a grin, stowing the amulet back inside his robes. 'I'm goin' to make you talk anyway, just so's ya know. But before I do, let's have a quick look at what you got in store for ya when I'm done!'

He gripped the tarpaulin that covered the wagon and ripped it dramatically aside to reveal a wheeled cage with thick metal bars. Borik moaned in horror at what he saw slumped inside. Bulging, rubbery flesh squirmed and twisted. Flesh-fungi pulsated, glowing from within as they blinked mutant eyes and slathered with sprouted tongues. Long, floppy tendrils beat weakly against the bars and coiled around them, trailing rubbery digits that bent and flexed revoltingly and left slime trails in their wake. Somewhere in amongst that bulbous mass of flesh and fungi, Borik saw two human eyes staring at him in deranged misery.

Kasmit. That had been the watchman's name.

Kasmit.

Borik looked away, breathing hard, hanging tightly to the last shreds of his sanity. He felt nothing but pity for the poor thing that had once been a man, trapped in that cage for the grots' amusement. Yet in that instant Borik also felt a sliver of hope. He could escape this yet. Silently, he thanked Kasmit and readied himself.

'So now you know what bein' unhelpful has earned you, it's time to make it up to me,' said Skragrott. He turned to his assembled minions and snarled out a series of words. Borik caught the name Nukkit, and cringed back as he saw the grot alchemist shambling over. Nukkit gave him a horrible leer as he cranked a spigot on the side of his alchemy set and let a reeking purple fluid drizzle into a test-tube that he held up to catch it.

'Troof water,' said Skragrott brightly. 'Makes you tell us whatever we want, don't it? Could've just given you this to start off, but… nah, not much fun, izzit? Already lost control of your body, stunty. Brain and gob go next!'

Borik coughed weakly, dribbling spores onto himself, and tried to gasp out some words. As he did so, he relaxed what remained of his left arm and pulled it slowly back towards him. He felt his rubbery flesh tug and give around the metal manacle that held his wrist down. Bright jolts of pain shot up his arm as fleshy toadstools were dragged under the manacle's metal edge. He stopped. Any further and they'd snap, and for all he knew spray blood or spores of Grungni-knew-what all over the place. He couldn't give himself away. Not yet.

'Too late to start talkin' now, stunty. Ain't goin' to earn you anything,' spat Skragrott, but all the same he stepped forwards alongside Nukkit. The bloated grot leaned in and gripped Borik's jaw, squishing the rubbery flesh and opening his mouth like a spout. The sensation was a new kind of revulsion, but Borik steeled himself.

Any second now, he would escape. He had them where he wanted them. He remembered again that feeling as he had sat in the torchlight and laughed with his friends, and he let it give him strength.

'Know... a... secret... you... want... to... know...' he gurgled, and Skragrott held up a taloned finger. Nukkit paused with the potion before Borik's face.

'If this is you bein' funny again, you'll regret it,' said the Loonking. 'Go on, what's yer big secret? Never know, might even save ya yet.'

'I took another... in case the first one... didn't work...' croaked Borik, then as Skragrott blinked at him in confusion he wrenched his arm backwards with all his strength. Skin split and stalks tore. Blood sprayed in stinking squirts, and with what remained of his strength Borik bent his rubbery arm around behind himself and pressed one thick thumb down upon the firing stud of Eleanora's spare bomb.

'I'll greet my ancestors with your skull at my belt,' spat Borik. The last thing he saw was Skragrott's face twisting in an expression of horror, and something huge slamming into the Loonking from the side. There was a searing blast of light and heat, and Borik Jorgensson made good his escape.

The echoes of the blast subsided. Black smoke filled the chamber. Little remained of the duardin or the chair he had been strapped to, barring blackened ruin and drifting cinders. A bloated grot lay in a heap of smashed glass nearby, his flesh dissolving in the soup of lethal compounds that had spilled from his alembics to douse him.

Another corpse lay beside him, a huge one so badly blackened and burned that even its troggoth flesh could not regenerate the damage. Still the body stirred, the stump of one arm lifting slowly up and then flopping aside.

Skragrott the Loonking crawled out from under his slain troggoth bodyguard with a look of pure, murderous rage on his scorched features.

'They're all going to suffer fer that, stunty,' he snarled, waving off the scorched and frantic grots that swarmed to help him up. 'I'll make zoggin' sure they all suffer fer that...'

CHAPTER FIFTEEN

PLANS

'We agree, then? We blow it up?' asked Romilla. She leant over the desk in the safehouse office, her expression grim and her injured side tightly bandaged. The wound was painful, but she had found the sensation brought clarity and revelation. So often did one have to suffer for Sigmar's gifts, she thought.

'Seems the only safe way to dispose of so huge a quantity of such a perilous poison,' replied Watchman Thackeray. 'Sigmar knows we can't risk physical contact with the stuff. Can't exactly tip it away, either. It'd end up in the canal one way or another and we'd end up doing the grots' work for them.'

'If I knew more about its composition, I might be able to formulate something that could neutralise its potency?' suggested Bartiman, who sat on a stool with a spare cloak bundled around his shoulders.

'That would take time, and I do not believe we have much of that left,' said Aelyn. Her eyes flicked to Eleanora, also seated, grey skinned and sweating profusely.

'A few brave souls have reached us from other safehouses, but there's a lot more have vanished without trace,' said Watchman Shen, his tone dubious. 'There's still no sign of Lieutenant Grange. At this point we're assuming he's lost. Either way, from what sketchy intelligence we've been able to gather I can tell you that even with survivors of the watch and the militia combined, our numbers aren't great.'

'If we throw everything into a strike at the grots' poison, we may lose any chance of recapturing the city from them,' said Watchman Marika.

Romilla felt a surge of sympathy for her, for all the people of this city who had not asked for nor invited the curse that had come upon them. But she had to make them see.

'I wanted to believe this city could be saved, but we barely made it to the guild house and back alive,' she said earnestly. 'You've heard the reports just as we have. The Slump, vanished into a seething pit of a billion hungry insects. Greenskins raising fungal gibbets in the squares of Marketsway and ransacking every home and business for victims. Spiders big as town houses spinning webs between what's left of the Rookswatch towers, while the smaller ones prowl the rooftops and string cocooned victims up from chimneypots and weather vanes. Then there's the devastation from the meteors, the spore clouds still swirling through the skies, the infection spreading through what's left of the populace… Borik may have been an unsympathetic oaf about it, but I'm sorry, he was right. Draconium is lost.'

Silence followed Romilla's words. Somewhere in the middle distance came the faint sounds of screaming, swiftly cut off. Elsewhere, jabbering voices rose in a gleeful chorus of the damned. Floorboards creaked above them and everyone jumped.

'Just our sentries,' said Shen, though he kept a hand on his pistol all the same.

'Captain Morthan entrusted you–' began Marika hotly, but Thackeray shook his head.

'They're right, Marika. It's a hard dose to swallow but we lost this fight before we even had a chance to draw our blades.'

'The guild house armoury still stands,' Marika replied. 'We could wage a guerrilla campaign, clear them out bit by bit, get the surviving citizens to safety. And if the rains return, then we'd see how long their filthy fungus stands up to a good honest Draconium downpour. Scald the lot of them, I say.'

'We might hurt them, for a while, but look at this place,' said Thackeray. He gestured to the patches of damp spreading across the walls, the nub-like toadstools that had begun to push up through the wood of the desk. They had cleaned glistening spiders' webs out of the corners several times already, but somehow, they kept returning larger and more sinister-looking than before. 'While the Bad Moon hangs above our city, I do not believe we can stop the corruption that is spreading, and I don't think we can count on the rains. Sigmar's hammer, we've not even seen cheffing night and day now for… well, does anyone know?'

'It has been in the region of three days and four hours since the Bad Moon rose,' said Aelyn.

'Right,' said Thackeray, faltering for a moment then ploughing on. 'Even if we could somehow banish that damned moon from the skies, even if we could stop the rot, there must be thousands of grots and monsters infesting Draconium by this point. We're outnumbered so severely it's a dark jest. We're prey in our own city, and they the predators.'

'Well then, should we not try to evacuate those who still live?' demanded Shen. 'We swore an oath to protect the people of Draconium, Thackeray. Are you going to let some sellswords talk you into abandoning that in favour of a vainglorious gesture of defiance?'

'Vainglorious? Sellswords?' Bartiman's voice was indignant, and Romilla was glad to hear at least a ghost of his normal vitriol return. 'Young man, we could have turned around and walked away any *number* of times this last turning, and left you fools and your doomed city to rot. But we haven't, have we? We've fought, and we've lost, right alongside you, long after the coin dried up, because above all we serve Sigmar, as do you! There is nothing vainglorious about that!'

'Even if you could gather the survivors, even if you could somehow lead them out of Draconium without suffering the same fate as those cultists, what then?' asked Romilla. 'The only safe direction to take them would be south, towards the settled lands around Hammerhal. The greenskins' poisons would catch up to you and that would be an end to it.'

She watched the expressions of the three watchmen carefully. She understood the frustration and struggle she saw there. Romilla knew what it was to feel powerless as those you had sworn to protect were taken from you.

'So, we blow it all up,' said Shen, eventually. His shoulders slumped in defeat. 'How?'

Marika turned away and paced to the window, waves of bitterness and anger rolling off her.

'Eleanora?' prompted Romilla. The engineer looked up, her eyes fighting to focus. Romilla had given her every tincture and potion she could think of that might halt the spread of poison from that damned spider bite; she had laid hands upon Eleanora's wound and prayed for Sigmar's intercession, but she had felt only the malevolence of the Bad Moon burning down upon them, and the faint but nauseating sensation of things *twitching* beneath the taut skin of Eleanora's shin. Romilla felt dread for the fate of her young ward, but also a fierce pride that despite everything Eleanora had not given in.

'My first thought was that we could use the stores of powder that you described in the guild house,' said Eleanora, her words sounding laboured.

'Those stores are meant for our cannons, not for indiscriminate demolition,' snapped Marika.

'It doesn't matter what they're meant for, they wouldn't be any good to us anyway,' replied Eleanora. 'The last we saw, the Moonclan grots were making stacks of poison barrels beside their idol in the middle of Fountains Square. Located directly beside the headwater of the canal into which we're assuming they wish to dump the poison. I believe we can therefore safely work on the basis that they do not intend to move the poison again until they are ready to use it. Providing they have not already done so, obviously.'

A few faces paled at this thought, but Thackeray shook his head.

'A runner reached us from the guild hall an hour ago. She reported no sign of the poisons being dumped yet. Lots of what looked like ritual preparation, though.'

Eleanora blinked at Thackeray, began to count off the fingers of her right hand, stopped herself and then carried on as though he hadn't spoken.

'Making a direct attempt to reach the poison seems unlikely to succeed,' she said. 'Too exposed, too many greenskins. Besides which, the powder barrels are large and unwieldy and would require wagons for transportation, which we do not possess.'

'All right, not the powder barrels, we understand that much,' said Shen impatiently.

'Just let her do this her way, you won't be disappointed,' said Romilla, her tone firm.

'I then factored in alternative methods of approach. Specifically, the sewer tunnels that run beneath all the major streets of this city. While I was working in the Ironweld Guildhouse I acquired reading materials on my rest breaks and learned as much as I could about the city's infrastructure and design. They hold... um, held... extremely detailed plans of Draconium's transport systems, defensive structures, some impressively advanced spark-lantern patents, and the sewer network.'

'You're suggesting we could approach through the sewers, get the powder supplies in under the square?' asked Thackeray. 'We'd need maps from the guildhouse, wouldn't we?'

Eleanora stopped long enough to check he wasn't going to say anything else, then continued.

'The powder barrels still could not be deployed in this way. Too confined a space, too slow a method, and we wouldn't be able to guarantee a large enough concentration of explosives in the pumping chamber located beneath Fountains Square, especially if it has sustained structural damage, which seems likely.'

'So what then?' snapped Shen. 'Sigmar's oath, we'll all be dead by the time you get to the point.'

Eleanora levelled a flat stare at him. 'Without understanding the reasoning behind what I am suggesting, you would only ask unhelpful questions that I would then have to provide answers for anyway. By showing you how I reached my conclusions, I save us all time having to explain why I am right.'

Romilla couldn't help but feel a little spark of amusement at Shen's expression, despite the grimness of the situation. He looked as though he had swallowed a frog, she thought.

'By all means, continue. We will not interrupt again,' said Thackeray stiffly.

'The thermal pipes,' said Eleanora, leaping suddenly to the point as though it should be obvious to everyone in the room. 'According to the plans that I memorised, they draw vast quantities of heat and pressure up from the volcanic reservoir beneath

Draconium, then diffuse it through a series of shunt-pipes and cogwork heat-locks while bleeding off the excess via venting valves at regular intervals. If given access to the shunting board controls in the pipeworks, and assuming damage to the pipe network itself has not been in excess of workable parameters, I ought to be able to close enough valves and direct enough pressure flows to create a catastrophic overpressure event directly beneath the square.'

'And that would be a violent enough explosion to guarantee the poison was destroyed, not just, say, blown sky high and scattered across the city?' asked Marika.

'It would,' replied Eleanora. 'I calculate that with the correct application of heat and pressure, magnified by the ferocity-factor applicable to all Aqshian natural magics, we will entirely incinerate the barrels and boil off the poison within. In addition, anything stood within one hundred paces of the greenskins' meteor shrine will be killed in the blast, which I believe will cave in the heart of the square entirely. To warn you of an undesireable side-effect – if successful, my plan will definitely render the thermal heating system permanently inoperable.'

'I think the people of Draconium have greater worries than their heating just now,' said Romilla.

'Will it definitely work?' asked Shen.

Eleanora just stared at him, then counted off her fingers, right then left.

'If she says it will work, then it will,' said Romilla. 'The question is, how do we make it happen?'

'I've heard nothing of the pipeworks, but I can't imagine it's any safer or less beset than any other part of Draconium,' said Thackeray. 'Send too small a band of soldiery and we risk being caught or devoured. Send too large a force and we'll draw the attention of the greenskins from half the city. And Sigmar knows, we can't let any harm come to Ms VanGhest there – none of the rest of us would have the first notion of how to effect the act of sabotage you just described.'

'What if we staged a diversionary attack?' asked Aelyn. 'Ensure that our enemies are looking anywhere but the pipeworks at the crucial moment?'

'The square itself?' suggested Thackeray.

'Sticking one's hand into the squig burrow, rather, isn't it?' asked Bartiman.

'Yes, but that's exactly why it's a good idea,' said Marika, sounding excited. 'Their idol is there, yes? Their poison? If I were to gamble, I would suggest their leaders can't be far from the site either, or who else would be commanding such industry from such anarchic creatures?'

'All their most crucial targets, all in one place,' mused Romilla. 'That *would* prompt a response wouldn't it?'

'It would be all the more dangerous, that's for damned sure,' said Bartiman, but his tone carried more excitement than his words. 'I mean, you do remember that is the same square that we're planning to blow up, yes? With fire?'

'Hit and fade,' said Aelyn. 'We muster as much strength as we can, send runners to the other safehouses, to the guild house... we coordinate on a signal, make as much noise as we can on the way in to really draw their attention. Meanwhile, Eleanora and a band of your watchmen make for the pipeworks, reach the controls and do what must be done.'

'We could instruct the garrisons to evacuate their civilians a short time after the signal, also?' suggested Marika. 'It's the best chance they're going to have to get the people of Draconium out of here.'

'Slim chance all the same,' said Bartiman. 'And damnation but there's a lot that could go wrong with this plan. What if the greenskins don't take the bait? What if Eleanora gets to the pipeworks and finds it seething with monsters, or just wrecked? What if the pipes aren't up to snuff after all the tremors and explosions and what have you?'

'That, I'm afraid, is where faith must come in, Bartiman,' said Romilla. 'I don't think anyone else has a better plan?' She looked around the room, receiving only blank expressions and shaken heads in reply. 'No, then this is what we will do, and we will offer up prayers to Sigmar, to Grungni, to Alarielle and all the other gods of good that it works.'

'Righto then,' said Bartiman with a wheezing chuckle. 'Just wanted to check. I don't think Eleanora should go alone, though, eh? No offence,' he said, gesturing airily to the assembled watchmen. 'But the Swords of Sigmar watch out for one another. One of us should accompany our young engineer.'

'It should be you,' said Aelyn to Romilla.

The priest had seen this coming, and took a deep breath.

'You know that I would be of great help in the march upon the square,' she said. 'My prayers, my oratory – I was trained for the battlefield, Aelyn.'

'And yet, if Eleanora's… condition… overcomes her before the work can be completed, this will all be for naught,' said Aelyn. 'You alone possess such skills.'

Romilla knew she could have added that the priest had acted as a virtual mother-figure to Eleanora for years, that the two shared a bond the rest of the Swords couldn't touch. She didn't need to. They all knew it.

'Very well,' said Romilla, and Eleanora favoured her with a wan smile.

'We'll detail half of the watchmen in this safehouse to accompany you,' said Shen. 'That'll give you twelve able-bodied protectors, Ms VanGhest. The rest of us will accompany the diversionary attack.'

'I'll have Yenstin and O'Mord hang back with the civilians,' said Marika. 'I'll have them wait for a steady count of six hundred then take the survivors out along Cotter's Rise and down through the Shiftings. It's the quickest route to the East Postern.'

'We'll send out runners at once,' said Shen. 'It will take time to disseminate the plan, and we don't have time to dicker with anyone squeamish. We shall just have to pray to Sigmar that they hold to the plan.'

'What shall be our signal?' asked Aelyn.

'We've a few signalling rockets still dry in the first-floor armoury,' said Marika. 'I'll have a team take them a couple of streets over where they won't draw undue attention to this safehouse, then let them off. The whole city ought to see those things fly.'

With that, the plan was set and the watchmen first class hurried off to issue orders and prepare their soldiery. The Swords of Sigmar were left in the office to gird themselves for one last fight. They were all injured, Romilla thought, all bone tired and numb from their losses.

'We are still here,' she said aloud, and her friends looked up from their preparations. 'We are still alive, still able to do Sigmar's will, still able to avenge our friends.'

'In the names of Varlen, Hendrick and Olt then,' said Aelyn. She didn't add Borik, Romilla noted. They all wanted to hope their comrade had made it out alive. To name him would have felt like a jinx.

'Good fortune to us all, and we will meet again when the battle is done,' said Romilla, raising her hammer amulet and tracing it through the air in blessing.

Bartiman gave a dry chuckle. 'And for those who don't make it,' he said, 'we'll be sure to meet again in the Land of Endings, where Hendrick, Olt and Varlen wait.'

CHAPTER SIXTEEN

LURKING

In the event, it took several hours to send out runners, receive replies and ready the city's meagre forces for their last fight back. Crouched in the gloom of the safehouse, the Swords of Sigmar could do little more than watch the damp creep up the walls, stand their turns peering out of the windows and watching for danger, and try not to think too hard about what came next.

Aelyn was relieved when, at last, Marika's team of signalmen slipped out of the safehouse's side door with their armful of alchemical rockets. When the projectiles exploded in bright red and green starbursts a few minutes later, she was standing in the house's hallway amongst the press of watchmen and her few remaining comrades, her weapons in hand. Aelyn did not show her feelings as the humans did, but the creatures that had attacked this city had cost her much and caused her great pain and sorrow. Now those feelings turned to a cold and furious determination. Bartiman had been right, their plan was a desperate one and liable to fail, but Aelyn vowed that it would not do so on her account. She would honour her distant Wanderer clan with her deeds this day, even if word never reached them of how she had fought and, likely, fallen.

'That's the signal,' said Watchman Shen, who stood at the fore. 'Thackeray, you and your men get her to the pipehouse no matter what, understood?'

'In the name of Sigmar and Draconium,' replied Watchman Thackeray.

'No harm will come to Eleanora while we draw breath,' added Romilla. Looking at her comrade's shaved, scarred and tattooed scalp, her broad shoulders, heavy warhammer and look of absolute determination, Aelyn could well believe it.

'We do this now in Captain Morthan's name,' said Shen, and the assembled watchmen gave a murmur of approval. They would not shout, or cheer, not yet while they still wished to remain unseen. Soon, though, thought Aelyn. Soon.

Hoods were raised, gloves and cloth masks adjusted to ward off the filthy moonlight and the choking spores. Pistols were checked one last time and halberds hefted.

Shen opened the safehouse door, pistol drawn, and led the way out into the twilight.

Watchman Thackeray led the way through the city's winding streets, and Romilla followed with Eleanora close on her heels. Their bodyguard of watchmen maintained a loose cordon around them, alert for the slightest sign of danger.

The footing was treacherous as they tramped over slimy cobbles and through thick outcroppings of fungi. A spore-thick mist drifted between the buildings and reduced visibility to a hazy suggestion of shadows through which the Bad Moon's light shone, diffuse and leprous. It made it hard to avoid tripping over the rotting corpses that lay scattered about the streets, their bodies thick with mould. The effect was worsened by the waves of strange energies that pulsed from the Bad Moon above, causing them moments of sudden dizziness and confusing aural hallucinations, and making it appear that ghosts wrought in psychedelic hues flickered through the mists around them.

The pipehouse stood on the edge of the Pipers' District, a good half-hour's trek through the city streets under such conditions. Eleanora had suggested another route, however, one they were now approaching. Thackeray stopped as snarls and jabbered words echoed through the muffling fog. He motioned for them to close up, and backed carefully into the shadows of a half-collapsed eatery. Romilla glanced through a shattered window into the eatery's dark interior as they hunkered outside. A rudimentary barricade had been raised here, she saw, fashioned from heaped tables and benches. It was sundered at its centre, smashed apart, its splintered wreckage damp with rot and seething with burrowing worms. Further back, she saw the suggestion of flyblown corpses.

Romilla's attention snapped back to the street as something moved in the spore-mists. She saw dark shapes, short and hunched with pointed black hoods and glinting red eyes. The grots picked their way along the street in a ragged column, a dozen or so chattering in their crude, spiteful voices. One near the front hefted a tattered flag depicting a leering half-moon on a field of black. Romilla saw freshly flensed skulls dangling from the banner's cross-pole, crude twine looped through their eye sockets and beetles skittering over their surface. Several of the greenskins looked to be arguing with one another, while one near the back was carrying a human-sized helmet upside down like a bucket, plucking small objects out of it and popping them into its mouth with gusto. Romilla did her best not to look any closer. She had no desire to find out what such creatures considered a delicacy.

One grot was being towed along by a hound-like thing that strained at its leash and snuffled and snarled. It was mostly snout, Romilla saw, with beady eyes that stared malevolently ahead, a mouth stuffed full of sharp fangs, and a pair of stubby little clawed legs. Her heart beat faster as she saw the beast catch their scent, snapping its snout around suddenly, nostrils flaring. She gripped her hammer tight and placed a hand on Eleanora's shoulder as the creature took off across the street towards them, but as its lead snapped taut its greenskin handler dragged it back with a bad-tempered yank. The grot snarled at his beast, which snapped and growled at him until a hard kick sent it scampering out in front again. Romilla relaxed slightly, and one by one the procession of grots vanished into the murk.

'Too close,' whispered Thackeray. 'We're almost there. Hurry.' The watchman rose and set off again along the street, pistol drawn. Romilla followed.

A few minutes more brought them to an intersection. The street they were on sloped steeply uphill from here, while the road that met it crossways dropped away on both sides between the clustered roofs of houses.

'It is located a short way up the hill on our left,' said Eleanora. They advanced, passing dark and crumbling buildings that reminded Romilla of the flensed skulls that had dangled from the grots' banner. This city was truly dead, she thought. The greenskins and their Bad Moon had killed it.

Ahead, they heard a ululating shriek. There was a muffled gunshot, its flare of fire barely visible further uphill. Everyone tensed.

'How much further?' hissed Thackeray.

Eleanora froze momentarily, eyes darting and lips moving soundlessly.

'El, he doesn't need it exact,' whispered Romilla.

'Fifteen yards, give or take a handful,' whispered Eleanora, looking none too happy at being forced to approximate.

'Move, uphill, fast,' ordered Thackeray. 'Keep low and quiet, and let's hope this entrance of yours is there.'

They loped uphill, bent double and desperately trying to mind their footing. Romilla felt something crunch wetly under her boot, heard an insectile squeal, kept moving. A taller structure loomed suddenly on their left, a stone tower with a series of large dials on its front that reminded Romilla of clock faces. Below them was a metal door with an iron ring set into its surface.

'That door,' said Eleanora, pointing.

'Rechter, get it open, the rest of you, eyes open, guns up,' whispered Thackeray.

A burly watchman hurried forwards. He grabbed the metal ring and tried to turn it, cursing softly as his gloved hands slid on the clammy metal. Romilla brandished her hammer and put out an arm to shield Eleanora, who had drawn a pair of especially large and formidable looking pistols clearly of her own design. The other watchmen clustered close, putting their bodies between Eleanora and whatever had uttered that terrible shriek.

Now came the sound of slapping footfalls and sharp, gurgling breaths. A weird giggle skirled through the mists, getting closer by the second.

'Rechter...' urged Thackeray, as loudly as he dared.

'I know, I know, I'm—'

Watchman Rechter never finished his sentence. One of the spore-sickened fell from above, dropping through the murk to land on him like some huge and horrible spider. Rechter was smashed flat with a cry and the crack of breaking bone. Three more infected burst from the mists as he fell, sprinting flat out down the hill. One had once been a portly noblewoman, whose tattered finery trailed behind her like a comet-trail and whose rouge had mixed with bloody froth on her cheeks. Another was a militiaman whose left arm was nothing more than a bloody stump.

The third was Taverton Grange.

The sight of their former commanding officer charging at them out of the mists was just enough to cause the watchmen to hesitate for a lethal split second. Yellow-eyed and screaming like a gheist, Grange launched himself through the air and hit a watchman with crunching force. The two of them bounced and rolled down the hill and out of sight.

The noblewoman ducked under a panicked halberd-jab and hit another watchman in a tackle around their midriff. The watchman was slammed onto his back, his head cracking painfully from the cobbles. The infected reared up, her throat bulged obscenely, and she vomited a stream of frothing filth into his open mouth and eyes.

The one-armed attacker Romilla intercepted with a thunderous hammer-blow to the face. His legs shot out in front of him and he crashed down amidst the fungi, thrashing out his death throes.

'Rechter! Rechter, get that door open! Oh, damnation,' spat Thackeray as Rechter and his attacker rose from the floor. Both of them gibbered, twitched and spat foam. Thackeray raised his pistol and squeezed the trigger. The shot rang out through the murk and watchman Rechter was thrown back against the metal door with a clang. He slid to the floor, smearing gore down the door as he went. Eleanora's pistols barked, their muzzle flares magnesium white in the gloom, and the other infected simply came apart in a welter of blood.

'Sigmar's hammer, El, those are fearsome!'

Lieutenant Grange burst from the murk again, this time sprinting uphill, and swiped his talons at Romilla's face. She reared back with a cry, feeling lines of fire rake across her skin. Romilla teetered on the edge of her balance, and the memory flashed up of her tripping in the feasting hall, of her falling as Hendrick was infected and turned. The thought of the same thing happening to Eleanora hit her like a thunderbolt. Anger, absolute boiling fury surged through Romilla, and a halo of blue-white light sprang into being about her temples as the power of the God-King flowed through her. She drove her forehead into Grange's aristocratic nose with all the force she could muster, caving it in with a crunch of bone and sending him reeling back. Her hammer followed, swinging up under Grange's chin so hard that it ripped his jaw clean off and sent it spinning through the air. Tongue dangling, foam bubbling from the ruin of his throat, Lieutenant Grange staggered and then toppled lifeless to the floor.

More gunshots rang out as the noblewoman and her victim came at the watchmen with feral howls. Romilla saw that Thackeray had shoved Rechter's corpse unceremoniously aside and was straining with all his might at the slippery metal of the door's ring. Grabbing Eleanora, she dashed across the street and threw her strength behind Thackeray's. The door ring gave a rusted squeal as it finally turned, and then spun.

Romilla looked back. Four watchmen had fallen. Another was staggering and clawing spore-thick foam out of her eyes. She would turn any moment, Romilla knew. Lieutenant Grange's first victim burst from the murk downslope, jutting jaw thick with new-sprouted tusks, yellow eyes staring. A bullet took the creature in the shoulder, but it kept coming. One of the surviving watchmen screamed at the sight, turned to run and took a taloned fist to the face. He fell like a sack of grain.

'Get through the door,' snarled Thackeray. Romilla nodded, understanding.

'I'm sorry,' she said and ducked through the doorway, Eleanora close behind. Thackeray followed and, with a last anguished glance into the street he heaved the door shut at their backs. It closed heavily, cutting off a panicked scream from the street beyond. Something hit the door from the other side with a dull clang, which repeated several times then stopped. Thackeray spun the wheel closed from their side, his teeth gritted.

Eleanora stared in shock but said nothing. Romilla laid a hand on Thackeray's shoulder, but he shrugged it off.

'Can those things open this door?' he asked.

Romilla hefted her hammer and swung it in a tight arc that dented the wheel and buckled it sideways into its housing.

'Not any more,' she said.

'Come on then,' said Thackeray. 'And let's hope that this tunnel of yours exists, Ms VanGhest, or we just entombed ourselves.'

They were standing in a stone passage, claustrophobically tight and with only the faintest grey glow in its corners. Thackeray lit his spark-lantern, painting everything in harsh white illumination. Romilla nodded her thanks and let him lead the way, gesturing for Eleanora to walk between them where she was least likely to be attacked. Eleanora had assured them this was the entrance to one of the pipe network's monitoring stations, a site through which the pipes ran all the way from their source and then on in a radiating spread to the more well-to-do businesses and homes of Marketsway.

Sure enough, the tight corridor quickly emptied out onto

an iron gantry that ran around the inside of the tower. Above, metal stairways and more gantries vanished up into darkness. Below, they dropped two more floors into a circular pit that was dominated by a huge ironclad device that looked to Romilla like an overly elaborate boiler. Thick forests of pipes spewed from one wall to plunge into the device, which spat them out as a tangle of thinner conduits that vanished off in many other directions.

'Down there,' said Eleanora, over the rumble and hiss of the machinery. 'We need to follow the big pipes back to the pipehouse.'

They descended swiftly, their footfalls clanging hollow on the metal floors. Even here, the metal of the gantries and stairs was slick with slime and the walls furred with mould. Bio-luminescent fungi sprouted around the boiler-machine's base.

'Is it still in operation?' asked Romilla, surprised.

'The function of the pipehouse is at least in part automated,' replied Eleanora. 'It has to be. If everyone got ill, or the building was evacuated or whatever else, if the system couldn't regulate itself, it would soon explode and cause substantial damage.'

'Which is precisely what we're going to do to these filthy greenskins, isn't it?' asked Thackeray, scowling. His eyes had taken on a haunted, slightly manic look that Romilla both recognised and did not like the look of.

'Absolutely,' she said. 'We just have to steel ourselves and do our duty in Sigmar's name, no matter how painful that duty might be. You did the right thing, Thackeray.'

'Don't need your approval, knew what I was doing and why,' said Thackeray stiffly. 'Doesn't mean they won't all be waiting for me in the Land of Endings when my time comes though, does it?'

They stood in silence for a moment, their ears full of the hiss and bang of the boiler mechanisms. Eleanora swiftly checked over some dials and gauges, frowning and shaking her head.

'Problem?' asked Thackeray.

'This doesn't look right,' she said, sounding distracted. 'There's… some damage… somewhere… We need to get moving, right away. The system's pressure levels are slowly dropping, and if they deteriorate much further then the plan won't succeed.'

'Of course,' sighed Thackeray. 'Where?'

Eleanora pointed to where the dense nest of pipes flowed into the chamber. There was a crawlspace, just large enough for a human, which ran along the top of the pipes. Thick leather tarps had been laid over the pipes to allow people to crawl along them without getting scalded. Still, Romilla winced as she placed her hand on one. This would not be a comfortable experience.

'Of course,' said Thackeray again. 'Soonest begun, soonest done. Eleanora, follow on my heels. Romilla, rear guard.'

Romilla raised an eyebrow and gestured for him to take the lead. Thackeray obliged, hauling himself up into the crawlspace with a grunt and a hiss of discomfort, and began crawling.

'I hope our friends are having an easier time of things,' said Eleanora before scrambling up onto the pipes.

'I highly doubt it,' sighed Romilla, quashing her worries as best she could and following the engineer into the hot, dark tunnel.

Aelyn ducked behind the wreckage of a cart. Stubby black arrows thunked into its opposite side, causing rot-wet wood to splinter. An arrowhead burst through the wood bare inches in front of her face, its barbed head dripping a viscous poison that sizzled where it dripped onto the cobbles.

'They've got archers on the roof of the alchemists' shop,' she shouted. Then she rose, nocking her arrow, drawing and loosing all in one smooth motion before dropping back out of sight. A human archer wouldn't even have had time to aim at a target. Aelyn's sharp ears picked out the distinct thud of her shaft striking a grot in the chest, the bubbling wheeze of its breath and the clatter and thump as it rolled bonelessly down the slate roof and plunged to the cobbles below. She nocked another arrow, rose, loosed, dropped, then repeated the process again.

Several militia-militant slid in next to her, their shaved scalps, chainmail and robes distinctive. They rose from cover themselves and shot more arrows at the grot archers. Two of them ducked back down. The other toppled backwards with a greenskin's arrow jutting from his cheek, its poison eating away at his flesh with a wet sizzle.

'How much further until we reach Fountains Square?' asked Aelyn. One militiaman just looked at her coldly. The other glanced back up the street as bands of watchmen and militia followed them in.

'One more intersection, then a short stretch of street and we'll be there,' she said. 'They said this was your plan. That true?'

'I had a hand in it,' said Aelyn, rising to loose off an arrow then dropping again as a shrill scream greeted her efforts.

'Cheffing stupid plan,' said the militiaman, and spat. 'Going to get us all killed.'

Aelyn replied with a level stare. The woman stared back, then flinched as another volley of arrows hit the side of the wagon. Fewer this time, noted Aelyn.

'Move up! Move up!' That was Watchman First Class Shen's voice, raised from somewhere amidst the main advance. They had started as a small party, slinking through the carcass of their dead city, but as they had got closer to the square they had been joined by one band of watchmen or militia after another.

Aelyn had recognised Watchman Kole amongst the newcomers, shooting her a nod and receiving a fierce grin in return.

The greenskins had responded swiftly to their advance, grots spilling from the shells of buildings, dropping from shattered windows and clambering up out of pits and shattered sewer gratings. Initially their attacks had been piecemeal and ill organised, easily repulsed with volleys of shots and a few well placed blows. As the defenders of Draconium advanced, however, the greenskin numbers thickened rapidly. As they passed beneath an arching stone bridge hung with dangling human corpses, bellowing troggoths had emerged from the shadows to plough into their ranks with clubs swinging.

Flapping monsters with bat-wings and gaping maws had swooped down to bite watchmen's heads clean off. Spider-mounted greenskins had ambushed the advancing forces several times, galloping straight down sheer stone walls and scuttling along the undersides of road tunnels while emitting shrill war cries.

Still the Draconium forces had pushed on, and now they were within sight of their goal. No wonder Shen was urging the advance; at the rate they were going, Aelyn thought, they might actually succeed in driving the grots off!

Another hail of arrows fell from the rooftops to the right of the street. She popped up for a moment to see more grots scurrying along the slates to add their shots to the volleys. Black arrows fell amongst the advancing watchmen, and several crumpled.

'We need to clear those roofs or this push will stall,' said Aelyn. A robe-bundled figure dropped into cover beside her, and she saw Bartiman's tired eyes glinting at her from under his cowl.

'I think I may be able to do something about that,' he said. 'This will put the terrors up them.'

Bartiman produced a hideous little doll from under his robes, a fetish made from twists of cloth and splinters of bone. The thing's dead glass eyes stared from a face made of black hair and jagged flint. It made Aelyn shudder. Bartiman gripped the fetish firmly in one fist, allowing its sharp shards to puncture his flesh until they drew blood. At the same time, he began a muttered chant that grew swiftly in volume and complexity until he was spitting twisted syllables while blood drizzled from his fist onto the cobbles. The surviving militiamen exchanged a nervous glance and edged away as far as they dared.

Then Bartiman punched his fist skywards and shouted out. 'Nar, Alhamar, Shyisha-Nar Kon Olynder-Nar!'

A green glow radiated from within Bartiman's clenched fist, growing into an eldritch beacon of cold emerald light. One by one, flares of the same grave-light burst into being above his head, whirling faster and faster until a howling vortex of unnatural energies haloed the death wizard. With a scream of effort he flung his hands out, towards the rooftops on which the grot archers crouched. The vortex of energy billowed outwards, and as it did so, it split into dozens of wailing spectral figures whose yawning maws and crooked bones were hidden beneath clinging shrouds. Translucent and terrifying, the swarm of gheists boiled along the rooftops, passing through shocked greenskins as though they were no more solid than smoke. Where each gheist burst from the back of a grot, it did so in a spray of ectoplasm and blood. Their victims' flesh crumpled inwards like old parchment, their eyes shrivelling and their teeth falling from their gums. Thumps and thuds echoed along the street as desiccated grot corpses rained from the rooftops.

The few surviving greenskins turned and fled, diving into attic windows or scampering away along ridges to escape. Bartiman stood tall and threw out his arms as the screaming gheists spiralled up and plunged back towards the humans in the street below.

'BEGONE!' he boomed, and as though a gale had ripped down the street, the malign entities tattered apart and vanished. Bartiman swayed, leaned heavily on his staff and sank back into cover.

'Impressive,' said Aelyn, while the two militiamen stared at Bartiman with undisguised fear.

'Tiring,' he replied, coughing wetly into his fist. 'And possibly unwise, given my condition. Still, we must all continue on until Old Bones takes us.'

Now the advance pressed forwards with great speed. Whether Bartiman's display of sorcerous might had indeed frightened the fight out of the grots, or whether their enemies simply didn't have enough bodies to keep flinging into the path of the Draconium advance, Aelyn didn't know. She didn't care, either, so long as they were keeping their enemies' attention focused away from the pipehouse.

Across an intersection heaped with bodies, up a street part-flooded and riven with deep chasms that spewed fungal blooms, and suddenly Fountains Square stretched out in front of them.

'That is truly hideous,' breathed Aelyn.

From afar, the half-chiselled greenskin idol had been unpleasant, its gaze weirdly knowing. Now, its grotesque features nearing completion and the real Bad Moon hanging menacingly above it, the idol was horrifying. Its lunatic gaze seemed to bore into her mind, making Aelyn want to cringe away and cover her face.

'Steady,' bellowed Watchman Shen as the watchmen and militia balked.

'There's the poison,' said Aelyn, pointing to the huge pyramidal stack of black and gold barrels that towered above the shrine.

'Hmm, and their defenders,' replied Bartiman. 'Not so many as I'd thought.'

Aelyn saw that he was right. She guessed that perhaps a couple of hundred greenskins had packed themselves in around their idol, drawn up in ragged ranks with banners flying and gongs clanging. A few troggoths loomed amongst them and, further back, she saw a gaggle of bizarre grots clustered before the tunnel mouth dug into the idol's base. These sat astride walking toadstools or were carried on large squig-skulls, or else were bent double beneath the weight of weird paraphernalia and baskets of potions and poisons.

Yet her eye was drawn to the ragged figure that surveyed them regally from the platform etched into the top of the idol. He was tall, for a grot, and he carried a moon-fungus staff in one hand from which filthy light spilled in waves.

'Their leader,' she said.

'Must be,' replied Bartiman. 'Wish we had Borik here, one good shot from that cannon of his...'

'I doubt it would be that easy,' said Aelyn. 'No, we must do this ourselves. I just hope that Watchman Shen remembers the plan.'

Looking at the man, though, she doubted it. He swept past them with a fire in his eyes and his halberd raised high, advancing at a trot into the square. His watchmen followed him, several hundred in number now and bolstered further by at least half that many militia. Somewhere near the back of their ragged formation, Aelyn knew they had a couple of cannons being heaved along by sweating crewmen.

'We can finish this!' cried Shen, and his men and women cheered his words. 'In Sigmar's name, there's a damned handful of them! Is *this* what we feared, my friends? Forwards, now, for the regent militant, for Captain Morthan and Arch-Lector Kayl, for Sigmar and Draconium!'

The city's defenders cheered again and surged forwards, holding to only the barest suggestion of discipline or coherency as they charged. Aelyn felt the fanatical fervour of the mob around her, the weeks of frustration and fear and suffering that fuelled their rage. The enemy were here, at last, visible and in numbers they believed they could defeat.

'He intended this all along,' breathed Aelyn as warriors jostled and barged past her and Bartiman on both sides.

'Whassat?' asked Bartiman, hanging on to her to avoid himself being knocked from his feet.

'Shen, that fool, was planning this all along! He didn't hear a word we said. He's trying to win this in a straight fight, drive the enemy from the city he still thinks he can save. This doesn't feel right,' said Aelyn.

'Not too late to cut and run, you know,' said Bartiman.

'There are good women and men here, Bartiman, servants of Sigmar who don't deserve to die. We need to aid them,' said Aelyn. 'Besides, if they all get killed...'

'...then likely so do our friends,' he finished. 'Damn. Well, come on then. Let's see if we can stop this turning into a disaster.'

They were near the tail end of the force now, most of Draconium's soldiery having swept past them, caught up in the fervour of the charge. Aelyn saw the two cannons being wheeled hurriedly into place, their crews scrambling to load shot and sighting their barrels on the distant idol. She heard the danger before she saw it. A shudder through the ground, a susurrus of rasping cloth and the pound of heavy footfalls.

A gunner turning to grab a powder barrel from the cobbles looked up, and his eyes widened. The man screamed in the instant before a huge club whistled down and crushed him, his field gun and another of its crew. Aelyn spun, and saw a huge troggoth emerge from the shadows of one of the ruined buildings that edged the square. The thing wore a crude helm, and its eyes swivelled to stare at her with dumb hatred. She saw more of the massive beasts, emerging into the moonlight to the flanks and rear of the charging Draconium forces. Around their feet came hordes of Moonclan grots and arachnid riders. A vast horde spilled from the ruins, a force that outnumbered those defending the shrine ten to one.

'Ambush!' yelled Aelyn, but in their battle-fervour none of the warriors of Draconium heard her.

CHAPTER SEVENTEEN

DESPERATION

Aelyn was not given to panic. She had long held a reputation amongst the Swords of Sigmar for her glacial calm in even the direst of situations. Now, though, she felt panic threaten.

She was loping across the square as quickly as she could without leaving Bartiman behind, but the old wizard moved frustratingly slowly. She had no idea how old Bartiman Kotrin actually was, struggling as she did to gauge human ages at the best of times, but she didn't doubt that his sorcerous abilities had lengthened his lifespan substantially beyond that which was natural. Until Draconium, those same abilities had also lent him an unnatural vitality that belied his aged appearance. Now, though, Bartiman's wounds, his illness and exhaustion had combined to reduce him to an ill-tempered hobble barely faster than a walk. His staff thunked against the cobbles with every step, and he kept up a wheezing diatribe of profanity as he lurched along in her wake.

'Hurry, Bartiman!' she urged.

'Do I look like I'm taking a damned stroll?' he gasped, coughing wetly and staggering. Aelyn looked over his shoulder and saw a mass of Moonclan grots bearing down on them, red eyes gleaming and blades drawn. The greenskins had swept over the remaining cannon crewmen like a flood-tide, and now bore down on the two Swords of Sigmar with malicious glee. Aelyn plucked an arrow from her quiver, drew and loosed. She repeated the action once, twice, thrice and four aelven arrows slammed into the foremost greenskins. They vanished beneath the trampling feet of the horde, which did not slow at all.

Aelyn reached for another arrow and cursed as she grasped empty air.

'All gone,' she said.

'Oh no,' grunted Bartiman. He stopped and turned, raising his staff and pointing it at the surging mass of grots. He took several deep breaths, trying to drag in enough air to harness his magics. Aelyn felt arcane power crackle and saw Bartiman stand a little straighter as its energies flowed through him.

'Th'rak'ul!' boomed Bartiman, and a blast of night-black energy ripped from the tip of his staff to slam into the grots with a percussive thunderclap. The blast wave rolled outwards, rippling black fire rushing through the tightly packed greenskins and blasting them to ashes.

Black-hooded greenskins screeched in terror and scattered in all directions. Their charge broke apart like a wave against rocks. Aelyn felt a moment of relief before Bartiman staggered and fell. She lunged, catching him before he hit the cobbles. His hood fell back from his lolling head, and she hurriedly pulled it back into place, warding him against the moonlight. Before she did, though, Aelyn saw just how pale the wizard was, how sunken his eyes and liver-spotted his papery skin. It was as though he had aged – truly aged – a decade in the last few minutes.

'Shouldn't have, but you know, my dear, needs must,' he croaked. 'Probably best if you–'

'Do not tell me to leave you behind, Bartiman,' hissed Aelyn, hoisting him to his feet and supporting him as best she could.

'Don't you dare!' he gasped. 'I was going to say best if you hurry up! They won't be scattered for long.'

Aelyn set off again in pursuit of Draconium's ragged army, away from the hordes of greenskins and monsters spilling into the square. If she and Bartiman could catch up to the watchmen, if they could somehow rein them in and make them see sense, then perhaps they could fight their way out of the tightening greenskin noose.

'At least we got their attention,' said Bartiman, making a sound that could have been a laugh or a cough.

'Eleanora and Romilla can thank us later,' said Aelyn, distracted. 'First we have to escape this mess alive.'

She could see the human soldiery up ahead, dashing across the open ground towards the greenskins' shrine. Some paused to loose arrows or fire shots from their pistols. Others dashed headlong, all thought of strategy forgotten as the maddening rays of the Bad Moon beat down upon them and their hated enemies stood revealed before their blades.

Closer they charged, closer to the shrine and the greenskins around it.

Closer to the site of the devastating explosion her comrades were trying to engineer.

'They're going to get themselves killed, and us with them,' she spat. Some of the soldiers had spotted the ambushing forces by now, their headlong rush faltering as they realised they were outnumbered on every side. It only served to string their formation out even more, the front-runners dashing ahead while panic spread in from the flanks and rear.

'Sooner than you think,' gasped Bartiman. 'Stop, stop!'

Aelyn pulled up short, hearing the panic in the wizard's reedy voice.

'What?'

'Magic, a catastrophic build-up of magic–'

Green light erupted around the grot with the crown and the staff. He hefted his moon-fungus high and spat jagged words. Aelyn didn't speak the tongue, but she understood the spite and cruelty well enough. The fungus atop the grot's staff glowed brighter and brighter, sickly light spilling from it like a diseased star. Cries of pain and panic rose from the charging human host as the light blinded them. It was as though the rays of the Bad Moon were magnified a thousandfold, and Aelyn dragged Bartiman down behind a heap of rubble as the filthy light swept across the square. She found herself face to face with the severed stone head of Sigmar the God-King, half of his visage blackened by fire, his one remaining eye staring accusingly.

Beyond the rubble, she heard cries turn to gibbering howls and screams. Wild ululations echoed across the square, and voices were raised in sudden terror, jubilation or utter confusion.

'The light of day, I *see* it! We're saved!'

'Oh Sigmar, get them off me, get them off me! They're under my skin!'

'You filth! It was you all along!'

'Praise the Bad Moon! Praise the Loonking!'

'Guuuhhhh! I'll suck the eyes from your *skull*!'

'Oh no,' breathed Aelyn as the chorus of insanity intensified. She heard pistol shots. Blades clashed. Screams of pain rang out. At last the searing light died, cut off as though a curtain had dropped. Aelyn peered over the rubble to see the army of Draconium tearing itself apart. Men and women throttled one another or hacked at their former comrades with looks of animal ferocity on their faces. Some tore off their hoods and cloaks and raised their arms wide, weeping and laughing as fungi burst out all over their bodies. A watchman dug his dagger into his own flesh, wailing in panic as he rooted bloodily for something that was not there. Aelyn's throat tightened as Watchman Kole stumbled past, weeping tears of gore where she had clawed her eyes from her skull, whispering over and over again about a gift from on high, a gift from on high.

Then came the sounds of gongs hammering and clanging, and a ragged battle-cry rose from hundreds of grot throats. Those around the idol surged forwards, spears levelled. Arrows rose from amongst their mass and rained indiscriminately down into the brawling Draconium soldiery. Fanatics burst from amongst their ranks, frothing madly as they whirled their huge wrecking balls into the humans. Blood sprayed.

Aelyn looked back to see more grots closing in across the square from all sides. In the pallid moonlight, gathered in such numbers, they resembled a mass of moving shadow dotted with hundreds of red eyes, wicked fangs and sharp blades. Troggoths waded amongst them, booming roars echoing skywards. Squig riders bounded over the grots' heads in a swarm, every wild leap carrying them closer.

Terror gripped Aelyn as she watched the horde close in.

'What do we do?' asked Bartiman, slumped weakly against the rubble with his staff across his lap. Aelyn looked down at the frail old human and shook her head numbly.

This wasn't some brave last stand. It was a massacre, and they had walked right into it.

There was nothing they could do.

They were going to die.

* * *

Romilla squeezed herself from the tunnel and fell to the stone floor. She was sweating and scraped, her skin scalded in several places. She gave a dry cough, wincing at the pain in her injured side and gouged face.

'I would give my hammer for a glass of water,' she croaked. Thackeray placed a hand on her shoulder and shook his head in warning, raising a finger to his lips. Eleanora was crouched nearby, pistols in hand and eyes wide.

Natural light filtered from somewhere above, illuminating a wide square chamber with a low ceiling and metal steps leading up and out of sight. The pipes they had followed ran along the chamber's ceiling before vanishing up through the stonework, rattling and hissing louder than ever.

Romilla immediately saw what had alarmed Thackeray, and she became very still. Barely visible in the half-light, thick strands criss-crossed the chamber. They gathered in thick drifts in its corners, and in places formed dense cocoons that dangled from the ceiling and swayed in a hot breeze.

Spider's webs.

Masses of huge, thick spiders' webs.

Romilla shook her head in despair and clutched her hammer amulet tight.

'Sigmar,' she prayed in a whisper, 'give us strength.'

At first, they tried to pick their way between the cobwebs without touching them. It quickly proved impossible. The sticky strands filled the chamber in layers, forming complex interwoven patterns that Romilla couldn't begin to trace or avoid. Thackeray broke first, recoiling in disgust as a mass of web clung to his face. He hacked angrily at it with his halberd. Eleanora and Romilla joined him in simply clawing the webbing out of their way as best they could.

It was no mean feat, even still. Romilla had rarely had cause to wish she fought with a blade rather than a hammer. She wished it now.

Worse, she had enough bestiary lore to know how spiders hunted their prey. With every tug upon the mass of sticky strands she expected to see arachnids large as men come scuttling down the stairs from above.

Still, nothing emerged to attack them as they fought their way across the web-choked chamber and reached the foot of the iron staircase. Romilla looked up the funnel of webbing that filled the stairwell and felt atavistic terror threaten to freeze her in place. Up there was their goal. An escape from these underground chambers and a return to air and light, no matter how poisonous both might be by now. Yet how could they make their way through this nightmare?

'Eleanora, do you know where we're going?' she whispered. To her alarm, it took Eleanora a long moment to focus on her before the engineer answered. She was feverish, her hands shaking as though palsied and her eyes shot through with red-black veiny streaks. Heat baked off her.

'Up the stairs two floors until we reach ground level,' she said, blinking and swaying. 'Right along a tunnel lined with pipes, then up another flight of stairs. Or... no, left. Left up another... is it? Yes, right, up another flight of stairs into the exchanger chamber. The controls are... up... near the ceiling. The roof is glass, Romilla. We'll be exposed... to the moonlight again.' She gestured vaguely with one of her guns.

'Is she going to be able to do this?' asked Thackeray, frowning in concern.

'Yes, she is,' whispered Romilla with absolute conviction. 'Even if we have to carry her there. You can do this, can't you, El?'

Eleanora's gaze sharpened, and she looked down at the

mechanisms of her guns for a moment before looking back up at Romilla.

'I don't want any more of us to die,' she said quietly.

'Then let us be about Sigmar's work,' said Romilla. 'Thackeray, you've got the only blade amongst us. Lead on.'

Thackeray shot her a dark look, but he paced up the stairs, using his halberd blade to puncture and drag aside thick wads of webbing that blocked their path. Romilla followed behind, keeping Eleanora by her side. She half-supported the engineer, who sweated and shook but took one determined step after another.

They were near the top of the steps, and the web was funnelling inwards, tightening down to a dense mass. Thackeray raised the blade of his halberd and slid it into the fibres near the top before dragging it downwards as hard as he could.

The web fibres split with audible snaps. He dragged the blade lower, unzipping a ragged gash in the sticky mass. Thackeray's blade gave a sudden lurch downwards as the web's resistance gave, almost spilling him from his feet. His halberd-point hit the metal steps with an audible clang, and all three of them froze, listening for the telltale sounds of skittering limbs and rasping chitin.

They heard nothing. Romilla breathed slowly out and took another step up the stairs.

'What are those?' asked Eleanora. Romilla followed her gaze and gasped as she saw hundreds of silvery specks spilling from amidst the webbing and up Thackeray's polearm.

'Drop it!' she barked, and Thackeray let the halberd fall with a yell of alarm.

Too late.

Dozens of infant arachnids, translucent and each no larger than a thumb nail, had swarmed onto Thackeray's gloved hands.

He staggered back, making sounds of revulsion as he tried to shake them off. He slapped the backs of his hands against the walls, crushing the swarming creatures. Still they bit him again and again.

Romilla had a sudden vision of the three of them being trapped in the cellar by a tide of biting spiders. That couldn't happen.

'Hood up and stay close,' she told Eleanora, grabbing her wrist, then drove into Thackeray from behind with all the force she could muster.

The three of them tumbled through the mass of webbing and spilled onto a metal landing beyond. Romilla felt things scuttling across her body and she rolled and slapped frantically, crushing spiderlings with every swat.

'Oh, Sigmar!' spat Thackeray, writhing and beating at himself in revulsion. Eleanora echoed their movements.

'Don't stop! Not here!' Romilla urged as she scrambled back to her feet. They were in the midst of what must surely be a spider nest, and the walls and ceiling churned with a silvery mass of constant motion. Dragging Eleanora and Thackeray behind her, Romilla pushed through the last strands of webbing and up another clanging flight of stairs. She ignored the squirming sensation on her skin, the sharp stabs of biting pain across her flesh, until she had hauled both her companions to the head of the next set of steps.

Only there did she stop and wriggle out of her cloak, throwing it to the floor with a moan of disgust. They were all over her, she could feel their legs tickling and their fangs sinking in. Romilla slapped and beat at the swarming spiders, crushing them with every motion until at last they were all exterminated. Her skin still itched with the invasive sensation of arachnid legs, but Romilla made herself stop before panic took hold.

'You've killed us all!' gasped Thackeray, still swatting madly at himself.

'They're too young to be venomous,' replied Romilla. 'Calm yourself, man!'

'How can you possibly know that?' asked Thackeray, still scrubbing at his skin, his mouth twisted in disgust. Eleanora leaned against a nearby wall, whimpering slightly as she methodically checked each part of her body for spiders.

'I don't, but I assume we'd feel the effects by now if they had been,' replied Romilla. She didn't want to go into how just such an arachnid had bitten Eleanora many days ago, and that the effects of its bite had taken days to manifest. Somehow, she didn't think any of them would find that comforting. 'The alternative was to remain trapped in that basement while they crawled all over us and our comrades fought and died without our help. Would you have preferred that?'

'You're a cheffing lunatic,' said Thackeray, drawing his pistol. His lantern lay discarded a floor below, still attached to the end of his halberd. Its light spilled up from below, dots seething across it where spiderlings covered its glass surface and making Romilla's flesh tingle all over again.

'Call me what you like, just help me get this done,' said Romilla. Thackeray shook his head and set off up the next flight of stairs. The cobwebs were sparser here, forming diaphanous veils rather than knotted clumps. Romilla turned to aid Eleanora, taking one of the engineer's arms and giving her a last look over for the telltale movement of spiderlings. She heard a wet crunch from above, and turned to look up the stairs.

Thackeray was hauled off his feet, up the last few stairs and into the air above. Something awful enfolded him, a mass of spine-haired limbs and busy mandibles. The watchman's eyes locked with Romilla's for a moment, his expression a mass of horror and pain and terror. Then chitinous blades flashed and his head parted company from his neck, to be sucked into a glistening orifice that yawned beneath a cluster of staring eyes.

Romilla froze. She couldn't move. The enormous spider took several steps down the stairway, squeezing its nightmare bulk towards them. It gave off a carrion stench. The sounds of it crunching and sucking at Thackeray's severed head made her gorge rise.

Eleanora gave a piercing scream. The stairwell filled with thunder and light as her guns fired again and again. The spider recoiled, dropping Thackeray's body and giving a piercing shrill as shots punched deep into its face. Several of its eyes burst. One of its forelimbs sheared off halfway up, the wound gouting sticky black ichor. Clots of matter splattered from its body as Eleanora's pistols hammered it relentlessly. The thing tried to retreat, tried to rear up and spread its legs wide, but it had trapped itself in its hunger to reach them. Another shot ruptured chitin and sprayed gore across the walls.

Another.

Another.

The spider's shriek climbed to a pitch Romilla could barely hear, and at last it managed to drag itself backwards out of the stairwell. The damage was already done. It thrashed and flopped, a flailing mass the size of several carriages that bled black sludge. It rolled onto its side and its remaining legs pulled inwards like a hand forming a claw. The spider gave a final, convulsive lurch that sent splatters of black slime oozing from its body, then lay still.

Romilla's ears rang. Her heart hammered. She turned to look at Eleanora, who was staring wild-eyed at the dead spider, her guns still outstretched. Smoke wafted from their barrels.

Romilla drew breath to say something, though she didn't

truly know what. Then she heard the sounds she had been dreading. In the gunfire's fading echoes, she caught noises of skittering and of heavy bodies dragging themselves over stonework.

'There's no time, we have to move,' she said, and grabbed Eleanora by the wrist again.

They ran up the last flight of stairs, leaping over Thackeray's decapitated corpse and splashing heedlessly through the acrid filth that had squirted from the dying spider. Past cracked windows that looked out onto a corpse-strewn street, past an ironoak desk that might once have served as a station for the building's receptionist, Romilla saw the corridor that Eleanora had spoken of. It stretched away from them in the half-light. She dashed along it, ignoring the drag of snapped spider's webs and the itching pain from her dozens of bites.

Perhaps the creatures had been poisonous after all, she thought. It hardly mattered now. Only doing Sigmar's work mattered, before they were overrun.

The two of them burst out of the end of the corridor, and several gnarlkyd-sized spiders came at them from the shadows. Romilla swung her hammer into the face of the largest, eliciting a crunch of chitin and sending the horrible thing skidding away. Eleanora dropped one of her guns, snatching a smaller pistol from her belt and pointing it at another spider that was dropping down from above on a line of silk. She squeezed the trigger, but nothing happened.

Romilla swung again, dodging aside from the scrabbling limbs of the third spider and managing to smash her hammer into one of its legs. The thing limped backwards, hissing. Eleanora gasped, dropping her other gun and thumbing the arming mechanism of her pistol. She fired in the instant before the spider dropped, then its dead weight hit her from above and pinned her to the floor. Romilla screamed in denial and waded in, hammer swinging at the thrashing mass of limbs and chitin. She realised with a gasp of relief that the monster was already dead, flailing its death throes from the huge hole Eleanora's pistol had bored through its abdomen. She heaved it aside all the same, revolted at its skittering touch, and felt twice the relief as she saw Eleanora pale but still alive, staring up at her in horror.

'Behind you!' urged Eleanora, and Romilla spun, instinct propelling her hammer in a wild swing. She caught the first spider in the mandibles even as it reared up to strike, and sent it toppling backwards with ichor gouting from its ruined face. She hit the monster again, and then again, just to be sure.

Romilla turned, breathing hard, sweat rolling down her forehead, to look for the last spider. She saw it squeezing itself through a crack in the stonework, just a tangle of legs and glittering eyes vanishing into the dark. Romilla reached down a hand and heaved Eleanora to her feet.

'There are more of them coming,' said Eleanora, gathering up her guns and hastily reloading them.

'I can hear them,' said Romilla, properly taking in the room for the first time. They stood in a bare stone chamber, one wall of which played host to a mass of piping and gauges. Two metal stairways led up and out of the chamber in opposite directions; one right, one left.

'Which way, El?' asked Romilla.

'I... uhm...' Eleanora swayed, and Romilla looked at her in alarm. Eleanora never forgot anything once she had learned it. Not ever. Now was not a good time for her to start, yet as she took in the engineer's greenish pallor and red-rimmed eyes, Romilla admitted to herself that she was amazed Eleanora was even still on her feet.

'I don't...' Eleanora furrowed her brow, looking panicked and ill.

'Sigmar, guide me,' breathed Romilla then chose the right-hand stairway. 'Always the righteous path over the sinister,' she said and tugged Eleanora after her.

The two of them clanged up the stairs and burst through a veil of webbing into another corridor. They ran along it, passing clumps of gauges and dials furred with cobwebbing. There were no windows here, though they must have been a floor or so above street level now. From ahead they heard a growing sound of clanging and hissing. Romilla felt the temperature increase by the moment, and as they rounded a corner she saw a fiery glow radiating from ahead of them.

'This must be the way, Sigmar be praised!' she gasped.

They burst into a huge open space. Romilla had an impression of masses of pipework, flowing into the chamber from every direction and meshing with enormous machines at its heart. The din of rushing steam and groaning metal was loud here, and even she could see from the shuddering of pipes and the whistling jets of steam that all was not right. Thick webs and desiccated corpses of humans and duardin were scattered around the huge chamber, visible in the fiery light that spilled up from a stone-edged trench that ran along the chamber's heart. It was into this man-made crevasse that the largest pipes plunged. The infernal glow blended with the sickly moonlight that fell through the arched glass roof high above, the two sources of illumination creating a curdled haze like blood mixed into spoiled milk.

'Up there,' said Eleanora, pointing one wavering finger at a gantry high up near the chamber's ceiling. Romilla's eyes traced the broken tangle of iron staircases, ladders and walkways they would have to traverse to reach the pipeworks' controls, and her heart sank.

'God-King, we ask your aid in this time of trial,' she began, then stopped as something huge shifted at the lip of the fiery trench. Romilla's eyes widened and her heart almost stopped as a spider the size of the city's south gatehouse dragged its bloated form up into the chamber. It moved on legs thick as ironoaks, its mottled red and grey body so huge that it almost drove the sanity from her mind. A vast marking spread across the spider's pale underbelly, a leering moon shape picked out in bioluminescent pigmentation. Its eyes transfixed Romilla, orbs as wide as wells and thrice as dark and deep.

'Hendrick would have tried to fight them all, wouldn't he?' said Romilla, her hand closing reflexively around her hammer amulet as hundreds of smaller spiders spilled up from the trench around the monster's legs. 'He would have fought for a way we could all survive this *and* prevail. Damn him, he would have hoped for us, even if he couldn't for himself.' Romilla felt an answering tingle through her palm and looked down to see a faint blue light radiating between her fingers.

Sigmar was with them. They did his work. And perhaps, she thought, he was trying to tell her something more. It was enough to get her moving, one more time, dragging the near catatonic Eleanora behind her as she made for the nearest stairway. They could still do this, she thought. Perhaps they could not escape the chamber – that much she could accept, though the thought of Eleanora's death filled her with misery. But perhaps, like Hendrick before her, she had to hang on to her hope. If nothing else, they could do this, and if their deaths meant that thousands of innocent Sigmar-worshipping settlers were spared the vile fate that had befallen the people of Draconium, then Romilla could accept that price. She ran hard, adrenaline driving her exhausted body onwards, and as she ran she prayed.

* * *

Another grot came at Aelyn and she spun her dagger, weaving aside from the creature's spear thrust and ramming her blade into its throat. Blood jettisoned out. Aelyn whipped her blade back, and the grot collapsed. It wasn't enough, though, she thought. Not nearly enough.

The greenskins had borne down upon them and, trapped between their maddened comrades and the onrushing horde of foes, they had had no choice but to fight or die.

Or, more likely, fight until they died, she corrected herself grimly.

Bartiman was still propped against the rubble, muttering incantations as best he could. He had reduced a handful of grots to mummified corpses, and blasted another band to ashes, but Aelyn knew he couldn't possibly keep his efforts up much longer. His voice had become little more than a rasp, and his last attempt at a spell had fizzled to nothing. Now she stood over him against a seething tide of foes and fought harder than she ever remembered fighting.

Aelyn's shoulder was a mass of agony. Her ribs ached, and her thoughts reeled under the malign gaze of the Bad Moon. Still she spun her daggers in her hands, wove and twisted and stabbed with furious determination. A spear tore a deep graze across her shoulder, and she stabbed its wielder in the eye. A rusty shiv found its way past her guard and sunk into her ribs, but only an inch or so before she had lopped off its wielder's hand and kicked him back into the press of his fellows. A squig launched itself at her, jaws agape, and Aelyn ducked under its hurtling mass before sweeping both daggers up to slice the tip from one grot's hooked nose and bury the other under another's jaw.

Another speartip came from somewhere to sink deep into her calf, and Aelyn hissed with pain as her leg gave out beneath her. She fell half on top of Bartiman, and heard him grunt in pain as her weight landed on his frail body.

Aelyn pushed herself back up and stabbed out, driving one blade into a grot's chest and another into an assailant's weapon arm. A greenskin sunk wicked fangs into her forearm with a crunch and Aelyn screamed in pain as its dirty teeth scraped bone. The dagger dropped from her nerveless hand and the grot gave a muffled giggle around a bubbling mouthful of Aelyn's flesh and blood. Horrified, she punched her other dagger into the side of its head then ripped it out and stabbed again.

Filthy hands grabbed at her. A fist caught Aelyn in the jaw. A knife sank into her back, and agony shot through her again. Numbness came after it, ice spreading through her body, slowing her heartbeat, stifling her breath.

Aelyn slumped back, trying to shield Bartiman with her body. She lashed out one last time, and something squealed with pain as her blade hit home. Another knife pierced her chest, and another.

Aelyn coughed hot blood across her face. As her last breath rattled out, she saw the leering face of the Bad Moon stare down at her from above the mobbing press of grots. A moment of regret sparked in her mind, and then darkness fell.

'Get back, you damned *monster*,' spat Romilla, smashing her hammer into a spider's face and sending it squealing into the dark. The arachnid fell from the gantry, dropping a good thirty feet to hit the stone floor with a wet splat.

The control panel was only one level above them now. Romilla could see it, tantalisingly close, bathed in corrupted moonlight. The face of the Bad Moon leered down through the thick glass of the roof, and she had to fight off the sensation that it was staring directly at her, willing her to give up.

'One more walkway,' she said, as much to herself as Eleanora. 'One more set of stairs and then we're there!'

Romilla's amulet was glowing brightly now, its light seeming to redouble with every crushing hammer blow she struck in Sigmar's name. But the platform they stood on was shaking as though in a high wind. She looked down to see the enormous spider scaling its way up the chamber's machineries, huge limbs moving with greater speed and grace than anything so vast had any right to.

Dozens more spiders were swarming up around it, and more kept bursting from the innards of the web-strewn tangles of pipes, or dropping heavily from the ceiling to thump down on the gantries she and Eleanora ran along.

Romilla glanced at Eleanora. The engineer's eyes were glazed, her breathing laboured. A dark stain was spreading across her injured leg and an awful sickly-sweet smell accompanied it. The poor girl was on her last legs, thought Romilla, and the thought threatened to break her heart and her resolve both at once.

No, she thought. Not now. Not when they were so close.

Romilla raced along the gantry, dragging Eleanora along like a deadweight behind her. The Ironweld engineer had dropped her guns, but at least she was still hanging onto the shoulder of Romilla's filthy robes with one hand. The priest took hope from that simple gesture.

Their footfalls clanged against the metal as they pelted along. Romilla gasped as a vicious convulsion shook the metal and almost hurled her over the guard rail. She looked down to see the vast spider drawing its leg back to strike again at the gantry's support stanchions.

'No,' spat Romilla, and ran for the stairs with all her might. The ground lurched again, and she fell forwards, dropping her hammer in order to grab for the stair rail.

There came an awful screech of tortured metal and the gantry tore away, dropping from beneath their feet. Romilla screamed with effort as she hung on to the hot metal of the stair rail with one hand and clutched Eleanora's wrist with the other. The engineer wailed and clung hard to Romilla with both hands, her legs kicking in thin air.

The two of them hung suspended. Pain shot through every inch of Romilla's body as she strained to hang on. Below, the huge spider hissed and clicked as though in triumph. Machinery clattered, clanged and banged. Steam hissed. Spiders skittered closer, gathering for the kill. Adrenaline made everything seem inescapably sharp and clear.

'Sigmar... Give... Me... STRENGTH!' Romilla roared, and the glow of her amulet became a dazzling star. She felt fresh vitality flow through her limbs and swung Eleanora as hard as she could. The engineer yelped in shock as she was propelled upwards, landing sprawled on the stairs with a clang. Romilla hung on grimly as the huge spider hunched itself, preparing to spring and snap her from the railing like a choice morsel.

Then Eleanora was gripping her by the scruff of her robes, sweating and swaying as she pulled Romilla higher. Romilla pendulumed her weight and managed to snatch the edge of the dangling stairs with her other hand. She hauled herself upwards, screaming. There came a rush of air and a terrible snap of chitin.

Romilla dragged herself up onto the stairs and looked down. Blood flowed, and she groaned in pain. Two toes from her right foot had been severed by the slashing blades of the giant spider's mandibles, taken off along with the tip of her boot as cleanly as if it had used a straight razor.

'That... is all you get...' she panted, and spat defiantly down into the huge creature's eyes.

Amulet glowing, Romilla pulled herself to her feet and hobbled up the creaking stairs to the platform above. At least the shock of near death seemed to have shaken Eleanora back to consciousness, she thought, though for how long she didn't know.

The two of them stopped above the shuddering, hissing mass of machinery. The fires from below underlit the complex mass of controls set into the brass console at the platform's heart. The moonlight from above turned its upper surfaces pallid green. Below them, Romilla could hear the masses of spiders closing in.

'It's up to you now, El,' she said.

'What about you?' asked Eleanora, looking at her blearily.

'I'll pray, and I'll protect you for as long as I can,' said Romilla. 'And I am sorry, my girl, that I couldn't–'

Her breath caught in her throat, and she couldn't finish the words.

'It's all right,' said Eleanora. 'They took away my father, but they gave me a mother. Thank you.'

Tears squeezed from Romilla's eyes and her heart thumped painfully as Eleanora turned and staggered to the controls. She fell heavily against them, leaning all her weight on the console, and frowned down with fierce concentration.

Romilla coughed against the tightness in her throat and limped to stand beside Eleanora. Her amulet was still glowing fiercely, and in its light the young engineer didn't look quite so ill.

'Can you do it?' asked Romilla.

Eleanora's eyes darted across the switches and dials, the flashing green and crimson bulbs that illuminated small glass domes. Her focus sharpened as the challenge consumed her mind, though her eyes were no less bloodshot or red-ringed for it.

'I… no…' she said miserably. 'I can't. See, here and here,' she pointed, but Romilla barely heard her. Her ears were ringing, so sharp was her sense of anger and disappointment. They had given all this, fought all this way, and there was nothing Eleanora could do. For the barest instant, the light of Romilla's amulet flickered like a candle flame in a high wind.

No, she thought. She would not give in to despair again. Not while Eleanora lived. She tried to focus on what the engineer was telling her.

'...and without that differential I can close off the locking valves and direct the force, but there simply isn't enough pressure in the system.'

'How could you *get* enough pressure?' asked Romilla. The platform was swaying now, and awful clanging sounds rang from below. She didn't have to look to know what was causing them as it crept closer and closer.

'There isn't enough left in the system,' said Eleanora, banging the console in frustration. 'Unless Sigmar wants to send us the most perfectly timed eruption in the history of the Mortal Realms, we just can't achieve the differential to release the build-up from *this* chamber and send it through the system. Unless...' Eleanora gasped and slapped her palm against the metal. 'It's the... I'm having trouble... so stupid...'

Something huge and dark moved below them, blocking out the rising firelight and causing the gantry to creak and shift.

'What, girl, *what*?' urged Romilla.

'If I disable the safety valves and purge everything in this chamber through the reserve pipes, it would draw a huge surge of energy up from the vents and blast it all through the machinery in this chamber. You wouldn't *need* a pressure differential, the quantity of steam and fire generated would flood through the system and trigger an explosion even larger than we planned.'

A massive leg rose into view, clanging down on the edge of the gantry and effortlessly folding the iron guard rail down like crumpled paper.

'What are you waiting for, El? Do it!'

Eleanora looked at her, and Romilla saw naked terror in her eyes.

'It will set fire to everything in this chamber the moment the surge comes through. We'll all burn. Like…' she trailed off.

Like her father, Romilla thought. Oh Sigmar, why must you be so cruel? Romilla looked up at the glass roof above them. Escape, tantalisingly near yet wholly out of reach. There was a good twenty feet between them and it, and none of the ceiling's arching gantries was close enough for them to reach. There would be no escape upwards, nor down through the tide of scuttling bodies that converged upon them. There would be no escape at all, she thought. The stark fact of it brought acceptance and sorrow in equal measure.

'We'll do it together,' Romilla said soothingly, placing her hand over Eleanora's. 'I am with you. Sigmar is with you.'

Another huge arachnid limb clanged down on the platform's edge. The gantry gave a terrible moan of buckling metal as it began to tilt under the spider's weight.

'All right,' said Eleanora. 'Better than… that.' She threw a series of switches, working with feverish speed. Below, Romilla heard a grinding roar building. Steam howled and whistled. The chamber shook.

As though understanding what was coming, the vast spider redoubled its efforts and the platform tilted harder. Ironwork screamed and tore. In Romilla's peripheral vision she saw skittering shapes spilling over the railing and stalking towards them. She and Eleanora had killed more than their share of spiders in the last few minutes; their broodmates were wary.

She ignored them. She kept her eyes on Eleanora as the engineer flicked a last handful of switches and grabbed a metal dial.

'Now?' she asked, shaking.

'Now,' answered Romilla.

In the glow of her amulet, Eleanora turned the dial sharply to the right. There was a roar like dragon's breath, an earthquake shudder, and the panicked squeal of dozens of huge spiders. Every indicator on the console flashed red. With a cacophony of screaming metal and rushing steam, the machinery in the chamber began to come apart. Pipes tore away from their housings and crashed together, belching boiling vapour. Glass valves smashed from the pressure behind them. Rivets shot through the air like bullets to ricochet from the stonework of the chamber. There came a sound like cannonfire as the huge panes of glass forming the ceiling cracked and shuddered. Romilla felt Eleanora's hand close on her arm like a vice and turned her head to look at the young engineer in surprise.

Eleanora was staring at her with feverish intensity, then back at the shuddering console.

'What?' asked Romilla, shouting to make herself heard. Her ears were ringing.

'The pressure shift is too much for the radial support pipes!' shouted Eleanora. 'The overpressure is bowing the structure! I think there's enough spare if I can just...'

Romilla shook her head in bewilderment, grabbing the console for support as the gantry groaned and tilted. Something vast and dark moved behind them, but she dared not look.

'What are you saying?' she yelled, but Eleanora was bent over the console, working the controls with feverish intensity. She gave a snarl of frustration and smacked one hand against the metal.

'I *hate* not being able to think clearly!' she exclaimed. 'I forgot to account for the structural warping. If I can trap enough pressure in the nearest vent-pipes now that they're blocked, I might be able to blow their internal seals and cause a localised explosion that will blast a support stanchion free without weakening our blast wave! If I get it right it will punch right through the wall and give us a bridge to exit by. But I can't calculate the variables in this condition. Romilla, the pipe might not blow, the stanchion might fall wrong, we might get caught by spiders or consumed in the explosion if we're too slow. I–'

Romilla looked at the amulet blazing white in her hand, then at Eleanora's anguished expression. Even at a time like this, she thought, the girl found it so hard to act without certainty.

'All we have now is faith,' shouted Romilla. 'If it fails, then we die. If we fail to act, we die. Just do it and pray to Sigmar for his aid!'

Eleanora bit her lip so hard that Romilla thought she would draw blood. Her hand hovered over a brass switch, fingers twitching as though she longed to count off on them even as fire leapt around them and the platform shrieked.

'Eleanora, now!' yelled Romilla.

The engineer vented a yell of frustration and snatched at the switch. There came a rumbling groan from the machineries below them, which rose to a tea-kettle shriek. Three glass gauges on the console burst in quick succession, showering Romilla and Eleanora with shards. Then came a deafening bang that echoed from amidst the background roar of fire and steam and buckling metal.

A level below the platform, a fifty-foot-high support stanchion screamed like the damned as it tore loose in a cloud of steam. It toppled sideways like a felled tree and crashed into the chamber wall. Tons upon tons of metal hit the stonework like a battering ram and sundered it. A ragged wound was torn into the side of the structure. Sickly moonlight spilled through the rent. Romilla's eyes widened as the stanchion ground to a halt barely a foot below them, sunk into the stonework at a drunken angle.

A bridge.

Eleanora had done it.

'Eleanora, you are a bloody marvel!' Romilla shouted, grabbing at the console as she hauled herself and Eleanora towards the platform's upper edge. An awful sense of vertigo gripped her, and the drop to the floor below yawned cavernous and filled with dancing flames.

Steam jetted madly around them. Overstressed machineries howled. Spiders hissed and chittered as they scuttled closer, scaling the steeply tilted platform. Eleanora cringed.

'We have to jump,' urged Romilla. 'Over the railing, we scramble along the bridge, and we get clear. You've given us a chance!'

'I can't,' gasped Eleanora, looking imploringly at Romilla. 'My foot.'

'You can, and you will,' Romilla replied, her voice like iron. Her amulet was glowing like a fiery blue star, now, its light reflecting in Eleanora's wide, frightened eyes.

The engineer gave a mute nod. They hauled themselves atop the railing, snatched one another's hands and, even as a tide of arachnid horrors bore down upon them, they leapt and scrambled across the bridge. Behind them, the overloaded machines vented a monstrous blast of energy through the pipes of Draconium's heating system, sending it racing away towards Fountains Square. An annihilating tide of fire billowed up from the rift and consumed everything in the chamber.

Bartiman felt the ground shudder beneath him. Aelyn's body still lay atop his. She, combined with the vermin corpses of the grots she had slain, had all but buried the elderly wizard and hidden him from sight. They had also pinned him in place, so feeble had he become, and it had taken him long minutes to squirm and shove his way up through the carrion heap.

Part of Bartiman just wanted to hide beneath the bodies until death took him. Sigmar knew he had no desire to see that damned moon again before he passed. But the fear of suffocation had got him moving, that and the horror of his friend's corpse laying sprawled atop him.

Damn me for a useless old fool, he thought. I can at least give Aelyn her rites before this nightmare ends.

But now, still trapped beneath several bodies and barely able to see the twilit sky, Bartiman felt everything begin to shake.

'No, I don't believe it,' he whispered. Despite everything, Bartiman felt a fierce pride as the rumble grew to a howling roar that seeped up from beneath the cobbles. Bartiman choked out a dry laugh, heaving aside a last corpse and managing to haul himself into a sitting position amidst the bodies.

He was in time to see the eyes and mouth of the greenskin idol glow like furnace fires. Jets of steam blasted skywards around the idol, blowing shrieking grots high into the air. He saw a troggoth consumed by a sudden eruption of flame, just as it was about to swing its club through a reeling mass of watchmen. The regal grot with the moon-fungus staff spun, a look of horror on its face, and Bartiman felt a savage satisfaction at the thing's look of sudden panic. That sense was only slightly spoiled when, a moment later, the grot vanished amidst a filthy puff of green smoke to leave its lackeys wailing in terror at its sudden disappearance.

'Spit... on your... plans...' rasped Bartiman. 'And... spit on... your ugly... damned... Bad Moon.'

The explosion was titanic. It was apocalyptic. It washed out

Bartiman's senses and threw him backwards into the heaped bodies with bone-breaking force. It obliterated the poison stocks, evaporated the ground water, and incinerated the warring armies of grots and humans still entangled together at the heart of the square.

Bartiman felt rather than saw the entire heart of Fountains Square bulge upwards like a huge bubble, then burst in a spray of flame and cobbles and flailing bodies.

Debris rained down, trailing smoke, pulverising the corpses around him, and Bartiman took a deep breath as he prepared for his end at last. It was long overdue, he supposed, and at least they had avenged their friends.

Then the heart of the square caved in, thundering down into a huge pit. Bartiman began to slide, felt panic overwhelm his fatalism, clawed frantically at the sliding corpses around him. Something blunt and heavy smacked him in the head, and he knew no more.

EPILOGUE

DUSK

Orlen Drell cowered in the mouth of a storm drain, shying away from the touch of the glowing fungi that half-filled it. Even driven mad and hollowed out by hunger, he had not dared to remain out in the moonlight. He had grasped soon enough that its rays brought pain. Yet neither had he been fool enough to crawl far into the dark spaces beneath the city. He was a beaten and bloody fugitive, hiding in terror from the monsters that moved in the darkness, and in his more lucid moments he wondered how he had possibly survived this waking nightmare for as long as he had.

Drell had scraped off the fungal growths that had sprouted from his flesh. The process had left him shivering and bloodied, but he was too frightened to seek out any kind of medical supplies, nor even food or water. He certainly wouldn't countenance trying to eat the mushrooms growing around him in the dark; that way led to a certain and horrible death. Instead he simply crouched, balled up and stiff in the dark, while he waited for the next horror to manifest itself.

Perhaps it was how far he had strained his senses in his quest to stay alive, but Drell felt the change coming before he saw it. Tremors shook the air. Drell tensed.

A dull rumble reached his ears, a sound that reverberated through air and stone alike and grew slowly but inexorably. The tunnel shuddered, and Orlen fumbled to steady himself in his awkward position. Then came a reverberant boom, and another, and another. The drain shuddered and cracks spider-webbed its walls. Orlen was torn between paralysis and flight. He didn't know where he should go – back out into the light that stung and sickened him, or back into the darkness where some terrible thing would surely take his life.

Orlen gave a whimper of alarm as the air pulsed. A thrumming pressure beat against his eardrums and made his heart flutter in his chest. The feeling increased, and Orlen's whimper became a wail as a vortex of air funnelled along the storm drain and sucked him helplessly towards its entrance. He fought against it, digging his nails in until they splintered, but the pull of the air was inexorable. His wail became a frantic screech as he was dragged through a slimy mass of toadstools that themselves shuddered and tore in the howling gale. Orlen was a few yards from the mouth of the drain, almost back into the sickly pale light of the moon and fighting frantically, when there came another boom, this time so deafeningly loud as to leave his ears ringing. It was accompanied by a vicious pressure wave that replaced the howling vortex and shoved Orlen back along the drain like a ramrodded cannonball.

Orlen's head spun. He was all but insensible, his senses overwhelmed by unnatural stimuli. For a time, he simply lay still as death, breathing and feeling his heart pump.

Then Orlen realised that something had changed.

He scrambled around into as best a crouch as he could

manage in the tight space. He squinted against the glow that filled the mouth of the drain.

Not moonlight. Not the poisonous pale green rays that had sickened the city for so long now. Orlen saw the gold and rose shades of sunset spilling along the storm drain, and even that simple sight was enough to slow his hammering heart a little. Then, new sounds filled the tunnel, faint and strange and somehow painful. There came a sizzling squeal, a bubbling, popping sound that Orlen realised was emanating from the fungi growing out of the tunnel walls. The ragged bargeman watched in incomprehension as, one by one, the toadstools shivered as though caught in a brisk breeze. Their flesh squirmed and ran like wax, bubbles rising and bursting to release a reek of putrefaction.

Fresh alarm filled Orlen as stinking fumes built up in the air. Instinct drove him in a scramble along the drain, through sticky patches of rotting fungi that slicked his palms, and out into the open.

Just in time.

Orlen hissed at the sight of a rippling black carpet flowing across the cobbles towards him. Insects of every sort scuttled and squirmed frantically towards the shadows of the drain, thousands upon thousands of them. Panic lending his weakened frame strength, Orlen scrambled like an animal up a nearby heap of rubble and then into the branches of a withered and listing tree. For a moment he felt his grip fail him as exhaustion and malnutrition sought to pull him down into the seething tide of insects below.

Somehow, Orlen hung on. Below him, insects were pouring into the drain he had vacated. So many pressed in at once that they piled in a drift about the drain's entrance, scrabbling over one another in a clicking mass of waving antennae and flailing legs. Many didn't make it, shrivelling and squealing as the last rays of daylight found them and pinned them in place. Soon, a desiccated carpet of lifeless husks covered the ground. Then came bigger creatures, greenskins in black robes and pointed hoods. They ran, faces grim as they cast hateful glances up at the open sky. Orlen sensed the panic that came off them in waves. They had taken his place, he realised. Now it was these sharp-fanged monsters that fled into the shadows for fear of what might hunt them. The greenskins snarled, jabbering in fear at the sight of the drain clogged with insect corpses. They dropped to their hands and knees and dug madly, scooping fistfuls of crunching matter out of the way. They fought and pushed and clawed at one another to go first, one of them driving a blade into another's throat and leaving him to thrash and bleed into stillness amidst the dead insects. Like maggots vanishing into an open wound, the creatures squirmed into the storm drain and were gone. Orlen felt the rays of evening light bathe his skin, and the feeling brought forth a vague recollection of a time before madness, and terror, and pain. He remembered a family, waiting for him in Hammerhal Aqsha, and tears spilled from his deep-shadowed eyes at the thought that perhaps, against all the odds, he might live to see them again. He looked up and saw clouds streaked salmon pink and pale grey. He saw the flanks of the volcanoes limned with the golden light of Hysh as the stately dance of the heavens swept it from view and the first stars of night flickered into being.

True night, natural night, with no sign of the monstrous moon that had hung above the city for so long.

Orlen looked down from his vantage point for a long time, until he was absolutely sure that nothing was moving. Then, at last, as the night wind rose and began gently to sweep the insect corpses across the cobbles with a susurrus whisper, Orlen scrambled down from his perch.

He was hungry, and exhausted, and every part of him hurt. But he had a family to return to. A life.

Stepping gingerly, jumping at every sound of movement from the dead city around him, Orlen began the long trudge homewards.

When Romilla opened her eyes and found herself still alive, she wept with gratitude. Her silent tears became a flood when she found Eleanora lived too. Both of them were a mess, certainly, covered with cuts and bruises. Her robes were torn and fire-blackened, and her back was a raw mass of pain that she knew must be burns. Her ears rang, and she felt as though her wits had been blasted from her skull.

It didn't matter. They lived.

A sudden shock of realisation caused Romilla to grab for the ragged hem of her cloak and try to throw it over Eleanora's prone form: they were lying out in the open, patches of their skin exposed to the skies above! Yet as Romilla looked upwards and her eyes at last managed to focus, a sense of wonderment stole over her.

It was gone. The Bad Moon was gone, replaced by straggling clouds and the last amber glow of evening.

They lay upon a spongy and disgusting mass of fungus, tangled amidst a heap of wreckage, of twisted metal and shattered stones and a forest of sundered pipes, ruptured machinery and the black-burned husks of giant spiders. The ruins of the pipe-house loomed over them, thick smoke rising in a billowing plume from its shattered glass roof.

'We're... alive?' asked Eleanora in a faltering voice, wide-eyed with bewilderment.

'The grace of Sigmar, my girl! Oh, thank the God-King, we're saved by the grace of Sigmar,' Romilla replied.

'We must have been ejected through the rent by the blast wave,' said Eleanora, staggering to her feet and looking around at the wreckage surrounding them. 'We were near the end of the stanchion... Yes, look at the damage to the building's flank, we were caught in the blast cone and blown clear amidst a bow-wave of detritus. Romilla, the chances of our escape... if we had been a mere foot to either side, or a little further from the hole... We would have burned...'

'You got it just right, as I knew you would,' said Romilla with a weary smile.

Eleanora was still frowning furiously, counting on her fingers and looking from the building's wall to the fungal pulp in which she stood. She shook her head, and Romilla knew that the engineer was reasoning out their fortunate escape, calculating every angle, trajectory and whatever other technical details helped her to rationalise what had occurred.

'We must have landed atop one of the greenskins' fungal outcroppings. That at least does not seem so unreasonable. I mean, they sprout everywhere the light of–'

Eleanora stopped. She looked up. She made a choking sound and put one hand to her mouth.

Romilla nodded. 'It's gone,' she said simply.

'We did it,' said Eleanora.

Romilla shook her head, and wrapped her arms around Eleanora in a tight hug. They held each other and sobbed, all the terror and horror and pain flooding out of them in a tide.

At last, feeling exhausted but somehow cleansed, Romilla leaned back and looked at Eleanora. The engineer's hair was still plastered to her face with old sweat, but her fever had broken, and the black lines had vanished from beneath her skin.

'Let me see your leg,' said Romilla, then winced at the sight. Fire had burned Eleanora's flesh, but it looked to have done so many weeks ago, not mere minutes. On closer inspection Romilla realised that she could find no sign beneath the gnarled and silvered scar tissue of the corruption that had been spreading there before. Instead, she realised with growing wonderment, the burns on Eleanora's leg described a jagged, scything pattern that wound around her injured limb from foot to thigh.

'Lightning,' breathed Romilla.

'It aches, but not like before,' said Eleanora in bewilderment.

'And your fever is gone.'

'How can that possibly be?' asked Eleanora.

Romilla held up her hammer amulet for Eleanora to see. It was cracked right down the middle, and its blue glow was gone. They stared at one another in mute astonishment, and even Eleanora, for once, could offer no rationalisation for what had happened. Romilla looked up at the crumbling ruin of the pipehouse, at the place where, by rights, she and Eleanora should have died.

'Let us get out of this awful place,' she said to Eleanora. 'Can you walk on that leg?' The engineer took a few tentative steps, wincing with pain, then nodded and picked up another twisted spar of metal to serve as a makeshift shiv.

'We need to find our friends,' she replied.

Walking the streets of Draconium in the light of that blessed evening was the most surreal experience of Romilla's life. All around her was the evidence of slaughter, destruction and butchery. Bodies lay in chewed heaps. Buildings lay in ruin, or slumped crumbling and broken across the streets. Yet the Bad Moon was gone, banished, Romilla assumed, by Sigmar's divine might. Or perhaps it had simply turned its gaze elsewhere when its worshippers' plans were undone, she thought; if the gods of Chaos could be so fickle, could discard their followers' lives so lightly when they were not appeased, then why not the gods of the greenskins? For surely the Bad Moon must be a foul god. What other being could have wreaked so much unnatural misery and ruin?

'The fungi are entering an accelerated state of decomposition,' Eleanora said as they limped down a cobbled street between shattered shop-fronts. Romilla saw she was right; everywhere she looked, foul toadstools were bubbling with rot and collapsing into blackened slurry.

'Perhaps they cannot live without the light of the Bad Moon,' she suggested.

'Good, I hope they all rot,' said Eleanora with more venom than Romilla had ever heard in her voice. 'The fungi, the insects, the greenskins, all of it. And I hope the Bad Moon suffers worst of all.'

Romilla thought that last was unlikely, but as they staggered in a bewildered daze through the empty streets, she saw that much of Eleanora's wish seemed to be coming true. Fungal slurry slicked the cobbles and the stink of rot filled the air. Corpses of greenskins and squigs lay everywhere, mingled in amongst the bodies of the Draconium dead. In places, they waded through the dried out husks of foul insects, heaped now like mountainous drifts of fallen leaves. What had killed them, Romilla could not say for sure, but she presumed that without the light of the Bad Moon these vile things, too, had withered and died. The only other suggestion of the greenskins or their foul creatures that she saw was hints of movement in the deepest shadows, red eyes glinting and wicked fangs bared in snarls of fear as the grots fled back underground.

They rounded a corner into a wide thoroughfare and Romilla tensed as she saw two of the spore-sickened lurching towards them. Yet she realised that the cursed creatures were stumbling and gasping, their flesh bubbling like the toadstools at their feet. As she watched, skin and muscle sloughed from their bones and noxious froth spilled from their mouths, noses and eye sockets. One of the infected reached a withering hand towards her as it fell to its knees, and for a horrible moment Romilla thought she saw a glint of terror in its eyes. Then it collapsed into a mouldering heap and she put the thought from her mind as best she could. Just one more nightmare to add to the pile.

Still, Romilla thought as they limped on towards Fountains Square, she was more glad than ever that she had given Hendrick Sigmar's mercy when she could. The thought of her old comrade brought sorrow, and she quickened her step, praying fervently that they might find their remaining friends still alive somewhere ahead.

The square was a blackened pit. Every building around its edge was blasted flat, and scorched corpses lay strewn about like fallen leaves. The devastation caused by the explosion was so absolute, so shocking, that it took Romilla and Eleanora long minutes to grasp the scale of what they had wrought.

Silent and full of dread, they searched for their friends all the same. Minutes became hours and the stars wheeled above them as, eyes grainy with exhaustion and hearts leaden with dismay, they sifted through the charnel horror of the square. Eleanora's limp became more pronounced and she stumbled more than once, but she did not complain.

At last, they found Bartiman Kotrin lying amidst a tangle of corpses near the edge of the ragged pit that had devoured much of the square. His tattered cloak had caught upon a jutting spar of wood and had saved him from a plunge into the yawning gulf below. Carefully, gradually, Romilla and Eleanora reeled their comrade's body in and pulled him up from the brink, trying all the time not to dislodge the tangle of limbs and wreckage that had arrested his plunge.

All the while, Romilla's heart was in her throat. Bartiman looked so frail, so battered and limp. There was no sign of life in him at all. She prayed with all her might that some spark of life still clung on within the old wizard's body, but she didn't believe it was so.

At last they had him, and as they pulled Bartiman back from the edge the corpse-mound gave way. Bodies slid and tangled, slipping one by one over the edge and into the dark depths below.

Romilla rolled Bartiman onto his back and slid the balled up remains of her cloak beneath his frail old head. He was so pale, she thought, looked so wizened. Praying fervently, desperately, she lowered her head and listened. Faint, so faint, she heard the rattling wheeze of Bartiman's breath rasping in and out. Relief blossomed inside her, but also urgency.

'El, he's close to the brink,' she said. 'We need to get him out of here, to somewhere with clean water and a fire's warmth. Help me make a litter.'

'What about Aelyn? We have to find her too,' said Eleanora as the two of them cast about for the right bits of wreckage to fashion a makeshift stretcher for their friend. Romilla stopped for a moment and looked around sorrowfully.

'We have searched all night, El,' she said. 'We've covered every yard of this square. It is near dawn, and we have seen no sign of her. Bartiman is here, now, but he won't be for long if we do not get him somewhere that I can care for him properly. Do you understand me?'

Eleanora looked at Romilla without expression for several heartbeats, then blinked and counted her fingers. Right hand. Left.

'Perhaps she escaped,' she said as she dragged a blackened branch out from beneath a scattering of rubble.

'Perhaps she did, and we will see her again,' said Romilla, yet as they lashed their makeshift litter together she felt a bone-deep sorrow at another lost friend. Sigmar had lent them his grace, she thought, but they had suffered terribly for it. She had not buried this many friends at once in a very long while. She had hoped never to do so again.

They lashed Bartiman in place and bundled him in what remained of their watch cloaks. Romilla applied what scant herbs and tinctures she had left, hoping at least to ease the pain of the old wizard's wounds. Then they hefted their burden and set off, moving slowly towards the south gatehouse, barely managing more than a shamble. They would not stay in Draconium another hour, thought Romilla, not another minute longer than they had to. The greenskins' plans had been stopped. Countless thousands of lives had been saved from a blight few would ever know had threatened them. Sigmar's work was done.

Yet the city was a corpse, gutted and dead, and it had claimed too many good friends.

It was time to leave.

Romilla and Eleanora carried Bartiman out through the half-collapsed ruin of the gate through which they had entered Draconium so many days before. They walked out into the first light of a new dawn, through drifting ground mist and faint golden light.

Romilla had hoped perhaps to see the refugees of Draconium waiting upon the road. She had prayed that perhaps their efforts would indeed have given the surviving city folk a chance to escape, that they could have saved a few hundred lives from all those who had dwelt in this cursed city. It would have been some small compensation to her, that they could have done something for the people of the city they had failed to save. Perhaps there would also have been someone to help them save Bartiman's life.

Instead she saw an empty road, dotted only with the corpses of those who had tried to flee. The marshes stretched beyond, the dew glinting gold upon long stems of grass in the dawn's light. The waters of the canal lapped and splashed quietly, the half-submerged hull of a single barge jutting up from their dirty depths.

'We have no food, and no medicine,' said Eleanora. 'It's a long way to anywhere, Romilla. How are we–'

'Sigmar will provide,' said Romilla quickly, cutting the question off before Eleanora could ask it. She thought that if the question was voiced, the unfairness of it all might finally undo her. Romilla would drop to her knees in the roadway amongst the dead and scream until her sanity snapped.

Instead, she hefted Bartiman's stretcher and pushed aside the bone-deep weariness that threatened to pull her down.

'We go south,' she said. 'And Sigmar will provide.'

They were an hour's walk south into the forest, travelling slowly along the trade road that ran beside the canal, when Romilla halted suddenly. Even through a haze of exhaustion, she had heard the crack of branches breaking underfoot amidst the ashenpines off to their right.

She set down her end of the litter and turned, raising her makeshift metal shiv. She motioned for Eleanora to do the same. The cracking came again, echoing between the tightly packed trees. She and Eleanora exchanged a look. The forest canopy was dense here, and little enough daylight got through.

If something foul had fled the city into the forest... They shuffled closer together, between Bartiman and the trees, and waited.

The branches stirred, then parted.

Romilla brandished her blade.

Then she sagged with relief as Watchman First Class Marika emerged from between the ashenpines. The watchman stared at them in frank disbelief. She lowered her pistol, then put her fingers into the corners of her mouth and whistled short and sharp.

Two more figures emerged behind her, a watchman and a militiaman. They gaped at Romilla and Eleanora, who stared back in equal shock.

'You're alive,' said Marika finally. 'Sigmar's throne, you survived!'

'Barely, and not all of us,' replied Romilla. 'And Bartiman still may not live. Please, tell me you have a camp near here. He needs a fire, broth, bandages and herbs if you have them. I–'

Marika held up a hand and smiled, the first honest smile that Romilla had seen in a long while.

'Follow me,' she said. 'You helped us beat them. You banished the moon. What we have is yours.'

Marika's companions moved to take up the litter but Romilla waved them away, and she and Eleanora hoisted their frail companion between them. They followed Marika into the underbrush, taking care not to let stray branches or thorns scratch at Bartiman's unconscious form. The watchman and the militiaman fell in behind them, betraying themselves as city-dwellers with every crack of a broken twig that snapped beneath their feet.

Marika took a winding course, through a thicket and down into a shallow river-ditch, then back up the muddy bank and through a stand of ironoaks into the dappled sunlight beyond.

It took Romilla's eyes a moment to adjust from the shadows of the forest to the glare of daylight, but as they finally did she felt weak with relief.

A clearing stretched before them, and there they were. Hundreds of men, women and children, battered and bloodied but alive. Many nursed injuries, broken limbs, bloody gashes and the like, but they were alive. They huddled around camp fires, some beneath makeshift shelters, and men and women of the watch and the militia moved between them with food and supplies. Romilla saw a handful of priests, too, figures festooned with faith-papers and tattoos who drifted from one huddled band of survivors to the next with healing poultices and words of comfort.

'Bring him over here,' said Marika, pointing to a fire that crackled in the shelter of a wagon piled with food. A few shell-shocked looking city folk huddled around the fire, but they made space for the newcomers willingly enough. As they set Bartiman down by the fire, an infant boy watched Romilla with big eyes. Shyly, he buried his face in his mother's chest as Romilla and Eleanora sat down.

'Thought we was all going to die,' said the woman, holding her child close. 'Thank Sigmar we didn't.'

Romilla inhaled, then very slowly released that breath. She watched Marika attract the attention of one of the priests and send him their way with a satchel of medical supplies bumping at his hip. Romilla stroked a hand through Bartiman's thin white hair, looked at Eleanora warming her hands before the fire, and allowed herself a faint, sad smile.

'Thank Sigmar indeed,' she breathed.

ABOUT THE AUTHOR

Andy Clark has written the Warhammer
40,000 novels *Fist of the Imperium, Kingsblade,
Knightsblade* and *Shroud of Night*, as well as the
novella *Crusade* and the short story 'Whiteout'.
He has also written the novels *Gloomspite* and
Blacktalon: First Mark for Warhammer Age
of Sigmar, and the Warhammer Quest Silver
Tower novella *Labyrinth of the Lost*. He lives in
Nottingham, UK.

YOUR
NEXT READ

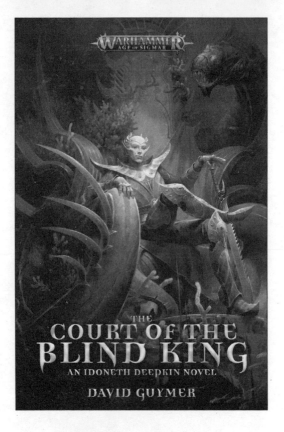

COURT OF THE BLIND KING
by David Guymer

As the diseased Knights of Nurgle wage war against the inhabitants of Briomdar, Prince Lurien sees the opportunity to claim the vacant throne of the undersea kingdom – even if it means facing his fellow Idoneth Deepkin as well as their myriad foes.